THE GENTLEMEN'S GUILD FOR CURSED ADVENTURERS

R. LINDSAY CARTER

ROCK AND FLOWER PRESS

Contents

Members of the Gentlemen's Guild   VI

Dedication   VII

1. Friday, January 22nd, 1915   1

2. Tuesday, February 2nd, 1915   8

3. Sunday, February 7th, 1915   15

4. Tuesday, February 9th, 1915   22

5. Wednesday, February 10th, 1915   36

6. Friday, February 12th, 1915   51

7. Saturday, February 13th, 1915   60

8. Sunday, February 14th, 1915   75

9. Wednesday, February 17th, 1915   86

10. Monday, March 1st, 1915   93

11. Wednesday, March 3rd, 1915   105

12. Saturday, March 6th, 1915   110

13. Tuesday, March 9th, 1915   116

14. Friday, March 19th, 1915   125

15.	Tuesday, March 23rd, 1915	127
16.	Friday, March 26th, 1915	131
17.	Saturday, March 27th, 1915	135
18.	Sunday, March 28th, 1915	143
19.	Monday, March 29th, 1915	156
20.	Tuesday, March 30th, 1915	170
21.	Monday, April 5th, 1915	179
22.	Tuesday, April 6th, 1915	183
23.	Thursday, April 8th, 1915	189
24.	Monday, April 12th, 1915	196
25.	Thursday, April 15th, 1915	205
26.	Friday, April 16th, 1915	210
27.	Monday, April 19th, 1915	214
28.	Friday, April 23rd, 1915	221
29.	Saturday, April 24th, 1915	228
30.	Sunday, May 2nd, 1915	234
31.	Friday, May 7th, 1915	241
32.	Saturday, May 8th, 1915	251
33.	Sunday, May 9th, 1915	255
34.	Monday, May 10th, 1915	270
35.	Friday, May 14th, 1915	273
36.	Saturday, May 15th, 1915	279

37. Sunday, May 16th, 1915   288

38. Monday, May 24th, 1915   292

39. Monday, May 31st, 1915   298

40. Tuesday, June 1st, 1915   301

41. Wednesday, June 2nd, 1915   307

42. Saturday, June 5th, 1915   309

43. Sunday, June 6th, 1915   317

44. Friday, June 11, 1915   342

45. Saturday, June 12th, 1915   346

46. Tuesday, June 15th, 1915   351

47. Saturday, May 27th, 1922   356

Acknowledgements   361

About the Author   363

Books by R. Lindsay Carter   364

Connect   365

Members of the Gentlemen's Guild

- Malcolm Drury: *The owner of Birchwald and president of the Guild*

- Rodney Paulson: *Cursed with a copious amount of sores*

- Pablo Reyes: *Cursed with asking every woman to marry him repeatedly*

- Hector Freeman: *Slowly turning to stone*

- Farley Hunt: *Cursed to injure himself every day and feed the blood to his letter opener*

- Marvin Ivey: *Sees visions of death and destruction which never come true*

- Ambrose Lyster: *Cursed to speak his mind, as well as the minds of others*

- Peter Withers: *Cursed with catatonia*

- Karanja: *The caretaker of Mr. Withers*

- Fred Jamison: *Cursed with night terrors*

- Herbert Norris: *A chicken*

To anyone who has lived with a curse,
and especially to those of you who have found the courage to break it.

CHAPTER ONE

Friday, January 22nd, 1915

Malcolm

Perhaps ten in the morning was too early to start drinking.

Regardless, Malcolm Drury's hand itched to grab the decanter from its tray on the sideboard, the cut crystal of the glass twinkling cheekily at him.

Instead, he flopped into his worn office chair, turning his back on the whiskey tray. He desperately needed to pull his thoughts together into some semblance of coherence. And alcohol would most decidedly not serve that purpose.

He sighed and rubbed a hand down his mouth, hearing the rasp of day-old stubble as much as feeling its bite on his palm. The chair squeaked as he shifted his weight backward to stare at the ceiling for a moment.

It was only twenty-two days into this new year, but already it was shaping up to be much the same as the last five years—hopelessly chaotic, if the events of yesterday and today were any indication. All that time ago, Malcolm had thought that assuming the mantle of president for the Gentlemen's Guild for Cursed Adventurers would introduce something much needed into his life, allowing other damaged souls to reside in his home for camaraderie. And while the role did fulfill some of his expectations, the emptiness within him overshadowed even the best aspects of the job.

Not to mention the utter turmoil it had introduced, which had profound effects upon other aspects of his home and life. Such as the current problem at hand.

Another maid had quit this morning. She had only lasted two months, despite her apparent desperation for work at the time of hiring. As if that weren't bad enough, her quitting meant the staff had been whittled down to just one maid, when the household could have used at least four. Malcolm doubted the final maid standing would last much longer unless more could be hired, and fast.

It wasn't as if he didn't give his staff ample warning about the lunacy of his household when he hired them. It could not be his fault if they refused to believe him until they were thrust into their roles. These young women simply weren't made of strong enough cloth.

He heaved a sigh. *Women.* Fickle, unreliable creatures. The only one he would ever trust was Mrs. Bixby, his loyal housekeeper.

He straightened and looked at the typewriter in the corner of the room. He hated the contraption with a passion. He couldn't pinpoint the source of his enmity, although the loud clack of the keys often gave him a headache, and it annoyed him to no end to hunt for each letter, given the lack of alphabetical order. Writing by hand was so much easier, but the newspaper preferred typed ads to be submitted.

I must make another advertisement to fill these positions. Otherwise Bixby and Mathers will have my head.

As if summoned by his errant thoughts, his butler, Mathers, rapped his knuckles on the teak door frame. The older man cleared his throat as he stood at the threshold, waiting for Malcolm's invitation.

Malcolm gestured for the man to enter with a flippant wave of his fingers. "Yes, Mathers?"

The butler approached, revealing two letters tucked in his hand. "Pardon the intrusion, sir. I have received the post. Two new letters for you." He held them out across the desk.

Malcolm eyed them but did not move to receive them. "You hear the news?"

A slight upturn of Mathers' mouth marred his otherwise stoic expression. "Mrs. Bixby is in fine form over it. Her language this morning was uncharacteristically colorful. It would be difficult *not* to hear the news, I'm afraid."

Malcolm grunted and finally plucked the letters from his butler's hand. Still, he made no move to further inspect them. "I suppose I'll have to calm her down, hm?"

Mathers gave his head a slow shake. "I wouldn't worry too much over it, sir. Mary Kelly was a rather flighty thing, and not the best worker. She apparently left in the middle of wound care, leaving our housekeeper in a bit of a predicament this morning. It wouldn't be the first time she's been unreliable. There wasn't a day went by that Mrs. Bixby didn't complain about her. If you ask me, she'll most likely be happier without her." He paused before adding, "Still, perhaps a kind gesture to your devoted housekeeper would be appreciated in these trying times."

Malcolm valued the fact that Mathers felt comfortable enough to speak his mind to him. Mathers had also buttled for his father, the late Gordan Drury, and Malcolm vaguely remembered that such informal conversations were very much not allowed between employer and butler. However, seeing as how Mathers had done more to raise Malcolm than his father ever did, advice would always be welcome, in his opinion.

Malcolm smirked at the older man's words. "Yes, you are probably right. Will you be going to town today? I'll be sure to type another advertisement for you to bring to the newspapers. That will be a first step, at any rate."

"Yes, sir," Mathers replied with a small head tilt. The question of whether or not anyone would apply was left unsaid. Word must have gotten out about the ... unusual circumstances of the job, and despite trying to hire more staff in recent months, no one had come forward.

"Say, Mathers," Malcolm began before pausing to formulate his question. "What do you mean by wound care? Which man are we talking about?"

A small mien of disgust flowed over the other man's mouth. "It was Mr. Paulson, sir."

"Of course." Malcolm knew full well about Rodney Paulson's condition; after all, he had personally attended to him many times over the years.

Mathers nodded knowingly. "He's developed a rather nasty sore on his right buttock, which makes it difficult for him to sit for any given length. I would have summoned you for the task, but Mrs. Bixby told me not to, as you were asleep."

Malcolm shifted in his seat, a passing embarrassment flitting through him. Both his butler and his housekeeper knew how poorly his sleep tended to be. He tried to downplay it. "So, it fell to Mary Kelly?"

"Indeed. The sore burst, and Mary Kelly was tasked with cleaning the wound after it had opened. It was entirely too much for her, though."

"Good god," Malcolm hissed. "I can hardly blame the girl, then. Wouldn't you agree?" Rodney, as much as he was a kind soul, was one of the more disgusting cases among his men. His condition was not for the faint of heart.

Mathers gave his silver head another small shake. "I must agree with you on that. I should mention though, Mrs. Bixby confided in me that this assigned task was more of a retribution after the girl had carelessly allowed Mr. Hunt to be injured without following up with protocol. It led to further injuries of a more grievous nature, as is expected with Mr. Hunt."

Malcolm squinted his eyes shut. "Oh yes. That was the hullabaloo I heard about two days ago, wasn't it?"

"It was. Your grandfather's prized polar bear toppled over upon poor Mr. Hunt, gouging a good chunk out of his scalp with the teeth and breaking the taxidermy in the process. You well know how much head wounds bleed, as superficial as they usually are. Most unfortunate, all the way around."

Malcolm sighed. He didn't care much about the stupid stuffed bear, but he hated to hear that Farley Hunt had been further injured over something so reckless. Perhaps it was best the girl was gone if this was the extent of her carelessness.

Mathers straightened once they made eye contact again. "Is there anything else I can do for you, sir?"

Malcolm waved his hand in dismissal. "No, go on. I'll take a look at these letters. Thank you, Mathers."

"Very good, sir."

As the butler closed the door behind him, Malcolm took another moment of peace before picking up his letter opener and swiping it under the first envelope's flap. He removed the paper and scanned the lines.

Ah. Another candidate for membership was on his way. All the way from Kenya—a British territory in Africa, from the looks of it—and the letter, written by a colonel in the British army stationed there, claimed the man was arriving within the month with a native African caregiver in tow.

It was unusual for a new member to arrive with help, unless they were completely incapacitated. The colonel had not gone into much detail, but Malcolm surmised this might be the case. Heaven knew he could use the help right about now. He only hoped the African man spoke English, to make communication easier.

Very well. On to the next letter.

This one hailed from London. The envelope was curiously addressed to his predecessor, Arnold Thompson, and forwarded on to Malcolm. The sender must not have been aware of Arnold's retirement and Malcolm's taking over as president of the Guild. He mentally shrugged and opened this second letter, unfolding the paper and perusing it as a whole before reading it. The writing was crisp and meticulous. Malcolm's slight sleep deprivation made it difficult to decipher at first glance. He read it over carefully.

Dear Sir,

My brother, Leighton Abernathy, has an unfortunate affliction brought about by a cursed relic. He has had to retreat from polite society as a result, and he has come to a point at which he is having difficulty caring for himself. Therefore, I am entreating you for membership into your Guild for Cursed Adventurers. I understand there is a membership fee due, but our family is of high standing, and I do not believe the cost will be an obstacle. As a matter of fact, I, too, would appreciate admittance into your fine establishment. I do believe membership would be advantageous not only for my brother, but for me as well.

I am currently enrolled in Oxford and had plans to stay for another semester, but with Great Britain at war, I have made the decision to travel home to New York post haste. I will be leaving London as soon as I am able to book passage. I shall be in touch once I am back in the States to further the procuring of our enrollment into your guild.

Sincerely,

N.J. Abernathy

He stared at the page for a few seconds longer, the name signed at the bottom tickling some long-lost memory. *Abernathy.* He'd heard it before, he was sure.

Malcolm stood, the rollers on his chair spinning it away from his body with the force of his departure. He strode to the bookcase on his left, his gray eyes skimming over the various scrapbooks it contained.

The scrapbooks were started by Arnold when he was president. Each book contained newspaper clippings or eyewitness accounts of various adventurers: their lives, and their downfalls in many cases. Some of the adventurers within the scrapbooks had gone on to join the Guild, while others simply remained curious stories. Now that he was running the establishment, any time an explorer was mentioned in the press, Malcolm would meticulously add the indication into the scrapbook, just in case things began to go very badly for said person. And, as he knew firsthand, the penchant for things to go badly was relatively high.

There. He finally set eyes on the spine that indeed read "Abernathy." He carefully pulled it from the shelf and opened it with reverence. His eyes widened as he read the contents.

Arnold had documented extensively on this name, and it wasn't just one individual listed within. There was no mention of Leighton, but the latest clipping was from 1892 when one Robert Abernathy died of mysterious conditions while on an expedition to Africa. His wife died less than a year later, at home. Malcolm flipped further back. In 1866, George Abernathy passed away following a long trip to Australia. In 1824, another Robert Abernathy died of a wasting disease, once he was back home from exploring the wilds of Brazil. Even more documented deaths were present, going all the way back to the early 1700s.

Clearly, this was not a case of a single adventurer, but a whole damn lineage. Despite its rarity, Malcolm could easily comprehend such a thing. Given the frequency of family news articles, it was no wonder the name had stuck out to him.

The Abernathys continued back at least five generations. When this N.J. said that money wouldn't be an issue, he wasn't lying. Transplants from England, the Abernathys had lived in New York since before it was a state. And all the while, their wealth had increased. This might be a good thing.

He shook his head. He already had a full house, with eight members currently residing within these walls. And with the anticipated arrival of the man from Africa, that would be nine. Given his lack of help, could he truly maintain ten at once?

He looked at the letter again. It was postmarked two weeks ago. It was possible that this mysterious Abernathy was already on his way, although the foolish war in Europe might have slowed things down. He could only hope the passenger ships were too full of fleeing immigrants for the time being. Perhaps this person would choose to wait for the war to blow over instead. It was bound to, sooner than later. Malcolm didn't think it would take long for Germany to be defeated.

In the meantime, he'd try to find more about this person asking for his help. Surely there had to be some news source he had overlooked, if the brother was already cursed.

A shortage of help, an angry housekeeper, a broken polar bear, one—possibly two—new members en route, and royals fighting in Europe. Malcolm let out a gusty sigh.

Perhaps ten in the morning *wasn't* too soon to start drinking.

CHAPTER TWO

Tuesday, February 2nd, 1915

Norah

THE ATLANTIC OCEAN SPRAWLED in every direction as far as Norah could see, a gray blanket of water both dull in appearance and breathtaking in its vastness.

She hated it.

It didn't help that the waves were small but choppy, causing a continuous nausea to bunker in the pit of her stomach, making her as miserable as possible. Only twice on this journey, when the rolling gait of the ocean became a gallop, did she finally purge, which only eased the motion sickness for a brief period of time.

Crossing the Atlantic in June nearly two and a half years ago had been much easier. The weather was certainly warmer, and the water was less sullen. This winter ocean was a vicious bitch.

The February wind whipped about her, making her forget why she had come up on deck in the first place and wishing to immediately surrender and go below. But no, the fresh air did help to quell the worst of the queasiness, and besides, her great-aunt was smelling particularly ripe this evening. Sharing a tiny cabin with a chaperone who sometimes reeked of rot did not make for a pleasant voyage, even when the weather behaved.

She took a deep breath through her nostrils as she gazed at the unforgiving ocean. In the distance she could see the peaked backs of icebergs, abundant in this part of the sea and deadly if hit. Less than three years earlier, the *RMS Titanic* had learned that lesson at a heavy cost. If memory served, the tragedy had struck not too far from here.

Norah shivered. Not for the first time, she wondered which passenger had carried a curse so heavy as to doom the ship. Or perhaps one of the workers had unknowingly laced a jinx upon the craft itself, somebody spurned to a degree as to imbue the hull with a malevolent power. Alas, *Titanic*'s secret was forever lost in the depths of this watery grave. She would never know the answer.

She sighed at her circumstances. It would have been wonderful to make the return trip in the late spring, or even summer. Such timing would have afforded her the opportunity to enroll for one more semester at Oxford. She was incredibly close to taking all the classes she deemed necessary for her education. Completing her studies would not have granted her the degree she so longed for—women were not allowed the privilege of graduation. But it would have given her a sense of accomplishment, an inner feeling of completion, and she could have at least pretended that she had gotten her doctorate alongside her male classmates.

Two things made this trip a necessity, however. The war had confounded her plans for fake graduation. As it were, many students had already abandoned their studies during the last term to join the swelling ranks of soldiers. These young men marched off with smiles on their faces and a mock bravery in their hearts, certain that they were the heroes in their own stories, and secure in the misguided notion that nothing bad ever happened to heroes.

Idiots. War did not care about heroes.

Norah did not wish to be swept up in the European war alongside the British patriotism. While people still talked as if it could end any minute, she'd already heard too many rumors and stories to make her believe such optimism. As it was, the United Kingdom had already blockaded the North Sea about two months ago, cutting off Germany from imports. The Brits knew Germany would retaliate any day, and when that day arrived, travel would become truly dangerous. Norah, not wanting to add any further peril to her existence, jumped on the first ship that had passage to New York for two women and a dog.

Even if the war hadn't happened, the last missive she received about her brother painted a wretched picture. She had tried to stave off asking for assistance until her imagined doctorate, but from the sounds of it, she could no longer put off returning home.

She hoped her letter had made it into Mr. Thompson's hands. She hadn't heard back from him, but that did not surprise her. Postal times, especially transatlantic, could be slow at best. It was possible his reply was en route at the same time she had departed. She would show up at the New York address all the same and plead her case for her brother's sake.

Her reverie was broken by footsteps behind her. She straightened, pulling her shawl tighter about her in a flimsy shield and turning to see who approached.

It was only the porter. He held a leash in one hand, the other end attached to her small dog. "Excuse me, miss," he said with a drawling English accent as he held out the leash to her. "Your dog has done his duties and is ready to head back to your cabin. I'd take him myself, but supper will be served soon, and it would be prudent of you to go below. It's getting dark up here, and it's not suitable for a lady to be out alone, if I may be so bold to say."

Norah sighed. She hated being a "lady" and needing a chaperone. She wished this long-time outdated notion would die a quick death. She was more than capable of taking care of herself, unmarried status or not.

Still, it was not the porter's fault for keeping up with society's rules. She nodded as she accepted the leash. Her dog, Eddie, planted his front feet on her skirt, happy to be back with his mistress.

"Begging your pardon, but what kind of dog is he? I thought him to be a King Charles, but the face isn't quite right," the porter asked.

Norah glanced at Eddie. He was a small thing, barely twelve pounds, with drooping ears made even longer by the copious trailing red locks upon them. He had fur in droves, cascading from his body in straight and shiny waves of red and white, the longest of which was on his voluminous white tail.

"You were correct with your guess, but Eddie here is not quite up to standard," she told the porter as she continued to gaze at her dog. "If you look at old paintings of the breed, the King Charles spaniel used to have a muzzle, but over the last hundred years or so, it was bred to be flattened. Every once in a while, though, a litter will produce one of these 'throwbacks.' They aren't desirable to breeders, but I personally think it makes him more handsome."

It wasn't much of a muzzle, only two inches at most, but what she said was her truth—this small protrusion was much more appealing to her than the flat faces she commonly saw. It was one of the reasons she chose to adopt the little scamp. He was unique.

The porter looked at the small dog dubiously. "If you say so, miss. He's a friendly one, at least."

She smiled wryly. "That he is."

The porter held out an arm to guide her away from the churning gray waters of the ocean. "This way, if you please."

Norah allowed herself to be corralled down into the belly of the steamer. She paused at her cabin door, steeling herself for the sweet smell of corruption she was sure to walk into, before opening it.

She needn't have worried. Aunt Nell had opened the hatch for some fresh air, and the smell was no longer quite so cloying. Norah breathed in relief.

The woman in question sat on her lower berth, her eyes downcast as she worked on a needlepoint under the low light of the electric lamp. Her long, black hair had not been pinned up, but trailed down her back in one long braid. She wore a simple travel gown of a gray color, nearly matching the Atlantic.

Aunt Nell looked up from her busywork, silently watching Norah as she unclipped Eddie, removed her hat and brushed down her blouse with her hands. Norah gazed at her aunt in turn. Nell was very beautiful, if one ignored the odd texture of her pale skin—almost papery in places—or the unsettling yellowing in the corners of her slightly cloudy eyes. Although she appeared to be a maiden on the cusp of adulthood, Norah knew that Nell was much, much older.

She was also technically not alive.

It was a sordid affair spoken only as rumors passed down through the generations, but from what Norah could piece together, Eleanora Montmorency had been a girl of eighteen when she started an affair with her stepfather, Ernest Abernathy. Her dying mother discovered the betrayal and cursed her own daughter, turning her into a mostly dead creature with an appetite for carnal pleasures.

She was in truth Norah's blood-aunt, but with more than a few "greats" added to the official title, since Norah's line descended from Nell's half-brother. Curiosity always getting the best of her, Norah once looked up her family tree to get an idea of just how old her aunt actually was. Considering that the half-brother was born in 1717, and Nell was supposedly eleven years older, that put her at nearly 210 years of age.

All things considered, she looked great for being two centuries old.

Aunt Nell was very private about her eccentricities, so Norah was not privy to everything the curse entailed. All she knew was despite her non-living status, men were drawn to her aunt, and Nell married often, although she never changed her maiden name. It was just as well, because her husbands never lasted more than five years before dying. Nell would wear her customary mourning black for the uncustomary time of three months before reverting back to her normal clothing. She'd be single for a span of six months to two years, and then the next mister would appear to sweep her off her feet in matrimony.

Nell's latest husband, a lovely English merchant, had succumbed just three and a half months prior, an early casualty of the war. Nell had changed out of her black dresses just a week prior to this trip.

The aspect that Norah did not understand was *why* Aunt Nell married. Norah had stayed with her aunt and her late husband Christopher—she'd been loath to call him "uncle" since he'd been only two years older than she, even though the term was technically accurate—at his townhouse in Oxford while she studied at the university. Christopher had been a nice chap, a bit simple in Norah's mind, and decent to look at. He clearly worshiped her aunt's feet. But Aunt Nell paid his love back with an air of indifference, as if she merely tolerated his presence. And upon receiving the news of his death after not even three years of wedded bliss, she simply shrugged off the news and unpacked her mourning clothes.

Aunt Nell made it clear that she was not fond of anybody, really, with one exception: she got along fabulously with Norah. Norah always chalked it up to the fact that they shared a name, an ironic fact given that one of her only memories of her parents was of them bitterly complaining about the undead black sheep of the family.

Then again, Norah was the first girl born to the family in two hundred years. Perhaps in that time the Abernathy clan had forgotten all other female names other than Eleanora and its derivatives existed.

Whatever the case was, Norah was glad in some small way for her strange aunt, which was why she normally didn't mind the smell that sometimes followed her about.

Aunt Nell narrowed her eyes at Norah, assessing her. "That was longer than a trip to the privy. Where were you off at, gel?"

Her aunt may have looked young, but she certainly did not *sound* young. Her voice should have been girlish and sweet, but instead her vocal cords made a rasping, dry voice, like that of a seventy-year-old who had smoked cigarettes her whole life.

Norah sat next to her aunt on the berth. Eddie also jumped up, settling his small frame neatly into Norah's lap. She stroked his fur and said, "I needed some air. It was getting—" she stopped herself before she could say *smelly,* "stuffy in here. Besides, fresh air does wonders to stimulate the appetite."

Aunt Nell sniffed disdainfully. "I wouldn't know."

Norah cringed inwardly. She knew her aunt didn't need to eat, but she joined others at mealtimes to keep up appearances.

Nell was not fooled by Norah's choice of words, either. "It was me, wasn't it? The smell?"

Norah hated to point out her aunt's flaws, but she hated lying even more. "It was a contributing factor," she admitted diplomatically.

Aunt Nell let out a small grunt of acknowledgement. "I may have lost the ability to smell, but I have eyes, gel. I took care of the problem while you were away. Is it better now?"

Norah nodded. It was true that her aunt's odor of decay had different strengths depending on the day and time. While she was with a husband, she seemed to smell less often. Norah did not wish to dwell on any implications of why that might be, nor did she wish to expand on what "taking care of it" might mean.

All she said in reply was, "Thank you."

Nell patted her knee. "Shall I watch your dog while you prepare for supper?"

"Won't you be joining me?"

Nell shook her head. "I don't enjoy the company. I intend to sit this one out."

Another quirk of Aunt Nell's. She much preferred solitude to interacting with the public. She also enjoyed staying away from the outdoors, if given the choice. Between spouses, she contentedly lived alone in the basement of the Abernathy townhouse in New York.

"Very well, Aunt Nell." Norah stood and stretched. Eddie, having jumped to the floor, gave his body a brisk shake. "We should be arriving in three days' time. It will be good to be home."

Aunt Nell tutted to herself. "I'm not sure I see it the same way. You'll have your hands full once we arrive."

Norah closed her eyes as if to block out her aunt's pessimism. "True. I'll have to assess LJ and take him to Mr. Thompson. I'm sure Mr. Thompson will appreciate my insight as well. It might help some other folks in his care."

Nell snorted in a rather unladylike fashion.

Norah scowled but kept her back to her aunt. She had a plan, at least. She'd get the help LJ needed, because he depended on it.

And so did she.

CHAPTER THREE

Sunday, February 7th, 1915

Norah

THE STEAMER HAD ARRIVED in the New York harbor without incident—a great relief to Norah. She and Aunt Nell once again established themselves into the family brownstone. Getting used to the familiar surroundings took Norah a small amount of time, especially in the company of LJ once more.

Upon seeing her brother for the first time in close to three years, Norah once again felt resolute in her decision. And so, less than thirty-six hours after arriving home, Norah left her warm townhome and headed out on foot to seek Mr. Thompson.

It took little time to walk the distance, despite the treacherous underfoot conditions slowing her down. All too soon, Norah found herself on the corner of 75th and Madison, staring at a brownstone much like her own. This was it. Her destination. She paused.

She'd had the address memorized ever since she'd first found the advertisement seven years ago. The words still burned brightly in her memory.

Attention, Adventurers!

Have you fallen into bad luck? Do you have a condition that requires some extra care? Join The Gentlemen's Guild for Cursed Adventurers!

Yearly dues are required for membership. Room and board included.

Please inquire within with A. Thompson, President

207 E 75th St

New York, NY

She had wanted to contact this A. Thompson from the moment she spotted the ad, knowing it was only a matter of time before her brother would fall to a curse, just like all the men in her family did. But seven years ago, LJ was fine, foolhardy, and eager for adventure, not to mention in perfect health. He left for Belize shortly after her discovery of the Guild, and Norah let him, albeit with a heavy heart. Almost three years ago, when he returned with an unspoken pallor and jilted stride, she had again planned to reach out, but LJ swore to her that he was hale, that it was only the stress of his trip that fatigued him so.

Norah was not convinced, but she respected her brother's wishes and she once again held off, instead deciding to go on her own adventure to the other side of the Atlantic. It was the first time Norah had put her wishes ahead of LJ's, and her greatest wish of all was to attend Oxford, even in the limited capacity her gender set for her. She had not regretted this selfish act for a moment.

There was no denying the curse this time, however. The moment she laid eyes on LJ, she could see the pain he was in, as much as he tried to hide it. LJ finally admitted his downfall. Getting proper help for him was at the forefront of Norah's mind. She only wished she had disregarded his denial years ago, but hindsight was always perfect.

And now, here she was, standing out in the dirty snow and staring at the modest townhouse before her. With a quickening of her heart and a clutching of her fur-lined winter coat, she took the steps, stomped the clinging snow from her boots, and rang the bell.

A moment later, a tall, aging woman with her graying hair pulled into a matronly chignon opened the door. "Can I help you?"

Norah took a breath, gathering her courage. "Good afternoon. I am here to inquire about membership into the Guild."

The woman stared at Norah for a beat more before blinking, her expression remaining neutral. "I'm afraid you are confused, miss."

The bottom dropped out of Norah's stomach. The roar of an imaginary ocean began to fill her ears. "Is this the residence of Mr. Thompson?"

The woman nodded with a guarded tempo. "Yes, but—"

Norah pressed on. "He is the president of the Guild, is he not?"

The other woman shook her head. "I don't know of this guild, miss. Perhaps you have the wrong address."

Norah opened and closed her mouth, at a loss. She could actively feel the blood draining from her face. "This can't be! I don't understand."

"Mrs. White? Who is it?" an elderly man's voice spoke from the interior of the hallway.

The woman, Mrs. White, turned to address the speaker. "It's a lady, sir. She seems to think there is a guild at this address. Shall I send her away?"

No, there must be some mistake, Norah thought miserably. *Please don't send me away. I won't know what else to do.*

But the speaker thankfully seemed to understand. "Ah, no, please bring her in. Here—" Mrs. White was shuffled out of the way of the open door, replaced by a man with sparse, ill-managed white hair, spectacles, and a kind smile. "Hello, my dear," he said, his tone matching the kindness of his smile. "I believe your information is a bit outdated. Won't you come in?"

Norah stayed on the stoop. "You *are* Mr. Thompson, correct?"

He held out a hand. "Arnold Thompson, present and in the flesh, yes. And who might you be?"

She took his proffered hand shakily, her manners failing her in her agitated state. "Norah Abernathy."

"*Abernathy!* I was wondering if I'd ever be graced with the presence of your lineage." He winked at her as he held the door open for her. "Please, come in. You look as if you need a stiff coffee."

Norah's feet finally came unglued, and she allowed herself to be led into the front room of the townhouse, a cozy sitting room with comfortable furniture. She sank into one of the sofas at Mr. Thompson's insistence while Mrs. White disappeared to gather the offered coffee.

"You'll have to forgive my housekeeper," Mr. Thompson said breezily as he sat across from her. "She's only been in my employ for a year, after I lost my longtime housekeeper to influenza. I hadn't bothered to fill in Mrs. White about my past responsibilities, as I did not think they would be significant."

Norah only nodded, still feeling faint with the shock of her plan possibly failing.

Mrs. White returned promptly with two steaming cups, heavily laced with cream, sugar, and a dash of stronger stuff. Norah gratefully took one with trembling fingers.

"Now then," Mr. Thompson began, picking up the other cup, "You've come here because someone in your family is cursed. Is that right?"

"Yes!" Norah blurted with perhaps too much force to be considered ladylike. It did not seem like the gentleman minded. "I've kept your advertisement handy for the last seven years, knowing I'd have use for it one day."

He tutted. "Seven years, you say? Well, I was indeed the president of the Guild that long ago. Would have been ... eh, in 1910 that I gave it up."

Norah felt faint. Even the strong coffee couldn't help the sinking sensation she felt. "So there isn't a guild anymore?" she asked in a small voice.

"Oh, don't fret, my dear. I never said such a thing. It's merely been transferred."

"Transferred." The repeated word hung heavy in the air.

Mr. Thompson nodded. "That's right. This *was* the headquarters for the Guild, and I was the president for many years. But as word got out, more and more adventurers began to show up. It was a lot of work. My house became too small for the cause, and, as you can plainly see, I'm old."

"And what happened?" Norah asked breathlessly.

"An old friend of mine's son showed interest. He was also a cursed adventurer, but he had a rather large estate to run after his father passed and couldn't make it to the city. Birchwald, that's the name of the place. He offered to host the Guild there instead and to take over as president. I was ready to retire and agreed to the change."

The wings of hope lifted once more. "So, the Guild, it's ... elsewhere?"

"Croton Falls, New York, to be exact. About two hundred miles north of here, if I had to guess. I made the trip once to help young Drury get set up with the lads. It's a bit secluded, out in nature and all. Nothing like our home here." He paused assessing her. "How presumptuous of me. Do you call New York City your home?"

She nodded, her head whirring. "Yes, although I've been abroad for a number of years. I actually live close by."

"Not Fifth Street, I garner?" he said with a chuckle.

Norah smiled back, her mind beginning to ease. Fifth Street was also known as "Millionaire's Row." It was a favorite place for Norah to walk, with the grandiose architecture on one side of the street and Central Park on the other. "No, nothing so illustrious. I'm only three blocks north of you and farther east. A brownstone, like yours."

Mr. Thompson took a deep, clarifying breath with a smile. "There's nothing finer than this great city of ours. I've lived here my whole life, and I intend to die here. Peacefully, I hope."

Norah frowned. "Then you weren't an adventurer yourself?"

He shook his head, the wispy hairs flitting in the breeze and a faraway look fogging his eyes. "No, none of that for me. It was my son who got me involved in the running of the Guild. His curse, specifically. A rather nasty one that left him unable to function on his own. It was his idea to take in other unfortunate men like him and make it a guild. God rest his soul."

"I'm so sorry."

He waved a hand in the air. "It was a long time ago. And you, my dear? For whom are you seeking help? A husband? Surely not a son in this situation."

"My brother. I sent a letter to you explaining this. Did you not receive it?"

Now it was Mr. Thompson's turn to look confused. "A letter? No, I have not."

"I sent it about three weeks ago. It should have arrived by now." Norah's voice rose in pitch.

Mr. Thompson thought. "Was it addressed to me? Or to the Guild?"

"The Guild, I suppose."

He slapped his thigh. "There you have it. It was forwarded on to the new address, I'll wager. My guess is that Mr. Drury already knows you will be seeking membership for your brother."

"Are you certain?"

He nodded. "Quite so, quite so."

His affirmation settled her rapid pulse ever so slightly. She sipped her coffee to gain a moment. "Thank you. Would you please tell me the best route to attempt to get there?"

Mr. Thompson, as insular in New York City as he seemed, was very eloquent when he described the train route from Grand Central Station to Mahopac, and how she could most likely catch a horse cab for the rest of the commute, a mere mile or two for the last leg. Luckily, the cabs were typically prepared for foul weather with sleigh-style carriages in the winter months, although the bulk of Croton Falls' visitors vacationed in the summer. In all, the journey would take close to five hours.

It would be more than worth it, Norah decided. "Thank you for your time, and for the beverage, Mr. Thompson," she said with diplomacy as she set her mostly empty cup down on the low table and stood.

The old man led her back to the front door. "Any time, my dear. I do hope you and your brother find what you need there."

"So do I," Norah agreed with a sigh.

Malcolm

The phone rang with a disconcerting clang next to Malcolm's ear.

With a start, he sat up, momentarily discombobulated before realizing he had fallen asleep at his desk.

No, he wasn't being very honest with himself. He scowled at the half-empty decanter at the edge of the desk. Sleep was not the proper term. Passing out was.

The phone rang again, shaking Malcolm from his alcohol-induced torpor.

He picked up the receiver in one hand with more force than necessary and jerked the transmitter to his mouth with the other. "Yes?"

The voice on the other end was tinny and faint, but understandable and familiar. "Hello, Malcolm? Is that you? It's Arnold."

Malcolm relaxed his grip on the body of the device. He had a soft spot for the old man, which was part of the reason he'd agreed to take over the Guild in the first place. "Hello, yes it's me. How are you, Arnold?"

"Quite well, quite well. Listen my boy, did you receive a letter from a prospective member recently?"

It took a moment for his whiskey-soaked brain to puzzle through the question, to remember the mysterious letter from N.J. Abernathy. "Yes, I did. Abernathy. Is that to what you are referring?"

"The very same! Most excellent, that. I wanted to let you know that she stopped by my house just half an hour ago, unaware that the Guild had been relocated. I let her know where you were and how to get there. I imagine she'll be on her way within a day or so. She seemed to be in a bit of a rush."

Arnold's words weren't quite making sense. Malcolm took a moment to muddle through the speech. "She?"

"Yes. Her brother too, of course."

"She?" Malcolm repeated the word. "Who is 'she?'"

Arnold paused on his end. "Why, Miss Abernathy of course. What was her Christian name? Nellie? Nona? Oh yes, Norah. Norah Abernathy. That was it."

Malcolm set the transmitter down to free his hand, which he now used to push through a stack of papers on his desk until the letter popped into view. He snatched it up, scanning the contents again.

"*As a matter of fact, I, too, would appreciate admittance into your fine establishment. I do believe our combined efforts would be advantageous not only for my brother, but for me as well.*"

He stared at the signature. N.J. Abernathy. N for Norah.

"Hello? Malcolm, are you still there?"

He picked up the neck again and brought it to his mouth. "Yes, I'm still here. Thank you, Arnold, for letting me know. Goodbye." He set the receiver back in its cradle, sure that he had cut Arnold off mid-sentence.

He found that he didn't much care. He had bigger issues to think of.

CHAPTER FOUR

Tuesday, February 9th, 1915

Norah

NORAH WAS ENTIRELY FED up with traveling.

She had managed to drag her brother out of their shared townhouse at the ungodly hour of six that morning, stuffing him and two small trunks into a taxicab before squishing herself in as well. The dirty and slushy snow had slowed the vehicle down, a fact that Norah had not accounted for when she originally made her timetable. Consequently, by the time the tickets were purchased and the luggage stowed at Grand Central Station, they had mere minutes to catch their desired train before it pulled out. Running was not easy for LJ with his condition, and Norah's boots made the sprint an unpleasant one. They made it—barely. She waited to chastise herself until they found an empty car and sat, giving herself a moment to breathe.

Once the train began to move, Norah relaxed slightly. Across from her, LJ slumped, still winded from the unanticipated exercise.

That simple act worried Norah; LJ used to run circles around her when they were younger, and he had always been the more athletic of the two.

She studied him. Ever since she'd arrived home, her brother had been trying to keep his distance, physically, but—more importantly—also emotionally. When she had left two and a half years ago, LJ had joked that she was escaping him. Now that they were back together, it was clear he was the one trying to evade her.

She had asked about his condition multiple times, and other than finally acknowledging his curse existed, LJ refused to talk of it, only downplaying the severity to her. But she knew. She had eyes. She saw the winces of pain, the stilted gait, the pallor brought about by bouts of agony.

LJ was not to be dissuaded from hiding facts, however many times she asked him to be truthful. He'd always been stoic. He was, after all, the male child. The heir to the family's generational wealth, as threadbare as it was these days. He was the golden son, both metaphorically and physically. He'd always been an Adonis compared to her, with his dark blonde hair and good looks. It was a wonder he was still single. The Abernathy formula to life was to marry and produce an heir first, and then go exploring. LJ, having adventured first, had spit in the face of that tradition.

"All I can say is this had better be worth it."

Norah snapped out of her reverie. "Come again?"

LJ fixed her with a narrow-eyed stare. He'd not been happy about waking so early. "I said, I hope this quest of yours is worth it. I don't enjoy being about when the sun is still vacant."

Norah couldn't help but roll her eyes. "LJ, I didn't travel halfway around the world, missing my chance to finish my classes, to be with you if I thought you were well. You clearly aren't. You may have fooled one of us, but it wasn't me. It was yourself."

LJ huffed. "I'm managing."

"And you can also manage at the Guild, where there will be people to help you and fellow adventurers to commiserate with."

"And become a shut-in."

She frowned. "I do apologize. I must have missed the letter in which you clearly outlined all of the soirées you've been attending lately. I'm sure with your gammy gait you have the ladies swooning on the dance floor."

"And you wouldn't know what a soirée was unless it poked you in the backside," he countered with a twin frown. "I want to live on *my* terms."

"As do I. Sometimes we don't always get what we want, hm?"

He pursed his lips. "Fair enough. Fine. We'll do things your way. For now."

They spent much of the remaining time on the train in silence.

Mr. Thompson had been accurate about the availability of carriages for the remainder of the journey, although they had to wait for one to return before they could venture out. The station master told them it was a walkable distance of less than two miles to the estate, but given the eighteen inches of snow on the ground, it was a foolhardy task. Norah agreed, opting to wait the hour instead. She knew there was no way LJ would be able to walk it, snow or no.

At last, the siblings were loaded into a sleigh-style carriage, with a fresh horse eager to ferry them to their destination. Norah settled in for the last leg of their journey, envisioning the meeting that was soon to take place, an occurrence she was sure would change her and LJ's lives for the better.

It was well past 1:30 by the time Norah caught her first sight of Birchwald as they rounded a bend in the road. She was struck mute by the sight.

She'd half-expected a small but charming summer house: perhaps ten rooms with a garden that would be cheerful in the warmer months. This first look shattered those expectations. Birchwald, while still technically classified as a summer house, would not be considered charming in the slightest by anyone, and certainly not by Norah. The word she wanted to use instead was *imposing*.

Norah had plenty of time to take it in—the driveway was long and lined with skeletal trees frosted with snow. From her limited vantage, she counted three stories, each bedecked in a dazzling limestone façade. A rounded atrium jutted out from the right side, creating a small amount of asymmetry that was pleasing to the eye. Closer to the domicile, the driveway curved like the eye of a needle, with the apex at a covered carriage porch adorning the front and center of the mansion.

In the city, Norah enjoyed the unique architecture along Fifth Street. One of her favorite houses to admire for its eccentricity was the Vanderbilts' *Petit Chateau*. It was a monstrous, gaudy Gothic thing full of turrets and frivolity at every window. Norah now studied Birchwald with the same eye. While she would not consider the two mansions to be similar—there were no turrets in sight on this summer home, at least—there was a clear connection between the two properties. Birchwald had a slate blue roof that caught the eye, just like the Chateau, and both estates screamed money.

A lot of money.

Norah suddenly felt very over her head.

There was to be no turning back now, at any rate. The sled had stopped under the entrance roof and the cabbie was opening the door to help Norah down. She thanked him, and turned toward the heavy wooden double doors, feeling faint at the prospect of walking through them.

Up the steps, one of the grand double doors opened, admitting a solitary older man in coattails into view. Norah smoothed her coat down to quell her nervousness.

"Greetings, madam," the butler said to her with a stiff bow.

"Hello. I am here to speak with Mr. Drury," Norah said, hating how stilted and awkward she sounded even as the words left her mouth.

The butler did not seem to mind. He gave a small head nod. "Of course. Won't you please come this way?" He motioned to the door.

LJ had by this time gotten out and tipped the driver, before hobbling over to her side. He looked at her.

"No time like the present, Nor," he said with his usual swagger and a hint of acerbity.

Norah nodded and placed a hand on his back, urging him to walk ahead of her. As the cab was whisked away by the fleet hooves of the horse, she took a breath and stopped wishing to be back inside the interior, instead focusing on why she was here in the first place.

At the doorway, the butler motioned for them to follow him to the left into a small room off the vestibule, which was stuffed with lavish sofas and chairs. In an ordinary home, Norah would have labeled this a parlor, but clearly—given the tiny glimpse into the interior she had so far been afforded—Birchwald was far from ordinary. "Reception room" would be a more fitting term.

The butler busied himself with the fireplace, and within minutes the flames licked upward, quickly filling the space with heat. He turned back to them. "I shall take your outerwear for you, if you'd like."

"Thank you," Norah said, peeling the gloves from her fingers and unbuttoning her heavy coat.

LJ needed help with his buttons. With the patience of a mother, Norah undid each and helped him shuck the coat down his arms.

"Whom shall I say is calling?" the butler asked next, once his arms were laden with their coats.

"The Abernathys, please. I was told Mr. Drury would be expecting me. I believe Mr. Thompson—"

"Mr. Thompson did indeed ring us. I will let the master know. Wait here, please," the butler interrupted her rambling.

She nodded.

As the butler left to announce them, Norah flopped into the chair closest to the fire, heaving a sigh. The journey was over and they had made it unscathed. She figured that had been the hardest part of this enterprise. It would be easy from here.

Malcolm

They were here, in his house. Just across the vestibule and in the reception room, in fact.

Malcolm practically buzzed with contained energy.

Ever since Arnold's phone call, Malcolm had been on high alert, waiting for this moment. It had affected his already tenuous sleep schedule, and made him snappish and brittle with the help. He avoided the guild members altogether for the last day, knowing it was unfair to take his mood out on them.

Consequently, Malcolm had been overly attentive to the goings on at his front door, more so than usual. He was aware of the strangers' presence from practically the moment they entered the door, so he did not have much use for Mathers' announcement.

His need for pettiness won out over politeness. Instead of seeing them right away, he pretended to be busy in his office for much of the next hour. Let them stew a bit in the reception room. Malcolm knew they'd be fine in there, probably sipping some of his expensive coffee while they waited.

In the meantime, the extended wait continued to jangle at Malcolm's nerves.

He finally sent Mathers to fetch them at a quarter to three. Even then, he cautioned the butler to take his time bringing them into the office.

He needed a drink.

But no, He'd meet them sober. Somehow, he felt it was important.

A soft knock on the door readied him for its opening. Mathers stood ramrod straight. "The Abernathys, sir."

The butler moved to the side, and there they were. Two people, his age or younger, a man who limped forward with the rash energy of confidence, and a skinny woman, her dark coif messy from travel, who pretended to have that same confidence but failed miserably.

He hated awkward silences, but his surly mood did not allow him to show the proper manners. Instead, he simply barked his name. "Malcolm Drury."

The woman flinched at the introduction. A smug warmth lit up Malcolm's chest. He expected the man to introduce himself next, but the woman caught a second wind.

"Mr. Drury, thank you for allowing us into your home. My name is Norah Abernathy, and this is my brother, Leighton. LJ for short."

He watched her shrewdly, the smugness turning into an angry fire. "What does the 'J' stand for?"

She seemed perplexed. Good. "In LJ? It stands for James."

"No," Malcolm barked, startling her anew. "Not his name. Yours. What does the 'J' in Norah J. Abernathy stand for?"

Her confusion was paramount, which gave him ample glee. She stuttered before speaking, "I don't quite understand what that has to do with anything—"

"Because, madam, I am just a tad irritated by the fact that you held your sex incognito within the contents of your letter." His voice grew in volume with this statement, and he brandished said letter in the air, having found it in the stacks while he made them wait.

There. He'd announced it out loud. How dare a woman of all things try to pull one over him? The anger he had felt ever since Arnold's call seemed vindicated.

Her face flushed. "Perhaps, Mr. Drury, given how you react to perfect strangers, I would not even have gotten in the door had you known. Perhaps, *Mister Drury*, my full name does not get me places like my initials do. And just perhaps, in a perfect world, it should not matter what the 'J' stands for."

He had to admit, she had gumption. He felt a begrudging respect grow. "Very well, Miss Norah J. Abernathy. What brings you to my home?"

She was still riled up, he could tell by her flashing eyes and firm mouth, but she was trying to rein it in like a proper lady. "You clearly received my letter, so I believe you already know why I am here. My brother and I are seeking membership."

Malcolm knew, all right. Her confirmation only served to aggravate him. He needed a moment away from talking with this confounding creature. He glanced at Leighton Abernathy, who had carried an air of amusement about him the moment the conversation turned heated. It spoke of someone who took pleasure in others' misfortune. It was interesting, to say the least. "Cursed?"

Leighton flashed a roguish sideways smile as he brought his full attention to Malcolm. "Belize. 1909. I discovered a cave. Clearly, it had been used as a burial site. But everything within the cave was covered in crystals. Quite the sight." He pulled out a small object from his vest pocket, the surface twinkling in the light of the office.

Malcolm peered at it from across the desk. "Is that a bone?" He tried to hide his grimace.

Leighton smirked, his expression unsettling. "Good eye. A finger bone, to be precise. The cave was littered with native skeletons. It was just a souvenir, but now my bones are crystallizing too. Have been since 1912, when I left the country."

Malcolm suppressed a shudder. He would never understand why some people thought human remains made good souvenirs.

Miss Abernathy cut in, "Our family has a penchant for curses. LJ's mobility and general health are diminishing rapidly. That is why we've come to you."

"I wouldn't say they are diminishing rapidly, Nor," Mr. Abernathy interjected. "It's my body, and I feel well enough."

The woman shot her brother a look, her brows drawn together. He in turn shrugged his shoulders and focused back on Malcolm.

Malcolm sat back in his chair. "Of course. Mr. Abernathy, you are most certainly welcome to join, provided you can pay the entrance fee."

"And me?" the woman asked with audacity.

Malcolm gave her a challenging stare. "Absolutely not."

Norah

Her face heated at Mr. Drury's words, matching the inferno in her chest. This man had not given her two seconds of civility before antagonizing her. How dare he—how dare he!

"I beg your pardon?" she said, trying to quell the anger that licked at her brain. She took a steadying breath. She must remain the civil one. She must. "I believe, Mr. Drury, that I have made my intentions clear from the start—"

He laughed. It would have been a nice sound to hear from his rich, deep voice if not for the fact it was aimed at her. "Have you, Miss Abernathy? Once again I ask you, is purposefully hiding your femininity from me a clear intention?"

"That should have nothing to do with the subject at hand!" Norah tried not to shout, but her volume did increase along with her ire.

Mr. Drury looked at her. He softened his voice into a more conversational tone. "Tell me. What is the name of my guild, of which I am in charge?"

Norah opened her mouth without a sound before snapping it shut to think on the question. "The Guild for Cursed Adventurers, is it not?"

He chuckled and shook his head. "You forgot the most important part. It's the *Gentlemen's* Guild for Cursed Adventurers. Unless I am thoroughly mistaken, there is no way you can be a gentleman, am I correct?"

She clenched the fingers of one hand. This was an avenue she had trod down many times before. As a woman, she could not vote. As a woman, she was dependent on her family's fortunes, with no hope to control her own wealth. She could attend classes at Oxford, but she could not actually obtain a degree in doing so. And now this.

"There is a growing number of people who believe such gender separation to be archaic and are starting to eschew the traditional segregation," she pointed out rationally.

"Ah, but not all of us agree with that, miss, and as I pointed out, this is *my* guild. My rules. But let us bypass that for now and examine the other criteria for membership expressly mentioned in the name, shall we? Are you an adventurer?"

She shifted in her seat. "No, I suppose not."

"Are you cursed?"

Her temper snapped. "How is it possible for you to turn down free money? The fact remains, I'd be an asset to you, to my brother. He is the most important thing to me, and for you to so callously deny me, is a true mark of your unfeeling character, sir."

LJ put a hand on her arm to calm her as Drury's eyes flashed. "Madam, you have no idea what it is like to run this guild. To have a company of men depending on me. These are broken men, Miss Abernathy, men who come here to live as comfortably as they can in the presence of other souls who understand the daily torment they must live with. It is a brotherhood. I am not turning down free money. I am turning down *your* money. I have enough to pay the few servants who stick around. Your contribution is not necessary, nor is your company."

His tone brooked no argument. Norah knew when she was beaten, at least in this round.

"Now," he paused his rant to peek at his pocket watch. "Regrettably, it is too late in the day to call back a cab for you. I will allow you guest quarters for tonight, and then first thing in the morning I will call for transportation." He glanced at LJ. "Mr. Abernathy, it is your decision whether you wish to stay or leave with your sister in the morning."

"Thank you, Mr. Drury," LJ said. "I'll give it some thought. Truthfully, this was Norah's idea from the start, so I'm not sure I'm inclined to stay."

Norah clenched her teeth.

"If you do choose to join, the membership rate is $600. Yearly. Can you afford that?"

It was a princely sum to give all at once, but they had some familial wealth to fall back on. Norah spoke for her brother, "We can surely afford double that."

Mr. Drury looked down his nose at her, trying to put her in her place, she was sure. "Duly noted. I'll put you both up on the second floor tonight—Mr. Abernathy, Birchwald does have an elevator if stairs are difficult. Did you bring luggage?"

Norah noticed the change in his tone every time he switched from speaking to her to speaking to LJ: a softening, a compassion. If only she had not seen the hardened, cynical side first, she might have liked this man.

LJ answered his question, "Yes, indeed. Two small trunks. Just enough for a night or two. Norah figured we could send for the rest of our things later."

"Hm, I imagine." Drury almost sneered at her as he looked over at her again.

She scowled, forgetting her manners.

Her expression did not seemingly faze the man. He gazed thoughtfully at her for a moment before leaning over and pulling on a cord behind him. When the butler popped in within a matter of seconds (probably lurking in the hallway, Norah surmised), Mr. Drury addressed him next. "Mathers, the Abernathys are to stay overnight. I'll have you assist Mr. Abernathy into the Iris bedroom—no, Poppy would be better since it's closer to the elevator. Will you please inform Mrs. Bixby that I request her assistance for Miss Abernathy? She can take the Aster Room."

The butler, Mathers, hesitated. "The Aster Room? Are you quite certain, sir?"

Drury waved a hand. "Yes, yes. Just for one night. If Mr. Abernathy decides to stay, we'll get him moved to the third floor tomorrow." He faced Norah and LJ once more. "Dinner will be served in your rooms at eight. I'd appreciate it if you did not go exploring. The privacy of my members is very important."

Mathers left to fetch Mrs. Bixby, leaving the brother and sister duo in the clutches of Mr. Drury once more.

Norah decided one last time to plead her case. "Mr. Drury, if I could just—"

"No, madam," he said with a swipe of his hand. He rubbed a palm down his face in exasperation, belying an exhaustion he had hidden from her earlier. "Mathers and Mrs. Bixby will be here to attend to your needs. I bid you both a good day." He stood, not waiting for any other conversation, and walked out of the room with a massive sigh and a harder closing of the door than was necessary.

Norah soaked in the newfound silence for a moment, temporarily paralyzed by the overwhelming sensation of failure.

As usual, LJ was her savior. "You tried, Nor. He makes some excellent points. There are certain criteria one must meet to join."

His tone was kind, but a lifetime with LJ had attuned Norah's ears to every subtlety, and she easily pinpointed the hint of glee hidden deep within the words. He wouldn't stay, not without her by his side. "I can do so much for this place, I just know it," she responded, feeling the tears welling in her eyes. She blinked furiously to keep them at bay. Tears were weakness. Tears meant the dastardly man had accomplished getting under her skin. She would not give him the satisfaction, even if he wasn't here to witness them.

Mathers returned, followed by a much shorter, plumper woman with pure white hair and dimpled smile.

"Madam, if you would please follow our housekeeper, Mrs. Bixby, to your room," he said with the same starched tone he used with his master. "Sir, let me assist you to your quarters."

Norah and LJ exchanged glances. He fumbled for her hand, giving it a small squeeze. "Be good, sis," he said as he stood slowly, wincing with the regaining of his feet.

Norah stood as well with a much more fluid motion, despite the daze she found herself in. She allowed LJ to hobble out first before turning her attention to the woman.

"Hello there, dearie," the woman greeted her, her dimple twinkling in her real smile.

Norah couldn't help but smile back. "You must be Mrs. Bixby."

"I am. Housekeeper of this insane asylum, but don't let the master know I said such a thing. It's just between us women," she said, leaning in conspiratorially.

Norah liked her immediately. "I do believe you have been sent to escort me to my prison cell," she joked.

Mrs. Bixby tutted. "Indeed I am. Will you be needing the elevator or shall we take the stairs?"

Norah shivered. Elevators gave her the willies. There was something chilling about being hoisted in a box between floors. She always imagined the cables snapping. "The stairs, if you please."

Mrs. Bixby led Norah out of the office, down a shallow set of stairs and into the grand entrance hall. Norah had glimpsed it earlier, and now that she was standing in the hall, she had to take a moment to center herself, dazzled by the opulence as she was.

The hall was massive, with solid marble archways surrounding it. Heavy velvet curtains flanked the arches in rich red tones. High above, two stories up, the ceiling was painted with a fresco of a cloudy sky, with gilded ceiling tiles framing the artwork, and massive chandeliers dotting the surface. Everywhere she turned, carvings and gilt caught her eye.

To her right, just beyond the arches, loomed a fireplace so massive she could easily stand within it. To her left, a grand staircase replete with red carpet runners beckoned between the arches.

The archways directly in front of her contained enormous glass windows which afforded a view of a covered area—a loggia, if she remembered correctly. Beyond the loggia and its own arches, she spied a sprawling terrace covered in snow.

"This way, please," Mrs. Bixby said, drawing Norah back to earth. Finding she could move again, Norah followed her to the grand staircase.

At the first landing, the staircase bifurcated. Mrs. Bixby took the left path, following the curve up to the second-floor landing. A generous walkway flanked the large opening of the hall below on three sides, with marble columns rising to the ceiling between spans of ornate iron balustrade. Norah could see an upper loggia through the windows where the walkway terminated.

Norah had little time to gawk before the housekeeper was once more on the move, taking the walkway to the right and turning the first corner of the gallery. "We have three bedrooms on this floor, along with master and mistress rooms," Mrs. Bixby said as they walked. They passed the elevator, and Mrs. Bixby motioned to the next door. "That's the Poppy Room, where your brother will stay tonight," she mentioned.

They passed a flight of stairs leading up to the third floor directly on the other side of the Poppy Room, and then turned the next corner of the gallery. Halfway down the walkway on this stretch, Mrs. Bixby stopped at an ornately carved door.

"Here we are," she proclaimed with her usual cheer. "The Aster Room."

"Are all the bedrooms named after flowers?" Norah asked as she looked around. Her eye caught on a similarly ornate door in the corner of the gallery, next to the third-floor stairs.

"Indeed, they are," Mrs. Bixby confirmed as she unlocked the room. "Lily and Iris in the north, Poppy in the south. Plus Aster and Rose."

The way she kept Aster and Rose separate from the others piqued Norah's inquisitiveness. She studied the other door again. "Is that the Rose Room?" she asked, drawing the older woman's attention to the other door.

"Yes, it is."

"Is the Rose Room also the master bedroom?"

Mrs. Bixby paused with the key in the hole. "A keen mind you've got, dearie."

"Then, that would make this the mistress bedroom," Norah deduced.

The housekeeper nodded, her lips tight.

"Is there not a Mrs. Drury?" Norah asked with natural curiosity. It was unusual for a guest to stay in the most important bedroom of the estate.

Mrs. Bixby's mouth became a fine line, further inciting Norah's curiosity. "There is not," was the simple reply as the housekeeper flung the door open and ushered Norah inside.

It was cold and dark, the windows heavily draped. Mrs. Bixby flicked a switch near the door, and the wall sconces flickered to life, illuminating the spacious room. Norah was impressed that the mansion had electric lights.

"My apologies for the chill; let me get a fire started for you," the housekeeper said as she bustled over to the fireplace.

"It's not a bother, really," Norah said, even though she rubbed her hands together surreptitiously for warmth. "I'm sure a servant could do the same if you have more important duties to attend to."

Mrs. Bixby let out a snort as she turned a knob on the side of the fireplace. A hissing sound filled the room. "Won't be but a minute, thanks to the miracle of gas. It's a bit of a skeleton crew around here, I'm afraid. Just me and Mathers, plus Cook and her scullery maid, bless them. Lost our last servant a week ago. The maids don't seem too keen on staying for very long."

"Why is that?"

The housekeeper took a long match from a container built into the surround and expertly struck it. "Well, it's a bit of an unusual household, you see. Mr. Malcolm has got his hands full with his guests, and requires some unusual care for them at times. Most girls aren't made of strong enough stuff to withstand the pressure." She touched the match to the ceramic logs. The fire roared to life, the flames already driving away the chill. "There we are. See this knob? Just turn it counterclockwise if you get overheated. I'll be back before bedtime to make sure you don't burn the place down in our sleep."

"You're too kind," Norah said with only a hint of sarcasm.

"Is there anything else you'll be needing before supper, miss?"

Norah tapped her lips in thought. "Do you have any magazines? Newspapers?"

Mrs. Bixby seemed taken aback for a brief moment. "Why, yes, as a matter of fact. The old missus enjoyed the Ladies' Home Journal, and Mr. Malcolm never stopped the subscription after her death. I also have the latest McCall's I can lend you for tonight. And as for newspapers, I'll gather a couple of Tribunes for you. Will that do?"

"Yes, thank you."

The housekeeper bustled out to gather the reading material. Norah was grateful. If she was to be stuck in this room for the next few hours and the night, she'd at least have something to do besides stew in her defeat.

That was the hope, anyway.

CHAPTER FIVE

Wednesday, February 10th, 1915

Norah

IT WAS AFTER MIDNIGHT, but Norah tossed and turned.

It wasn't for a lack of comfort or warmth. The fireplace, although the gas had been turned off, still emitted a gentle heat from the ceramic logs, and with her heavy wool nightgown and the thick blankets, Norah was snug enough. The mattress, while not new, was pliant and lump-free. Money really could make one's life as comfortable as possible.

No, the physical comfort was not the issue. It was the mental torment that chased away the sleep.

She should have handled things better. Mr. Drury was right; she'd purposefully kept her name a mystery, hoping it would at least get her foot in the door. Technically, it had worked, but she'd invoked the wrath of the bear in the process.

Perhaps if she'd been forthcoming from the very start, he would have had the heart to listen to her. Then again, Mr. Drury did not exactly exude a liberalness of the mind. It was equally possible that he would have just shut down her request all the faster for her honesty.

There must be *something* she could do in the morning to change his mind. She'd be polite, she wouldn't antagonize him. She'd cure her ills with honey, not vinegar.

The problem with that plan was the simple fact that his reaction to her riled her up, no matter what the conversation was. She found herself quick to argue with him, uncharacteristically so. She seemingly had no control over herself when it came to Malcolm Drury.

It was maddening.

Sighing, she gave up trying to sleep. She threw back the covers and crept over to the wall, flicking the switch to turn on the lights. As the sconces buzzed to life, she decided reading might calm her mind enough to allow her a few hours of sleep.

She surveyed the small stack of material Mrs. Bixby had lent to her. She'd already read the two magazines from cover to cover, the mostly inane articles chafing her. Any reading was better than doing nothing, however. There were still two newspapers under the magazines that Norah had not yet touched. Surely, they'd have less vapid stories. She reached for those.

The first was dated two days ago, and the second was a week prior. She picked up the newer one first, glancing at the sensationalism journalists liked to splash on the front page about the war in Europe. She read an article about Germany officially declaring the seas around Great Britain to be a war zone, threatening to sink any ship they deemed a threat—including merchant and passenger ships. She checked the date of this declaration, stunned it had transpired only days after she and Nell had safely departed. Their timing couldn't have been more perfect.

Now that she was back in the States, the war seemed so very far away and out of her mind. It was funny how the distance of an ocean could make the woes of another region feel unreal or insignificant, even when she logically knew they weren't.

Having had her fill of war news, she moved on to the local pages, and finally—to be thorough—the classifieds. She could not care a wit about a widow's room for rent or some lady's lost engagement ring. More interesting to her were the segments of suffragists calling to action, trying to get those housewives out of their homes to spread the cause. Norah was not one to picket, but she appreciated the sentiment.

The job listings were less exciting, but then a single word caught her eye as she scanned the postings: *Birchwald*. She brought the paper closer to her eyes to read the fine print.

WANTED: Strong, reliable young women as maids at Birchwald, Croton Falls. Must not back away from a challenge. Duties include general housework, plus care of unusual patients. Inquire at any hour.

Norah thought back to what the housekeeper had said—they were working on a skeleton crew. Her interest perked up. She put the paper aside and grabbed the older one. If the same ad was in this one from a week ago, chances were high that there had been no nibbles. She opened the paper to the appropriate page.

There was the ad, same wording and all.

She pursed her lips, deep in thought. An idea was forming.

Malcolm

Malcolm was too agitated to sleep. He knew it was futile to even try.

Instead, he lounged in his office chair, staring at the fire on his left.

It happened on occasion, his brain awhirl with memories of past discrepancies, things he wished he'd done differently, or people he had hurt, whether on purpose or by accident.

The whiskey did not help anything, either. Sometimes, if he had a drink late enough, like tonight, he would either need to stay awake for a good long time, or further drink himself into an alcohol-induced sleep, which was never a restful way of going about things.

He was about to opt for option B, however. Otherwise he'd never get that woman off of his mind.

A soft knock sounded on his office door. Puzzled, he glanced at the clock near his desk. 12:47 a.m. His butler always went to bed around ten, but perhaps something was amiss. "Mathers?"

A faint voice filtered through the door, too delicate and high-pitched to be Mathers. "No, it's me. Miss Abernathy."

Malcolm slumped slightly. This was the last thing he needed. He stayed silent for a second longer, which was enough time for the woman to fill the gap. "Could I talk to you?"

He could say no. It was in his right. But somehow, this midnight meeting was too odd of an encounter to pass up. "Enter," he barked.

She slowly opened the door and walked in, setting herself in the same chair she had occupied earlier.

Malcolm stared at her. "What on earth are you wearing?"

He shouldn't have brought attention to her state of dress, but he had never had a woman ask for an audience while wearing a wool nightgown and a flimsy wrap. Her mouse-brown hair had been unpinned from her crown, but was tied back in a loose braid. This too was an entirely different look than he was used to.

She looked down at herself, her face reddening. "I apologize for the informality. It's the middle of the night, after all."

"I'm aware of the time. Seeing the lateness of the hour, would you care to get to the point of this meeting?"

She huffed out a breath before meeting his eyes with a determination she had lacked in the earlier encounter. "You are at a disadvantage, sir."

He didn't catch her meaning. "Come again?"

She placed a hand on the edge of the desk, splaying out her fingers. Malcolm couldn't help but watch them. She spoke with her same blasted assurance from before. "You are at a disadvantage. I know something about your affairs you didn't want me to know."

Alarm flared with red-hot alacrity. Malcolm struggled to take a proper breath in the wake of her declaration. She couldn't possibly know, could she? Who could have told her?

Malcolm needed some clarification before the panic completely overrode his senses. He leaned forward, trying for nonchalance but surely allowing some of the unease to filter into his wide eyes despite his best efforts. "What is it you think you know?"

She was smug, that mouth of hers twisting into a knowing grin that did his emotional turmoil no favors. "You are short on help, and have been for some time."

He flinched back, the words she uttered not what he was expecting. His chest unclenched, although confusion addled his mind.

She continued, "I've seen the classifieds for the past week. I'm assuming you've lost a lot of staff recently, and Birchwald has gotten a reputation. It means you've gotten no applications. You're drowning, Mr. Drury, and adding new members to your organization will only throw more water in your face."

The secret she divulged was nowhere near the one he'd been worried she knew, but still, her words twisted his insides with their truth. He leaned back further, aiming to appear aloof. "I see. And I'm assuming you have a reason for bringing this up? Perhaps a plan to help ease me out of this pool of water I've found myself in?"

She nodded, her deep brown eyes twinkling. "You won't let me join the Guild. I understand that, and I begrudgingly accept that. Instead, *I* am applying to be a servant. An assistant, if you will. I planned to stay to help my brother; what are a few more bodies to take care of?"

He stared at her for a silent moment before letting out a guffaw. She did not join in his mirth, her face neutral. He collected himself.

"I think you may be underestimating what you are asking to do," he told her.

She raised an eyebrow. "I think you might be underestimating *me*," she replied.

He tapped a finger on the desk, buying time to think. Unfortunately, his mind was in tatters tonight. "I won't pay you," he finally countered, grasping at one last reason to get her to back down.

"Fine."

"And you can change your mind and leave at any time. My men know this place is not a prison, and the same goes for you."

"I wouldn't expect anything less."

"And you'd have to help all of the members."

"I already said I w—"

"Sores and all."

"Sores ...?"

Aha. He'd gotten her with that one.

She only hesitated for a second. "I accept."

Blast.

He let out a ragged breath. "Very well. A fair warning, you'll not have any seniority in this house. You'll answer not only to me, but to Mathers and Mrs. Bixby."

"Of course."

He stared at the woman, noting the determination in her eyes. He blew out a breath. "Are you sure?"

She did not hesitate. "I'll see to it that my brother's membership fee is wired to you post haste. And I'll be sending for more of our things in the next couple of days."

"Yes, yes," Malcolm said without truly listening to her. Did he really just agree to letting her stay? It all happened so fast. "Miss Abernathy, I will have you officially meet the members in the morning. For now, though, I suggest you get some rest. It might be a long day tomorrow." *Your first, and hopefully your last,* he added in his mind.

"Thank you, Mr. Drury," she said with true appreciation as she stood, clutching her wrap about her. "You won't regret it."

Malcolm was afraid he already had.

But he had one small consolation. Perhaps if she actually met the men in the Guild, she'd realize her mistake and run screaming for the hills. Given the limited staying power of his servants, he couldn't see this failing to work.

He was quite possibly a genius.

Norah

He was an idiot. It was the only explanation.

Mr. Drury seemed to think he had won some battle, making a point to tell her he was not going to pay her for her service. Norah would have happily *paid* to be in this position, so she had come out on top with that one.

In a much more cheerful mood, Norah slept soundly until seven, when a knock sounded on her door.

"Miss?" Mrs. Bixby's shrill voice was muffled by the door.

Norah sighed and stretched before getting out of the warm bed and making her way to the door.

Mrs. Bixby charged in like a miniature locomotive the moment the door was no longer an obstacle. "Good morning, miss, I hope you got enough sleep. The master has requested your breakfast be brought up now. He's also requested your presence in the entrance hall promptly at 8:30—he's very keen on promptness. I'd have otherwise let you sleep more."

Norah waited for a beat to make sure the housekeeper had officially run out of words to spew. "Oh, well, that's quite alright, Mrs. Bixby. I understand."

The older woman started the fire again and threw back more drapes to allow the dim morning light to filter through. Only then did she wheel the cart inside, setting up a plate of eggs, biscuits, and bacon plus a steaming cup upon the small round table that resided against the far wall of the room.

"Enjoy, dearie," she called out as she wheeled the cart away and closed the door behind her.

Norah smiled at the brief exchange, so different than any she'd had with the master of the house. She walked over to the table, sitting and tucking the napkin into her lap. As she took bites of the breakfast—offering silent thanks to the cook, who knew their business—she gazed at the room that had been hers temporarily. She imagined after this morning she'd be moved. A shame, really. This was the nicest bedroom she'd ever inhabited.

The room shape was peculiar, a perfect oval with a span of flat wall for the bed and dresser to rest against. The door resided down a short hall at one end of the curved portion, and here, at the other curve, she found herself looking out of the tall windows as she consumed her breakfast. Her view confirmed that the Aster Room jutted out slightly from the rest of the story, sitting atop the solarium on the first floor, although the solarium extended further out in its half-circle design. The solarium roof was gorgeous from this perspective: black iron curved in intricate patterns with thick glass between the swirls. She imagined only the mistress of this room knew about the beauty of the solarium's roof from this angle. It gave her a small thrill to be privy to that secret.

Now that she was properly taking in the contents of her room, Norah understood why it was named the Aster Room. What looked to be white wallpaper at first glance was actually delicate aster flowers in artful rows, the hearts of each bloom painted with a subtle gold sheen. Pops of sage green in the form of leaves and stems broke up the white of the flowers here and there.

Swallowing the last bite of food, she stood to inspect the rest of the room. Norah had already discovered the marbled bathroom to the left of the entrance last night, complete with a massive clawfoot bathtub, a toilet, and a bidet. And to the right, across from the bed, was the extensive dressing room, now empty of clothing but waiting to be filled with gowns opulent enough to fit the mansion.

She only poked her head into this room. Her wardrobe was too limited at the moment, and besides, she did not think Mr. Drury held many lavish balls these days.

Having satisfied her curiosity, and mentally bidding a farewell to the room, Norah finished her morning grooming and dressed herself smartly in her navy dress. There was nothing else to do but face the dragon in his own castle. She was ready.

The man in question met her at the foot of the grand stairs as she descended, his square jawline slightly hidden by stubble but otherwise attired like the gentleman he was. "Miss Abernathy, thank you for being on time."

She inclined her head graciously. "A lady does not keep anyone waiting."

He gave a smirk. "Indeed."

The great hall was suspiciously empty. "Where are the others? I thought I was to meet them."

Mr. Drury shifted his eyes away momentarily. "I thought it best to keep them in one of the smaller rooms. The third floor is nowhere this spacious or opulent, and while they have free roam of Birchwald, most prefer to spend their time up there. The great hall can be a bit intimidating."

Norah understood the feeling.

"Let me give you a quick tour before we get to them," he continued. He held out an arm. She hesitated as she looked at it, debating whether or not to be rude. Ultimately, she linked her arm with his and allowed herself to be led about.

He cut across the hall, entering one of the archways into the wide hall with the grand fireplace. Norah noticed a stuffed polar bear, its lower jaw hanging askew. Mr. Drury took no notice of it as he led her right and through a doorway.

"Here is the library," he said, not pausing to stop, despite Norah's slowing of her feet. She only had a moment to take in the dark wood wainscoting and enormous bookcases before being whisked through a second door into a new hallway.

This one had curio cabinets along the length, holding an assortment of art, sculptures, and natural specimens, much like what one would find in a museum collection. The assemblage clearly spanned geographic regions and cultures; Norah spied ancient coins, carved jade figures, an elephant's foot, and a monkey's desiccated hand in quick succession.

"What are these?" Norah asked as Mr. Drury sped past them.

"My father's collection." He sounded bored. He paused outside a glass door. "This is the solarium," he said without entering. His walking speed resumed.

They entered the music room at the end of the hall before reemerging into the fireplace area, where Mr. Drury took her diagonally across the great hall and into the foyer, past the elevator. "The breakfast room," he announced as they marched by the door and into yet another hallway. This one resided behind the grand staircase. "The dining room is here on the left," he informed her. "It does not get much use, but you are welcome to dine within if you wish."

Norah slowed down, forcing Drury to pause his walking. "And the kitchen?"

He seemed puzzled by her interest. "On the other side of the dining room. You must enter the butler's pantry to access it. But this way, please. The trophy room is at the end of this hall, and my other guests are waiting for us."

"Of course," Norah replied demurely. Internally, her head spun. This had been a whirlwind of a tour, as if the master did not truly care if she saw anything.

They arrived within the trophy room, which was as Norah expected: light wood walls filled with various mounted animal heads, and over-stuffed red sofas pushed to the sides of the room. A well-stocked bar took up much of the back wall.

The room was also filled with men, standing or sitting in a clump, as if they felt as much out of place as Norah did.

"Gentlemen," Mr. Drury boomed to the crowd, "let me introduce to you your new companion, Miss Abernathy. She has graciously offered to lend a hand in assisting you in your daily life."

The silence overwhelmed the space for a moment as most of the men turned their attention on Norah.

"A companion, eh?" exclaimed a voice within the cluster. "Seems a little too straight laced to be of much fun, if you ask me. And not much of a figure, eh?"

A couple of chuckles ran through the gathering.

Norah let out a gasp, unused to being objectified—at least out loud.

Drury laughed that deep, honest laugh again. She would enjoy the sound more if it wasn't always at her expense.

"Take no heed, madam," he said to her. "Ambrose's curse can be rather … rambunctious."

"That wasn't me thinking that, miss!" the same voice called out.

Norah nodded, pretending to understand.

Malcolm took the lead in conversation once more. "Well, shall we go one by one and introduce ourselves? Let's start with Pablo Reyes, at the end. Go ahead, Pablo."

The first man in line stepped forward, his olive complexion and name denoting a Spanish heritage. "Will you marry me, miss?"

Norah blinked, unsure how to answer. "My apologies. I don't even know you."

The man hung his head. "*Mis disculpas.* It is my curse. I am Señor Pablo Reyes, renowned explorer from Catalonia. I do not actually wish to marry you, but I must ask. And I will do so again. And again. It gets … tiresome for you."

"And I'm sure my answer will be the same each time, Mr. Reyes," Norah responded kindly.

The Spaniard inclined his head in acknowledgement. "It is to be expected." He stepped back.

The next man in line was physically hard to look at upon first glance, but Norah forced herself to make eye contact. It would not do to make any of the men feel like she looked down upon them on their first meeting.

"You poor soul," she said to him. "I think I can see what your affliction is."

The man was covered in welts and pustules, some large, some small, and some already burst, the contents within dripping down his skin. It was impossible to tell his age due to the sheer number of blemishes. Even his scalp was covered in the sores, and no hair grew upon his head.

Despite his outward appearance, he smiled at Norah. "The name is Rodney, miss. Rodney Paulson."

"A pleasure, Mr. Paulson," she simply replied, returning the smile in the hopes of setting him at ease.

Her eyes moved to the next in line, a rather handsome young fellow, despite the numerous scars that adorned his exposed skin. These were not the rounded scars that Mr. Paulson would have if his skin would ever stop erupting, but the thin silvery marks made by something cutting into the flesh.

He dropped his eyes once Norah met them, a small blush staining his cheeks and throat. Oh, this one was adorable.

"Hello, miss," he said shyly. "My name is Farley Hunt. I could definitely use your assistance on the regular. My problem is a small letter opener. It wants my blood, you see."

Norah cocked her head. "I don't quite see at this moment, Mr. Hunt, but I'd be happy to learn more about you later."

"She wants to see him naked, is what she meant," that other man, the loud one, said. A couple of the members chuckled.

Norah sighed, doing her best not to let this one under her skin. "And what might your name be?"

The man, a rather short bloke with a mop of red hair and freckles, stepped forward. His voice was high, with an obvious cockney accent. "The name's Ambrose Lyster. I'm good for nothing and a ginger, to boot." He scowled and looked around. "That wasn't very nice, chaps."

Mr. Hunt elbowed Lyster kindly. "Only joking, Ambrose." He turned to Norah. "You'll get used to his eccentricities soon enough, miss."

Norah almost wanted to laugh if the greater emotion overtaking her wasn't embarrassment. "I'm sure he is a lovely man, behind that tongue of his."

"I'd love to get my tongue in front of something else right about now." Ambrose flushed as the words left his mouth, as if he didn't wish to say them. It confused Norah even more, not to mention flustered her with his salaciousness. She was sure she was redder than a beet by now.

"*Moving on*," Mr. Drury growled. Lyster shrank slightly and disappeared back into the crowd. "This next gentleman was our newest member, before your brother arrived. His name is Peter Withers, an English man who came from Africa. He is unable to speak or to do much else, honestly. And that is his assistant, Karanja, behind him. They only arrived last week."

Norah gazed at the unfortunate older man who sat in his wheelchair, his blue eyes vacant, a line of drool trailing from his parted lips and sticking in his silver beard. Behind him, a tall man with dark skin stood protectively. He seemed more uncomfortable than even Norah, an understandable feeling given the situation.

"How do you do," she said politely.

"Ma'am," Karanja answered in a deep voice, refusing to look into her eyes for long.

Her gaze moved on to the next person. "Is that a chicken in your arms?" she asked, dumbfounded.

The man, a scrawny fellow in his forties with dark circles under his eyes, nodded eagerly as he proudly displayed the pure white chicken he held. "My name is Fred Jamison, miss. I was captured by wildmen in Borneo some five years ago, along with my longtime friend, Herbert Norris. We were tortured for a time before being individually cursed and eventually escaping. This is my best friend and fellow adventurer, Mr. Norris."

The chicken let out three clucks in rapid succession.

"But that's a chicken," Norah said weakly.

"That he is, miss. A tragedy, truly. Mr. Norris got a worse curse than me, to be sure."

"But Mr. Norris is a *hen*," she pointed out.

"The fates are cruel, sometimes, miss," Mr. Jamison said as he stroked Mr. Norris' red comb with affection.

Norah raised her eyebrows but did not continue this line of inane questioning. Instead, she glanced over at the next man, who also sat in a wheelchair, his lower half extended outward and covered with a blanket. She smiled kindly at the older man.

"You're a spot of sunshine in this dour community, miss," he said with a voice that wheezed and crackled. "Hector Freeman's the name. I traveled to Australia some three years ago and took a piece of that big rock with me as a souvenir. I didn't think much of it at the time, but now I'm dying, so I suppose I should have given it more thought."

"I'm sure it can't be that bad—" Norah began to soothe.

Mr. Freeman whipped the blanket off of his legs and rapped on one of his knees. The surface did not give for his fist, like living flesh should have, and the sound his knuckles produced was a firm knock. Norah let out a gasp.

"They're stone now, miss. Can't move them. Started at my toes, and every day it creeps higher up my body. There's no reason to lie to myself or anyone else. This will surely kill me."

Norah instantly thought of LJ, how the crystals were consuming his bones, how in some specific amount of time he would no longer be able to move them, and then he'd wither and die if help was not found soon enough. Her eyes filled with unshed tears at the very real comparison sitting before her.

"No need to cry over me, miss," Mr. Freeman said to comfort her, misunderstanding the target of her sentiments. "I've made peace with my fate."

Mutely, Norah nodded, desperately wishing her emotions away. She took a deep breath, dispelling some of her sadness. The rest stayed; this was a sorry lot of people, after all.

There was one last person standing before her. He worried at the bald spot on the top of his lowered head, his eyes squeezed shut.

"Hello, and you are?" Norah asked.

The man glanced at her feet for a fraction of a second and turned away again. "Ivey, miss. I don't wish to see your death, so I'm avoiding looking at you."

Norah took a step back reflexively. "I beg your pardon?"

Mr. Ivey scrunched his eyes closed and noisily breathed through his rather large nose a couple of times. "I've seen the deaths of each of these men more times than I care to admit. Fire. And blood. So much blood. It never comes to pass, but the images stay with me. You're much too pretty to see covered in blood, or burned to a crisp."

"I ... thank you?" Norah stuttered.

Mr. Ivey said nothing, only shrinking into himself more.

Now that introductions were finished, she counted the members. Nine. Nine men, some with curses worse than others. Some who seemed to accept her presence, and others who would perhaps prove to be difficult. And LJ made ten.

It was more than she'd bargained for, she could admit. She would not say that to Mr. Drury, however.

As if summoned by her thoughts, Mr. Drury appeared by her side, a charming smile on his face. "That's the lot of them. Your new wards."

Norah stared at each man again, taking them all in. It would be a challenge, but she was resolute. "Thank you for the introductions. Now then, can anyone tell me what their recovery plan is?"

The men—minus Withers and Ivey—stared blankly at her.

Norah frowned. "I don't think this is the time to be shy. Has anyone made steps toward breaking their curse?"

Reyes shouted, "Will you marry me?"

Lyster said, "What the devil is she talking about?"

No one else spoke up.

Baffled, Norah turned to Mr. Drury. "Why is no one answering me?"

Mr. Drury stared back at her. "Madam, when I said you could help them, I only meant in the way to keep them comfortable while they are here."

She looked into the man's eyes, as gray as the ocean she had recently crossed, and as stormy as well. "You mean to tell me you don't actively seek to break the curses? Only to live with them?"

"The Guild was created to be a sort of retirement place for cursed adventurers, especially those who can no longer function in normal society. I give them a place where they can be themselves amidst other people who can empathize with what they are going through. I thought you understood that, Ms. Abernathy."

"But that's preposterous!" Norah sputtered. She turned to the members. "Have not one of you longed for a day when you would be free of your curse? It *is* possible, you know."

Mr. Drury's voice dipped lower, almost a growl for her ears only. "Giving them false hope would be very dangerous business, madam."

"It's not false. Curses can be broken." She said this loud enough for the group to hear. Mr. Drury clenched his jaw at her words. She ignored him, giving her attention back to the group. "Of course I will make it my duty to lend you comfort in your troubles, but also, I'd like to learn more about your individual curses. I do know some things about curses. I studied at Oxford. Maledictology."

"Mal-uh-what?" Mr. Drury asked.

"Maledictology. The study of curses. A rare science, which is why I had to attend a prestigious place like Oxford to learn about it. Curses are everywhere, Mr. Drury. It doesn't mean one has to roll over and accept them."

"It has been this way for centuries, though."

Norah closed her eyes as if to block out the words she was hearing. "Leave it to a man to embrace the status quo and not strive for change, even if it would benefit him. Mr. Drury, I cannot with good conscience watch these men undergo these curses without at least trying to better their lives." She scrutinized him. "Mr. Thompson mentioned *you* were cursed. Is that true?"

Mr. Drury ruffled up a bit. "Well, yes."

"Would you care to tell me upon which continent your misfortune manifested? Africa? Asia?"

"I would not care to, no."

Norah hmphed. "I should have guessed that response. Very well, keep your secrets. In the meantime, I will do what I was hired to do. I will offer my help to these men."

And don't you dare try to stop me, she added silently.

CHAPTER SIX

Friday, February 12th, 1915

Malcolm

THIS WOMAN WAS HARDER to scare off than Malcolm had anticipated.

He thought for sure after being proposed to, leered at, visibly disgusted, and otherwise surrounded by what most would consider sheer lunacy, Miss Abernathy would run for the hills. Some of the fresh hires certainly did just that, not even sticking around to learn the basics of their jobs.

After the meeting of the members, she'd looked a tad green around the gills, but otherwise resolute. And now, two days later, she was apparently still upon her ridiculous mission to save the gentlemen, if the upstairs chatter was to be trusted.

He shook his head. Maledictology. What a joke.

Whether or not she was to be believed, there was a renewed energy on the third floor, that much was noticeable to Malcolm. Some of the men were intrigued, while others were skeptical of Miss Abernathy's claims. Her presence had piqued something in all of them, a slowly forming vigor that had been lacking in their daily lives before.

Regardless of how anyone felt about the woman in their midst, the integrations were slow-going. Miss Abernathy seemed to be taking her time. She had only spent a few minutes here, a few minutes there, easing herself into the situation, instead of inundating them with her odd presence.

It spoke of thoughtfulness on her part.

These men had largely been shunned by polite society due to their eccentricities. Having a lady in their midst was an incredibly huge adjustment for them, one that he was sure made a few of them self-conscious.

He counted himself as part of that number.

Malcolm begrudgingly admired her for the tactic. This in turn made it more difficult for him to resent her intrusion into their sanctuary.

Personal feelings aside, Malcolm had tried his best to avoid her since the meeting. His part was done, and now it was up to Mathers and Mrs. Bixby to tend to her, and to keep her in line.

In contrast to Miss Abernathy's slow and quiet approach, her brother had barreled into the guild dynamics, instantly inserting himself into the group with limited finesse. His brashness won over the likes of some of the members, thankfully. Leighton, as he insisted he be called, was a bit too much like a happy puppy to be bosom friends with Malcolm, however. There was also something about this demeanor that made Malcolm alert and watchful, as if his joviality was only an act to hide a jagged edge in his personality. Perhaps Malcolm was reading too much into him, though. Perhaps he truly was a likable chap, and it was only his sister who put Malcolm on guard.

Normally, Malcolm accepted a new member without any fanfare, provided they could afford the membership. But between Leighton's too-sunny attitude and Miss Abernathy's aloofness and downright hostility of him, Malcolm sensed some secrets about the Abernathys. With these two new people in his midst, he decided a little research may be in order, if only for his own peace of mind.

And if he could find some dirt—especially on the lady—it might provide him with the tools necessary to either keep her in line or cast her out altogether.

Unfortunately, his resources were extremely limited. He only had his small library and his scrapbooks at Birchwald. He could certainly send Mathers to the city to explore the vast contents of the New York Public Library—he doubted the local library at Croton Falls would have anything available—but the trip would have to be planned to perfection. Malcolm hated having his butler away for too long. Perhaps it was best to work with what he had currently.

Malcolm once again scanned the scrapbooks Arnold Thompson had created, to see if anything of interest caught his eye now that he'd met the living Abernathys in person. It was all the same as the last time he looked, of course, but his attention snagged upon the last of the family to perish—Norah and Leighton's parents. Intrigued, he read again about their deaths.

Robert Abernathy died in November of 1892 off the coast of Africa at the age of thirty-six. His wife Angela passed away in her home in January of 1893 at the age of twenty-nine.

Both parents were relatively young at the time of their individual demises. Malcolm did some quick math; the father died twenty-three years ago, which made the siblings at least that old. He wondered which of the two was older. It was difficult to tell.

Perhaps it was time for him to ask some questions and get the facts straight from the source, if one of them was amenable. He left his office.

Of course it would be Miss Abernathy he ran across first.

She was in the library of all places, the very first room Malcolm stepped into, seeing how it was located next door to his office. Miss Abernathy had taken the sofa in front of the fireplace, a large book open on her lap and entirely oblivious to anything else.

He watched her for a moment as she peered intently at the book, savoring each page before moving to the next. His angle was all wrong to see her face fully, but he could observe the dip of her dark eyelashes as her eyes moved from the top to the bottom of her reading. Her movement was graceful as she expertly turned the page. Her tongue darted out to touch the corner of her mouth, at which point Malcolm felt too much like a voyeur to keep staring. He cleared his throat.

She jumped and turned, her eyes rounded with surprise as she landed upon him. They narrowed upon recognition.

"My apologies, I didn't mean to scare you," he said, although he couldn't keep the grin at bay.

She tilted up the corners of her mouth perceptively. "Quite alright. I was lost in my research."

"What is it that you research?" he asked.

She sighed, closing the book. *The Wilds of Indonesia*, he read from his vantage spot as he moved closer. "I've never once ran across a curse that transforms someone into an animal," she admitted. "I was hoping to learn more about Borneo, and how the native people perform curses."

"Mr. Norris is a bit of an oddity, even here," Malcolm agreed. He paused, studying her. "So. You're an educated woman."

She tried to keep her face neutral, but a hint of a frown snuck through anyway. "Yes, I am."

"I applaud you." The words had tumbled out, but upon further reflection, he was surprised to learn he meant them. The few other women he had known would not have had the determination for such rigorous schooling.

"Thank you," she said, her tone still guarded.

"Tell me, then, Miss Abernathy," Malcolm continued, genuine curiosity making him ask, "why curses?"

She blinked, her lids like a metronome, as if needing the time to parse out his question. Then she let out a ghost of a chuckle. "They fascinate me. After the number of curses my family has suffered from, I suppose it was only natural for me to want to study them."

"Very good. And what can you tell me? Why do they happen? And why are adventurers more commonly affected than others?"

She set the book down next to her, seeming to give his impromptu questions her full attention. Her eyes focused on somewhere to her left. "Curses can happen to anyone, no matter their age, race, or gender." She sounded as if she were reciting from a textbook. She looked at Malcolm. "They can happen anywhere in the world, and they seem to be created by intense emotion, usually negative, but surprisingly this is not always the case. Items can be imbued with this emotion if it's strong enough, and words can also be afflicted."

Malcolm nodded. So far, everything she had said rang true.

"In terms of why adventurers are more prone to curses than other professions, well, that is probably a two-fold issue," Norah continued. "First of all, older items tend to absorb the energies around them over time. Human remains are especially susceptible to that. Disturbing them can be disastrous if done casually, as in my brother's case." She shook her head, clearly annoyed at the carelessness of Leighton's actions.

"And the other part?" Malcolm asked.

She sighed. "In addition to these relics, all cultures around the world have special people who are trained to wield their emotions, making them more adept than the average person at cursing others. Shamans, wizards, priests, call them what you will, but their power is the same. I haven't yet talked with the friend of the chicken—Mr. Jamison, was it? He mentioned a Bornean tribe. I wager he and Mr. Norris did something to anger the tribe, and they cursed the two men as punishment. And this may shock you, Mr. Drury, but I do not blame the tribe one bit." She paused, as if waiting to see if she had scandalized Malcolm. He only raised his eyebrows, a silent request for her to continue.

"Let's not forget the fact that normal, untrained people can also cast curses, given the proper motivational energy. Put all that together, and a man who encounters a different culture—whether its contemporary or ancient—has a higher probability of being cursed than the average person. In other words, Mr. Drury," she said, now with a genuine smirk on her face, "adventurers stick their noses where they don't belong, and mess with things they have no reason to mess with. It's no wonder they are cursed at a higher frequency."

Malcolm was impressed. It would not do to show too much of it, though. "A fine analysis, Miss Abernathy," he told her. He stalled, getting to the meat of his seeking her out. "I was just doing a bit of research myself, and I was hoping to ask you or your brother some questions, if you allow."

Miss Abernathy stiffened in her seat. "My educational proficiency was not the purpose of your visit, was it? I suppose it depends on the questions."

He took the wingback chair perpendicular to the fire and the sofa. "Fair enough. I shall allow you the power to decline to answer. Agree?"

She nodded.

"Very good." Malcolm shifted forward in his seat. "For starters, who is older? You, or your brother?"

She dropped an eyebrow. "I didn't realize these questions would be so personal."

"Shall I move on, then?"

She shook her head. "There's no harm in asking. Normally, a lady does not divulge her age, but quite frankly, I find such polite notions tedious at times. Both LJ and I are twenty-seven."

Malcolm blinked, not expecting this answer. "Twins?"

She laughed, a rather pleasant sound to his ears. Laughter was not common within these walls, especially of the female variety. "Well, yes. Does that surprise you?"

"I suppose it does. But you still haven't answered my question."

"Mm, you're right. LJ is the older sibling, by twenty minutes. The official heir to the Abernathy fortunes, even though it would have gone to him anyway." Her tone turned caustic.

"So, your mother did not die in childbirth," Malcolm mused.

Miss Abernathy frowned. "What would make you say that?"

Her demeanor became guarded instantly. Malcolm rushed to placate her. "I was reviewing your family history, what little I have here. Mr. Thompson created books about each cursed adventurer he could find, regardless if they became a part of the Guild or not. Your family in particular seems to have a long history of curses. I was curious how your parents died."

"We were only five years old when we became orphans, Mr. Drury. I wasn't yet of an age where I could catalog all the ways a person can die. If it helps, she was of good health; that much I do remember. Her death was rather sudden, and in the aftermath I believe I've blocked out many of my memories of that time."

She said these words woodenly, not a hint of emotion lacing them. Malcolm felt like an ass.

"Of course, Miss Abernathy. I apologize. I've been surrounded by death myself, and I sometimes forget that others are less immune to its effects."

She looked at him. "You've lost your parents as well." It was a statement, not a question.

He nodded. "My father was cursed with a withering disease after traveling to Egypt. He died when I was thirteen. We were not close, so I was more burdened by donning the mantle of master at a young age than by his death."

"And your mother?"

Malcolm tilted his head down. He had loved his mother with all his heart. And she had loved him, making up for the coolness his father had always exhibited for his only child. Paula Drury spent years making this summer house a true home for the both of them, a fact Malcolm greatly admired. They'd had a wonderful thirteen years together after Malcolm's father had passed, but Malcolm's love was not enough to keep her perpetually safe. His mother had succumbed to pneumonia five years ago, at the young age of fifty-one. It had been the darkest day of his life.

"She passed away when I was twenty-six," he mumbled.

Miss Abernathy must have sensed his despondency, because she only replied, "I'm sorry."

Malcolm was saved from explaining himself by Mathers entering the library. "My apologies for the interruption, sir, but the Abernathys' belongings have arrived."

It took a moment for Malcolm's thoughts to catch up. He remembered now; Miss Abernathy had dispatched a telegram back home to send for her items, after the meeting two days ago.

"Of course. Please help the porter bring them in."

Mathers stayed in place, shifting his weight to his other foot, a sure sign of discomfort. "Sir, should I send the luggage up to the Aster Room, or ...?"

That was an excellent point. He'd had every intention of moving Miss Abernathy from the second floor to the third, where the servant's quarters were kept. With so few staff members at present, it was woefully empty. But for some reason even Malcolm couldn't explain, he'd decided to keep her on the second floor. Even more baffling was his decision to house her in his mother's room in the first place, when there were three other perfectly usable guest bedrooms available. He chalked it up to temporary insanity.

Mathers was giving him an out. Good chap.

He knew Miss Abernathy was expecting to be kicked out of the Aster Room at any moment. Somehow, keeping her there was something he wanted to do. He figured it made him look good, his one charitable act toward her.

"Yes, Mathers. The Aster Room will be just fine."

Miss Abernathy sucked in a small breath near him.

He would have liked to explore that small sound, but another, more obnoxious noise filled the air in the distance. A yapping sort of noise.

Miss Abernathy gasped and bolted to her feet, rushing past Malcolm and Mathers and out of the library, toward the unexpected cacophony.

"What on earth?" Malcolm muttered.

"Sir, I was about to warn you that among the Abernathys' possessions, there is a dog," Mathers said with some reluctance.

"A dog," Malcolm repeated.

"Yes, sir."

Malcolm ran a hand down his face and followed the blasted woman out of the library.

He found her sitting on the steps leading to the vestibule, with a small, shaggy dog jumping all over her and yipping frantically while it tried to lick her face. Her closed-lip smile as she struggled to avoid his tongue was mesmerizing, but he was in no mood to appreciate it.

"What is this?" he demanded.

Miss Abernathy stood, scooping up the frantic dog into a tight hug as she did so. It calmed down almost immediately, although its long white tail waved in the air like a flag of surrender.

"This is my dog, Edward Longshanks the Second," she said with a smile. "Eddie for short."

"Edward Longsh—" Malcolm stopped himself from speaking the rest of the name out of exasperation.

The woman didn't seem to notice his mood. "Yes, that's right. You see, Eddie is a King Charles spaniel, and Edward Longshanks was king of England in the late thirteenth century—"

"I didn't ask for a history lesson, woman!" Malcolm snapped, effectively shutting her up. He needed a drink. "*Why* is there a dog in my house?"

He immediately regretted his outburst as the storm clouds rolled over her face.

Her brows lowered. "I told you I had sent for my possessions, did I not?"

"You did," Malcolm admitted.

"Eddie is my finest possession. I figured you already shared a house with a chicken, and dogs are more sanitary than poultry."

Malcolm started to raise a finger for rebuttal.

She ignored the gesture. "He will be my responsibility entirely, so you needn't worry about him taking up Mrs. Bixby's time or Mathers' time. He is fully trained, so he won't have any accidents inside."

"But—" Malcolm tried to say.

"*And*," she plowed forward as if he hadn't made a sound, "research shows that animals can be incredibly therapeutic. Eddie here is small, cuddly, and cute, and he can make even the dourest of people smile."

Malcolm looked the dog over again. He was indeed small, only slightly bigger than a cat. His long, droopy ears and small muzzle gave him a comical appearance, especially now while his tongue lolled out of his open mouth. The red patches covering his eyes lent him a roguish flair, like a bandit. All complaints died before they left his mouth. He sighed, declaring defeat. "Very well."

Miss Abernathy smiled again, this time showing her white teeth, and for the first time Malcolm wished he could see that look on her face more often.

CHAPTER SEVEN

Saturday, February 13th, 1915

Norah

EDDIE BREATHED FRESH LIFE back into her. Norah had missed her little companion fiercely while they had been apart.

She was only sorry that his arrival had apparently caused yet another rift between her and the stormy president of the Guild. She had actually seen a hint of humanity behind his fierce exterior yesterday during their brief interaction.

Granted, Eddie did not make for good first impressions. When he became overly excited, he couldn't help but emit a high-pitched yip, jumping up on her and acting wildly out of control. Once he got that out of his system, though, he was a perfect gentleman. Malcolm Drury would have probably allowed *him* to join his little guild.

Eddie was calm and collected this morning, resting his small frame up against her while she lazed under the blankets. Norah felt a small pang of guilt at having the dog up on the furniture of the mistress suite—it was a failing of hers in this one aspect of Eddie's training—but Mr. Drury'd had ample time to change his mind about allowing Norah to stay in this room. His choices still mystified her, but she wouldn't look a gift horse in the mouth.

It was Saturday, and so far Mrs. Bixby hadn't scuttled in to shoo her out for the master's bidding. Not that he had asked for her recently, not since her first day here. No, other than yesterday, Mr. Drury seemed of the mind to avoid her completely. It was just as well. Mrs. Bixby was a much kinder boss, and at least made sure she was fed.

At the thought of food, Norah's midsection rumbled. Reluctantly, she threw back the covers and emerged from her warm cocoon, her stomach winning the battle over comfort. Eddie stretched and jumped down, waving his flag tail happily as he took the lead, even though he didn't know where Norah was planning to go.

She shook her head in amusement as she walked into the dressing room. The room was no longer empty, thanks to Aunt Nell sending Norah's wardrobe. Still, the room was much too grand for the limited clothing Norah had. As such, it was much colder in this room than in the bedroom. It made for quick dressing.

At least Norah did not have to wait for Mrs. Bixby to help her. Norah stripped out of her warm wool nightgown, quickly donning her stockings, drawers and camisole, and choosing her dove-gray woolen dress for the day's wear. It was one of her favorites, with a navy collar, asymmetrical blouse design, and a double row of buttons down the skirt.

She was just finishing tying her boot laces when the knock on the door came. Eddie let out a miniature growl at the intrusion, but his wagging tail belied any true hostility. Mrs. Bixby's voice came through the door. "Miss? Are you awake?"

"Come in," Norah called out to her.

Mrs. Bixby marched over to her, wasting no time. "Good morning, dearie. I do hope you aren't starving. It's later than usual for breakfast, but the master tries to sleep in on Saturdays and insists breakfast be delayed. He hates cold eggs."

Norah peered around, noticing there was no cart full of food waiting in the hallway. "I am hungry, but content to wait. Is breakfast still not ready?"

The housekeeper tutted. "I should have warned you yesterday, but I plum forgot. Mr. Malcolm would like you to join him and the other members for breakfast this morning. It's a Saturday tradition. You'll be set up in the upper dining room, where we serve most of the communal meals. It's a bit easier for the men to access."

"The upper dining room?" Norah repeated. "Where is that?" She had not done much exploring on her own, mainly for fear of inciting Mr. Drury's wrath once more. She knew her way to the library, the study, and, of course, the great hall in the center of the mansion. She'd been to the third floor only twice, both times to seek out her brother, and slowly get to know the men better, although many still hid away in her company.

Mrs. Bixby shook her head, rueful. "I've been too busy to give you a proper tour. That's my failing. The lower dining room is behind the grand staircase on the main floor, you follow? Well, the upper dining room is in the same position, just on this floor. There's a hallway behind the grand stairs for access."

"Of course," Norah said, remembering seeing a hallway branch from the gallery next to the stairs. "Thank you. What time shall I arrive?"

Mrs. Bixby replied, "Half an hour, if you can. I should have given you more warning, but I'm afraid my head was in the clouds today. Lucky for us, it seems you've already dressed. That's downright providential."

"Indeed." Norah chuckled lightheartedly. "Say, while I have you here, may I ask a question?"

Mrs. Bixby puffed up with importance. "Of course."

"I noticed yesterday, while I was placing my items in the dressing room, there is a small door against the far wall. What is its purpose?"

The housekeeper hemmed in her throat. "Come with me." She strode into the dressing room, not bothering to check if Norah followed—which she did, her curiosity at a high throttle.

At the door, Mrs. Bixby took out her ring of keys and thumbed through them before choosing one and fitting it into the keyhole. She turned the key and opened the door.

An icy blast of winter wind whipped through immediately, chilling Norah even through her woolen dress. She saw a single glimpse of a snowy balcony before the housekeeper pushed the door shut with resolution.

"Goodness, that was colder than I thought!" the older woman exclaimed with a theatrical shiver.

"What an odd thing to attach to a dressing room," Norah observed. "What is the point of the balcony?"

Mrs. Bixby looked lost in thought for a moment as she stowed her keys safely away in her pocket. "Your room and the master's room take up one corner of the house. When the place was built, the architect—what was his name? He was very popular among the upper class around thirty years ago."

"It wasn't Hunt, was it?"

"Farley Hunt? No, he's not an architect. Besides, he's much too young. I believe the man has since passed away."

Norah smiled. "No, no. A different Hunt. Richard, I believe his given name was. And yes, you are correct in his passing."

"Oh yes, of course. Silly me." Mrs. Bixby chuckled. "Yes, Birchwald was constructed starting in 1889. The master and mistress rooms were built near each other, as we've discussed, and Master Gordon—that's the old master, mind you—enjoyed sitting outside with his wife in the summertime, when he was actually home, that is. This was supposed to only be the summer house, you know."

Norah suppressed a snort. There wasn't anything "only" about this grand estate.

The housekeeper continued her rather dizzying line of thought. "And so, they designed the balcony out there to connect through the respective rooms—although yours had to go through the dressing room to work—so the married couple could continue meeting here together."

Norah nodded in understanding. "Why *did* Birchwald become the main manor for the Drurys?"

Mrs. Bixby frowned into space. "Mistress Paula, rest her soul, never felt at home in New York City, although they had a grand house there. After the completion of Birchwald, she loved it so much that she convinced her husband that they should stay here. Master Malcolm loved it here as well, being a young boy at the time. I don't think Master Gordon cared much one way or another. He was usually off traveling anyway."

"I see."

Mrs. Bixby clapped her hands together, startling a small bark out of Eddie. "Goodness me! Here I've been chattering away when I told Cook I'd help with the dumbwaiter. She'll have my hide if I'm not there. Finish getting ready, dearie. I'll see you in twenty minutes or so."

Norah smiled fondly as the housekeeper bustled out, muttering to herself. She wondered if Mrs. Bixby had a curse upon her as well to make her so flighty at times.

Malcolm

Breakfast with the household was something Malcolm looked forward to every Saturday. It would also be the perfect test for Miss Abernathy. If she couldn't hold her own during this weekly event, she didn't belong here.

Malcolm did not hold out much hope for her failure, unfortunately.

He would also insist that she help out more from here on out. He'd given her a couple of days to acclimate. Now it was time to be thrown into the water.

With a gathering as big as his household, he'd had to come up with a way to seat everyone and still be able to converse with the group as a whole. This was accomplished by creating a U shape with three rectangular tables. Four chairs could easily sit side by side at each table, which in the past was plenty of room. Now, with Peter Withers and his helper, and the Abernathy twins joining the fray, it was a bit more cramped, although still doable.

He made sure every man was present at half-past nine, fifteen minutes before the lady was due to arrive. Malcolm wanted to figure out the best possible seating for Miss Abernathy, a position that would perfectly highlight the chaos that was a natural aspect of Saturday breakfast. Claiming the middle of the U bottom for himself, he placed Mr. Withers and his assistant next to him on his left, and Leighton on his right. He'd like to get to know these newcomers better.

At the left-hand side sat Hector Freeman with his stone legs tucked under the table, Fred Jamison with the chicken, Mr. Norris, on his lap, Pablo Reyes, and Marvin Ivey at the end, as he was prone to hyperventilation when pressed from too many sides.

The right-hand table saw the loudmouth Ambrose Lyster closest to Malcolm's table, with Farley Hunt—minus his letter opener, Malcolm noticed—next to him, an open space for Miss Abernathy, and lastly poor sore-ridden Rodney Paulson at the end.

It was almost too perfect. If the dear lady had a case of feminine sensitivity, it would be clear to everyone here she wasn't what this guild needed after all.

The one thing Malcolm didn't account for was the dog. He came trotting into the room first like he already owned the place, three steps in front of his mistress. His appearance was all fine and well, if not for Mr. Norris letting out a squawk of fear and flapping his wings at the sight as he fled Fred's lap and landed on the table.

Eddie stopped mid stride and began barking as ferociously as a petite dog could. Miss Abernathy ran the last few steps, bending down to calm her pet.

"Must he be here?" Malcolm roared over the commotion.

Mr. Norris beat his wings louder, his clucks of alarm intensifying. Fred leaned over to help calm the bird, murmuring soothing words to his avian friend.

Miss Abernathy straightened with the dog in her arms. Eddie stopped barking, and from his new vantage point, pointed his blunt muzzle toward the chicken with a whine, all the while furiously wagging his tail.

"The chicken startled him, is all," she said over the continued cackling of Mr. Norris.

"Mr. Norris has a right to be afraid of dogs," Fred pointed out as he stroked the chicken's comb in an attempt to calm him.

She blushed as she brought her attention to the last speaker. "Of course, Mr. Jamison. I don't blame Mr. Norris at all. But please be aware, Eddie may want to just play with your friend. He'd never hurt a fly. May I be allowed to acquaint these two further?"

Fred reluctantly looked at the chicken in front of him. Mr. Norris had settled, although he kept a wary yellow eye on Eddie. "I suppose we could give it a try."

The woman rounded the table into the interior of the U and leaned her dog over the top. Eddie's tail tempo increased even more as he stretched his neck to smell the white hen. Mr. Norris stared down the sniffing dog before craning his neck toward him, inspecting Eddie's face up close. He then gave the dog a single peck on the nose, which made Eddie flinch back in surprise.

Miss Abernathy laughed as she straightened, separating the two animals. "There, you see? Mr. Norris has established that he is not to be trifled with. I do hope he won't be afraid of Eddie anymore. Eddie has been properly put in his place."

Eddie was not the worse for wear for the single peck. He continued to wag his tail like a white flag as he stared at his mistress with utter adoration as she placed him back on the floor.

Fred was reassured by her speech. "I do believe you're right, miss. Perhaps having another animal around will do Mr. Norris some good, after all."

Malcolm was surprised to hear this. Fred was very protective of his friend-turned-chicken. He begrudgingly accepted that Eddie also had a place in the room.

He stood to draw attention to himself. "Please be seated, Miss Abernathy. Your dog can stay under the table, provided he continues to behave himself."

She inclined her head in response and gracefully walked to her seat between Farley and Rodney. Both gentlemen stood as she approached, taking their seats again as she sat.

With the last person seated, Mrs. Bixby and Mathers appeared from the background to remove cloches from dishes, releasing the mixed scents of bacon, scrambled eggs with cheese, fluffy biscuits, and pastries filled with jam.

The men dug in, helping themselves to whatever was closest to them before one of the two servants began swapping the dishes around. Miss Abernathy looked a trifle confused by the sudden hubbub as she sat primly in her seat.

"If you want to eat, you must help yourself, madam," Malcolm called from his seat as he spooned eggs onto his plate.

She glanced at him with a grateful smile before unsticking her hands to reach for a pastry.

Malcolm watched as Rodney Paulson also reached for the same tray, his hand colliding with hers as they picked the same pastry. He yanked back his hand as if her touch scalded him.

Here it comes, thought Malcolm as he eyed the scene with distinct interest. Other women would have fled in disgust over coming into contact with the oozing man.

"Ooh, I'm so sorry! Did I hurt you?" Miss Abernathy's voice was nothing but concern.

Interesting reaction.

"Oh, no, miss. I only don't usually allow people to touch me, is all. My apologies for taking up your space. It can be bad for the stomach." Rodney smiled shyly as he ducked his head.

"I insist you take that pastry, Mr. ... was it Paulson?" she said kindly.

He nodded. "That's right, miss. And thank you. Raspberry is my favorite. You should try the strawberry one; they're quite good too." He paused, as if weighing a decision in his head. "If it's easier for you, you can call me Rodney."

Malcolm's head snapped up. So, Rodney was already offering his given name informally? He was moving rather quickly.

Then again, Malcolm remembered when he'd first been introduced to Rodney. The man had said he wasn't fond of his last name anymore after some chaps began referring to him as "Mr. Pus-son." Perhaps he was in the right to quickly abandon his formalities, given that information.

To his further surprise, he heard Miss Abernathy reply, "I appreciate that, Rodney. There are so many new names to learn. You may call me Norah, if you wish."

Next to him, Leighton sighed audibly. The negativity of the sound provoked Malcolm's curiosity. He leaned toward Leighton. "Is your sister usually this forthcoming?" he asked in low tones.

Leighton rolled his eyes in immediate response, a stark departure from his happy-go-lucky persona. "We Abernathys have always been quick to buck the system," Leighton answered, following up his eye roll with a wink as if to soften the effect of the former action. It only made Malcolm leery. Leighton went back to watching his sister, his eyes narrowing almost imperceptibly. "We're proper, but sometimes manners get in the way of establishing connections. It doesn't make her any less of a lady."

Pursing his lips in thought, Malcolm straightened and took a bite of eggs.

The group ate in companionable silence, for the most part. Ambrose Lyster muttered to himself, and Marvin Ivey ate small bites while keeping his eyes screwed shut to stave off visions. Fred Jamison shared his plate with Mr. Norris, who was back in his lap. To his left, he watched the African man feed himself sparingly, pausing to wipe the drool off the chin of the mostly comatose Mr. Withers. The older gentleman's eyes were bright this morning, a twinkle bordering on fear within them.

Malcolm leaned back to peer around the man at his helper. "Is he alright?"

The man—what was his name? Oh yes, Karanja—leaned back as well to talk around his ward. "Bad sleep, sir. Mr. Withers needs extra rest today."

Malcolm nodded. Perhaps the poor man had been plagued by nightmares. It was hard to say what he suffered from, given the fact he couldn't talk.

Others were doing more than their fair share to make up for it. Amidst the chatter, one voice rose above the rest. "These eggs taste like shite!" Lyster exclaimed.

Norah—Miss Abernathy—coughed on her bite.

Mrs. Bixby whipped Ambrose over the head with a hand towel. "They taste the same as always, Mr. Lyster. You'd do well to bite that tongue of yours."

"Dammit, woman, I can't bloody bite my tongue!" the man bellowed back. "You can't know it was my thoughts, either. Perhaps if you had more brains than bubs, you'd remember that fact." He closed his eyes, mumbling incoherent sounds for a couple of seconds. "I'm sorry, Missus. You know I can't help myself."

Mrs. Bixby patted him on the top of his ginger head like he was a child. "I know, dearie."

"Perhaps, it's Mr. Norris' eggs throwing the lot?" Lyster offered.

Miss Abernathy paused her eating, her fork halfway to her mouth. "Did you say, 'Mr. Norris' eggs?'"

Fred looked slightly offended. At whom, Malcolm couldn't tell. "Mr. Norris enjoys contributing to our meals. He's not laying as much as he used to, but his eggs are as lovely as the rest."

Miss Abernathy set her full fork down on her plate and blinked her eyes a couple of times, as if to steady herself. Malcolm grinned in anticipation. Here came the hysterics.

She picked it back up though, daintily biting the contents off the utensil. "*I* think the eggs taste wonderful. Thank you, Mr. Norris. And compliments to the cook."

Well.

Hector Freeman raised his glass. "Hear, hear!"

Fred Jamison beamed.

Once more, the conversation picked up, and Malcolm got lost in the pleasant noise. This was what he enjoyed: unusual men enjoying a dash of normalcy. To his surprise, no one seemed to mind the woman in their midst. Perhaps most surprising of all, neither did Malcolm.

Of course, with this lot, something was bound to happen to end that feeling of normalcy. He heard Miss Abernathy gasp, and turned his head to see why. Farley Hunt, using his knife to cut his pastry, had grazed his thumb when the knife slipped. As Malcolm watched, three drops of blood welled from the scrape.

"Goodness, are you alright?" Miss Abernathy moved to place her napkin upon the blood.

"*NO!*" most of the members at the table yelled at her. She froze at once, a look of consternation upon her face.

Malcolm rose. "Apologies for yelling, Miss Abernathy. It would be imprudent to use a cloth to wipe away the blood. Farley's curse requires that blood, you see."

"Oh?" she said faintly as she moved her hand with the napkin away from the young man.

"Actually, this would be the perfect opportunity to get to know about it better. Mr. Hunt, why don't you show Miss Abernathy to your room? Mrs. Bixby can chaperone."

Holding his hand carefully, Farley stood. "Very well. Come along, miss."

Malcolm couldn't help but notice the look of intrigue upon the woman's face as she followed the man out of the room.

"Goodness, that dress makes her arse look fabulous," Ambrose commented loudly as she left.

Norah

The grand staircase did not continue to the third floor. Instead, Mrs. Bixby led the way around the gallery, past the elevator, past the Poppy

Room, and to a less imposing set of stairs that led up. She huffed as she took the stairs one by one, assuming the two people behind her would follow.

Mr. Hunt gestured with his uninjured hand for Norah to go before him. She lifted her skirts and took the steps, listening to the man's heavier footfalls behind her.

She had been to the third floor twice already—both times to visit LJ—but had not yet explored its contents. She did so now. It would seem that the designers cared less about maintaining an illusion of grandeur here. There was no gallery, considering the lack of an open area from the previous floor. Instead, the stairs opened into a sitting area in the middle. Three bedrooms resided beyond this informal space, the middle of which now belonged to her brother.

That was where her knowledge of the third floor ended, but Mrs. Bixby did not allow her much time to gawk. "This way, dearie," she called as she resolutely marched around the bend to the right. Halfway down this hall, a new, short corridor opened up to the right, which the housekeeper took. Only two doors rested here: one on the right and one on the left. She chose the lefthand one.

The three of them bustled in, Mr. Hunt looking at ease despite the awkward way he held his left hand.

"Welcome to my room, Miss Abernathy," he said with a mock flourish.

Norah had to admit the room was larger than what she had anticipated. Not nearly as grand as her room, she conceded, but that was to be expected. Slightly longer than it was wide, it was furnished with a double bed, a small sitting area, and, judging by the extra door she saw, had a bathroom attached.

"Are all the guest rooms this nice?" she wondered out loud as the gentleman rushed over to his table to look for something.

Mrs. Bixby waffled her head about. "Not exactly. There are nine guest rooms in total on the third floor. The east wing has the nicest rooms up here. Mr. Paulson, Mr. Hunt, Señor Reyes, and Mr. Freeman take those up. Mr. Paulson and Mr. Freeman have private baths, and Mr. Hunt shares a bath with the Señor." She pointed to the corresponding door. "On the south end are two more smaller rooms, which hold Mr. Ivey and

Mr. Jamison with Mr. Norris. They also share a bath. The smallest of the rooms are the three north-most rooms, but I'm sure you are already familiar with those, since your brother is in the middle one. Mr. Ambrose and Mr. Withers and his aide reside within the other two." She paused, thinking. "The west wing is taken up by servant quarters. It's where my room is located, as well as Mathers'."

Norah picked through the excessive information dumped upon her. "How did you decide who gets which room?"

"Seniority," Mr. Hunt said, scampering over to her. He held a dagger in his hand.

Norah took a step back before looking closer, realizing it was only a letter opener, although a wickedly sharp-looking one. The blade was tarnished silver, stained on the edges with a rusty color, like old blood. The handle mimicked the normal anatomy of a dagger, with the quillons on either side decorated with elaborate scrollwork, and the handle bearing an etching of a fanciful heart symbol.

Mr. Hunt allowed her to inspect it from his hand. "This is Bloodletter. It's a beauty, eh? Too bad I didn't realize what it was before I chose it."

"Bloodletter," Norah mused, catching the wittiness of the name. "A cursed object, then?" She leaned in for a closer examination.

"Well, yes. What else would it be?"

Norah closed her eyes for a second, listening to the memory of one of her professors as he explained about the ways to be cursed. Emulating him, she said, "There are different ways in which to be cursed. Cursed items or relics seem to be one of the more common ways. It would seem our ancestors were more easily able to imbue objects with a curse. Cast curses are another way, given to bearers by powerful people, their emotions giving weight to the words they speak. And then there's generational curses, which are rare. Those, a person is simply born into the curse."

"Most of us here are the first kind," Mr. Hunt said thoughtfully. "Although Mr. Jamison and his friend suffer from a casting. Ambrose too, I wager."

"So, what is it about this letter opener that has you cursed?" she asked, nodding her head at the object in his hand.

He started, and glanced at the blade. "Every day, I must feed it my blood."

She scrunched up her face. "How does that work?"

"I'll show you." He placed the blade against his scrape, nudging at the blood that had dried in place. "It doesn't like dried blood," he whispered. He scraped the old blood off, putting pressure upon the small wound with the flat of the blade until a fresh drop oozed out. This he wiped on the tarnished silver. "There."

Norah frowned. "That's it?"

Mr. Hunt nodded.

Such an improbable method of placating a cursed relic. Norah was intrigued. "How did you come to be cursed?"

Mr. Hunt sighed as he stared at the letter opener in his hands. "I'd just graduated college, and I was engaged to be married to a nice girl. I went on a trip to Europe to celebrate, and while in Paris, I found this small antiques shop. The letter opener was for sale there. It caught my eye with its beauty. It was a woman's tool, so I bought it for my fiancée. Only after I had it in my possession did I learn its past." He looked at Norah. "The original owner, a wealthy, young, and beautiful woman, murdered her lover with it."

"How horrible," Norah said with a revulsed twist of her lips.

"Indeed. I never would have bought it, had I known. Nor would I have let it get a taste for my blood."

"I couldn't help but notice the scars on your face and hands," Norah said softly. "Is that because of this?"

Mr. Hunt nodded. "Since I've been cursed, I've been overly accident prone. Except I suppose they aren't accidents exactly, are they? The curse demands I shed blood daily, without fail. No matter how careful I am, something happens at some point in the day. Paper cuts of unusual sizes. Giant razor nicks while I shave. I was once stabbed by a rose bush so badly my arm gushed blood for a solid minute. Today's injury? That was nothing." He leaned in. "The worst part is, if I don't get the blade fed soon enough, it gets angry, and then something much worse comes along."

"What do you mean?"

He sighed. "Before I joined the Guild, I tried to live normally with this. I didn't believe in the curse, not really. It took some trial and error to learn that if my minor wound didn't feed the blade, a major wound would. I've been stabbed multiple times over the years by a variety of objects. I've had glass break near me and skewer me with shards. A dog once came out of nowhere and bit me hard on the—" he blushed, refusing to finish the sentence. "The last time I took too long to feed Bloodletter, a stuffed polar bear fell on me as I walked by, breaking my scalp open with its teeth. All accidents, and all much worse injuries than cuts and scrapes. And all because I didn't give the blade what it wanted the first time around."

"Goodness." Norah felt sorry for this young man.

"I remember when it fully awakened, just two days after purchasing it." He rolled his eyes up. "Clear as day. I was still in Paris, set to leave the next day for home, reading the newspaper over a cup of espresso. I got a paper cut, a really deep one. I ignored it, cleaned the blood away, and went on with my day. At lunch, I stopped by a café, where a man with a knife jumped in front of me, yelling at me. I couldn't understand—my comprehension of French is admittedly abysmal—but he brandished a knife at me. I deflected his swing, and he gave me this." Mr. Hunt showed Norah a rather long, puckered scar that ran the length of his left jawline. "Nearly slit my throat over a misunderstanding. It was then I remembered the letter opener, which was in my pocket, and I took it out as some form of protection. The man's face took on a look of fear, and he fled. By then I was bleeding all over, and some of it got on the blade. I've bled at least once a day ever since."

"Why did it choose you?" she asked, trying to get to the bottom of this curse. Surely, other people had picked up the item without being cursed in order for it to make its way to the antiques shop.

He shook his head, chagrined. "Foolish carelessness. While I handled it, I slipped and poked myself with it. It got the taste for my blood, and I was doomed."

"What would happen if you fed it someone else's blood?"

"Nothing. It likes mine, and will continue to bleed me until it kills me one day. It cost me my engagement, my way of living, and one day, it will cost me my life, I'm sure." He sighed and walked over to place his relic down on the table again.

Norah thought over his words. *It likes my blood.* There might be something to that, but she'd have to tread carefully if she was to help Mr. Hunt. More information was necessary before she could formulate a plan for him.

"Mr. Hunt, wouldn't it be easier to purposefully bleed yourself each day?" Norah asked. "A timed feeding, if you will?"

The man raised his eyebrows as he glanced at the relic.

Norah sighed. "You've never tried that, have you?"

"It never crossed my mind," he admitted.

Norah suppressed the weary laugh that bubbled in her midsection. "My only thought is that you could better control your injuries in this way, instead of waiting for one to happen naturally."

"Of course," Mr. Hunt said, a note of wonder in his tone. "Why didn't I think of that?"

"Sometimes, when you live with a condition a certain way for a long time, it's difficult to imagine a new way of living." She smiled kindly at the man.

Internally, she pondered the situation. Had all these men simply given up ever leading regular lives again? If a simple solution like a daily pin prick was not thought of, what else could she suggest that would make the Guild's members routines that much easier?

She supposed it was time to get to work fully.

CHAPTER EIGHT

Sunday, February 14th, 1915

Malcolm

MALCOLM DRANK TOO MUCH last night. Again.

A tornado of unbidden thoughts and repressed emotions spiraled through his mind as he tried to sleep. And at the center of that cyclone was Miss Abernathy.

There was something about knowing Miss Abernathy had freely given her name to poor old Rodney, the walking pus pocket, that really got his goat. He shouldn't care. He didn't care, he told himself. But she had known the man for less than a week and they were already on a first-name basis.

He hadn't seen her again for the rest of the day yesterday, which was just as well. He might have slipped up and called her Norah, now that the idea was planted in his mind.

Norah J. Abernathy. She never did tell him what the "J" stood for.

And so, like he did every time his mind became stuck on a rolling ball of futility, he drank until it quieted.

Now that he was awake and had managed to eat a meager meal—plenty of coffee, some dry toast—he remembered another reason to be surly today. The date.

February fourteenth.

Mathers was keen not to bring it up. But the calendar in Malcolm's room did not do away with the day to spare his feelings.

Malcolm groaned. He would have stayed in his room, if not for the fact it was a Sunday. Sundays at Birchwald meant a special visitor, which in turn meant he had to be involved.

In Malcolm's mind, there were two types of cursed victims: those who became angry at God and turned their backs on religion, and those who sought its comfort even more. Malcolm was never truly religious in the first place, only going to church as a youngster to appease his mother. Once she was gone, he wrote the whole organization off.

But some of his men fell into the latter camp, and since attending church in their conditions could be tricky at best, and downright disastrous at worst, Malcolm made sure a man of God would come to them.

Without fail, through rain or heat or—as the case was now—snow, Father Berkely came to Birchwald to tend to his very small and unusual flock. He hailed from the nearest rectory, and he was chosen for his kindness and grace. A man well into his fifties, his supportive demeanor was a true blessing to those who required his guidance.

Despite not personally needing spiritual counseling, Malcolm still felt the need to speak with him each week, to check on how his members were doing. It was the only aspect of this Sunday ritual that was important to him.

Father Berkely arrived each Sunday no later than noon. He always met with the members who needed his spiritual fortitude first. After, he would talk with Malcolm, and then Mrs. Bixby made sure to feed him a grand midday meal before they sent him on his way again.

Malcolm checked his pocket watch. It was ten in the morning.

For the first time, Malcolm wondered if his newest member, Leighton, and his sister would benefit from the father's visit. Perhaps he should ask them.

He stepped out of his room, his head pounding slightly from the light emitted by the chandeliers that hung in the empty space above the entrance hall. He grimaced in pain.

"Sir, are you well?" Mrs. Bixby asked, having just exited the stairway to his left with a bundle of papers. Her sharp eyes had clearly noticed his face upon her arrival.

"Headache, is all. Do you know where I might find the Abernathys?"

Mrs. Bixby looked astonished. "The Abernathys? Both of them?"

"Yes, both of them."

She hesitated. "Well, certainly, sir."

He waited a second for her to tell him, but she did not. "And?"

"And what, sir?"

Surely, she was playing games with him now. He was in no mood for her flightiness. "Where are they?"

Now she exhibited a nervous demeanor. "They'll be in the upper dining room, sir."

That was not the answer he expected. Other than Saturday breakfast, the room was not used, generally. "What on earth for?" She opened her mouth, but he gave her no room to speak. "No, it doesn't matter. Thank you, Mrs. Bixby. You can continue your chores."

He strode down the gallery. She followed at an agitated gait that scraped at his nerves, as much as he tried to ignore her.

"Sir, I really think you should get some rest," she tried to say through puffed breaths.

He ignored her, finally reaching the dining room.

It wasn't just Mr. and Miss Abernathy present. Half of the members were also there.

The tables were a mess, with bits of paper, pots of paints and glue, and scissors strewn about. Miss Abernathy stood over Pablo Reyes, who was busy writing something, while Ambrose Lyster dipped a dainty paintbrush into a pot of red paint. Leighton, looking more dour than Malcolm had ever seen him, used a pair of scissors to cut a piece of paper into the unmistakable shape of a heart. Mr. Norris carefully strode over his section of the table, his clawed feet making pink chicken prints upon the paper placed under him. Farley Hunt sat close at hand, holding a bloodstained cloth to his finger, his letter opener by his side resting next to a pair of scissors. Underneath the table, Eddie snoozed.

Malcolm took it all in, speechless and unmoving for a moment, paralyzed by the sheer incredulity of the scene.

His paralysis broke. "What in hell is going on here?" he roared.

All members of the party froze, turning their rounded eyes to him. Miss Abernathy straightened her body and addressed him first. "It should be obvious. It's Valentine's Day."

"And so you took it upon yourself to wreck my dining room?"

"Oh dear," Mrs. Bixby said softly from behind him.

He turned on her. "You knew this was happening, didn't you?"

Before the older woman could comment, Miss Abernathy spoke again, "Just what are you accusing us of, Mr. Drury? We have not 'wrecked' a thing, I assure you. All we are doing is participating in the holiday as it were. And do not blame Mrs. Bixby; it was not her idea."

He turned away from the housekeeper, fixing his attention on the other blasted woman, who stood prim and proper in her cream-colored suit, a red paper rose attached to her blouse. She had the audacity to look him squarely in the eye with a slight uptilt of her chin.

"And whose idea was it? Yours?"

"That's correct. I thought an exchange of valentines would brighten the day of some members. Everyone likes to be appreciated."

"Of all the ..." Malcolm pinched the bridge of his nose. He steeled his eyes at Miss Abernathy. "Madam, that is the stupidest thing I've ever heard. These men are not children. This 'holiday' is vapid and unnecessary, and your efforts are wasted."

She stared at him, a fire flashing in her eyes. Before she could respond, Pablo stood with a scraping of his chair.

"That is not true, Señor!" he said with gravitas. "This project has been much enjoyable, and I look forward to passing them out to *mis amigos.* Miss Abernathy, will you marry me?" he added, turning to look at the lady in question with true adoration.

She patted his shoulder. "No, thank you, Señor Reyes. Mr. Drury, I fail to see the point of your outburst. If it is to prove that you are a curmudgeon, then by all means, I heartily congratulate you."

The table fell deathly silent, with not even a peep coming from Mr. Norris. Leighton cleared his throat. "Nor ..."

"Oi, she's caught the tiger by the balls, she has!" Ambrose chortled.

Malcolm gritted his jaw and did his best to sound civil. "Miss Abernathy, may I speak to you? Alone?"

Pablo turned to shield the lady.

Malcolm's eyes wanted to bug out of his head at the gesture. Did Pablo truly think he would harm his guest?

Miss Abernathy murmured to the Spaniard, and he backed down. She faced Malcolm. "Of course."

Malcolm gestured toward the walkway.

Pablo called after her, "Will you marry me?"

She turned just long enough to give a small shake of her head with a smile. Pablo sat back down as she left the room.

Malcolm marched south, into the corner of the house that held the nursery, a room which had never once been used. Malcolm shook the thought away as he turned his awareness to the woman in the alcove with him.

He spun to face her. "What exactly is your game plan, hmm?" he spewed as soon as he had her attention. "Are you here to undermine my power? Is that it?"

He was standing much too close, but he didn't care. His temper had him by the throat and he would allow it to take the lead.

"Do you think so little of yourself as to be thrown by a woman standing up to you?" she shot back with a frown, looking up into his face. She grimaced as she peered at him. "Your looks match your temper today."

"What does that mean?"

"It means you look a fright, and the way you are treating people is no better. Mr. Drury, as I recall, I am here to help these men, but how can I do that if I have you acting the monster every time I do something?"

He studied her, the rose of her cheeks, the shine of her passionate eyes. A thought came to him. He grinned wickedly. "I see now. Is that your game?"

She cocked her head. "What game?"

"All any woman wants is a stable marriage and children. You're too old to easily land a husband now, so you figured you'd ingratiate yourself to this lot to try your luck with the rich castoffs."

She slapped him, hard. His head tilted to the right with the force as his cheek acknowledged the sting. He stepped back from her, realizing he had practically boxed her in with his body and the wall.

Her features were smooth, like river stone, yet the ire was present in her eyes. "You know nothing of what I want," she hissed. "*Nothing*. How *dare* you. I have been transparent about my desires: to find a cure for my brother, and in the process help the other poor souls in your care. There is one reason and one reason alone that I remain unmarried in my 'old age:' I have no desire to shackle myself and continue my family's line, especially if any possible husband were to be as thick-headed as you!"

The slap to his face had reawakened his headache. He pinched his eyes shut for a moment. "Madam—"

"These men are not infantile either, Mr. Drury," she continued, cutting him off. "I suggested the valentines to Mr. Hunt yesterday, and he brought it up to the others. They agreed it would help to cheer up some of the members. Receiving a small card with well wishes upon it, especially a hand-made card, does wonders to brighten a person's spirit, so we were making enough for everyone." She thrust a fist out at his midsection unexpectedly. He expected her to land a punch with the action, and sucked in his gut and raised his hands for the impact. Instead, she dropped a crumpled piece of paper into his hands. "And I do so mean everyone."

She gave him one last disgruntled look before turning on her heel and leaving the alcove without another glance back.

Malcolm watched her go before inspecting the paper in his hands. It was a crudely cut heart with red and pink paint. The words were smudged, but he could make them out clear enough.

To Malcolm Drury,

You keep their hearts safe with your home, so they are giving them to you on this day

Happy Valentine's Day

He never expected to feel the sting of her slap reach his heart.

Norah

After the altercation, Norah excused herself from the card-making party, taking Eddie with her. She had so wanted to watch everyone receive their valentines, especially Mr. Jamison. He had not wanted to make them himself—he looked terrible, as if he had not slept a wink overnight—but readily agreed to allow Norah to carry Mr. Norris to the dining room. She had never held a chicken before, but Mr. Norris was quite willing, and Norah had to admit she enjoyed the feel of his soft feathers in her hands.

His chicken-print cards had turned out darling to boot. Oh well.

Mrs. Bixby caught up to her as she was halfway to her room. "Dearie, wait a moment!"

Norah kept walking. "I'm not much in the mood, Mrs. Bixby."

The older woman trotted until she was in front of her. "His behavior was inexcusable, and that's coming from the woman who relies on his payments. But you must know, this is a very hard day for him."

"Why, because he's allergic to fun?"

She shook her head. "It's not my place to say. In the past, we've always avoided mention of the holiday. That is all I *can* say."

Norah pursed her lips. "Very well. I suppose I shall tiptoe about lest I offend the master. Lesson learned. I'm going for a lie-in. Please don't disturb me." She shut the door in the housekeeper's face, only feeling slightly guilty for her rudeness.

In the privacy of her room, she let loose the full extent of her ire. She had not meant to slap Mr. Drury, but when he accused her of husband-hunting, she reacted without thinking. Even now, recalling his words, she could feel the heat of her fury.

Norah paced the room, trying to work off the agitated energy. The scene replayed in her head as she marched about, fueling her emotions instead of lessening them. Her eyes blurred and she stopped, sinking to the ground with frustration as the first hot tear escaped her eye.

Eddie whined, sensing the hurt rolling off his mistress. She scooped him up and hugged him close, letting the tears fall on his soft fur as she crawled up onto the bed with him.

She must have dozed, because she awoke with a start, a subtle knock on the door the culprit. She rolled off the bed, noting the time of 11:45 a.m.

"Mrs. Bixby?" she called as she approached the door. She opened it.

It was not Mrs. Bixby.

Malcolm Drury looked even worse than before. The skin behind his lengthy dark stubble seemed haggard, and the bags under his eyes more pronounced.

She almost felt sorry for him. "Yes?" she asked in an icy voice.

He sighed and reached out a hand. It held a piece of paper, a crude heart shape. She took it and glanced at it. In red paint, it read, "I'm sorry."

"I shouldn't have snapped the way I did," he said sheepishly.

"No, you shouldn't have."

"It's just that ... I don't have love for this holiday. It's rather painful to me, to be honest."

"I concluded that."

He met her eye. "You aren't an easy person to apologize to."

She smirked, the tendrils of her anger loosening their grip. "I can imagine."

He looked away again. "I was ... engaged. And Valentine's Day was the day she called it off. She ... she ..."

Norah put out a hand to stop his stuttering. "Mr. Drury, you do not owe me any more than a succinct explanation for your outburst. Any apology to me does not need to warrant your life story if you are not ready to tell it. I understand your distaste for the holiday now. I wish I'd had warning beforehand since I am not a mind reader, but that is in the past. Perhaps in the future when I accidentally stumble upon another of your sore spots, you could ease me into it more gently. I accept your apology this time for your stormy mood."

"Thank you," he breathed, obviously relieved.

"However," she added with a stern look, "I am still quite offended by your characterization of women in general. I do not believe my actions have warranted any accusations of husband-hunting."

"Oh, yes," he said with a slight hunch of his shoulders and a grimace that he smoothed out before speaking again. "You have to understand, Miss Abernathy. This was the way my fiancée was, and my mother as well. It has been my only experience of women thus far."

She shook her head. "Then you have little experience at all."

"That is probably true. Is what you said to me also true? About not wishing to marry? How can you survive this world without a husband?"

She bristled. "I've done quite well so far, thank you. So long as my brother lives, I'll continue just fine. Past that, well, I shall cross that bridge when I get there. Hopefully that won't be until I am an old woman."

He cringed. "Yes, well ... I do apologize for that as well. The old part. It was rude of me. You aren't geriatric."

"No, I'm not."

"You're younger than me, in fact."

"I expected that to be the case."

"And I don't consider myself old, so you … are not, either."

Norah studied this man who had turned very awkward before her eyes. "But men don't grow old, according to society. They age like wine. It is only women who come with an early expiration date."

"Dammit, N—" he stopped himself when he clearly realized her expression was teasing. "Oh. Yes. It is indeed a failing of our societal whims." He cleared his throat. "Um, I had another reason to stop by."

"Oh? What is that?"

"It is Sunday, and as such I have a priest who comes by to tend to the spiritual matters of certain members. I told him about you and your brother, and he asked for you to join him at lunch before he departs."

Norah was taken aback by the change in topic. "Oh. I'm not exactly inclined toward religion, Mr. Drury," she replied, her voice shrinking under what she was sure to be his scrutiny.

He showed no signs of surprise, however. "Leighton already spoke for the both of you. If it helps, neither am I, and Father Berkely has yet to cast my damned soul into the fiery pits. He's an understanding sort, which is perhaps why he works so well with this lot."

She nodded, buying some thinking time. "Very well. I shall join him."

"And me, as well."

She looked up into his eyes suddenly.

He tried to backtrack. "That is, if that is amenable to you."

She couldn't very well tell him to shove off, since it was his house. She repeated her previous words. "Very well."

Malcolm Drury's volatile presence couldn't possibly make lunch with a man of the cloth any less awkward. But she was a lady. And if it was one thing ladies knew how to do well, it was to take bitter medicine with a smile on their faces.

As it turned out, the lunch was not as awful as she had originally anticipated. Father Berkely was a quiet, thoughtful older man who, while clearly having an affinity for his craft, was incredibly considerate of other people's beliefs—or lack thereof.

"Miss Abernathy," he greeted as Norah entered the lower dining room, a rather extravagant room of dark woods and a painted ceiling. "As soon as Mr. Drury told me there was a lady staying, I knew I just had to meet her. I had the pleasure of speaking with your brother Leighton already. He assured me that the both of you will have no need for my services. Is this true?"

She inclined her head slightly with a smile gracing her lips to soften the blow. "I'm afraid so. I fear my family has not been one to put their faith too closely in the divine."

He did not seem taken aback by her confession. "While it pains me to hear such secular feelings from anyone, I can accept that this is the way. Nevertheless, I want you to know, as long as you are a guest in this house, if you have the need for council, whether it is of spiritual nature or otherwise, I am happy to lend an ear."

"Thank you, Father," Norah said.

They sat and dined on a hearty soup and freshly made bread. Father Berkely chatted easily, and, while Mr. Drury did not say much in return, he at least seemed more at ease with the priest present. Norah wondered if perhaps he saw something of a father figure in the older man, something he had apparently been lacking for longer than his actual father's demise.

"Tell me, Miss Abernathy. What are your thoughts on this guild?" the priest asked abruptly.

Norah, about to eat a bite of soup, put her untouched spoon down slowly, mulling the question over. "It is not quite what I thought it would be," she admitted.

Mr. Drury looked up, a captive audience.

"In what way?" Father Berkely pressed.

"I was under the assumption that the men who joined would be eager to rid themselves of their afflictions."

"And what makes you think they aren't?" The older man's question was not said with defense, but rather in a kind, gentle manner.

She shook her head. "I haven't been here long enough to know for certain, but each man seems to have a system they have carved for themselves, and they seem reluctant to divert from it, even if it meant a betterment of their lives."

Father Berkely chuckled softly. "That is the human experience, though, my dear. Even when one is under great stress or hardship, if they have learned to live with it, they will be hard-pressed to change their ways.

It is one of the reasons my calling is so important, as God can be a way to lift a man out of his self-made prison. To be sure, though," he added quickly, "there are other ways to find the courage to change a difficult position. One must find the inner strength to do so, if they choose not to lean on our Heavenly Father."

Norah glanced at Mr. Drury, who was now staring at his bowl of soup.

She cleared her throat. "And what if they choose not to change, even if for the better?"

The priest splayed out his hands, then picked up a piece of bread. "God gave all men free will. If they choose a life of misery, one must respect their wishes."

Norah looked down, thinking of LJ. She hoped he would find the power to want the help she would offer him, if not for his sake, then for hers.

CHAPTER NINE

Wednesday, February 17th, 1915

Norah

NORAH WAS SLEEPING SOUNDLY in her cocoon of warm bed covers, only to be awakened by a frantic pounding on her door.

"Miss? Are you awake?" Mrs. Bixby's voice slowly filtered into her mind.

Norah's heart began to pound as frantically as Mrs. Bixby's fists and a knot of unease slithered about her midsection. Something was wrong. She scrambled out of the bedding, sprinting to the door and throwing it open.

"What is it?" she asked breathlessly.

Mrs. Bixby was also in her nightclothes, an oil lamp held in one hand. Her eyes were wide with consternation, a look that made Norah's anxiety creep into minor terror. Her thoughts immediately tumbled to the idea that something was wrong with LJ.

"Sorry to wake you in the middle of the night. It's Mr. Paulson."

Norah opened the door wider, a trickle of relief dousing the worst of her dread. The rest of her fear transferred to Rodney's state of wellbeing. She had grown fond of the disfigured man. "What's wrong?"

Mrs. Bixby trundled into the room, intent on finding Norah's wrap. "The poor man has some periods where his ... condition worsens. He wakes up in the middle of the night in utter agony, and he needs help in taming his sores, so to speak."

Norah had no idea what that last sentence meant, but she didn't care. "How can I help?"

Mrs. Bixby faced her, holding the lamp out to illuminate both of their faces. "It's not a job for the weak of heart, dearie. We've lost more than a few maids to this sort of thing. He's rather disgusting on a normal day, but this? It's worse."

"I assure you, I can handle it," Norah insisted.

The housekeeper sighed with a tired smile. "I know you can. You've got the kind of heart that can look past the outer obstacles to see the true beauty of a person within. Put your robe on, dearie, and follow me."

Norah did as she was told, trailing after the housekeeper as they trudged up the stairs past Mr. Drury's door. Eddie, of course, followed dutifully behind.

At the top of the stairs, Norah was startled by a muffled scream emanating from the room next to her. She stopped in her tracks, the darkness of the hour amplifying a primal fear.

Mrs. Bixby tsked. "That's just poor Mr. Jamison. It's a nightly occurrence. You get used to that. This way."

Mrs. Bixby bravely led Norah to the back bedroom at the end of the right-hand hall. The door was already open, and a dim glow emanated from the entrance. Norah entered and found herself in the company of Mathers and Mr. Drury, the latter of which came as a surprise. The two men were hunched over bowls of steaming water, wringing out cloths and setting them on the brims by the light of a single oil lamp. Beyond them, the hapless Rodney lay on his back in bed, his heavy breaths of pain punctuating the silence.

Mr. Drury looked at her with speculation. "Mrs. Bixby, are you sure she's ready for this?"

"I think our lady has shown she's made of stronger stuff than most, sir," the housekeeper answered with steel in her voice.

He did not look convinced but gave a one-sided shrug. "We shall see. Miss Abernathy, I need to know you can stomach this. Go over and look at Rodney, please."

Brows dipping in perplexity, Norah did just that, taking the second lamp with her. Once she caught sight of Rodney, she gasped.

On the best of days, Rodney had so many bumps and pustules upon his exposed skin that it was difficult to know the true shape of his face. On this night, though, it was as if his flesh had erupted.

Every single lump had seemingly abscessed over the span of a few hours, and every single one had broken open, oozing like a landmass of mini volcanoes until they pooled between the swellings. It wasn't just his face either, but his entire body, Norah now saw. Rodney was clothed in a simple but short night shirt, and much of it was damp with the horrifying bodily fluids. Some of the abscesses had grown to huge proportions on his arms and legs. Even the bottoms of his bare feet had erupted with rashes of pimples.

"My god," Norah breathed, a hand held to her mouth.

"You see?" Drury stated from behind her, a slight sneer evident in his tone. "You may go, Miss Abernathy."

She wrenched her eyes away from the terrible sight of Rodney's body to glare at the other man. "What needs to be done in times like these?"

A silence pervaded the room, save for the dripping of a wet cloth into a washbasin. It was Rodney's weak voice that broke the quiet. "Hot cloths help greatly, miss."

She smiled at the ailing man. "Of course."

"Here, dearie," Mrs. Bixby said, handing her a freshly wrung cloth. It steamed in her hands. "Place this on his skin and let it sit until it cools. You can then use it to clean the area before getting a fresh cloth."

Norah did as she was told, carefully positioning the cloth on Rodney's forehead. The man tensed at first contact and then sighed as he relaxed into the warmth the hot towel provided.

Mr. Drury joined her with another cloth, focusing on the man's feet. Norah ignored him.

Rodney had closed his eyes, focusing on breathing through the pain, but now he opened them to gaze at Norah, who gently mopped up some of the purulence between the sores. She tried to keep her face neutral, a difficult feat considering the blood-streaked white liquid made her want to gag.

"You don't have to pretend, Norah," Rodney said in low tones. "I know I'm disgusting."

"*You* are nothing of the sort, Rodney," Norah declared firmly as she threw the cooled and dirty cloth into a bin at her feet. Mrs. Bixby wordlessly handed her a fresh towel.

"It's only your curse, Rodney," Mr. Drury added. "It has nothing to do with you."

"But me and my curse are one and the same," he whispered, closing his eyes again.

They worked endlessly, Mathers wringing out cloths, Mrs. Bixby rushing to the bathroom to fill the basins up with fresh hot water, and Norah and the master of the house soothing and cleaning Rodney. Even the cook's scullery maid, the only other servant in the house, had been roused to fetch the dirty linens and wash them out in the bathtub when the clean stock got too low. They could hear the poor girl retching as she did this task.

Whatever made his sores much worse this night, it also sapped Rodney of strength. He could not even lift his own arms to help, which meant it was up to Norah and Drury to manhandle the gentleman to properly tend to every inch of diseased skin. There came a point where the cursed man had to have his nightclothes removed, leaving him completely naked, save for the dry towel Drury draped over his nether regions to safeguard the lady's morals. Norah frankly didn't care; there was nothing about this body that could offend her more than the pure corruption of the flesh, but she said nothing.

The sores on his chest were massive, the bloody rivulets of pus freely streaming from crater-like wounds. Norah tried her hardest not to let her stomach twist. She couldn't imagine the pain these caused.

"Why are his sores so much worse tonight?" she asked Drury, unable to contain her curiosity any longer.

He flattened his lips, his stormy gray eyes meeting hers in the lamplight. "It happens like this, about once a month. His condition never fully goes away, but it's typically manageable. And then, for one night, he breaks out even worse and they all erupt like this. Tomorrow, he'll be sore, and some will still leak like always, but they heal up as much as they ever do and the cycle will start over."

"God," she breathed.

Rodney spoke softly, keeping his eyes closed. "It's like my body must rid itself of the demons that build up within it. I'll feel much better after this, miss. You needn't worry about me."

"Of course I worry about you," she shot back. "This is neither normal nor pleasant for you. How did you end up this way?"

He sighed. "The Tiger Vessel cursed me."

"Tiger Vessel?"

Without looking, he pointed a finger to the other side of the room. Norah followed its direction.

Halfway up a bookshelf sat a small greenish object resembling a teapot. A stylized animal figure sat at the top. It was hard to make out the features in the near dark, but Norah guessed it was a tiger, based on the name.

"What is it?" she asked him.

Rodney grimaced. "The Tiger Vessel is a bronze water vessel from China, around three thousand years old. I nicked it from the old Summer Palace when I visited it in 1899."

Norah paused. "Why would you take it?"

"I was an idiot, that's why," Rodney replied without preamble. "I was sixteen, young, and reckless, and I believed nothing bad would ever happen to me. My father, who enjoyed traveling, took me to China with him, and while we were at the Palace, I saw the vessel just sitting there and thought it would make a nice souvenir."

"Oh, Rodney."

"Yes, well, perhaps I was just a bit too cocky for my own good. I began to break out as soon as we boarded the ship for our next destination, and it got worse and worse. By the time we landed back in New York four months later, I was like this."

"He is the Guild's longest-standing member," Mr. Drury said. "Rodney was already living at Mr. Thompson's house when I took the Guild over five years ago."

"Yes, ever since I turned eighteen and it was clear my affliction wasn't going away," Rodney added with a pained sigh.

"Fifteen years like this, Rodney? Nearly half your life?" Norah shook her head sorrowfully.

"It isn't all bad, miss. I have great company, and I'm well taken care of."

"That may be, but still. I can't believe how cavalier you men are about your curses. And to leave a priceless cursed artifact out in the open like that!" Norah refrained from tsking like a schoolteacher. She turned her attention to Mr. Drury, who was suppressing a smirk. "Don't pretend that isn't the case. And you still haven't shared with me what your curse is about."

He met her eyes, his twinkling in the low light. "Nor have you shared with me what the 'J' in your name stands for. Perhaps my curse is that I growl like a bear when I'm angry, thanks to the Norse gods."

Norah gave her head a tiny shake but turned away to hide the smile that began to form.

It was close to five in the morning before the entirety of Rodney's body had been soothed, minus the area covered by the towel. Norah hesitated.

Mr. Drury looked at her, the bags under his eyes pronounced, but the fierceness of his usual countenance greatly softened. "It's all right, Miss Abernathy. I can handle this last bit. Get some rest."

"Are you sure?"

"Quite so. I do believe Rodney would feel more comfortable with me handling ... things."

Norah nodded, her face flushing. She hoped it wasn't noticeable in the lamplight. She turned to go.

"And Miss Abernathy? Norah?" he called once her back was turned.

She stiffened at the sound of her given name and slowly turned.

He gave her a small, but genuine smile. "Thank you."

She nodded in acceptance of this thanks and left the room, her thoughts a muddle over the oddness of the night.

Malcolm

He hadn't meant to say her first name, but with the dull ache on his brain muddling his actions, it had simply slipped out.

She hadn't seemed to mind, but Malcolm couldn't be too sure.

He tried to shake the thought out of his head while he lifted the towel to tend to the last parts of Rodney. He really did not want to be thinking about Norah—Miss Abernathy—while he hot-packed another man's bits.

Rodney watched him with some small amount of embarrassment. Mathers had gone to refill the basin, and Mrs. Bixby had left shortly after the lady, leaving just the two of them in the room.

"You like her, don't you?"

Malcolm turned his head to look at the lumpy visage of Rodney, which held a small smile. "What?"

"Norah. She surprised you tonight."

"She surprises me every time I interact with her."

"She's been good to me. I knew she'd stick around to help. I believe she truly wants to help us all."

Malcolm huffed in agitation. "But why? Why should she care about a group of men the world would like to forget about?"

Rodney groaned as Malcolm pressed against a rather nasty specimen in his groin. "Perhaps there is something in it for her as well," he grunted.

"A selfish reason? She wants her brother cured, I know that much. But why?"

"He's her only family. You would have done anything to see your mother live longer, wouldn't you have?"

His heart gave a jolt of longing at her mention. "Yes, I suppose I would."

CHAPTER TEN

Monday, March 1st, 1915

Norah

DAYS PASSED AT BIRCHWALD, faster than Norah had expected. After the Rodney incident, Mr. Drury was more pleasant toward her, stopping his antagonistic ways. For the most part, he largely accomplished this by leaving her alone, a fact that Norah filed away in her mind. After some of their past interactions, she should have been glad for this small favor, but on occasion she found herself with an urge to learn more about her enigmatic host. She let him be, regardless.

She instead renewed her efforts in getting to know the various members, realizing that connecting with Mr. Hunt and Rodney had been beneficial in understanding better what it was like to have such conditions thrust upon a person.

Some of the men were more amenable to the idea of a woman integrating into their lives than others. Pablo Reyes especially welcomed her company as much as Rodney and Farley Hunt. Some of the other men were still rather tight-lipped about their own personal curses, but Señor Reyes was an open book.

"This charm, you see? Ancient Pompeii amulet, discovered by my team. Will you marry me?"

Norah shook her head, learning to ignore the proposals that came from his mouth at a rapid pace. They were not personal, she now knew. Reyes also asked Mrs. Bixby, Cook, and even Cook's scullery maid for their respective hands any time he caught sight of them.

Instead, she focused on the oval piece of glass upon a chain around the man's neck, leaning closer to study it.

"What is the figure upon it?" she asked, seeing the faint outline created in the glass itself.

He smiled. "A satyr. Very common in Roman times. You know of Pompeii, yes?"

"Oh, yes." Norah had learned a great deal about the doomed Roman city at Oxford. Countless artifacts had been excavated there since the 1500s, and Norah knew from her studies that Señor Reyes was not the first man to be cursed by one. "Why not just take the amulet off?"

He flashed a grin. "Try it." He stood, bending his head slightly toward Norah.

She shrugged and grasped the chain with both hands, careful not to let the amulet itself touch her. The chain lifted easily enough, but as soon as it reached the underside of his ears, it seemed to catch upon something and would not move further. She let go of it, and Señor Reyes sat back smugly.

"I see. Of course you would have tried that before." Norah cocked her head in puzzlement.

He nodded, then looked at his feet with a downturn of his mouth. "I am lucky."

She gazed at him quizzically. "Lucky? How?"

He met her eyes. He was not a bad looking fellow, she had to admit. Rather short, a large nose, unruly black hair, but his eyes, with their long dark lashes, were his best feature. They looked sad at the moment.

"'Will you marry me?' '¿*Quieres casarte conmigo?*'" He shook his head. "That is the extent of my curse. To ask this one thing over and over. It is annoying, yes, but not life-threatening."

"How many women have you asked?"

His face turned stony. "Every single one I meet. Young, old, very old. It does not matter." He leaned in, lowering his voice. "Sometimes, I find myself asking *men*. Not often, but it has happened. And, most embarrassing of all, I asked my mother before I left for America."

She suppressed a smile.

"But despite this, my curse is not much. I am lucky."

Norah admitted he had a point.

On the other spectrum from Reyes was Mr. Freeman. His case was dire as the stone curse crept farther up his body. It still only encompassed his legs up to mid-thigh, but any higher and the poor older gentleman would suffer from some serious complications.

Norah knew that an interruption to his digestive system would be lethal, once the curse consumed more than his legs. She brought up the idea of surgery to Mr. Freeman, an incredibly risky choice by itself, given the likelihood of peritonitis or other surgical complications. Still, she was willing to do the legwork in finding a reputable surgeon, a tricky feat in and of itself.

Mr. Freeman declined.

"You realize that once the fossilization surpasses your ... your ..." she took a deep breath before saying the word, "*anus,* you will be in complete pain. Not to mention the inability to urinate around the same time. There won't be anything we can do to help without a surgeon."

He patted her hand. "I know, my dear. It has been three years of this 'fossilization,' as you put it. I've had that long to come to grips with it."

She sighed. "But don't you want to stop the curse? Surgery could buy you some time."

He shook his head. "I've had a good life. I traveled the world. I outlived my wife. My sons are both gentlemen who will carry on the name. I got to step foot on every single continent, barring Antarctica, but that was a personal decision. I can't abide the cold," he added with a whisper. "Australia was to be my last stop before I retired from adventuring. It's only fitting that I die because of it."

The only thing Norah could persuade the older man to try was some heat pad therapy. Specifically, the warmth of a small canine body on his lap. Eddie was a willing tool, calmly cuddling up to Mr. Freeman and laying on the stony lap for as long as the man tolerated. And while he claimed it did not change much, Mr. Freeman did admit he enjoyed the warm sensation at the cusp of the stone, as well as the company of the little beast.

Norah still saw similarities between Mr. Freeman's curse and her brother's, which worried her tremendously. Freeman's fossilization had started in his toes, turning everything to stone before moving upward to encase his feet and legs. Unbidden, it would eventually consume his torso before the curse killed him. Similarly, LJ was sure that the product of his curse would be complete crystallization of his bones, just like the skeletons he saw in the cave he took the finger bone from. He assumed his soft tissue would be fine—unlike Freeman—although the crystallization would be tremendously painful. Like Mr. Freeman, the curse first took hold of his toes and gradually moved up his legs. According to LJ, the sensation stopped around his hips, although his spine twinged with mild pain at times. Thankfully, unlike Freeman, there was no interruption of his bowels or bladder.

As with Mr. Freeman, Norah decided to try the warming therapy via Eddie. LJ had made it clear that he was not enamored with Norah's pet from England, but he put up with it all the same. And, much to Norah's delight, he admitted that his bones ached less after just half an hour of the dog on his lap. She insisted he attend daily therapy sessions after that. LJ grumbled about smelling like a dog, but did it anyway, most likely to shut his sister up for a while at least.

The only people who did not warm up to Norah immediately were Peter Withers, who continued to be catatonic and was cared for by the African man, and Marvin Ivey, who did not enjoy anyone's company lest he envision their untimely and possibly gruesome demise. Norah did not mind keeping her distance for now; after all, she had only enmeshed herself into the household not even three weeks earlier.

Sometimes it was impossible for her to grasp that she'd been here for such a short time. Norah had an affinity for change, having had her parental figures ripped away from her at a young age. She'd never had the privilege of stability. Governesses and nannies came and went through her childhood years. As an adult, she had moved to England without so much as a backward glance and had adjusted well to that lifestyle. Now, she had settled into an even stranger setting without much trouble, the brunt of it being from the broody president and master of the house.

Norah may have been adaptable, but she was also a creature of habit, and as such, once she had carved out some semblance of normality in her new setting, she sought the comfort of a routine. This took the form of daily rounds amongst the members. It started with Rodney after his incident and expanded to include Mr. Hunt—and a new bloodletting technique—then Señor Reyes, LJ, Mr. Lyster, and Mr. Freeman. She had yet to include Mr. Jamison and Mr. Norris, but she had the feeling they would soon be added to rotation.

As a matter of fact, perhaps today would be the day.

Admittedly, Norah did not know much about the curses afflicting the two men. Mr. Jamison had been cursed with nightmares, she had been told, and after hearing his screams on the night she helped Rodney, she now knew them to be worse than the garden variety of night terrors. And Mr. Norris? Norah had never heard of a man being cursed into changing species, outside of fairy tales, that was.

Still, she liked the pair and found herself wanting to help them in any way she could.

As she made her rounds with Eddie this morning, she almost sensed an optimism in the air, spurring her on. Perhaps it was the fact that it was now March, and with the new month came the promise of a warming of the weather and a chance to see the grounds without the blanket of snow covering everything. Already, she noticed a lessening of the snowfall as the days slowly became longer. She did find the snow pretty, but after months on end of the same color, she couldn't wait to see the world in verdant hues again.

Her routine started at approximately nine in the morning, after she had breakfast in her room. The layout of the third floor largely shaped her walk; she always chose Rodney's room to visit first, considering it was the farthest way at the northeast corner of the house. From there, she visited Mr. Hunt and Señor Reyes, who shared the far east bedroom corridor. Mr. Freeman took up the southeast corner, directly above Mr. Drury's master bedchambers. Once she exited his room, she was back at the stairs. To the left of the stairs was the room shared by Jamison and Norris, so it only made sense to make it her next stop.

She knocked on the door. "Mr. Jamison? Are you up?"

She did not have long to wait before a bleary-eyed Mr. Jamison opened the door. She was glad to see he was fully dressed, despite his otherwise disheveled appearance.

"Miss Abernathy. How may I be of service to you?"

She shook her head kindly. "It is not how you can be of service to me, but how I can be of service to you. May I come in?"

He paused for a moment before stepping aside to allow her entrance. She walked in, Eddie at her heels, and Mr. Jamison shut the door behind her.

She had never been inside their room; the only other time she had knocked on the door was the disastrous Valentine's Day, on which Mr. Jamison merely handed her Mr. Norris at the door.

Now that she was inside the room, the first thing that caught her off guard was the smell. Born and raised in the city, Norah had smelled some pretty terrible scents—garbage, fish from the harbor, horse manure in the summer, to name a few—but she had never actually placed herself into a henhouse. This room was the closest thing to it, and Mr. Norris' daily habits did nothing to freshen the air.

Norah knew that Mr. Norris did his business whenever and wherever the mood struck him, and therefore wore a "diaper" of sorts—a cloth contraption with a small cone covering his backside for dropping collection, and held up by a harness about the neck. Norah had been told the article had been created by Mr. Jamison years ago, to keep Mr. Norris from completely soiling the interior of homes. Mr. Jamison simply changed the diapers out about twice a day, washing them by hand in his bathroom. Here, in their room, the smell from the diapers lingered about, even though not a dropping was in sight. Clearly, Mr. Jamison did his best to keep the room clean, if not smelling the greatest.

At the moment, Mr. Norris was busy walking about and picking something up off the floor with gusto. Eddie ran over to see if the chicken might share, but Mr. Norris gave him a subtle peck on the nose for an answer. Deciding whatever the food might be was not worth his time, the dog instead sat and watched Mr. Norris with a wagging tail and perked ears, vicariously living through the chicken instead of participating.

"Ah, we weren't expecting visitors this morning. My apologies for the mess," Mr. Jamison said bashfully.

Norah waved it away. "I hope my visit isn't a bother. I only thought it was time to get to know you better, and to see what I might be able to do to help you two through your curses."

He looked dubious, although he tried to hide it behind a polite veneer. "That is incredibly considerate of you, miss. Have a seat, please."

"So, tell me," she said, doing as directed upon the desk chair, "how exactly did you come to be cursed?"

He sat at the foot of his bed. "It was terrible," he began with a theatrical shudder. "Herbert and I have been friends ever since boarding school. Inseparable, you might say. When we graduated, we decided we would like to see the world, venture to places few ever have. We started in India, and then slowly worked our way east, until we made our way to Borneo. It was a lovely country. Have you been?"

"I'm afraid not," Norah replied with a small grin.

"Ah, yes. Of course. Most women wouldn't, I suppose. Except the locals. Well, anyway. We started in the north area of Borneo, which most consider to be a safe location, given it's a British colony. Herb and I, however, wanted to experience Borneo as it must have been before the white people came. So, we traveled inland, where the jungle is thick, and many people haven't yet explored.

"After a few days of wandering, we ran across a native tribe of Dayaks. It should have been obvious to me and Herb that if we strayed too far, we'd run into wildmen, but until it happened, the thought didn't cross our minds. This group, they had seen white people before, but stayed away from them. And, much to our dismay, they took offense to us."

"Why?" Norah asked, already hooked on the story.

Jamison shook his head. "To the best of our knowledge, we did something to the jungle that displeased them. Dayaks are known to be the guardians of the forest. It's possible we destroyed something simply by chopping through the brush, and that was enough to set them off like a swarm of wasps. Whatever it was we did, they captured us and held us prisoners in their longhouse."

"Oh dear." She said this to be polite, but on the inside felt vindicated that she had guessed the nature of the Borneans' wrath in her earlier conversation with Mr. Drury.

"Exactly so. Although," he chuckled, "I suppose we were lucky in the regard that they no longer headhunted. If we had been thirty years earlier, our heads may as well have been detached from our bodies."

He sighed as he recollected his trials. "They starved us for a while, and then we were separated, with me in the longhouse, and Herb outside with the tribe. I could hear Herb screaming as if in pain, and then ..."

Norah leaned forward.

"... the clucking of a chicken," Jamison finished in a whisper. "The shaman came back into the longhouse with Mr. Norris under one arm and dropped him at my feet. Then, he said something and touched my forehead with his finger."

"What did he say?" Norah asked.

The man's eyebrows raised. "I couldn't tell. It was in a different language. The point is, he cursed my poor Herbert, and then he cursed me. I suppose I should be glad to get the lesser of the curses."

"What happened after you were cursed?"

He became quiet again. "I waited until the village had gone to sleep, and then I took dear Mr. Norris and escaped into the jungle. I can't remember exactly how I made it back to civilization, but eventually I made my way there and decided I'd have enough of adventuring. I traveled to New York, where I heard about the Guild, and we've been here ever since."

"Fascinating." Norah leaned back. "I'd like to know more about the curses. Did the shaman use any objects when he cursed you?"

He pursed his lips. "Not that I can recall, but it was dark in the longhouse. And I can't say for sure what they did to poor Herbert, either, since I wasn't present and he can no longer talk."

She studied the chicken at these words. He'd stopped picking up the food and was now grooming his feathers. "Yes, about Mr. Norris. Does he seem to understand you?"

"Some, I'd say."

"Does he have above-average intelligence? Like a human?"

Mr. Jamison shook his head. "Not exactly, no. He wasn't the smartest human either, although that didn't matter to me." He gazed at Mr. Norris with affection as the chicken let out a few contented clucks.

Norah began to suspect there was more to their friendship than the man had let on, but she decided it was none of her business.

"Now then," Mr. Jamison said briskly, walking over to pick up Mr. Norris, "we were about to go out to the sitting room for some exercise and social time. Would you care to join us?"

Norah stood as well. "I'd be delighted."

The sitting room in the middle of the third floor held two round tables with wooden chairs, a chessboard on an ornate pedestal, and two armchairs of a burgundy velvet to lounge in. It seemed to be the main area in which the men gathered during the day, although they had full access to the rest of the house. As Norah, Mr. Jamison, Mr. Norris, and Eddie approached, she saw that Ambrose Lyster, LJ, and Mr. Hunt were already there. Mr. Lyster shuffled a deck of cards.

Mr. Hunt, seated at the chessboard, nodded at Norah. She had helped him with his bloodletting this morning already—a simple poke of a needle to his finger was all it took, which appeased his curse and would not leave a scar.

LJ hoisted his feet up onto the table he and Lyster sat at. "Nor, darling. You haven't stopped by yet. I thought perhaps you'd finally forgotten about me." He did not seem too sad about the prospect, Norah noted.

"Feet off the table, LJ. We do still have manners here," she replied cooly, but gave him a smile all the same.

"Your sister was kind enough to pay me a visit this morning," Mr. Jamison told LJ as he took a seat at the table, placing Mr. Norris on top of it. Mr. Norris flapped his wings.

From behind Norah, came a familiar gruff voice. "Is that so? Adding to your collection, are you, Miss Abernathy?"

Norah spun as Malcolm Drury approached her, his face freshly shaved for once and no bags under his eyes. She gave him a small head dip in greeting.

"Oi, up for a poker game, guv?" Lyster shouted at the president.

He nodded, taking the fourth seat at the table. The chair creaked as he sat.

Lyster eyed Malcolm. "You clean up good, sir."

Malcolm raised a brow. "Is that coming from you, or one of my other admirers?"

The ginger man grinned. "Who's to say? Mr. Norris' beak is quite shiny, innit? And my, but Norah's eyes are like rich chocolate."

Norah was taken aback, if only for a moment. It was mainly the use of her given name from the man she barely knew.

"That's Miss Abernathy to you," Drury growled at him.

Lyster raised his hands in mock surrender. "Perhaps now I know where that last thought came from," he said with a wink at Drury.

Mr. Lyster was one of the men who, while not disregarding Norah, had remained tightlipped about why he was a part of the Guild. And this current conversation was congruent with others she had overheard when Mr. Lyster was involved. As usual, Norah was thoroughly perplexed by the multiple trains of thought he spewed at random. "What is it you speak of?" Norah asked, no longer able to hold her curiosity.

The men became silent, but it didn't last. "Quite the busybody, she is," Lyster commented. He scowled. "Fess up, who thought that one?"

The room stayed silent.

He sighed. "Cat's out of the bag, miss. It's my curse. Think of me like a ... radio. You've sailed before, yes?"

His train of thought was dizzying, and she failed to keep up. "Yes?"

He nodded. "They have radios on the ship. To communicate wirelessly. A bleedin' miracle, that. This radio analogy is terrible—hey, no it's not!" He looked around the room. A few men smirked. He focused back on Norah, who was more confused than ever. "My curse, it infects my brain with other people's thoughts, and they come spewing out of me. I don't know who thinks them, and I can't stop them. Sometimes my own thoughts come out unbidden, but I at least know when they're mine."

"I think I see," Norah said slowly. "So, when I first met you, that was someone else's thought invading your mouth?"

"She's a smart cookie, for a woman," he said before clapping his hands over his mouth. He straightened. "Really, fellas. Someone needs to stop."

She thought through the implications of the Englishman's curse. She remembered his first line to Drury just minutes ago and her skin flushed.

"Now he knows I think he's handsome," Lyster said and guffawed. "I can see that one coming from only one of two people present." He winked at Norah, which made her blush harder.

"Shall we play, or shall we listen to the talking radio all morning?" LJ said.

Lyster began to dole out the cards.

"It must be difficult to broadcast other people's secrets, Mr. Lyster. I can imagine it complicates your life greatly," Norah observed as she watched the cards glide across the table into neat piles.

Drury snorted. "I think he takes pleasure from it at times."

"And I think you take pleasure in being a hard-nosed arse at times," Lyster replied caustically. "See, the thing is, miss, in a group like this, there's no telling who thought that. It can be a fun guessing game at times, and there are instances where I get to speak my mind without consequences, because these blokes understand and generally don't care."

"Don't care?" Jamison spoke up as he glanced at his cards. "I'd rather not have my, er, predilections cast about. Check."

"Nobody here cares, you fop," Lyster commented.

"Might we take some time, the two of us, to discuss your curse further, Mr. Lyster?" Norah asked.

"Whatever for?" he answered. "Malcolm?"

"I raise five," Mr. Drury answered.

LJ sneered and tossed his cards. "Fold."

Norah pushed on. "I'd like to see about ways of breaking it."

Without missing a beat, Lyster said, "The nerve. She's not done a single useful thing here and she never will, at this rate. A waste of time."

The table fell silent.

"That was not me, miss," Mr. Hunt said quietly.

Norah believed him. She had a feeling she knew who authored that thought. Her eyes suddenly felt tight. She stood, glancing at Mr. Drury, her expression icy.

She would prove to him she was not a waste of time, but for now, she needed to leave, not wanting to make a scene. She'd avoid showing her emotional side, which would only bolster the low opinion of her.

"Gentlemen," she said as she turned on her heel. She left with a straight spine, her dog her obedient shadow.

It was only once she was back in her room that she allowed herself the release from her frustration at once again being minimized. She refused to cry in front of others, especially those who caused the tears.

Malcolm

"You really stepped in that one," Ambrose said quietly, waiting to hear Norah's footsteps on the stairs lest she overhear.

LJ, scowling, swore and stood abruptly, flinging his cards on the table to follow his sister to the second floor. Malcolm assumed he had gone to make sure she was alright. It's what he himself would have done, if he wasn't inclined to avoid any confrontation.

Malcolm agreed with Ambrose's sentiment. It had been an incredibly unkind thought. He felt the overwhelming need to go and apologize, only tempered by his natural hesitation.

The problem was, he did not think those words.

CHAPTER ELEVEN

Wednesday, March 3rd, 1915

Malcolm

TODAY WAS THE DAY. The anniversary.

Malcolm groaned as he rolled over in bed, clutching his pillow to his face. He briefly thought about using it to suffocate himself, but no. If anything was to keep him alive, it was spite.

There was no way he could let *that* woman win.

However, his tenuous will to live did not preclude him from desiring to be drunk all day. He planned to hit the whiskey as soon as he made it into his office, and preferably not leave until he passed out and forgot all about his predicament until next year.

Unfortunately, the Fates decided not to make it that easy on him. The minute he stepped foot outside of his bedroom, he was waylaid.

"Mr. Drury!"

It was Norah. Malcolm tried very hard not to think of her as Norah, but ever since he called her that to her face, it had stuck in his mind. It took him a great deal of brain power to remember to use her formal name in her presence.

Perhaps the angry look on her face would make it easier.

He plastered a pleasant expression to his countenance. "What can I do for you, Miss Abernathy?"

She let out an exasperated breath. "Have you been avoiding me?"

"Not at all."

Yes, he had. His last interaction with her had left him confused and feeling guilty, of all things. Why he'd experienced that particular emotion, he couldn't pinpoint. Perhaps because he hadn't spoken up for her when she clearly had been hurt by the anonymous comment from Ambrose. She had doubtlessly blamed Malcolm, too, which had stung.

And with the anniversary looming, he'd found it easier to avoid her altogether rather than pick apart why exactly she made him feel anything at all, other than the initial annoyance he had when she first arrived.

She stared at him, her eyes searching both of his, back and forth like a pendulum. They were very dark in the low light of the hall, her pupils swallowed up by the chocolate brown.

"I don't think I believe you," she declared at last.

He sighed. "Madam, today I don't think I have it in me to care." He began to walk toward the grand staircase.

She kept pace. "Mr. Drury. I only wish to have a frank discussion about what was said the other day."

"I'm sure I would be very happy to have this conversation any other day. Unfortunately, I have a meeting." He reached the stairs, treading down them quickly.

Norah huffed but kept up behind him. "A meeting? With whom?"

With my whiskey bottle, Malcolm thought. He said, "It does not concern you, madam."

He reached the first landing and kept up his harried pace down the last flight. Norah still followed.

He strode across the great hall, pretending she was not there. The decanter beckoned him sharply from afar.

He nearly forgot about Norah by the time he made it into his office. He slammed the door behind him and made a beeline for the tray.

His office door opened with just as much force as he had closed it. Malcolm growled but made no other move that would detract him from pouring his drink.

Norah yanked the decanter from his hand. "What is this?" she accused, taking a couple of steps away from him.

Malcolm turned slowly, fixing his eyes on her in a predatory manner. "Madam, I would rethink your actions."

"Or what? You'll hurt me?" she said in a mocking tone, but the fear in her eyes was real.

He closed his own, pinching the bridge of his nose. "I would not dream of hurting you. But I need that bottle." The last few words sounded more like growls to his ears.

"It's 9:30 in the morning, Drury. What could possibly make you want to begin drinking this early? Have you no morals?" She studied him. "Is that your curse? Drinking?"

He scoffed, despite her guess being too close for comfort. "Yes, you now know my secret. I once sailed to the Caribbean, whereupon I was hijacked by pirates, and they cursed me with an unquenchable thirst."

She stared at him for a beat before her brows drew together. "It's all fine and good to make fun of me for asking. I know you think of me as a waste of time as it is."

He paused, his temper dampening. "Why would you assume that was my thought?"

She let out a puff of exasperation. "You've made it very clear that you don't want me here. You accused me of husband-hunting, you made my time as difficult as possible—don't deny it, Drury. Your messages have been received loud and clear."

Drury. He rather liked her shortening of his formal title. Now he just needed to make her see her error in logic. "Norah. I'll admit, I did not want you here in the beginning. But I've seen how some of the men have taken to you. I know your heart is in the right place. I still do not understand *why* it's where it is, but I see you. Please, believe me when I say I did not broadcast that thought to Ambrose."

She stilled, her rounded eyes slightly stricken by his words. Doe-eyed, he thought. Liquid, warm, doe eyes.

"If you did not," she began in a small voice, "who did?"

He shook his head, unsure.

She walked back over and snatched a glass from the tray, pouring two fingers. She handed the decanter back to him.

"What are you doing?" he asked, bemused.

"Joining you. Somehow, thinking it was you was palatable. Enraging, but palatable. I was beginning to trust those men in the room that day. Knowing one of them thinks so poorly of me is more than I can take at the moment."

Malcolm nodded in understanding as he poured himself a glass. He clinked his with hers. "Bottoms up."

Norah

"So, tell me," she said later, as the acerbic burr from the alcohol relaxed her, "why are you drinking so early in the day?"

They were still in his office, he in his chair with his legs up on the desk, she on the other side in a rather unladylike pose, curled up in her chair.

He sighed. "Do you truly wish to know?"

"Of course. We know why *I* am imbibing. Let's make it even, hm?"

He smiled devilishly at her. With his square jawline full of dark stubble and those flashing gray eyes, that smile turned his whole face into one of sheer beauty. It was a good thing Mr. Lyster was not here to tell him how handsome he looked when he smiled.

"Today is my anniversary," he said simply.

The whiskey must have dulled her senses more than she'd realized, because she could not comprehend what he was talking about. "What anniversary?"

"Six years ago, my fiancée left me."

She snorted without meaning to. "And that is cause for celebration?"

"Are we celebrating?"

She looked at the whiskey in her hand, her second glass. No, third. "Oh, I suppose we aren't."

"No, indeed. March third represents a dark day for me. I prefer to forget it exists."

"Hence, the drinking?"

"Hence, the drinking."

She took a sip, letting it roll about on her tongue as she watched the amber liquid through the facets of her crystal tumbler. She swallowed and sighed. "You do realize drinking to forget your problems doesn't actually work, and in fact only leads to more problems?"

He eyed her with one lowered brow. "Says the woman drinking with me."

"Pah." She sat up, placing her half-drunk glass down. "I will not make a habit of this. But you do, I've already deduced. You use alcohol to cope. From what, I still haven't figured out. What is your curse?"

He too straightened in his chair, setting his feet on the ground. A somber expression crossed his face. "I was exploring in the Seychelles, diving with the natives, when I stumbled upon a cursed pearl. Ever since then, at the new moon, I grow gills and must breathe water for the full night. Drinking helps my throat to grow the gills."

She stared at him, taking in this new information as he gazed back at her with all seriousness. Then his face cracked with a wicked grin.

"Oh, you almost had me!" Norah shouted. She clapped her fingers to her mouth. "Oops. A bit too loud there, wasn't I?"

"A bit," Drury agreed cheerfully.

She stood, bracing herself on the desk as the room distorted for a second. "Well, I am sorry for your loss. You must have loved her greatly for her leaving to cause you such distress. I should go. I do apologize for barging in like this."

"What will you do?" Drury asked, suddenly attentive to her motions.

She shrugged. "Go ask Cook for some coffee, I suppose. And some food to soak up the whiskey in my system. I think I've learned from the master that alcohol will not get you where you need to be. I will leave that to you. Happy drinking."

"Norah, wait."

She paused, her heart giving a little leap at the sound of her name. She never gave him permission, but she was not about to tell him to stop.

He stood. "I think perhaps I've had a change of heart. About the drinking. May I join you for coffee and food?"

She smiled at him. "You may."

CHAPTER TWELVE

Saturday, March 6th, 1915

Norah

NOW THAT SHE HAD been a part of the household for nearly a month, Norah figured it was high time to learn more about the last two members she had yet to make contact with. Considering it was Saturday, she had the perfect opportunity to have a captive audience.

Norah made sure to get to the upper dining room early, so as to choose her place carefully. She had attended three such breakfasts so far, and had sat next to Mr. Hunt, Rodney, Mr. Lyster, her brother, Mr. Jamison, and Señor Reyes in turn. Overall, she had enjoyed the company of these men, but it was high time she cracked through the barriers of Mr. Withers and Mr. Ivey.

Drury was already there when she came walking into the dining room. "You're awfully punctual this morning," he greeted drily.

"I thought my chances of choosing my seat would be greater that way," Norah responded. "I would like to sit next to Mr. Withers and Mr. Ivey, if I may."

Drury plopped himself down in the middle of the U, as usual. "I suppose that can be arranged."

"Wonderful."

"Indeed."

The conversation stopped. Norah continued to stand as the silence became oppressive. She could take it no more. "Where shall I sit?"

Malcolm closed his eyes. "You seem to be an independent lady. You are more than capable of figuring it out on your own."

She huffed with irritation, just as Señor Reyes and Mr. Hunt entered the room.

Brightening, she called out, "Ah, gentlemen! Please do be seated next to Mr. Drury today."

They cocked their heads like puppies at Norah taking command, but did as they were told.

While Mrs. Bixby worked the dumbwaiter and Mathers supplied the tables with food, Norah directed the men who trickled into their seats, making sure to leave a space between Mr. Withers and Mr. Ivey, the latter being at the far end where he always sat.

Satisfied, Norah took her place. The group dug into the food with usual gusto, filling their plates with eggs, bacon, sausage, and biscuits.

She turned first to Mr. Ivey, who had only grabbed a biscuit for his plate. He had his eyes squeezed shut—a normal occurrence for him, Norah had come to notice. In fact, the only time he didn't have his eyes tightly closed was while walking, and then they were firmly trained upon the ground.

"Mr. Ivey," she greeted pleasantly. "How are you?"

He hunched his shoulders, turning his head away slightly. "As good as I can manage, miss."

"Would you like some help in procuring more food for your break-fast?" The man was incredibly thin, she noticed.

He shook his head. "I'm not typically hungry in the morning."

Norah was getting nowhere fast. Perhaps a different approach was needed.

"Mr. Ivey, I appreciate your concern over my wellbeing, but I would like to get to know you better, in order to help you. I feel that a temporary discomfort would be a worthy sacrifice in order to heal oneself. Wouldn't you agree?"

He sighed. "Not necessarily, no."

"Please, look at me."

"No thank you."

"Please?" She placed her hand delicately over his.

She could feel his desire to pull away, but somehow, he didn't. Instead, he slowly turned his face toward hers. Like the petals of a flower, his eyelids lifted.

Mr. Ivey's eyes were the most vivid green Norah had ever seen on a man. They caught a hold of her own eyes and stared for a heartbeat, before screwing shut again. He clasped his fists to his sockets.

"The stab wound ... staircase ... your hand is so bloody. Reaching out to me ..." He sobbed and rocked in his seat.

"Who has been stabbed, Mr. Ivey? Me? I'm fine. There is no blood. It's only a vision," she said, trying to calm the man.

Mr. Ivey's broken sentences continued, though. "Bloody ... your dress is red from it. Malcolm, holding a knife ..."

Despite herself, goosebumps broke out on her flesh. She glanced over at Drury, who had taken an interest in the goings-on at the end of the table.

"Did I murder you?" he called out to her.

She nodded. "I believe so."

"It happens more often than you think. Perhaps it's best to leave Mr. Ivey be for now, Miss Abernathy."

She nodded again and turned back to the despondent man. She placed a hand on his arm. "I apologize, Mr. Ivey."

At her touch, he calmed and stopped rocking. His hands came away from his eyes, which he opened but kept downcast, not looking at anybody. He took a deep, ragged breath, letting it out slowly.

"Here," she said, swapping their plates. "I haven't yet touched the food. You need sustenance, Mr. Ivey. I'll leave you to eat."

"Thank you, miss," he said in a very quiet voice. He picked up his fork and took a bite of eggs.

Norah filled her new plate, taking the time to eat herself before gathering her courage to interact with the person to her left.

Eventually, she turned that way and set her eyes on Mr. Withers. The man sat in his wheelchair, having been settled at the table by his assistant. He was one of the oldest members, around the same age as Mr. Freeman, if Norah had to guess. He had gray hair bordering on white, thinning at the top, with watery blue eyes that stared out into nothing. A small trickle of drool glimmered at the corner of his parted lips.

"Mr. Withers?" Norah did not know if he could hear her, but she was determined to stick with the assumption he could, unless she learned otherwise. "I'm Norah Abernathy. We haven't yet had the pleasure of meeting, other than when I first arrived."

Mr. Withers merely stared straight ahead.

"He cannot respond, miss," his caretaker said from his other side.

Norah glanced past Mr. Withers to meet his eyes. She had not said much to him either, not since her first encounter with the group as a whole in the trophy room. Mr. Withers and his assistant hardly interacted with anyone as far as she could tell. Anytime she occupied the third floor, they both seemed to remain in their shared room.

She could admit she was not familiarized with keeping company with Black people. New York City had a small population of them, but none in her neighborhood. She hardly saw them while living in the city. This man was her first true encounter with a race other than her own.

The men at Birchwald seemed to pay no mind of him. She wondered if it was because in this household, everyone was different, an outcast, a freak to "normal" society. If so, this one African individual was the most normal of them all—after all, he was not cursed.

Now, with the perfect opportunity for personal growth, Norah made up her mind that she would certainly treat him no differently because of the color of his skin.

She reached a hand behind the older gentleman. "It's nice to see you again. I'm Norah Abernathy."

He looked at her hand for a moment before reciprocating, although he cast his eyes downward at her welcoming smile. His hand was smooth and warm. "I am Karanja."

"Karanja. You are Mr. Withers' assistant?"

"Yes, ma'am."

"What a blessing for him to have you here. You must be an incredibly caring person to travel such a long way from home. What can you tell me of his curse?"

Karanja looked away, and Norah wondered if he'd answer. Perhaps she had said the wrong thing after all. But he turned back, his face stony, before he smoothed it out to a polite smile. "I am sorry. Too many languages in my brain sometimes."

"You speak many languages?"

The man nodded. "My native tongue, of course. Neighboring African dialects. Some German. And English."

Norah's eyebrows raised. "Goodness. That is very impressive. You speak English very well."

"Thank you." He paused, as if gathering his thoughts. "Mr. Withers cannot do anything on his own. He is trapped in his body. I am in his debt, so I take care of him."

"That is kind of you."

He looked her in the eye, his gaze fierce. "It is what is owed to him."

Mr. Withers made a noise in his throat, bringing Norah's attention to him. His eyes began to jitter back and forth as he tried to vocalize.

"Mr. Withers?" Norah asked, putting a hand on his arm.

Karanja stood. "This happens sometimes. He becomes agitated. I must tend to him."

"May I be of service?" Norah asked as she began to stand as well.

"No—" Karanja said with force, before stopping and taking a breath. "No, thank you. I would be happy to speak with you at another time, miss. Thank you for conversing with me."

Norah realized that as insular as he was, Karanja had little opportunity to fraternize. He was new here as was she, only she had made strides to socialize. He was most likely incredibly lonely, what with only Mr. Withers as his usual company.

"Karanja, would it be possible for us to talk again soon?" It was forward of her, but she wanted to befriend a fellow outsider, and he fascinated her.

He gave a small bow. "It would be my pleasure, miss. Have a good day," he replied as he wheeled Mr. Withers from the table.

She sat again, sighing. How did one cure a comatose, cursed man? She was bound and determined to get to the bottom of it.

She glanced back over at Mr. Ivey. Horrific visions that never came true. Another puzzle for her to solve.

The chair Karanja had vacated scuffed on the floor. She turned to see Drury sitting in it, a grin upon his face and his eyes shining.

"Oh, hello," she said with lackluster spirit.

"Hello, yourself. I see you managed to send poor Marvin into a vision *and* scare Mr. Withers away. You're in fine form today."

She forced a contrite chuckle. "Just trying to solve some mysteries, is all. And what about you? What's your curse?"

"What's the 'J' stand for?"

She narrowed her eyes. "I asked you first."

He sighed theatrically. "I touched a rare gem in Malaysia and lost my thumbs."

She glanced at his hands. "You have thumbs."

"Yes, but these aren't mine. Some poor bloke I was traveling with got my thumbs, and I got his."

"Drury, your wit is unmatched," she deadpanned.

He grinned wider, enjoying himself.

She faced forward, scooping another bite of eggs into her mouth and ignoring the exasperating man beside her.

CHAPTER THIRTEEN

Tuesday, March 9th, 1915

Norah

Dear Aunt Nell,

You will be pleased to hear that I have settled into Birchwald, and I am acquainting myself with the members with predominant success. There are a select couple who have proven trickier than others, but I have faith I shall win them over in time.

The president of the Guild has been very gracious to me

Norah sighed, tapping the top of her fountain pen against her lips. Had he been very gracious? He certainly wasn't in the beginning, and even now, his attitude toward her was more of a teasing curiosity rather than true agreeability. Still, he had eased off on the hostility, which was a very good sign. Norah actually enjoyed catching sight of him, rather than wanting to run the other way.

She decided it wasn't exactly a lie, what she wrote in her letter. She continued her sentence.

The president of the Guild has been very gracious to me, allowing Eddie and me to stay in the mistress suite, named the Aster Room because of the wallpaper. LJ is housed at the top of the house, with the rest of the members. His room is much smaller, but he seems to like it well enough.

Another fib. She soldiered on.

I have yet to break anyone's curses, but since I have only been here a month, I must allow myself grace. It will not be a swift process, by any means.

I do miss your company, and I hope you are well. I think fondly of the time we lived together at Oxford, and sometimes I yearn for those days again. However, I am content here at Birchwald and I do not see myself leaving any time soon. Perhaps in the near future you could visit us.

LJ sends his love along with mine.

Your niece,

Norah

She scanned the letter, and bit her lip over the LJ sending his love part. He didn't even know Norah had decided to write to Aunt Nell. Perhaps she should see if he wanted to add anything as a postscript.

She fanned the paper to dry the ink before capping her pen and striding out of her bedroom.

Upstairs, she surveyed the common area. Post-lunch, it was usually a quiet affair and today was no different. Mr. Jamison napped upon one of the armchairs, with Mr. Norris upon his lap, his head tucked behind a wing and his eyes fully closed. The man twitched and frowned in his sleep, a sign that even in the daytime his rest was plagued by bad dreams. Mr. Hunt read a book in the other chair. Some of the page edges were streaked with a rust-brown stain, a sure sign that he'd cut himself upon the paper during other reading sessions. At one of the tables, Rodney played solitaire, while Señor Reyes sketched intently from the opposite chair. Nearby, Mr. Freeman rested in his wheelchair, with Eddie upon his lap. Every few seconds, he automatically lifted a weathered hand to stroke the snoozing dog's back.

Norah smiled at the serenity before her, a reminder that even troubled souls could be at peace for moments of time. She felt lucky enough to witness it.

Rodney saw her first. He waved a hand, beckoning her closer. "Norah!" he whispered so as not to disturb anyone.

She smiled at the genuine affability he exuded as she joined his table. "Enjoying the lull?" she murmured to the two men.

Reyes also smiled with warmth. "Miss Abernathy, will you marry me?" he whispered.

She shook her head with a grin and then looked at the paper in front of him. "Why, Señor, I had no idea you could draw." She sidled closer to him to get a better look.

It was a pencil sketch of Rodney, complete with his many sores. Despite the rough exterior of the subject, the Spaniard had managed to capture the gentleness in Rodney's eyes.

"It's beautiful," Norah breathed with appreciation.

Reyes blushed at her scrutiny of his work. "*Gracias, bella dama.* I am no master, but the art brings me joy."

"You're too modest. You have a gift, Señor. Don't you agree, Rodney?"

Rodney craned his neck to look at the sketch. He frowned and shrugged before returning his attention to his card game. "He's talented, for certain. But his choice of subject leaves much to be desired."

"Pshaw," Norah whispered firmly. "Beauty is in the eye of the beholder, and you, sir, have beauty, despite your flaws. I can see it, clear as day."

Now it was Rodney's turn to blush, even through the facial lumps. He cleared his throat softly, changing the subject. "What brings you up here, Norah?"

She gazed past the sitting room to the three doors beyond, focusing on the middle one. "I was writing my aunt and thought I'd see if LJ had anything to add. If you'll excuse me, gentlemen, I'll go see if he's available."

They stood in unison as she left the table, then settled again immediately.

The subtle commotion was enough to awaken Eddie, who wagged his plumed tail the second he caught sight of his mistress. He leapt down from the stone lap, rousing Mr. Freeman from his stupor.

Norah placed a hand on the older gentleman's arm affectionately. "Mr. Freeman, how are you feeling?"

He blinked to clear the cobwebs from his mind. "Hector, please. I'd like to be on friendly terms with you. It's my dying wish. May I call you Norah?"

Norah's heart melted. "Of course you may. But you're not dying yet. Not if I can help it. Eddie was with you for over an hour. How do you feel?"

He glanced at his legs. They looked normal to Norah, encased in trousers as they were. The clothing did not give away their secrets. "I'll do," he answered enigmatically.

Norah let out a breath through her nose. "Well enough for now, I suppose. But let's keep at it, shall we?"

Hector gazed at Norah like a doting grandfather. "If you wish, my dear."

"I'm about to pop in to talk with my brother. Do you need anything before I do?"

He shook his head. "No, no. I'm fine. Go and tend to Leighton."

She patted his arm before moving over to LJ's door, Eddie by her side. She knocked softly.

"What is it?" His voice was muffled by the door.

"It's me. Can I come in?"

A pause. Then, "All right."

She entered, allowing Eddie in as well, and shut the door behind her. LJ's room was much smaller than some of the other bedrooms and sparsely furnished. A single window illuminated the space, with the bed wide enough for a single occupant, and the only other furniture a dresser on the other wall. LJ lounged upon the bed, staring at the ceiling.

"I hope I didn't disturb you," she said.

LJ snorted. "Not a bit. I was just contemplating my prison sentence."

Norah rolled her eyes. "This is hardly a prison."

"No? You try living in here."

She swept an arm out. "You have access to the entire house. No one said you had to stay in your room."

"And what would I do out there, hm?" He sat up, dropping his legs over the side of the bed. "A man can only play so much chess and poker before feeling like he is losing his marbles."

"You were on your way to making friends with the other members when we first arrived," Norah pointed out.

"Ah yes." LJ's voice dripped with disdain. "But then they got to know my sister, and suddenly I wasn't good enough."

Norah stayed silent at this accusation. LJ had always been the popular one. He'd never had to work for friendships. Then again, he and Norah had never moved in the same circles. Norah did not understand why he would push the others away just because she also was getting to know them.

She took a deep, calming breath. Clearly, LJ was of the mind to tantrum. It was understandable, really. He had always been the adventurous one, never wanting to stay in the same space very long. She should have known he'd act in this way. "Well, let's get you cured, and then you can be on your way," she said with sweetness like poison.

LJ let his head fall back against the wall with a thunk as he stared upward again. "Right. So, what brings you around? Cures?"

"Actually, I was writing a letter to Aunt Nell." She waved the written page about as if showing proof of her statement.

"Okay, then."

"Would you like to add anything for her before I send it?"

He glanced her way. "What would I possibly say to her? 'Dear Aunt Smell, we never got along, so being away from you feels no differently than being in your company?'"

Norah winced at the vitriol in his tone. "Don't call her that! It's not her fault she smells bad sometimes." LJ had come up with that cruel moniker when they were ten and referred to her as such on many occasions—behind their aunt's back, of course. He'd thought himself quite clever. "She's your family, after all."

"No, Nor, she's *your* family. You were the chosen favorite. She couldn't have cared less about me. So now, the feeling is mutual."

"That's not ..." Norah paused. She was about to refute his claim, but it would be pointless. LJ was right; Aunt Nell *had* been rather disdainful of her twin, just as she was with males in general. She sighed. "Very well. Sorry to have bothered you."

Suddenly feeling dejected, she turned and opened the door, marching out quickly. She only made it two steps before ramming into a sturdy blockade.

"Oomph!" the blockade uttered.

In a daze, she took a step back and looked up into Drury's face.

"Good lord, woman," he growled.

She backed up even farther, once again within LJ's room. "Drury, I'm so sorry! I wasn't paying attention ..."

He rubbed his sternum. "Clearly, Norah. Quite the greeting there. Is your head made of stone?"

Norah glanced back at her brother, who was watching the exchange with calculating eyes. She refocused on the man before her, feeling incredibly discombobulated. "No more than your chest is."

"Mr. Drury, what brings you here?" LJ asked, his voice artificially cheerful to Norah's trained ear.

"Call me Malcolm, please." He said this at LJ, but looked at Norah while he said it, a clear message to her. She felt her face flush, which irritated her to no end. Why should he fluster her so easily?

Drury continued, "I was just making my rounds and wanted to check in on you. I had no idea you already had company."

"Not at all. *Norah* was just leaving." LJ's tone at her name was pointed.

It was time to flee before her face caught on fire. "Gentlemen," she garbled out as she sidestepped Drury's mass and exited swiftly before anything else could be said. Eddie, who had waited in the sitting room, dutifully trotted after her.

It was only once she was back in her room that she realized she must have dropped her letter when she ran into Drury.

Malcolm

Malcolm wasn't sure what was stranger, the tension in the room, or the concern he had for Norah.

She had left in quite the hurry, a far cry from the other times she had seemed so self-assured with her little spats—mostly directed at him. Her fleeing had unsettled him, possibly because the last time she had done so, it was because she was upset with him. Her grip upon his psyche unnerved him, yet he was powerless to stop it. Getting to the bottom of this current quandary might assuage him.

Luckily for him, he had a good reason to go knocking on her door. He'd spied the letter on the floor as soon as she'd left. It took little time to extricate himself from Leighton's room—the man did not seem to care for company and took no mind of Malcolm's hasty departure. He found himself outside of the Aster Room with stunning quickness.

Here he paused, a fist raised but stationary, the wood surface of the door so familiar to him. How many times had he knocked upon it in order to summon his mother over the years? He was surprised there wasn't an indent in the shape of his knuckles. Yes, the door was the same as it ever had been, unaltered by time's passage. It was only the person inside who had changed.

He stopped stalling and knocked. As he predicted, she answered quickly, although her eyes rounded at the sight of him.

"Oh. I wasn't expecting you," she said. She did not move out of the way.

He brandished the dropped letter in between them. She smiled sheepishly as she took it. "Thank you. I suppose I wasn't quite myself just then."

"Are you all right?" he asked, keeping his voice purposefully soft.

She motioned her head back and forth slightly, not a head shake, but not a nod either.

"Family spat?" Malcolm hazarded.

Norah sighed and held up the letter. "Just a difference in opinion, is all."

He pointed his jaw at her hand. "Who were you writing to?"

She stared at him.

He felt the urge to take back the question. "I ... that is... it's none of my business, really ..."

"Drury." His name so casually thrown about stopped his rambling. She smirked knowingly. "It's kind of you to ask. The letter is for my aunt."

"Your aunt?"

"Yes. Well, she's my great-aunt, really. Actually, she's my half-great-aunt five or six times removed ..."

"Now who's rambling?" he asked, his confidence back to normal. He paused as her words registered. "How many times removed, did you say?"

She quirked her mouth to one side in thought. "Five or six? I haven't actually counted. It could be more, now that I think about it."

He frowned. "Seems impossible. What is your aunt's name?"

"Eleanora Montmorency. It's a mouthful, I know."

"Eleanora." The name roused a memory from a deep recess in his mind. Suddenly, it came rushing to the forefront. "*Nell?*"

She cocked her head. "Why, yes. Do you know her?"

"Know her? No. Know *of* her? Yes. She's an urban legend. I had no idea she was real." Before moving to the country, Malcolm used to play with a small group of boys, usually while their mothers gossiped over drinks in the afternoon. Legends like the skunk ape and Bloody Mary always tickled their fancy, and he distinctly remembered the tale of the undead widow who was always looking for her next husband. Even the sordid little rhyme they used to chant came back to him.

Nell, Nell, the widow is swell

She'll marry you quick, and then drag you to hell.

"Aunt Nell? An urban legend? She might enjoy that. For all I know, she started it," Norah said with an amused chuckle.

Malcolm was floored by her cavalier demeanor over this revelation. "How on earth is Nell the widow your aunt?"

She waved a hand. "It's a long story. But other than LJ, she's my only family. You recall I lost my parents at a young age, and my grandparents were also deceased by the time I was born. After my mother died, Aunt Nell came into our lives. She does have husbands every once in a while, but she had just been widowed again, and so she came to live with us. She isn't exactly motherly." She paused with a small smile on her face, which Malcolm found endearing, "But she was the only mother I remember." She frowned. "Unfortunately, LJ remembers her a little differently than me. Hence the disagreement."

"I see. Are you content here?"

The slight change in topic clearly caught her off guard. She blinked a couple of times before answering. "Well, yes, I am. I fear my brother is not, but I'm hoping with time he'll come around."

Malcolm was glad to hear she too had noticed the signs of discontentment in her brother. He'd gone from charming and gregarious to downright moody since entering the Guild. He paused to study her. "You do know he's free to leave if he wishes to, don't you?"

She snapped her head up, a stormy expression flitting across her face. "Of course. But he should stay. It's important."

"Important to him? Or you?"

The storm clouds continued to roll in. "I'm not sure what you are insinuating, Drury. I'm only looking out for his well-being."

He held out his hands to placate her. "I understand that, Norah. Please."

She narrowed her eyes. "What's your curse?"

Ah, she was changing the subject. He smiled shrewdly. "I'm allergic to carrots."

She gave him a look that said she thought he was an idiot. "That's not a curse."

"It is if you're only allergic because you desecrated the sacred carrot god's altar."

Her sigh of exasperation was adorable. "Drury ..."

"What does the 'J' in Norah J Abernathy stand for?" he countered.

She gazed at him, her brown eyes no longer stormy or sad, but amused. "Have a good afternoon, Drury." She closed the door.

"You as well, Norah," he said softly to the wooden surface.

CHAPTER FOURTEEN

Friday, March 19th, 1915

Norah

AT LAST, THE DAY had arrived: the snow was gone.

Norah peered out of her second story window to see that the last of the white had been reduced to lonely islands within the deepest recesses of shade. The sky was an anemic blue and clear, with no sign of impending flurries. Spring had officially peeked its head out, and Norah could not be giddier about it.

She hadn't truly explored outside of Birchwald since the day she arrived. Her ventures outdoors had comprised of standing in the open door of the solarium or stepping out of the lower loggia onto the terrace while Eddie ran out to do his business, the small dog nearly disappearing into the depths of the snowbanks on some days. He never dallied either; he was not much of a fan of the cold white stuff himself.

But today, the green of the grass lawn out back could be seen, and this minor change sent a thrill through Norah, and awakened a desire to reconnect with nature. She wished to share the feeling with someone.

She made her morning rounds with a small jaunt in her step. She had taken to visiting with each man now, all except for Mr. Withers and Mr. Ivey, who still stayed mostly to their rooms. None of the members seemed to join her enthusiasm; they were content to stay indoors, as was their habit. Even LJ, who yearned for adventure, refused to remove himself from his room, opting to sulk instead. Norah did not let this dampen her spirits, though. She thought she might know someone else who would share in her delight, someone who she had recently connected with in small ways.

At half past eleven, she knocked on the door to Drury's office.

"Enter," he barked, although the bite of his voice was absent.

She walked in, smiling widely as she sat across from him. He looked up from his papers with a crook of an eyebrow.

"You seem awfully chipper this morning," he remarked with a quirk of his mouth.

"Have you looked outside yet today?" she asked.

He glanced at the window behind him. "It looks cold out." He turned back to his desk, his face smoothing out.

She huffed at his nonchalance. "What you meant to say was, 'the snow has melted and it looks like the perfect weather for a stroll.'"

He kept his eyes on his work, staying silent as if she hadn't said anything at all.

She cleared her throat. "Well, Drury? What do you say?"

His pen scribbled across the paper. "About what?"

"A walk about the grounds. Get some fresh air."

He sighed and put his pen down. "Miss Abernathy ..."

She sucked in a breath, astounded. He hadn't called her that in ages. A feeling of dread crept into the pit of her stomach.

He finally looked at her, his face a combination of almost-contained anger and sadness not quite hidden by forced passiveness. She wracked her brain for a reason he would deliver such an expression to her. It did not do anything to quell the growing knot in her midsection.

"I must decline," he said simply before returning his attention back to his work.

She waited a moment more. Perhaps an explanation, an apology, *anything* would come from his mouth. But, no. He stayed silent, the scritch of the pen to paper being the only noise.

That, and the pounding of her heart.

She rose, almost unsteadily. He made no move to stop her.

"Sorry to have bothered you," she said in a voice laced with steel, an armor to protect the feelings that had already been battered by the encounter. He did not answer as she left the room.

CHAPTER FIFTEEN

Tuesday, March 23rd, 1915

Norah

AFTER THEIR LAST DISASTROUS encounter, Norah decided it was best to avoid Drury. On his part, he had kept his distance as well, even at Saturday breakfast, in which he hardly looked at her.

She instead took walks with Eddie alone, relishing the feel of the warming air on her skin. Winter still had a tenuous grasp on the weather, with mild flurries here and there, but nothing stuck around.

Still, Norah was lonely.

To help pass the time, she assisted with household chores to ease Mrs. Bixby's burden, especially on wash days. The number of men in residence resulted in a solid day's worth of laundry every week, and the housekeeper was happy to receive some help.

They were in the basement, a place that was a far cry from the rest of Birchwald's elegant atmosphere. The laundry room was muggy but spacious, and Norah would rather be here than anywhere near Mr. Drury at the moment. Heaven knew *he'd* never step foot into the basement.

Norah handed wet clothing to Mrs. Bixby, who ran it through the wringer with careful precision.

"Something on your mind, dearie?" the older woman asked after a quick glance at Norah.

She had been in thought, once again, over what she could have done to turn the master so cold to her. It would not do to admit such a thing, however. "Does it bother you to be in a house full of curses?" she asked instead.

Mrs. Bixby *hmm*ed in her throat. "No, not exactly. I feel for the poor souls. I get annoyed by Señor Reyes always asking me to marry him, although I should feel flattered. I dare not spend much time with Mr. Lyster, since I don't want my thoughts to be said out loud. And I hate washing Mr. Paulson's clothing."

She had excellent points, especially the last one. Norah saw firsthand how soiled from purulence Rodney's garments became. It was hard to wash the crusty and sometimes bloody stains fully.

"But I also feel a kinship with them," Mrs. Bixby continued. "They are lost lambs, and my mothering instincts come out around them."

"Are you cursed as well, Mrs. Bixby?" Norah asked on a whim.

The older lady chuckled. "Seeing curses around every corner, are you?" she teased. "No, dearie, no curses for me. As far as I know, none of the help are cursed." She paused her wringing. "Now my husband, he had what you might call a doomed life. I often wonder if he had a curse placed upon him that he didn't know about."

"He is no longer among us, then?"

She shook her head. "He's been gone longer than we were married. Freak accident. Used to be a driver for the master's father, until the carriage backed over him one day."

Norah clasped a hand to her mouth. "How horrible!"

"For sure, dearie, for sure. But his death led to my employment with this family. And I have to say, that has been a blessing in my life. Especially ever since the Guild moved to this location. Master Malcolm needed the company, after his mother died."

"And his fiancée left him?" Norah added.

The housekeeper grunted. "Oh, so he told you?"

She nodded once. "A very brief description. I caught him trying to drown his sorrows on the anniversary earlier this month."

"Yes, he likes to do that."

"What was she like?"

Mrs. Bixby tapped her chin. "Nice enough. Her parents were family friends with the Drurys, from New York City. She was seventeen at the time of the engagement, around seven years younger than Mr. Malcolm. Her father had died, you see, so I believe the mothers hatched the scheme to wed their children."

Norah sucked in a breath. "It wasn't a love match?"

"Well, I'm not sure. They saw plenty of each other while they grew up. Amiable enough, you might say. But there was definitely the money component at work as well. Miss Fiona and her mother moved to Birchwald three months after the engagement was announced."

Fiona. Norah imagined a teenaged girl spoiled by money, her blonde hair perfectly coiffed, relying on her looks as her only redeeming assets to get by.

In the back of her mind, she wondered why this imagined visage of Drury's ex-fiancée riled her up so.

"And Drury offered her the mistress suite?" The words flew from her unbidden. They sounded oddly petulant to her ears.

Mrs. Bixby did not react adversely to them, though. "Oh my, no, not the Aster Room. Mrs. Paula was still alive, and that was her room. Miss Fiona took up the guest room at the end of the hall, the Iris Room." She lowered her voice. "Truth be told, we were surprised seven ways to Sunday when Mr. Malcolm put you up in his mother's room. I never thought I'd see the day it would be occupied again."

Norah knew on some level that she had been staying in the same room that had previously been occupied by Drury's mother. Hearing these words straight from Mrs. Bixby's mouth gave her an enormous sense of satisfaction. Not even the ex-fiancée Fiona had had the privilege, and she had been a more special guest than Norah.

Still, she felt the need to self-deprecate as she handed the housekeeper another article of clothing to wring out. "I'm not sure why he did. He's made it clear how he feels about me being here."

Mrs. Bixby slowly turned back to the wringer, as if digesting Norah's comment. "And what conclusion have you made?"

She stared at the back of the housekeeper's head. "He started with open hostility, followed by begrudging acceptance. Now I'm afraid we are back to ignoring each other."

"A word of advice?"

"Of course."

Mrs. Bixby cranked the lever with vigor. "Master Malcolm has a rough exterior."

Norah snorted. "That's a fact, not advice."

"Dearie, with all respect, I wasn't nearly finished."

"Sorry," Norah replied with a hunching of her shoulders.

Mrs. Bixby cleared her throat. "He's prickly on the outside, but his heart is good. He's had some hard knocks in life, and he's developed that armor to mask how vulnerable he can actually be." She turned and scrutinized Norah. "I have the feeling you two may have that much in common. Anyway, you shouldn't let his prickles be taken to heart. He's a good man, as is evidenced by his taking over of the Guild. Not many would open their homes to such lunacy."

Norah considered this. "Thank you for telling me."

The older woman patted Norah on the arm. "Just don't tell him I said anything."

She smiled. "Wild horses couldn't drag it from me."

CHAPTER SIXTEEN

Friday, March 26th, 1915

Norah

"I HAD A THOUGHT, Rodney," Norah said. She and the man in question were downstairs in the library. Norah had recently discovered his love for literature, especially adventurous or speculative works of fiction. Mr. Drury's collection was not extensive by any means, but Norah had identified such authors as Jules Verne, Walter Scott, and Robert Louis Stevenson among the drier history tomes and encyclopedias.

Rodney was parked in front of the fire with *Frankenstein*. He devoured the pages with his eyes and had to tear himself away to focus on Norah, who sat in the chair perpendicular to him, a book about China open on her lap.

Ever since Mr. Drury had turned cold toward her, she had been throwing herself into finding cures for the members. She admitted to herself that she had been distracted as she acclimated to Birchwald, and this had led to an indolence on her part. She theorized perhaps her previous inaction had been a cause for Drury's sudden souring. It was possible he did not look kindly at her previous passivity.

Rodney reluctantly placed his open book down on his lap. As he did, a large sore on his forehead burst, sending a small trickle of pus down his face. He didn't seem to notice. "Hmm? What did you say?"

Norah did her best not to stare at the oozing purulence. "I said I had a thought. Now, please forgive me, Rodney, but I'll be asking some ... personal questions to help formulate my ideas. Are you willing?"

He smiled. In the midst of his damaged face, his teeth were nearly perfectly straight. For the first time, Norah thought he might have been a handsome man before his misfortune took over. "Fire away, Norah."

"Very well." She paused to collect her thoughts. "How often do you bathe?"

Rodney's eyes unfocused as he thought. "The usual, about once a week."

"And do you use any special soaps or tonics while you bathe?"

"Just Ivory. Nothing else."

"What about after your bath," Norah pressed. "Any creams or lotions applied?"

"None at all. Why?"

"I'd like for you to try some new bathing habits, if you're amenable. Perhaps we can cure your lesions from the outside. Are you familiar with stinging nettle?"

He chortled. "I do believe anyone who had a boyhood of exploring the outdoors is familiar with stinging nettle."

She smiled. She supposed most children would learn to stay away from the painful plant. "I took a class at Oxford during my studies: 'Botanical Cures for Curses.' Stinging nettle is a great tool for minor curses, as is angelica and agrimony. Now, I would have to order the last two, but on one of my walks about the property, I stumbled on a clump of nettles. I'd like to try infusing them in your bathwater for your next bath."

Rodney looked dubious. "I suppose I'll try, if you think it may help. They aren't going to sting me all over, will they?"

"Oh no, nettles no longer sting once they are boiled. In fact, they are incredibly nutritious to eat that way. Only the raw, living plant is vicious in that regard," she assured him.

"Very well, then."

Norah clasped her hands together. "Wonderful! I'll go and pick them tomorrow after breakfast."

Rodney gave her an uncertain smile before flipping his book back around and immersing himself in the story. Norah continued to peruse her own book, her mind whirring with thoughts and ideas.

Malcolm

He was an ass. And a coward. There was no way around it.

The look on Norah's face when he'd turned a cold shoulder had haunted him for the last week. Every time he tried to sleep, he saw the hurt in her eyes and the stiffness of her posture as she removed herself from his company. She had acted as if he'd slapped her. He may as well have.

The fact that he couldn't bring himself to explain made him an ass. His avoidance of her ever since made him a coward.

Malcolm knew that the longer this went on, the worse he'd feel, but a deep paralysis of his actions prevented him from doing the right thing and explaining his motives to Norah. He was powerless to end it.

It was just as well, he reasoned. There was no point in getting close to a woman, especially one as driven as Miss Abernathy.

He had pretended to be busy in his office for the past week, although most of the time was spent staring at ledgers that did not need updating or watching the last of the snow melt out the window. It was an incredibly dull existence.

He'd been ignoring the other members as well, all because he was afraid of running into the woman. Miss Abernathy. Norah. He missed saying her name out loud.

Perhaps a letter would suffice, just to end this mental torture. But what could he say? *Dear Madam, I apologize for my cowardice. Let us forget about my rudeness that day in my office.* Something told him it wouldn't suffice.

Mathers poked his head into the office, breaking Malcolm's reverie. "Sir?"

"What is it, Mathers?"

The butler walked in, standing at attention dutifully. "The gardener has gone back to work, now that the snows are gone. He reported to me today that the willow tree has more than a few downed branches clogging the area. Apparently the snows were heavier than usual, and the branches had snapped off. The rosebush is in need of trimming as well."

Malcolm blanched. The news was unexpected and much earlier than he anticipated. He typically tried waiting until April to tackle these things, but it would not do to leave the special site so disheveled. He wouldn't allow it.

"I'll take care of it tomorrow."

Mathers, as stoic as he was, nearly grimaced. "Sir, you really needn't do it yourself. The gardener is more than capable—"

"*I* must do it, Mathers. That hasn't changed." Malcolm eyed his butler with an iron stare.

Mathers shifted his feet as he tried to keep his face neutral. "Very well, sir."

Malcolm sighed as the butler left his office. At least his new task would keep his mind off Miss Abernathy for a bit. That alone would make it worth it.

CHAPTER SEVENTEEN

Saturday, March 27th, 1915

Norah

MALCOLM DID NOT ATTEND Saturday breakfast.

Mrs. Bixby must have been able to read Norah's concerned face well, because she explained without prompting that the master had a pressing matter to attend to that morning. She was rather tight-lipped about what that matter might be, however, and Norah's interest was not assuaged in the slightest by the vague explanation.

Nevertheless, the breakfast's success was not thwarted at all by the lack of the president overseeing it. As a matter of fact, the majority of the members looked to Norah—of all people—as their stand-in leader, and insisted she take the head of the table in Mr. Drury's stead.

After the breakfast, the bulk of the men decided upon a game of charades for group diversion, and invited Norah to join in. She politely declined and made her temporary farewells to them, intent on fulfilling her promise of nettle collecting for Rodney. As she made her way to her room to grab her coat, she wondered if Mr. Lyster would be able to play without blurting out all the answers in advance.

To Norah's delight, the late March day was cloudy and cool, but not overly cold, and with no precipitation in the air. She crossed the terrace at a casual stroll and entered the expansive lawn on her way to the wilder areas of the property. As Norah crossed the grass, Eddie pranced with abandon, gleefully following his doggy whims.

The walk gave her time to reflect upon the breakfast. Her keen eyes had watched each member as he interacted with the others. These men were beginning to feel like friends, now that she had remained at Birchwald for close to two months. She was delighted at the easy banter that flowed about her, and at the way many of the men had accepted her as well.

Not all, Norah thought with a grimace. Despite her offer of friendship to Karanja, he still kept to himself, barely talking to anyone, much less Norah. Mr. Ivey also still refused to look at anyone, keeping to his own headspace lest he invite unwanted visions. Mr. Withers, of course, could not interact at all.

And then there was LJ. He had promised to try the Guild for Norah's sake, but she knew he was putting no effort into fitting in anymore. His bare minimum hurt Norah in a way she couldn't quite grasp, but she had to give herself one small silver lining. At least he was safe here, and did not seem to make any moves to leave.

There was also the thought of Mr. Drury—unbidden, but present. Norah tried her hardest to put him out of her mind, a task easier said than done.

Norah remembered the way to the nettle patch easily. She donned the kid leather gloves she had brought in her pocket and swiftly cut half a dozen stalks using her small pocketknife. These she placed in the basket, careful not to let the stems touch her, although she was bundled up well enough to avoid the stings.

The task was accomplished so easily, and the weather was so enchanting, that Norah decided to further explore and head back to Birchwald a different way. She followed a stream to the west for a bit, skirting the edges of the property, before turning south at a diagonal.

It was in this way that she stumbled upon a hidden cemetery. She had been trailing a line of hazelnut and viburnum bushes, when they suddenly opened upon the scene of a giant willow tree, a bench, and, upon closer inspection, two gravestones.

Honestly, it wasn't much of a cemetery. Norah would have passed right by it without a second glance if not for the person who happened to be toiling under the willow tree, his back to her.

She almost didn't recognize him, with his heavy coat, thick gloves, and a ratty flat cap upon his head. It painted a different scene than his usual immaculate suits he wore. But a quick view of his profile confirmed it was indeed Mr. Drury.

She crouched down, her heart pounding with the surprise of finding him out here. She could have sworn there was a gardener on staff, so why was the master of the house at work cutting down scraggly branches?

He hadn't noticed her, but worked ceaselessly to remove the limbs, dragging them to the side and depositing them in a growing pile. Norah took the scene in: the way he almost angrily used the clippers to break the branches, the muscles in his back hidden behind the heavy coat he wore, yet still somehow on display. The air plumed from his mouth like a steam engine as he worked.

After watching him from the last bush for a few moments, Norah came to her senses. She understood that Drury would not want to be bothered, and he certainly would not wish to be spied upon. She made the decision to turn around and leave him be.

Eddie, however, emerged from the bushes at this time. He saw the man and darted out, running straight at him with his long ears flopping about in a jovial manner. He raced up to Drury's back, circled him playfully, and let out a happy bark.

"Eddie?" she heard Drury say, the confusion heavy in that one word. "What are you doing out here?"

Norah thought to flee, but he turned and spotted her before she could act. Now it was time to pretend she had just stumbled upon him, lest she be forced to explain her brief voyeurism.

He huffed a breath as she emerged from the bushes, a long section of willow stick still clasped in his hands. "Miss Abernathy, why are you here?"

She knew her face was flushed, and it wasn't from the walk. He had a sternness about his eyes as he watched her approach that spoke of disappointment at her appearance. Clearly, he had not wanted company for this task.

She stopped a handful of feet away from him, trapped in the moment by an unwavering awkwardness. Finally, she gestured at the basket. "I was collecting nettles."

He eyed the basket dubiously. "Nettles."

"Yes."

Eddie, oblivious to the burden he'd placed upon his mistress and the general tension of the encounter he'd inadvertently created, sat on the cold ground with his tongue lolling out, glancing from one human to the other.

Norah felt the need to explain. "I found the nettles the other day and thought I'd try a remedy for Rodney's pustules. Stinging nettles are useful in lesser curses, so I figured it was worth a try. But goodness, are you well?"

While she spoke, Drury's face had gone from a surprised pink to a pasty complexion. Beads of sweat dotted his upper lip.

He frowned. "I'm fine. So, you were out nettle collecting. But why are you *here*? The nettles grow in the northeast corner of the property."

She scrunched up her nose. "I like to take walks. As you know." She inwardly flinched at the unintended barb. Drury seemed not to notice as he wiped his forehead with his sleeve and waited for a better explanation. "I thought I'd come back to the house by a different route. I had no idea where that particular path was leading me. Are you quite sure you're feeling alright?"

Drury let out a breath. Whether it was from discomfort or exasperation, Norah couldn't tell. "I've been hard at work. It creates sweat. So, you just happened upon me?"

His pallid face pointed to more than a heavy workout, but Norah decided not to push the issue. "Yes, exactly. I'm so glad you understand." She glanced around. "And what are *you* doing out here?"

He raised an eyebrow. "If you must know, I am cleaning up the area." He paused to stare at her, his forehead still knotted with suspicion. "I find it awfully convenient that you found me out here today of all days."

"What are you implying?" Norah frowned. "I'll have you know I have better things to do than trail you all day."

"Like collecting nettles."

"Exactly." She was struck by an inclination of teasing, as they were wont to do before he began to ignore her. Perhaps it would lighten the mood. "That, and discovering your secrets. What is your curse, again?"

He half-grinned, a sparkle of interest showing through the irritable fire in his eyes. "My skin is blue."

She squinted her eyes at him. "You look rather yellow at the moment."

"I'm only blue under my clothes. I'd show you, but I'm too bundled up at the moment."

Her face warmed further. She thought to counter this rather scandalous comment of his, but there was something off about his face, which concerned her. "Drury, I think you should take a moment to rest."

He scowled, but then winced as if in pain. "You may be right, but I also believe it's time for you to be on your way. I have more work to do."

She eyed him. "As do I. I hadn't penciled an interrogation into my busy schedule. Don't work yourself to death, Drury."

He gave her a mocking gentlemanly bow to see her off.

Malcolm

Malcolm watched Norah walk away from the cemetery, her back ramrod straight and her gait carefully measured. Eddie's bouncing and meandering trot was the antithesis of his mistress' bearing.

The moment the aggravating woman was out of view, he gave a gasp and sank into the bench seat. It had been hard to maintain the illusion of normalcy, but he'd be damned to show weakness in front of her.

He willed his heart to beat normally, and the shaking to subside. He still had much to do. The willow tree's damage had been worse than he'd thought, and he hadn't even gotten around to trimming back the rose.

He took a smattering of steadying breaths. He'd work through the pain, the lightheadedness. He didn't have a choice otherwise.

Standing with a sigh, he picked up the clippers once more.

Norah

At six in the evening, Norah decided to dry the nettles she'd collected earlier in the day. She'd kept them in her room, watching them slowly wilt as she tried to determine the best course of action. She'd realized the plants would need to be moved when Eddie tried to sniff at them.

Luckily, she'd been watching him and managed to shoo him away before he could do damage to his exposed nose.

Her room was no place in which to perform this task, so she settled on bringing them to the kitchen, where she was sure Cook would offer her a small space in which to hang them. She had never been to the kitchen before, but knew the general location, at the side of the house next to the grandiose main dining room.

She walked down the grand staircase with them still in the basket, the kid gloves in her dress pocket. She reached the entrance hall, intent on turning right toward the kitchen, when a loud banging brought her to a halt. Turning in the opposite direction, she caught sight of Mathers staggering in from the loggia at the back of the house, clutching a barely functional Drury to his side.

Norah gasped and dropped the basket, the stalks of wilted nettle spilling out at the careless act. She rushed forward to Mathers' side.

"What's happened?" she demanded, her voice pinched with unexpected worry.

Mathers grunted under the weight of his master. "Madam, would you be so kind as to help me to the elevator," he rasped out as he stumbled forward another step.

Norah rushed to the ailing man's other side, lifting a limp arm to drape over her shoulders. Drury's pallor had increased since she saw him earlier in the afternoon. His eyes were barely open and did not seem to focus. He barely held any weight on his own feet. The arm around Norah's shoulder did nothing to keep him upright, so Norah had to grasp it with her right hand and wrap her left around his waist in a similar fashion to Mathers' grasp.

Together, the three of them managed to stagger over to the elevator. Mathers fumbled to open the doors and then practically pushed Norah and Drury inside, where they hit the back wall and sagged.

"Shall we call for Mrs. Bixby?" Norah panted as Mathers entered the elevator.

Drury lifted his head slightly. "N-n-no," he slurred. "Shtay with me."

She assumed this was directed at Mathers until Malcolm turned his head to look at her, his bloodshot eyes trying to meet hers. She merely nodded.

Mathers closed the doors and worked the lever. "I apologize, miss. It was not my intention to waylay you. I can call for Mrs. Bixby once we have him in his room."

"I don't mind," she stated firmly, and much to her surprise, she meant it.

Mathers was silent as he stopped the elevator and opened the doors. He reached over to hoist up half of Drury as Norah did the same, and together they did the awkward shuffle down the gallery. The burden was so great, Norah counted each little goal as they moved in order to perceive a feeling of victory. Past the south guest bedroom. Past the staircase to the third floor. There—Drury's room. A simple jiggling of the knob and they were in. A few more steps and they reached the bedside, at which point all three flopped down so to keep the near-comatose man from dropping to the floor.

Norah and Mathers worked in tandem to turn him lengthwise on the bed, his head propped by pillows. Mathers began to remove his master's shoes.

"Would you please go and fetch Mrs. Bixby now, madam?" he asked Norah as he undid the knots.

Drury's hand lashed out and grasped Norah's wrist with more strength than she would have given him credit for. "Don't leave," he whispered.

Mathers eyed the connection. "If you are comfortable with staying, I shall go for Bixby."

Norah nodded, watching Drury's face. He closed his eyes in delirium, and she made her decision. "I'm okay with staying."

Mathers nodded and stood. "I shall return with reinforcements."

She kept her eyes on the ailing man as his butler left. Drury was much too pale, slicked with sweat, and clearly in pain. She brushed the back of her hand over his forehead, noting the clammy quality. He was cold, not feverish.

"Drury," she murmured. He kept his eyes closed, a ragged breath escaping his lips. She tried again. "Malcolm?"

He cracked an eye, his throat bobbing.

She brought her face closer and asked, "What is your curse?"

He wheezed, an alarming sound until Norah realized it was a ghost of a laugh. "I think you know."

She pondered those words for a moment as Malcolm reached his left hand over his body to search for hers. She allowed him to grasp it, the act lending him the illusion of strength.

All this time, she'd never figured out where he had traveled to. None of the other members knew, either. And until today, she wasn't sure he ever left Birchwald. And now, it made sense.

Yes, she believed she did know what his curse was.

The house. The house was his curse.

CHAPTER EIGHTEEN

Sunday, March 28th, 1915

Malcolm

MALCOLM AWOKE WITH A start, a stark confusion momentarily befuddling him. He was in his bedroom. It was dark, the only light being a single oil lamp near his bedside. And there was a heaviness, a warmth pressed down on the bed next to him.

He turned his head as much as he dared, the small action causing the sweat to bead on his forehead once more. Malcolm caught sight of dark hair, messily coiffed, and the curved lines of a woman resting on her side. Norah still wore the dove gray dress she'd had on the last time he'd seen her. He straightened his head, staring straight up at the ceiling. His mind refused to connect the dots.

He recollected being outdoors for much of the day. He remembered Norah stumbling upon him unannounced, and even then he'd been feeling poorly. But he chose to continue working after she left. And that was where his memory became foggy.

He blew out a shaky breath. He should have gone back to the house with her. He could have recovered by dinnertime, and no one would have been the wiser.

Instead, he'd pushed too hard and nearly died for his effort. As it was, he still felt like death would be the kinder alternative.

But how did he get here, in his bed? And where the hell had Norah come from? That part he couldn't comprehend.

It was best to wake her. Get it over with.

He tried to move, but his limbs were as weak as newborn kittens. "Norah?" he rasped. The effort made him cough.

It was enough to rouse her, though. She sat up abruptly and turned her upper body toward him. He glanced from the corner of his eye at her. The shadows were deep on her face, but he could still make out eyes rounded with concern.

"What do you need?" she asked without preamble. Her hand shot out to feel his forehead.

He tried to swallow through a dry throat. "Why are you here?"

She blew a breath through her nose, a sign of mirth or vexation—he couldn't tell which. She removed herself from his bed, and he nearly protested, until he realized she was getting him a glass of water from the dresser.

The sound of pouring water stopped, and she came back to sit on the bed by his side. She placed a hand behind his head, propping him up slightly, before bringing the glass to his parched lips. "You asked me to stay," she said as he took small sips of the cool water.

He leaned his head back, signaling he was done with the water for now. The effort to drink was incredibly taxing, and her words did not spark any recognition. He took a few steadying breaths. "I did?"

"Yes."

"And you stayed?"

"Of course."

"Why?"

That last word hung in the air, a question suspended in the miasma of feelings. Finally, she answered plainly. "Because I wanted to."

It was then that his mind recalled the last thing they had said to each other before he'd passed out.

Malcolm, what is your curse?

I think you know.

He squeezed his eyes shut, a fresh wave of pain overtaking him. Only this one was emotional, not physical.

Norah didn't know the difference, however. "What's wrong? Malcolm?"

Hearing his first name in her soft voice helped to dull the pain, somehow. Still, he needed to clarify something. "You know, don't you?"

"Know what?"

He opened his eyes to see her peering at him from above, her concern etched into every shadow of her face. He tried to grin, but the corners of his mouth pulled down into a grimace instead. "My secret."

She huffed a laugh. "I have an inkling. Be honest. Have you ever traveled anywhere?"

He was cornered and he knew it. "I have not."

She quirked a brow. "No Seychelles, no Malaysia?"

He grunted. "My father. Not me."

"Oh? Did he lose his thumbs? Was he allergic to carrots? Clearly, your skin isn't blue, otherwise I would have seen evidence of it."

His eyes flew wide and he made the effort to lift his head to inspect himself. He had been stripped of his coat, boots, vest, and trousers. He was hidden under the blanket, but only wearing his shirt, and someone had helped to undress him, since he clearly didn't do it himself.

He flopped his head back down on the pillow, a puff of breath escaping his lips as he did so. "Madam, I'm afraid you have the advantage over me."

He could hear the grin in her voice. "Mathers did the bulk of it."

"But you peeked."

"Your virtue is intact, I promise. I only caught a glimpse of leg as he tucked you into the covers. It was very much flesh-colored. No blue in sight."

"And where is my butler now?" Malcolm assumed he was not here, otherwise he would have been tending to Malcolm's every whim. It was just as well; Malcolm would not have appreciated the pampering at this moment.

Norah responded, "Getting some rest. I told him I'd take the night watch."

Once again, the infernal single word escaped him. "Why?"

She narrowed her eyes. "Because your manservant is getting up in years and I figured he'd need his sleep in order to put up with you all day, that's why. Goodness, it's like you don't trust me or something."

He flopped his mouth open for a rebuttal before actually thinking one up. "It's not that I don't trust you, Norah. But if others were to catch wind of this arrangement, it would put you in a compromising position."

"Oh, please." She shifted her body to better see him. "I hardly think you are in a fit state to compromise me. And who will care? Your butler? Mrs. Bixby? They already know I'm here, and I can assure you, they were more than happy to leave me to care for you."

"What about your brother?" Malcolm retorted. The moody visage of Leighton flashed through his mind unbidden. "He might not be happy to learn of your nocturnal enterprise."

Norah paused, her lips reflexively sticking out as she thought over his words. Malcolm couldn't help but stare at the slight pucker. She looked at him. "You might have a point there. But in all honesty, he is not my keeper. He's done things I don't approve of either, so he should get a dose of his own medicine."

Malcolm sacrificed some energy to smile at her fiery words. "I'm sensing some sibling conflict in that statement."

Norah huffed. "He's placed me in a position that I never wanted to be in."

Malcolm had no clue what she was talking about. What position? The Guild? It seemed to him this was exactly where she wanted to be. He shook it off.

"Anyway, we were talking about you," Norah continued. "If you've never left the States, you've never been an adventurer. So, Mr. President, the only logical conclusion I can deduce is you've been cursed here, at home."

Malcolm stared at her. "You are much too intelligent, Norah."

"For a woman?"

He frowned at her addition. "No, for anybody. None of the members know."

"Why do you keep it a secret?" she asked as she fussed with the blanket covering him.

He growled, wishing he could run away. He was angry at his body for betraying him. "It's ... it's ... embarrassing." There. He said it.

She stayed silent for a moment, and in that silence he focused on his heartbeat, which sounded much too loud in his ears. The steady rhythm began to lull him.

It nearly startled him when she spoke at last. "Why are you embarrassed?"

Here it was. There was no escaping it. "My father got to go off and explore, and I assumed I'd join him when I was old enough. He missed most of my childhood as he gallivanted about. Yes, he got to swim with natives in the Seychelles. Yes, he navigated the jungles of Malaysia. And more. He would bring back trinket after trinket, each time he came home. You've seen them."

"The gallery pieces?"

He tried to nod. "The same. He somehow never became cursed himself. Not until that last trip to Egypt. He came home from that and died just a month later."

"When you were thirteen?"

"Mm-hm. I was finally of the age at which I could think about exploring. But that had to be put off. Mother needed me."

"Then, how were you cursed?"

He gave her the eye. "You're a pushy one, aren't you?"

She looked ruffled. "Drury, I've spent the last month trying to figure out your curse. I'm impatient, is all."

"Hm. Call me Malcolm, and I'll agree to tell you."

She hesitated.

He pointed out the obvious. "You've called me that at least twice since yesterday. I know you have it in you."

She sighed, resigned. "You drive a hard bargain."

He wanted to laugh, but his body clenched. A wave of fire traveled down his spine and he gasped at the pain.

"What's happening?" Norah asked as she frantically began placing her hands on him.

Her touch was like a brand, and as much as he wanted her to keep handling him, it was too much at the moment. "Woman, you're killing me with your hands."

She jerked them back. "What can I do?"

He ground his teeth together. "One moment."

The spasm subsided, and he relaxed into his bed, his forehead drenched in sweat. He panted with the exertion and a tide of weariness tried to pull him under.

"Malcolm?" Her voice was small, timid.

He kept his eyes closed. "You can touch me now."

"I'm not sure I want to."

He used the last of his strength to slowly raise his arm, searching for her hand in his self-imposed blindness. Finding her wrist, he groped further until he clasped her fingers, and brought her hand to his chest. He did not let go.

Through this connection, he could feel Norah's tense posture. She stayed silent, as if weighing something in her mind. He was about to release her with great reluctance, but she sighed. "It's Jane."

Either he had fallen asleep and missed something of the conversation, or his mind was more addled than he'd thought. "What?"

She hesitated again. "I—I know your curse now. Or at least part of it. It's only fair you have your long-standing question answered. The 'J' in my name stands for Jane."

Malcolm rolled this over in his mind like a stone in a river. Norah Jane Abernathy. "Beautiful."

She made a soft noise of deprecation in her throat. "Now that you know, shall I leave you to sleep?"

He tightened his grasp on her fingers, just enough for her to feel a change in pressure. "Stay. Please."

"I won't go anywhere. We've talked long enough. It's late. You need rest."

He felt the bed shudder as she positioned herself on her side, careful not to break their connection.

"Thank you," he mumbled as sleep overtook him again.

Norah

In the low light of the oil lamp, Malcolm almost looked angelic as he succumbed to sleep. Norah knew better, though.

Before he had taken possession of her hand, she'd glanced at his pocket watch on the bedside table. The face read two in the morning. It was no wonder she felt as drained as she did, although their conversation had energized her at the time.

She settled next to him, watching his steady breaths. His body contraction had terrified her, had made her wonder in the moment if he was about to die. She was surprised by her reaction, the amount of care she felt for this man who was little more than a stranger to her.

Except he wasn't a stranger, was he? She had shared meals with him, learned parts of his history, slept in the same bed. Yes, she mused with a small smile, she could no longer claim they were strangers. After this night, there was something there. Something more.

It was with no great surprise that his rhythmic breaths calmed her and pulled her under. She couldn't remember falling asleep, but clearly she had, because the next thing she knew, someone was gently shaking her awake.

Norah started, opening her eyes so suddenly that they remained unfocused. Her hand felt heavy, and she realized it was still clasped with Malcolm's.

"Easy, dearie," Mrs. Bixby soothed from behind her.

Norah rolled over, carefully drawing her hand away from Malcolm's grasp. He slept on.

There was a knowing smile on the housekeeper's face. She must have seen their hands. Norah felt her face heat but tried to ignore it. "What time is it?" she whispered.

"Six in the morning. I'll take over for a time. I did a favor for you last night and let Eddie out before his usual bedtime. I'm sure he's ready to see you again, though. The poor darling was heard barking this morning."

Norah sat up in a rush. She had completely forgotten about Eddie. "Oh dear. He's not used to being alone all night. Thank you for caring for him." She paused as she stood. "Will he be okay?"

"Who, Master Malcolm?" Mrs. Bixby tsked. "Give him some time and he'll be right as rain."

Norah nodded and bit her lip, wanting to ask more questions but not sure if she should. Her curiosity won out. "If I may ask, what exactly are the effects of his curse? We spoke briefly in the early hours, but he had a relapse of sorts."

Mrs. Bixby eyed her. "Did you, now? Plain and simple, dearie—and I don't think he'll mind me saying at this point, if the cat's out of the bag—he can't leave the premises. Even being outside on the grounds is too much for him to take for long."

Norah thought it was something along those lines, but it was good to get confirmation, something she lacked from last night's conversation. His poor reaction to Norah's offer of a walk now made perfect sense.

But there was one point that she couldn't understand. "Why was he outside in the first place, then?"

Mrs. Bixby glanced at her employer, then grasped Norah's arm and quietly led her to the hallway. "Between you and me, he was tending to his mother's grave. He does it every year, without fail. Normally, he's back inside before he gets that bad. I thought we'd lose him last night when I saw him. It's a good thing Mathers went looking for him when it got dark, otherwise I'd be preparing a funeral instead of breakfast this morning."

"Goodness," Norah breathed. "Thank you for telling me. Will you please inform me when he's awake again? I think I'll tend to Eddie and then get a bit more sleep myself before I tackle my rounds upstairs."

Mrs. Bixby patted her arm with affection. "I shall. You've been a heap of help to us, you know. I won't forget it."

Norah pretended she didn't see the knowing smile on the housekeeper's face as she turned away to return to her room.

Malcolm

Fiona, the ex-fiancée, had come back.

She was gloating at Malcolm, mocking him with her wonderful life, while he rotted away in Birchwald. Her hat was enormous, blotting out the sun. Her hands waved about, the white gloves blinding to look at.

"Paris is lovely this time of year," she was saying in that obnoxious high-pitched voice of hers. "I love France, and Italy, and Spain, but you wouldn't know about them, would you?" She laughed cruelly.

He wished to speak, but his tongue was gone.

"You'll never leave this house," she hissed, her face growing longer as her eyes turned red beneath her burgundy hat. Her hair loosened and fell, a sweeping expanse of blonde that began to wrap tendrils around his furniture, his knick-knacks, his wrists. He tried to jerk away, but his limbs wouldn't move. Her hair wrapped its way up his body, encircling his neck like a noose. "You'll die here," she whispered.

From the corner of his eye, he saw Norah enter the room. She didn't see Malcolm and Fiona, as close as they were in a parody of a lovers' embrace. He wanted to warn her, but his tongue was still missing.

Fiona noticed his stare over her shoulder and jerked her head around like a snake. Malcolm wished to save Norah, but he was powerless. He watched with horror as Fiona shot tendrils of her hair at Norah, to wrap around her delicate throat and choke the life out of her. A tear trickled down his immovable cheek.

"Sir? Sir!"

A gentle shake broke the dream and his paralysis. He lurched forward slightly, only to fall back with weakness. His face was damp as tears streamed down from his upturned face.

Mathers stood over him, the concern evident in his countenance. "Sir, I'm sorry to wake you. You were breathing heavily and crying. I assumed you were in the middle of a nightmare?"

Malcolm let out a breath of relief to find himself in his bed, not necessarily healthy, but whole, and not being strangled by hair. And, if he was being honest, relieved that Norah was not in mortal peril. "Yes, thank you for that. Fiona was trying to kill me. And Norah."

Mathers halted, his face inscrutable. "Does Miss Abernathy's mortality factor into many of your dreams, sir?"

Malcolm sighed loudly at the uncharacteristic comment. "Something you wish to say, old chap?"

Mathers made a show of straightening the bedsheets. "She was in quite the state over your health last night."

Malcolm tried to sit up. He made it halfway before Mathers rushed over to rearrange his pillows and help scoot him higher on the bed. He eyed his butler. "And your point?"

"A lady who had no interest wouldn't put herself in physical discomfort to help me drag you upstairs to your room, nor would she stoop to potentially ruining her reputation."

"She helped you carry me here?" Malcolm tried to access these memories, but apparently his mind had jettisoned them into the sea of forgetfulness. He tried to rationalize her help away, if only to quash the emotions stirring within. "I have the feeling Miss Abernathy would help a slug if someone stepped on it. It doesn't mean anything."

"Hmm. If I may be frank, your statement begs for clarification. It doesn't mean anything to her, or it doesn't mean anything to you?"

"For god's sake, Mathers," Malcolm groaned, touching his forehead for an extra dash of theatrics. "It doesn't matter! She was kind enough to stay with me and make sure I didn't expire. It means nothing more than that."

Deep down, he knew it was a lie the moment he spoke the words. For all Malcolm knew, he was right about the amount of thought Norah put into it, but his butler had a very valid point. The fact that she'd stayed overnight with him meant a great deal to Malcolm.

He was not about to give Mathers the satisfaction, though.

Mathers, for his part, conceded. "Very well, sir."

"What time is it? I'm starving."

"Half-past ten. It is no wonder you're hungry; you skipped dinner last night. Shall I have Mrs. Bixby bring you up some breakfast?"

Malcolm nodded, his stomach giving an audible gurgle at the mention. "Porridge, perhaps? I'm not sure I can handle something overly rich."

Mathers agreed with a rare smile. "And some weak tea, as well. Very good."

Malcolm itched to ask Mathers if Norah was available, but he didn't dare, not after the to-do the butler had just made about her overnight stay.

Still, Mathers was anything if not uncanny. It would seem that years of servitude had given the butler the ability to read minds. As he made to leave to procure breakfast, he turned back to Malcolm with a knowing glint in his eye. "I'll be sure to inform the lady of your return to wakefulness. I'm sure she would appreciate knowing you are on the road to recovery and will not be dying any time soon." He shut the door before Malcolm could get a word in.

Norah

As relieved as Norah was when Mathers informed her of Malcolm's slow recovery, she dared not stop in to see for herself. It was not for a lack of interest on her part—once she slipped past his prickly exterior, Malcolm was enjoyable to engage with—but rather due to poor timing.

It was Sunday, after all, and Sundays meant a visit from Father Berkely.

Even before his arrival, she had her hands full. Eddie, unused to being alone all night, had apparently gone a bit feral in the Aster Room, and Norah had to scrub dog droppings out of the green carpet as soon as she got back to her room. Eddie was simultaneously overjoyed to see her and apologetic over his accident. Norah forgave him immediately.

Following that, there was a momentary panic when she remembered the nettles she had dropped the previous night in the frenzy of Malcolm trying to die. She could see that someone had cleaned them up from the foot of the stairs where she had last seen them strewn about the floor, but it took some sleuthing to discover the cook's maid had collected them and hung them up to dry in the kitchen. Norah went and thanked her personally for her foresight.

And then there was the matter of attending to the members. They, of course, knew nothing of what had transpired, but more than a few asked of Malcolm's whereabouts. Norah tried not to dwell too much on why they all thought she of all people would know. Instead, she explained he'd fallen ill and was on bedrest during his recovery.

As it happened, she did not get that nap in by the time the priest showed up. She'd barely gotten a chance to make herself look more presentable by a quick rag bath and a change of clothes. Her hair was woefully bedraggled after sleeping with it up, but it would have to do. She simply did not have time to fix it properly.

Mathers explained that Malcolm usually greeted Father Berkely in the reception room before leading him upstairs to tend to his little flock. The butler did not ask her to take over, but Norah assumed it was his intent in informing her.

And so, when the priest was shown in at a quarter till twelve, Norah was the one to greet him in the reception room.

As to be expected, Father Berkely was perplexed by the change in routine. "So good to see you, my dear Miss Abernathy. But where is the master?"

She clasped his hand. "I'm afraid Mr. Drury is unwell today, Father. Shall I show you to the third floor?"

He nodded as he offered her his arm. "I'm most aggrieved to hear of Mr. Drury's condition. Is he contagious?"

"Not at all," Norah reassured the man. She placed her hand on his arm. "His condition was brought about by a personal affliction."

"Ah," the priest replied knowingly.

Together they headed for the stairs. Father Berkely said, "And how are you, Miss Abernathy? Have you begun to see the fruits of your labor here?"

Norah dropped her head with a small smile while he scrutinized her in a paternal way. "I'm trying, Father," she said modestly. "I feel that some of the members are more open to my help than others."

He chuckled. "I very well know the feeling."

She laughed as well. "I'm sorry to contribute to that. My brother as well."

"Posh, tish," he said, waving her words away. "You needn't feel the need to stroke my ego. Anyway, I have no doubt you are doing an excellent job here. As a matter of fact, Mr. Hunt, Mr. Freeman, and Señor Reyes all speak very highly of you."

Her heart tightened with something akin to joy. "Truly? I do so enjoy their company. Really, there are only two men whom I can't seem to break through. Mr. Withers, for obvious reasons, but Mr. Ivey also refuses to interact with me."

"Hmm, yes," the priest said thoughtfully as they started up the stairs. "Mr. Ivey fights off many demons. He's worried about hurting you."

"You speak to Mr. Ivey?" Norah asked with surprise.

"Indeed. He finds the act of confession to be a balm on his soul. I can't tell you more than that, but perhaps I could put in a good word for you."

"Oh, thank you."

"As for Mr. Withers," the priest continued, "there is something going on there that sets me on edge."

Norah frowned. "What do you mean?"

He hesitated. "If I am being honest, I don't trust his helper."

It took Norah a moment to digest the priest's words. "Karanja? He seems nice enough. Shy, but nice."

"Call it a hunch. I don't know, maybe it's his ethnicity that makes me distrustful."

Norah nearly stopped walking in surprise. She knew instinctively that people—especially white people—had the habit of bigotry, but it seemed wrong coming from Father Berkely. She could not keep silent on the matter but aimed to keep her tone as polite as possible, so as not to ruffle any feathers. "I would think you of all people would know not to judge a person by their appearance, Father. Karanja may look different, but he is still a human being who is deserving of respect."

She must have hit the proper note. Father Berkely patted her hand. "Quite right, my dear. Please, don't take me the wrong way. We are all God's creatures, and our differences should be celebrated. Still, there are secrets being kept, mark my words."

Norah's heart rate sped up. Secrets, indeed. She allowed the topic to be dropped, making the rest of the walk to the third floor a quiet one indeed.

CHAPTER NINETEEN

Monday, March 29th, 1915

Malcolm

HE NO LONGER FELT like death warmed over, but Malcolm still needed at least one more day to recuperate. The necessary convalescence grated on his nerves. He hated being bedridden. There was too much to do, including finishing what he had started outside. His mother's grave beckoned him.

Of course, perhaps this time a trip outdoors would actually do him in, especially so soon after he nearly died.

Malcolm sighed, defeated. He'd have to pass off the job to the gardener after all.

He looked at his watch, noting the early afternoon hour. It would not do to put off the task any longer, as much as it pained him to pass it off to someone else. He rang the bell near his bed.

Mathers appeared minutes later. "What do you need, sir?"

Malcolm shifted in bed. "Mathers, I would like to finish the task I had been doing. But clearly, I'm in no state to handle it. Would you be a chap and ask the gardener? It only needs a bit of raking, and the rose still needs pruning. The pile of branches is ready to burn, as well."

Mathers adjusted his shoulders and shifted his eyes away from Malcolm, but said nothing.

Malcolm frowned at the silence. "Well, what is it?"

The butler cleared his throat. "I have no need to inform the gardener, sir. Miss Abernathy left this morning to tend to it herself."

Malcolm stared, digesting this information. "She what?"

"Miss Abernathy is out there as we speak. She took it upon herself to finish your job."

"Why would she do that?" Malcolm asked, his voice louder. He raised his upper body off the pillows.

Mathers rushed forward to fluff the pillows behind him. He spoke as he performed this task, "I was not privy to her inner thoughts, but if I had to guess, she understood the importance of the task you risked your life for. The lady is nothing if not shrewd, sir."

Malcolm fell back into his pillows. "She is at that. Do me a favor, old chap. Have her come and see me when she's finished. I'd like to have a chat with her."

Mathers nodded and left the room.

With his butler away, Malcolm was left with only his thoughts for company. And, as they often did these days, they spun toward Norah.

She never came back to see him yesterday. That had stung. Instead, Father Berkely had visited briefly and gave Malcolm a glowing review of the lady's achievements while he recuperated. That had also stung, oddly enough. Apparently, Malcolm was not needed for the smooth operation of the Guild. It was not a pleasant sensation, knowing one's efforts were obsolete.

Even if he could master this new form of self-pity, he could not pinpoint why her absence aggrieved him so. Perhaps it denoted that in her life, he was simply less important. That was fair; they had only known each other not quite two months, and she had made it very clear that her mission in this world was to cure each of the members of their individual ills. Her tending to only Malcolm would certainly delay her goals.

Perhaps, an insidious voice whispered, *you're feeling wounded because every important woman in your life has abandoned you.*

He would have to pick apart that errant thought very carefully. Was it true? So far, yes. His fiancée exited first, leaving him with a rather nasty parting gift. His mother departed this mortal plane soon after. He'd sworn off women for a time—it wasn't like there was a glut of them around, anyway—but now, here came Norah, who had turned his world upside down with her big, round eyes and her sharp tongue.

But was she an *important* woman? That was the big question, and on this matter the insidious voice stayed silent. She was not here for him, that much was certain. And Malcolm had tried all his tricks to not be invested in her. Somehow, he'd failed in that task, hence his current dilemma.

Round and round his mind went, until he was pulled under by a healing nap. He startled awake at the sound of his door being opened.

"Shall I come back later?" Norah asked quietly from the door.

He pushed himself into a sitting position and tried to look awake. "No, please come in."

She appeared timid as she entered and closed the door behind her. He patted the bed next to him.

She raised an eyebrow sardonically. "I'm not sure it's proper."

"I do believe 'proper' flew out the window when you shared a bed with me," he mused.

Her face flushed at the reminder, but she sat down, her hands clasped together with anxious fingers. "The way you say it, it sounds very titillating," she said, her mouth cracking into a wry smile. "The reality was far from it."

He sighed. "'Far from titillating' is what every man yearns to hear. You seem tense. Is everything all right?"

She bit her lower lip. "Mathers told you where I was earlier."

"He did."

She clenched the fingers of her right hand together tightly. "And?"

He frowned. "And what?"

She blew out a breath of agitation. "I assumed you wanted to see me in order to reprimand my actions."

He let out a bark of a laugh. "Is that what you think?"

Her lips puffed out on a quick exhale. "Of course! It's clear to me that you were cleaning up your mother's grave. It is a task that *you* insist on doing, despite having a gardener on staff, and despite your curse. I still don't quite understand the parameters of that, by the way. Regardless, it's a job that you prefer to do even though you risk death. That means it is very important to you. And I made the choice to finish the task on your behalf. I knew doing so would most likely incur your formidable wrath, but I did it anyway. So now, here I am, waiting for you to unleash your fury upon me."

He could only stare at her for a moment after her tirade, taking in the determined fierceness of her eyes as she stared back, waiting. He was struck by a sudden similarity of her to a hawk: beautiful, bold, wary, and deadly when she wanted to be.

"I never finished my explanation," he said calmly.

Her fierceness wilted into confusion when his words did not lash at her. "What?"

"The other night, I was explaining my curse to you. I never finished."

"Malcolm, why—what ..."

He smiled. "Ah. You haven't reverted to my last name again. That's good."

She blinked. "Are you mad at me or not?"

Malcolm's smile grew. He was curious how long he could string out her bewilderment before it turned to anger on her part. He thought it best not to push it. "Norah, I did not call you in to castigate you. I'll admit, I was astonished to learn of your actions, and it caused me a great amount of questioning as to why you would do it, but you succinctly explained yourself, so thank you."

"You're welcome?" She still sounded unsure.

"My true reason for asking you to visit me is to continue our talk, now that I'm not in danger of passing out at a moment's notice. I'm hoping to get out of this bed tomorrow." He shifted under the covers as if to prove his point. "So, with that in mind, where were we?"

Norah paused for a moment more. Malcolm waited patiently, giving her time to clear away her remaining confusion and coax her analytical side to the forefront, a trait he used to think of as pretentious but now he found endearing. She pursed her lips, bringing Malcolm's focus to them.

"I've been told you cannot leave the premises," she finally spoke. "Clearly, you can go out on the property—for a short time, at least. But what exactly are the rules governing your curse?"

He smiled at her academic demeanor. "You enjoy this, don't you?"

She returned his smile with one of her own. "What can I say? I am intimately conversant with curses."

"Hm, so I gather. Very well. Simply put, I'm fine if I stay in the house; I can be outside on the property for short periods of time before I begin to feel terrible; and if I step foot off the property, those symptoms become tenfold and I risk dying within minutes."

She raised her eyebrows. "I take it you know this from experience?"

"Unfortunately, yes," Malcolm answered. "It only took the one time for me to get the message. And thank god Mathers was there to drag me back onto the premises in time."

He could practically see Norah's mind calculating, no doubt searching for possible cures. She finally spoke what Malcolm had been waiting for. "It begs the question, how were you cursed?"

He smirked. "Oh, that's simple. It was my fiancée."

Norah

Norah expected Malcolm to say he had been cursed by one of the items his father had brought home. She expected him not to know which one it was, though, and to have to analyze each object to find the answer. She had neither expected him to already know exactly how he'd been cursed nor to hear it was the fiancée.

"How?" she asked, stupefied.

Malcolm grimaced. "It was careless stupidity on my part."

She snorted. "That goes without saying."

He gave her a narrow-eyed look, seemingly recognizing it for the good-natured ribbing it was. He continued speaking. "Fiona was a family friend, and when her father died and left her and her mother on slightly shaky ground, our mothers decided it would be perfect for us to marry. They came to live with us soon after.

"Fiona and I were cordial to each other, but I was not enamored with her. She was beautiful and had grown up to be a proper lady and bred to be a fine wife, but matrimony was the furthest thing from my mind at the time. I was twenty-four when we became engaged. She was still practically a child, in my mind."

Norah silently agreed with his assessment.

He continued, "So, I held off on choosing a wedding date, instead focusing on planning my first sea voyage to untamed lands, just like my father. I had my sights set on Belize, of all places."

Norah's heart skittered. What were the chances that Malcolm would have met up with LJ while in Belize, had he not been cursed?

"In the midst of all this planning and—I admit—procrastination, Fiona became agitated. She did have affection for me, more than I for her. She began to accuse me of deliberately holding her at bay, of not allowing myself to feel more for her. She wasn't wrong. I was careless and unfeeling."

He sighed, and Norah suspected they had gotten to the meat of this particular nut. "It all came to a head on Valentine's Day, 1909, six years ago. I did not do anything for Fiona—no card, no present, nothing to denote it was a special day. It did not even occur to me. Instead, I had a bouquet of hothouse flowers delivered for my mother."

"You didn't," Norah breathed.

He nodded grimly. "I was foolish. Fiona had been living here for slightly over a year at that point, long enough of an engagement to know each other, and to develop an attachment. Instead, I unintentionally snubbed her, throwing her affection back like an unwashed rag. And the worst part? At the time, I didn't much care. I was sorry for hurting her feelings, but that was as far as my thoughts went to it."

He shook his head at the memories he must have been seeing. "She, however, became unhinged in her rage. She threw things, screamed at me, and accused me of being an unfeeling monster for my lack of attachment to her. She made me realize just how much I ignored her, and our engagement."

Norah cleared her throat. "It's no wonder you hate Valentine's Day," she mused.

"Exactly. It was a terrible day. We had barely been engaged for our first Valentine's Day as a couple, so no one cared to do anything. In her mind, though, our relationship had progressed by the time our next holiday rolled around.

"At the time, I thought nothing of it, once the fight had passed. I continued to plan my trip, which was supposed to happen at the end of April. I was so excited that everything else took a back seat. But my lack of thoughtfulness sealed my fate in Fiona's eyes. Unbeknownst to me, she began making plans to leave."

"March third, correct?" Norah asked.

"Yes, it took her about a month to finalize her plans, and she and her mother left on the third. It was her parting words that sealed my fate: 'May you rot in this house, Malcolm.'"

Norah sighed. "So, a cast curse, then. She must have been incredibly angry with you to be able to conjure up that power with those words."

He chuckled ruefully. "Oh, she was angry, all right."

Norah shook her head. "And you never got to travel, did you?"

Malcolm's head dropped in defeat. "No. But not necessarily because of the curse. You see, my mother died that April, just two weeks before I was to set sail."

Norah's hand flew to her mouth. "Oh, Malcolm."

He flattened his lips. "I canceled my journey to tend to my mother's rites. My father had been buried on the property, and she had wanted to be too. It was at her funeral where I first discovered my curse. I felt weak and shaky during the ceremony, but I thought nothing of it, having been in deep grief over her passing. It wasn't until a week later, when I tried to leave the property, that I understood the depths of my fiancée's anger. I haven't left the premises since, and I only go outside to tend to my mother's grave and visit her once a year."

Norah's empathy soared for this man. To be cursed, to lose his mother, to lose his freedom, and all in the span of a month. It was truly heartbreaking.

A thought occurred to her. "Is that why you took over the Guild?"

Malcolm nodded. "I spent the remainder of the year in a depression, barely functioning, drinking too much—"

"A trait you still cling to at times, you have to admit," Norah added.

"I do. But it was much worse before," he admitted. "Anyway, when 1910 came to pass, I decided it was no use for me to be stuck in this mansion with only Mathers and Mrs. Bixby for company. I'd kept in touch with my father's old friend Arnold and knew about the Guild he ran. When he mentioned wanting to retire, I leapt at the chance to have companionship again."

"I'm glad you did," Norah said with a gentle pat to his hand. "Now that I know, I can work on figuring out a cure for you as well."

Malcolm stayed silent, a sign that he took some fault in her words. Her stomach knotted at his unspoken reaction. "What is it?" she asked.

He cringed almost imperceptibly, but Norah saw it. "It's just that ..." he paused. "You haven't actually cured anyone yet, and, well ..."

"You don't think I can do it," Norah finished for him, a note of iron invading her voice.

"Please, don't take offense—"

"Malcolm, you can't caution me to not be offended when you've just insulted me to my face," she said, standing from the bed.

"Dammit, Norah, it wasn't an insult! I just don't have any proof that you can actually do what you say."

"In other words, you have no faith in me," she coolly amended. "Very well. I believe it is time for me to go."

"Go?" The look on Malcolm's face bordered on panic.

She realized her words were misleading. Her chest warmed at his blatant concern. "From your chambers," she clarified.

He relaxed slightly. "I'm sorry I've upset you."

She huffed a laugh. "I admit, when it comes to my abilities, I can be easily provoked. I'm not leaving for that reason, however. I promised Rodney I'd help him this afternoon."

"Oh. I see."

She hesitated, drawn in by the wounded demeanor Malcolm exhibited. "I'll see you tomorrow, I hope?"

He nodded. "With any luck, not in my bed again." He winced at his words, hearing too late the unintended double entendre.

Norah laughed as she exited the room, the last of her ire evaporating.

On her own again, Norah reflected on the conversation. Overall, she was glad she had gathered the courage to face a tongue lashing, even though it never manifested. Malcolm's lack of faith in her still smarted, though. Well, she hoped her current mission would be enough to prove him wrong.

She took the time to head to her room, solely to grab the kid gloves, just in case the nettles still had some bite left to them. After that, she headed downstairs to the kitchen.

Cook was busy preparing dinner, and the smells from her heavenly concoctions wafted over Norah like a cloud. But Norah did not stay to bask in the delectable odor; she had work to do. With mostly dried nettles in hand, she made her way up the two flights of stairs, slightly winded with the effort by the time she stopped for a breather in the sitting area.

Mr. Hunt and LJ were the only two present in the communal room, both taking up a stuffed chair but largely ignoring each other.

"What's that, miss?" Mr. Hunt asked with curious eyes. LJ took a glance as well but quickly lost interest and turned back to his magazine.

"Nettles, Mr. Hunt," Norah replied. "Do you know where Rodney is?"

LJ answered without looking at her. "He's in his room."

Norah frowned at the off-putting tone from her brother but thanked him nonetheless and took the proper hallway to Rodney's room.

She knocked carefully. "Rodney? It's Norah."

He answered quickly, a smile upon his face as soon as he opened the door. "Welcome, welcome! I see you've brought me gifts."

She shrugged as she entered, smiling because of his enthusiasm. "I'm only sorry I put it off for a couple of extra days. But perhaps because they've dried more they'll be the stronger for it."

Rodney waved her apology away. "I'm just happy to try anything. I know the bad time will be coming around again soon, and I'd like to have some relief from the pain and unsightliness."

Norah felt the need to caution him. "This may not work, Rodney. I would hate for you to get your hopes up. The only thing we can do is try."

"Of course, of course. Well, how shall we go about it?"

Norah looked at the basket in her hands, and then at the door that she knew led to his bathroom. "Let's start the water running," she said after a moment's consideration. "I'll add the nettles and let them soak first."

Rodney's bathroom was much smaller than her own, which was no surprise, all things considered. Still, it was big enough for Norah's purposes, with a fine clawfoot bathtub perfect for full-body soaks. She ran the water until it was scorching hot, placed all the nettles in the bottom of the bathtub, and then plugged the drain. The water's volume rose slowly, and a faint green halo began to bleed from the plants.

When the water was deep enough, Norah turned off the faucet. The temperature was much too hot for anyone to comfortably bathe in, but she was pleased to see the amount of seepage coming from the nettles, turning the bathwater a lovely pale green shade, like weak tea. She smiled to herself. It was basically what she was doing, making the world's biggest cup of tea.

She allowed the water to cool marginally before scooping out the soggy stalks. These she threw in the sink temporarily, only making a minor mess on the floor by doing so.

It was Rodney's turn for action, now. "The bath is ready for you," she told him back in his room.

He looked hesitant. "What must I do?"

"I think the best course of action is to submerge yourself completely, including your head for brief amounts of time. Of course, if you feel uncomfortable in any way, please abort. For all I know, this could make your skin condition worse."

He gulped but nodded resolutely. "Very well."

"I'll be right outside the door. Will you give me updates?"

"Yes, of course. I—I'll just go change in the bathroom, then." Even with his deformities, Norah could see the blush that spread across his face. He shut the door with a bang.

Norah positioned herself on a small chair, right by the bathroom door. She could hear rustling as he removed his clothes, followed by the small splashes of water. Rodney gave a yelp.

"Is everything all right?" Norah called out.

"All good. It's just very hot!"

Norah suppressed an eye roll. The temperature seemed perfect to her, but then again, perhaps she just liked hot baths. She often looked like a lobster by the end.

Rodney must have sunk his body into the water, for a sizable sploosh sounded through the door. He let out a loud sigh, which Norah hoped was a good sign.

"It feels good, now that the water no longer burns," he called out. "I'm about to dunk my head, so give me a moment."

"Take your time, Rodney."

Silence met her for a few seconds, followed by a large splash as he emerged with a gasp.

"Oh, urgh!" he cried out with disgust.

"What is it?"

A pause. "Well, it's not polite to say, really."

Norah took a deep breath. "I'm here to help, remember, Rodney. I can't do that unless I know what's happening."

There was another beat of silence from his end. Finally, he answered, "There was a large sore ... *down there* ... it burst."

Norah clamped her eyes tightly closed at the visual his words produced. After all, she had asked for his transparency. "Does it ... feel better now?"

"Hmm, can't say that it does. It stings rather fiercely, if I'm being honest. Oh—there goes another one, on my leg."

Blast. She couldn't say for sure, but she believed the nettles were either helping speed up the process and causing the already purulent sores to burst before beginning to heal, or it was simply making his condition worse. She staked her claims on the latter, unfortunately.

But it gave her a thought. "Rodney, have you ever tried using your cursed relic in the bath?"

He made a yelping sound, which was not what she wanted to hear. "Things are speeding up, Norah," he called out. "What did you say about the vessel?"

"Have you ever used it in the bath?"

"Uhhh ... no? Why would I?" The confusion was clear in his tone.

"Well, I had a thought. Give me just a moment." She sprung up and put her kid gloves back on before walking over to the bookshelf where the bronze vessel sat. With reverence, she picked it up.

Even through the gloves, she could feel a heaviness about it that had nothing to do with its weight. She had no way of categorizing the feeling it gave off in a scientific way, but her instincts told her the vessel was angry.

She approached the bathroom door with the Tiger Vessel held away from her body. "Rodney, I'm coming in."

"What? No! You can't—"

"I'll keep my eyes closed, I promise," Norah said before doing just that and opening the door. She used her memory of the bathroom, plus the frantic splashes coming from Rodney, to guide her to the tub's edge.

"Okay, Rodney. I'm going to dip the vessel in now," she told him as she kept her eyes closed and face turned away.

She did not allow any more time for Rodney to protest, but she dipped her hand down until she felt the buoyancy of the water against the relic in her hands. That, and she clunked it against Rodney's leg. He yelped and scrambled to move out of her way.

"Sorry," she said as she submerged the vessel, hearing the satisfying *glug-glug-glug* as it filled with water. As soon as the noises stopped, she lifted it back out.

The nettle water made it incredibly heavy, but the emotional weight of the object began to dissipate, which brought a smile to Norah's lips. "I think I'm onto something," she said.

Rodney's voice was much too high-pitched as he replied, "That's great. Do you have to be in the room while you're onto it?"

Norah grinned wryly. "I'm still not peeking, I promise. This vessel is not happy, but the nettle water seems to be soothing it. Perhaps if I calm the relic, it will calm your curse. Isn't that worth a little embarrassment?"

"Hmm, I suppose so. What's your plan now?"

"I suppose I'll just ... pour the water out onto you?"

"You don't seem too sure about this, Norah."

She laughed. "I suppose I'm not, really. Are you ready?"

"Would it make a difference if I said no?"

"Hmm, I suppose not," she answered as she blindly poured the liquid over the area she assumed his body was located.

Rodney sputtered and choked. "Gah, Norah! You poured that in my face!"

"Oh, sorry," she replied and moved the stream farther down.

Rodney moaned.

"Rodney?" Norah checked in. "Are you well?"

He sighed. "The stinging sensation has stopped. I think ... I think you might be onto something."

The admission buoyed her spirits. She emptied the vessel near what she thought might be his feet before plunking the object back into the cooling water. "I take it as a good sign." She lifted the Tiger Vessel back up, ready for a second round.

"Norah? *What the hell are you doing*?" a new voice shouted from the bathroom door.

In her shock, Norah dropped the vessel into the bathwater and opened her eyes, which were thankfully pointed toward Rodney's feet. She caught a glimpse of sore-infested legs and a tub full of greenish water that was cloudy from putrescence before she spun around.

LJ stood in the doorway, his normally placid face a work of red-tinged fury. He stared first at her, and then at Rodney. Norah dared not turn to see Rodney's reaction.

"LJ," she gasped. "What—"

LJ strode forward the handful of steps, grasped Norah's nearest glove-clad arm, and yanked her painfully to her feet. Once she was standing, he pulled her out into Rodney's bedroom, whereupon he turned quickly, like a snake striking its next meal.

"Are you out of your mind?" he hissed in her face.

She tried to shrug his grip off her arm. "What is wrong with you?" she retorted.

He tightened his grip in response. Norah bit her lip to keep the cry of pain at bay. He growled, "What's wrong with *me*? What's wrong with you, Norah? I catch you in the same room as a naked man? Have you lost all your senses?"

He finally loosened his hand, and Norah jerked her arm out of his grasp, backing up a step. "I had my eyes closed," she tried to explain calmly, although her arm smarted and her heart beat painfully.

He guffawed. "And that makes it okay?"

"Nothing untoward happened, LJ. I was helping heal him. His curse seemed to be reacting favorably to my actions."

"Oh, for—" LJ stopped talking, instead opting to study his sister like she was a fly about to lose her wings. "This can't be happening, Norah. I won't allow it."

Now it was Norah's turn to become angry. "*Won't allow it?* LJ, let me make this clear. I am an adult. You are not my father. I can make my own decisions. And when it comes to helping these men, you will not have a say in the matter!"

LJ breathed through his nose like a bull. Norah imagined he was seeing red as well. With a falsely calm voice, he replied, "I am the head of this family, which makes you my responsibility. And I'll be damned—" his voice rose again, "if I let my sister whore herself out to a bunch of freaks!"

"*How dare you!*" she shrieked and began to raise her hands, whether to push or slap her brother, she did not know. LJ, wise to her body language, caught her wrists before they could make contact.

"Temper, temper, sister," he cautioned with twin squeezes that threatened to grind the bones of her arms together.

Tears formed in the corners of her eyes. "Please, LJ. You're hurting me."

He laughed, a low, cruel sound that curdled her stomach, but he let her go and backed off. He pointed a finger at her. "You stay out of that bathroom," he ordered her as she tore off her wet gloves to rub her wrists. "I won't warn you again."

He did not wait for a reply but left the room, confident that he had cowed her into submission.

Well, his confidence was accurate. The minute he was gone, Norah sank to the floor with a sob, allowing the tears to trail freely as she willed the soreness to leave her bones.

CHAPTER TWENTY

Tuesday, March 30th, 1915

Malcolm

A CLEAN BILL OF health was given by Mathers that morning, and Malcolm jumped at the chance to finally escape his bed. He still felt a little weak and had to go more slowly than he otherwise was accustomed to, but he was on his own feet once again, and that was worth a little weakness.

His first order of business was to check in on his members. After all, he hadn't seen them since Friday, and it was now Tuesday.

Rodney, Farley, and Pablo sat around a table, quietly playing a game of gin rummy. Hector napped with Eddie on his lap, who wagged his tail at the sight of Malcolm but otherwise did not move. Malcolm reflected on what a good boy that dog was.

He sat at the table with the other three. "Morning, gents."

They all mumbled their greetings, with Pablo flashing a winning smile. "*Buenos dias, Señor.*"

Malcolm surveyed the men at the table before doing a double take. "Rodney, your face!"

Rodney was still severely pockmarked with blemishes, but there were no burgeoning pustules ready to leak, and overall their size was much smaller than usual.

The man blushed. "Thank you, Malcolm," he said shyly.

Malcolm could not help but be in awe at the obvious change. "God, man, what happened? It's incredible!"

At this, Rodney looked a shade uncomfortable. "Well, uh, it was Norah, actually. She had me bathe in nettle water, only that was hurting me more than helping, so she took it upon herself to try to uncurse the Tiger Vessel."

Malcolm stared at the man, taking in his words. "How did she do that?" he asked, genuinely curious and oddly hopeful.

Rodney's flush deepened, extending into his neck. He kept his eyes on his cards as if they held all of life's secrets. "She filled it with nettle water and poured it on me."

"Fantastic." This was the first clear sign that somebody could be cured. A welling of pride grew in him for Norah.

But Rodney sat hunched and unsmiling, his eyes refusing to meet Malcolm's. Malcolm focused on Rodney, assessing him. "Are you well?"

Rodney glanced over for a second before answering, "Will you please let her know I'm sorry for getting her in trouble? And that I'm deeply grateful to her? I doubt I'll be seeing her anytime soon."

The smile on Malcolm's face slipped as he puzzled through Rodney's words. "Something happen?" he asked carefully.

"Just tell her I'm sorry. Please."

Clearly, Rodney would not divulge anything more, and forcing a confession out of him would do more harm than good. Malcolm needed to go straight to the source if he was to know what happened.

He stood abruptly, causing all three men to look up in surprise. "Gentlemen," he brusquely bade, and headed for the stairs. Checking in with the rest of the men would have to wait.

Malcolm had not yet seen Norah this morning, having taken extra time in preparing for the day. He had smelled rather foul after days-worth of captivity in his bed, and a bath was necessary before greeting other people. Remembering his morning bath also brought back Rodney's words: *she had me bathe in nettle water. When that didn't work, she filled the vessel and poured it on me.*

Malcolm hadn't thought through Rodney's explanation deeper than surface level, but after his odd reaction to Malcolm's praise, Malcolm began to feel an uneasiness in the pit of his stomach.

He reached Norah's door and knocked. "Norah, are you in there?"

He could hear her feet shuffling on the carpet as she reached the door and opened it. She blocked the entrance with her body, not opening the door fully. "Hello, Malcolm. Feeling better?"

Her tone denoted a polite detachment, which was not her usual habit of speech. Malcolm smelled a rat.

"May I come in?" he asked with forced sunshine.

She paused for a moment before moving out of the way. Malcolm walked in as if he didn't have a care in the world. Up until his chat with Rodney, he hadn't yet.

"I saw Rodney," he began, carefully watching her face.

"Oh?" Norah responded, standing too rigidly.

Malcolm nodded. "His face is much improved. He had you to thank for that. How on earth did you manage such a feat?"

She smiled at his kind words, but she was still guarded. "Oh, that. The nettles. They did the trick after all."

"Mm-hm. Wonderful." He paused, weighing his words. "He also told me to tell you he was sorry if he got you in trouble. Would you care to expand upon that?"

Norah's face blanched, the opposite reaction to Rodney's. "I don't believe there is anything to say in that matter. I'm quite tired; would you please let me rest?" She gestured at the door.

As she stretched her arm out, her sleeve rode up, exposing a purple spot on her wrist that Malcolm zeroed in on immediately.

"Norah," he said, his voice calmer than his rising emotions, "what happened to your wrist?"

She flinched back, covering the wrist with her other hand.

He silently walked closer, slowly so as not to spook her. "Norah. May I see?"

She looked away as he gently touched her, moving her sleeve up on the hand that was in front. This wrist was also bruised.

Anger took hold of him, not at Norah, who seemed defeated, but at whoever had dared to hurt her. "Who did this?" he asked in a low voice.

She stayed silent, not meeting his gaze and rubbing her right wrist in a repeating pattern.

"Norah," Malcolm tried again, softening his voice further, despite the anger inside of him making it difficult to do so. "Please. I have a zero-tolerance policy when it comes to physical altercations. I need to know who hurt you. Was it Rodney?"

Norah's gaze flew to his eyes. Her astonishment was evident, but Malcolm could not tell whether it was due to confirmation or refutation of his claim.

Malcolm further pressed. "He told me to apologize on his behalf. Did he ... force you to do anything? While he was in the bath?"

Even as he said these words, they tasted foul and untruthful. But it was the only scenario he could come up with.

Norah shook her head fervently, though. "You think Rodney would be capable of forcing a woman to tend to his desires? That man is as sweet as they come. If anything, I made *him* uncomfortable."

It was more of an explanation than he'd so far received, but Malcolm still was in the dark. "Then, who?"

She huffed a breath, looking down again. "LJ."

It took a moment for the name to register. LJ. Leighton. "Your brother did this to you?" He took a step back, the fury whipping into a tornado inside of him.

"He did catch me in what looked like a compromising position—"

"Stop." Malcolm laid his hands carefully on her forearms, as if to brace her. She stayed unmoving, allowing his touch. "I don't care if he caught you naked in the bathtub *with* Rodney. No one has a right to cause another person physical harm in this house."

A tear slipped from Norah's eye. Malcolm watched it track down her cheek as she turned her eyes up to his again. "What will you do?" she whispered.

Malcolm was torn. He wanted to break Leighton's wrists—an eye for an eye but with added interest. He was not the type to carry out this vision, however. If it had been anyone else in the house, the obvious answer would have been expulsion. But, seeing as how Leighton was Norah's brother, and she loved him ...

"He gets a warning," he decided.

Norah collapsed slightly. She must have assumed Leighton would be expelled, and her along with him. But in Malcolm's world, that wouldn't do.

"Thank you," she whispered.

It was those two words that did him in. He had seen her brash and intimidating, but to see her with her defenses laid bare? He fought the urge to wrap his arms about her, to mentally fortify her armor for her.

To kiss her.

He settled for a small touch on her chin. "You're welcome." He turned to go.

"Malcolm?"

He stopped and turned.

She hesitated. "Don't you want to know what he saw?"

He shook his head. "I trust you."

He left before she could say anything else.

Norah

Despite the easing of her heart after her chat with Malcolm, Norah still suffered from a knot of anxiety in her gut. It had loosened since last night, but it continued to cloy in her midsection even after Malcolm left her with those unexpected parting words.

If she was being honest with herself, the reason for this continued agitation was not entirely to be blamed on what had occurred last night. Some of her inner turmoil stemmed from the conversation she'd just had with Malcolm.

She could not come to grips with the implications. A lady's reputation was the best tool in a woman's arsenal, in most cases. Norah's careless actions in the bathroom should have destroyed her reputation, and LJ was only too right to point that out.

She expected no less from any man, and she had anticipated Malcolm to be just as furious with her for her indiscretion, or at the very least disappointed. Instead, his fury was over her brother's actions, not hers. Norah was stunned. Had Malcolm truly not cared about what she and Rodney might have been doing?

Malcolm's turning of a blind eye gave her pause.

Norah had always hated the idea of the lady's reputation. What did it matter if a woman chose to fraternize alone with a man? It was yet another way for the patriarchy to keep the lesser sex under its thumb.

Norah deemed it archaic and snubbed the practice as much as she could. If the rest of the upper class could see her here at Birchwald, walking freely about in a house full of men—not to mention the utter scandal of staying the night in Malcolm's bed, no matter how innocent the event actually was—she would already be ruined.

Truth be told, she'd already flirted with ruination. Not just here at Birchwald, but a year ago, in Oxford.

While attending classes, Norah had suffered through a period of low morale. The "morbs," as Aunt Nell liked to call it. Norah felt trapped against a fate she did not want, squished into a tidy hole of duty. She was a woman, after all, and women were only good for one thing in this world of men.

Norah wanted to be more. She wanted to be seen without having to be stripped of her identity.

What she had told Malcolm back in February, about never wanting to marry, was a slight falsehood. She saw the occasional happy couple and her heart ached for a connection like that. It was only her family's predicament that pushed her into a life of unmarried status.

In an effort to empower herself, she decided that she would rebel against the idea that chastity was a virtue. If her lifelong title was to be spinster, she could at least do away with the "old maid" part of the connotation. Pushing societal standards was a favorite pastime of hers, after all, as was learning new things.

It was just one man, a fellow student named Gerald who was easy on the eyes yet charmingly daft when it came to conversation. He was perfect; Norah was attracted to his body but not his mind. It safeguarded her against falling in love. And Gerald was incredibly easy to seduce.

Given the fact that Norah had no desire to reproduce, she made sure to be careful. Prophylactics were a must, and Gerald readily agreed to their use.

It was the only thing that went well in this disastrous experiment.

Gerald's simplicity, most unfortunately, carried through to his lovemaking skills. Other than the benefit of newfound wisdom into the secrets of human couplings, Norah gained very little from the experience. She was not impressed.

She had to be careful, however. Gerald now had the upper hand over her. If they were to be found out, Gerald would most likely receive a slap on the wrist, but Norah would be banished from the college, and her reputation would be dashed to pieces. In addition, Gerald had no qualms after the first session—unlike Norah—and was eager to further engage in the affair. Norah worried he'd rat them out if his needs weren't met, so she allowed a handful of trysts more as she wracked her brain for a way out that would benefit the both of them.

Ironically enough, Norah was saved from her predicament by the outbreak of the war. Gerald was one of the first young men to drop from university to join the fight. She never saw him again, and her reputation remained intact. She learned a very valuable lesson as well: her desires should never come at the cost of her personal liberty.

It didn't change the fact that she still had desires, though.

She sighed. Perhaps LJ was right to scare her away from another tryst.

Not with Rodney, though. She had no designs for any of the members living on the third floor.

But Malcolm? The more she interacted with him, the more he invaded her thoughts late at night. His smile, his broodiness, his care, and his touch: they all provoked the primitive aspect of her mind. The *want*. She found it harder as of late to tell herself she was not attracted to him.

She rubbed her sore wrists, bringing her thoughts away from Malcolm and back to her brother. He had never, *never* used force on her before. There had been a light in his eye as he squeezed, a malignancy that terrified her more than the physical pain. It was as if he was enjoying hurting her.

He had a dark streak, to be sure. She caught LJ on occasion tormenting animals as a small child, and he sometimes said hurtful things about other people. His "Aunt Smell" moniker, for instance, was downright cruel. She wondered if he had a similar name for her that he said behind her back.

"Norah?"

She yelped and spun, so lost in thought about past affairs and current conundrums that she had not heard the door open. LJ stood before her, looking a trifle sheepish. She froze.

"I—I'm sorry, Nor," he said. He held his hands out.

Norah hesitated. LJ may not have ever been physically cruel to her before, but a second thing he never did was apologize for *anything*. His actions rang of falseness.

He dropped his hands, dejected.

Norah still watched him, unsure of his motivation. It was an unnerving feeling, she realized. She and her twin had been inseparable since birth. Orphaned together, growing up as each other's only playmates and companions, and in adulthood being separated by continents, but never by their hearts. The distance had strained their once-tight relationship, but she still could read LJ as easily as when they were children. In the time they had moved to Birchwald, though, she felt the brother she knew slipping further away, being replaced by a stranger.

"What is it you are sorry for?" she finally asked him.

He shook his head. "Your wrists. I was only trying to drive home a point. I took it too far."

"I see." She kept her distance.

LJ huffed and let a half-smile peek out, displaying his golden boy persona. That look was how he had gotten out of many scrapes, both in childhood and as an adult. He should have known by now it never worked on her. "It gave me a fright, is all. I see how Malcolm looks at you. I know you have some of these men eating out of the palms of your hands."

She blinked, unsure if this was truly an apology, or if he was trying to convince her that he had been right to harm her. She could practically hear the phantom words he wanted to say: *I did this for your own good.*

She turned her back on him, rubbing her bruises. The tender pain served as a reminder of who she was. Who she wanted to be.

Free. I want to be free.

His voice cut through her. "Just ... I don't know. Be more careful. I can't always be around to protect you, Nor."

She did not bother turning around but nodded. "Thank you, LJ."

She heard him leave.

She was angry, hurt, confused. The brother she grew up with would have never called her a whore.

She should have been glad to feel these negative emotions, but instead, she felt further trapped.

Because deep down, she still loved him. He was still her family, even if he was becoming a stranger.

CHAPTER TWENTY-ONE

Monday, April 5th, 1915

Norah

NORAH'S BRUISES HEALED, TURNING a sickly shade of yellow as they faded. Her heart healed as well, mainly because she took time away from LJ. Absence could sometimes bring back the rosy glow of fond memories, and for Norah, they were a balm.

She didn't forget, however.

In the act of avoiding her brother, Norah also shied away from the rest of the Guild. It was an unfortunate side effect, but one she needed to heal herself.

It was difficult these days to feel down for very long, though, simply due to the change of the season. Winter was indeed continuing to loosen its grasp on this corner of New York, and the warmer weather made for more outdoor time. Norah enjoyed not only the walks with Eddie, who frolicked about in gleeful doggy abandon, but she also rediscovered the balcony.

When Mrs. Bixby had shown it to her the first time, it had been covered in two feet of snow. But now, the entire balcony was on display, and Norah was delighted to find that it contained a wrought-iron bench and two small tables, perfect for a sunset viewing on the days when the sky was clear.

There were no rain clouds to spoil this evening's sunset, Norah was pleased to discover. She donned her thick coat, poured a hot cup of tea, and called for Eddie to follow her out onto the deck.

The small door in her dressing room unlocked with a click, and she stepped out onto the balcony, eager to sit in solitude while admiring the rich sky colors. Eddie leaped out, his tail waving briskly, and she shut the door behind her.

"I see I'm not the only one," a deep voice said from behind her.

Norah shrieked and jolted half of her tea all over her hand before spinning around. "Bugger!"

Malcolm pinched his lips together at her curse, clearly trying not to smile. "I didn't think you had it in you."

Norah sighed and willed her heart to return to a normal pace as she set her half-empty cup down on the nearest table and wiped her scalded hand free of tea. "What are you doing out here?"

Malcolm, who also had a cup of tea—still in the cup, Norah noted disdainfully—took a sip before replying. "It's my balcony. I take pleasure in it at times. Won't you join me?"

Norah flopped down next to him on the bench. "I didn't think you could be out here," she said as she stared out into the scenery.

"Hm. You are wrong for once."

She chuckled. "It may shock you to learn I'm wrong more times than that."

"Well, I'll believe it when I see it." He took another sip. "No, there are only two ways I can get some fresh air that the curse doesn't count as being outside. Sitting on the upper loggia—not the lower one, mind you—or sitting out here. Apparently, as long as I have no means of escape to the property, it still counts as being in the house. The loggia is nice for sunrises, although most days I'm not awake for them. This balcony is perfect for sunsets, though."

Norah smiled. "So I've discovered. It's why I'm here too."

Malcolm cleared his throat. "Would you prefer it if I left?"

Norah looked at him. He faced her, his gray eyes shadowed by the diminished sunlight. She smiled serenely at him. "No, stay."

He returned her smile, his teeth shining in the dim light. He grew serious after a second, putting on a frown that was almost mocking. "You've been avoiding me again."

Norah rubbed her hand, which still stung from the tea. "I've been avoiding everyone," she admitted.

"Your brother apologized, didn't he?"

She nodded as she scanned the faraway tree line. The sun had touched their tips, and the sky was lighting up with pinks. "He did." Norah suspected LJ's apology was more forced upon him by the very man she now sat next to, than heartfelt. It changed nothing with how she felt about the whole affair. She breathed in, finding the courage to say more. "He's not the person I grew up with."

Malcolm turned from the sunset to focus on her. "Oh?"

She shook her head. "Truthfully, I've not known him well since he left for Belize, so perhaps I'm now witnessing the man he's become. I still have hope that it's an act."

"What would be the purpose of that?"

Now she was treading on dangerous territory. "It could be a means of escape. Our family was never one to shy away from adventure."

"Obviously," Malcolm said with a snort.

Norah perked the corners of her lips, although the expression verged on rueful rather than amused. "LJ is behaving like a caged animal. He seeks freedom. The only thing holding him back is me."

Malcolm stretched his legs out and carefully extended his arm behind Norah's shoulders, resting it on the bench back. She quirked an eyebrow at him, although the lowering sun made it hard to see.

Malcolm smirked. "Does this bother you?"

She sighed theatrically. "I suppose not." She leaned into his arm, the bubbly feeling in her midsection a pleasant sensation and welcome reward for her own brazenness.

"Norah." Malcolm's voice dipped lower, causing the bubbles to increase their tempo. She looked at him, her eyes widening as he leaned her way ever so slightly. "Rodney looks well."

The subject took her off guard. "What?"

Malcolm kept his face closer to hers, with a knowing smile gracing his mouth. Her midsection calmed, disappointingly. "Rodney. Whatever you did to him, it was working."

She forced her mind to comprehend his words, rather than his lips. "*Was?*"

He heaved out a breath with a rueful nod. "His skin stayed clearer than I've ever seen it. You would have known if you weren't avoiding everyone. Since yesterday, though, it's getting worse again."

"Oh dear." Norah thought of something. "When was the last time he had a full breakout?"

Malcolm sat back again in thought. "It was shortly after you came. Mid-February, wasn't it?"

"And how often do his attacks come?"

"Usually about once a month. Sometimes as little as twenty days, but the longest stretch was fifty."

Norah hummed in her throat as she did some quick mental math. "We're approaching that limit now, I do believe. I'd like to see if we can't continue to push it. I'll stop hiding, Malcolm. I'll see Rodney tomorrow morning and come up with a plan for him."

Malcolm sat up and patted her knee. Despite the many layers she wore, Norah felt it like a scorching fire. "I have to say, I didn't think you had it in you."

"That's the second time you've said that to me this evening," Norah retorted. "What might you be referring to, exactly?"

He rubbed his five o'clock shadow. "Swearing, for one. Ladies don't swear."

She snorted.

"*Most* ladies don't swear," he amended. "Clearly, living in a house of cursed adventurers has done a number on your morals. But mainly, I assumed I couldn't be impressed by anything. Not anymore. But quite frankly, I'm in awe."

"Of what?" Norah asked, leaning in with curiosity.

He smiled. "You. You're actually curing someone, Norah. This is going to work."

CHAPTER TWENTY-TWO

Tuesday, April 6th, 1915

Malcolm

AT TEN IN THE morning, Malcolm waited on the third floor, along with Pablo, Ambrose, and Rodney, the latter of whom had started a game of Solitaire to pass the time.

He'd told the men that Norah would make an appearance, but they had nearly given up on seeing her again. Malcolm knew better, though. She would come. It was written all over her face yesterday, on the balcony. He remembered the pleased bloom of Norah's face when he'd told her in certain words he was proud of her.

It had taken everything in him to hold back from kissing her.

And suddenly, there she was, emerging from the stairs like Aphrodite from her clam shell. Malcolm grinned broadly, reveling in the joy from the men at her appearance.

Rodney stood upon seeing her, the cards in his hand scattering over his half-played game. "Norah! What a pleasant surprise."

"Señorita, will you marry me?" Pablo blurted out.

"My, aren't you a sight for sore eyes," Ambrose added. It was a sentiment any of the fellows could have thought. He thankfully made no mention of how beautiful she looked in the moment, with her flushed cheeks and chocolate eyes shining. Malcolm wasn't sure how well he'd take those words coming from another man's lips, even if he originally authored the thought.

Norah took each of these greetings in stride, paying attention to each man in turn, but settling her sights ultimately on Rodney. She clasped a hand to her mouth as she got a good look at him, lowering it a second later to reveal her radiant smile. "Rodney, I can't believe it! Your face, it's so ... handsome."

Malcolm wished she could have seen it two days ago, before the swelling had started back up. He had never truly known the true map of the man's facial features until the sores no longer dominated. Rodney had even started to grow hair from the top of his head again, the blonde fuzz a true testament to his healing. Today, however, the pustules were beginning to grow and open again.

Rodney still blushed at the compliment. "It's all you, Norah."

"Well," she said briskly, "it would appear that we need to do more. Are you willing, Rodney?"

His smile fell. "Ah ... I'm not sure it's such a good idea."

Norah gazed at him with understanding. "Oh, Rodney, I'd rather get in trouble any day than see you suffer. But fear not; Mal—Mr. Drury and I have a plan."

Malcolm strode over. "Miss Abernathy will not be stepping foot in your bathroom," he told the reluctant man, who brightened visibly at the remark. "*I'll* be helping you, if need be. It's not anything I've never seen before," he added with a grin.

Rodney blushed and looked down. "Thank you, to both of you," he said. When he looked back up at Norah, his eyes were shiny with grateful tears.

Norah patted his arm with affection, her pressure light in case of unseen sores. "I collected more nettles earlier this week. Are you up for another bath?"

"Oh yes."

Norah nodded her approval at his response. "I've also put in an order with Mathers for the angelica and agrimony. I found a supplier in New York City, who will ship it to me shortly. I suspect it will further do you wonders. I'd like to see that face of yours as it was intended to be seen, Rodney."

A tear slipped from his eye, tracking unsteadily down the bumpy road of his face. "I'd like nothing more as well."

Norah wasted no time in bringing up the dried nettles to the third floor. She stayed long enough to show Malcolm how to prepare the bathwater, and how to hold the vessel without inadvertently cursing himself. Then, she excused herself to go attend to the rest of the guild members in need.

Malcolm had to admit, if he hadn't seen the evidence of success the first go around, he never would have thought this would work. He turned the faucet off, watching the tub water turn into the shade of green tea as the nettles steeped.

"Is this the right color?" he asked Rodney, who waited in the doorway wearing nothing but a robe.

Rodney walked fully in and inspected the water. "I think it was a bit darker last time. I'll need to allow the water to cool more before I get in anyway. Last time, I swear she was trying to boil me to death."

Malcolm chuckled, imagining Rodney as a crustacean meeting his doom. He tapped a foot, impatient to do something. As much as he'd helped Rodney with his outbreaks over the years, he found waiting in a small room with the mostly naked man to be an awkward encounter. Judging by Rodney's stilted demeanor, the feeling was mutual.

Malcolm snapped his fingers. "I'll prepare your vessel while we wait. Perhaps soaking it before I begin to pour will be a good thing."

"Good thinking," Rodney agreed quickly.

Malcolm retrieved the item, holding it at arm's length with the gloves Norah had provided. She had mentioned to him the unsettling feeling it exuded, but until now, Malcolm was sure it had been in her head. Now that he was holding it, he surmised she may have been right.

"Say, Rodney," he said as he entered the bathroom again, "how could you stand to hold this thing long enough to steal it?"

"It's got an energy about it, doesn't it?" Rodney mused. "I can tell you with full honesty, it did not feel like that back in China. Otherwise, I never would have nicked it. It only turned angry once we boarded the ship and my sores began to appear."

Malcolm studied the vessel before plunking it into the nettle water. As it filled, the aura lessened, and it became more of an ordinary bronze vessel. "Curious."

"How's the water?" Rodney asked, peering into the tub.

Malcolm shrugged his shoulders. "Hard to tell, through the gloves."

The other man dipped a hand in. "Well, it's not scalding. I suppose it's time." He dropped the robe and gingerly stepped into the bathtub.

Once he was settled, Malcolm began pouring the water from the Tiger Vessel onto Rodney's body, just as Norah had instructed. Rodney relaxed into the procedure, rubbing the water into his skin as Malcolm poured. The man sighed, a sound of comfort rather than the gasps of pain Malcolm was used to him making.

"There's something about her, isn't there?" Rodney asked abruptly.

Malcolm paused his pouring. "Who? Norah?"

"Norah." Rodney said her name like a poem. "You feel it, too."

Malcolm tipped the vessel, emptying it out over the man's knees. He bent over to refill it. "Perhaps."

"Malcolm." Rodney stared at him, an expression on his face telling Malcolm that he wasn't fooling anyone. "I see the way you look at her. She's available, isn't she? I know if I weren't me, I'd court her in a heartbeat."

Malcolm ruefully shook his head as he drenched Rodney's legs. "There's something unsettling about having this conversation while you're naked as the day you were born, old chap." He paused, considering the words he was about to speak, almost hating them as he did. "You know, something tells me that Norah is not one to care about looks. You're a good man, Rodney. What's really stopping you? Why not you?"

Rodney gazed at Malcolm with a strange smile on his face. "Because I've seen the way she looks at you, too."

Norah

The joy emanating from Rodney, Mr. Lyster, and Señor Reyes upon seeing Norah again was so genuine that it stripped her of all the apprehension she had been suffering from. Their acceptance of her back into the fold strengthened her resolve. She would not hide anymore. These men needed her.

While Malcolm left with Rodney, Norah got to work with her normal rounds, starting with Mr. Hunt and working her way clockwise through the third floor.

She had just left Hector Freeman's room when she spied Karanja, for once out of his bedroom. The three rooms to the north did not have adjoining bathrooms, and so the men residing within had to share a communal bath located next to Hector's room. Karanja was just leaving it at the same time as Norah's departure from Hector.

The timing was too serendipitous to pass up. Norah had been wishing to get to know the enigmatic man better for weeks now—and hopefully learn more about Mr. Withers in the process—and despite his agreement on the subject, Karanja had never made the time to allow it to happen.

"Hello, Karanja," Norah greeted, beaming a friendly smile at him.

"Oh, hello, ma'am," he responded with politeness, not looking her in the eye. He began walking back to his room.

Norah kept pace with him. "Would it be okay if we had a visit?" she asked, her voice breathless as she tried to match the long-legged pace of Karanja.

He paused, allowing her to catch up. "Now?" he asked.

Norah looked around at the near-empty room. Only Eddie prowled around the nooks and crannies of the communal area, the men having left to tend to their various businesses. She turned her attention back to Karanja, who shifted his weight from one foot to another. "If that is alright with you?"

"Well," he said slowly, "I suppose a quick visit will work."

Internally, Norah felt giddy. Externally, she regally bowed her head. "Thank you."

Calling to Eddie, Norah followed Karanja to the room he shared with Mr. Withers.

"I can't tell you how happy I am to spend some time with the two of you," Norah said as she breezed in after Karanja. She stopped short the moment she entered the room. Compared to the lightness of the communal area, this bedroom was oppressive, with little natural light entering through the stiff curtains drawn over the single window. A bed and a small cot flanked the walls on either side, with a small stand directly under the window, holding an odd assortment of items, including a small wooden drum, a comb, and an old, cracked wooden bowl. Mr. Withers sat in his wheelchair, a slight wheeze in his breaths. The air was stagnant, and Norah had to work to keep her face neutral. No one spoke as she waited for her eyes to adjust to the low light levels.

It wasn't just Norah who felt the change in atmosphere. Eddie pranced in after Norah, but his carefree gait changed the moment he entered the room. He tensed, stopping by his mistress' side, and sniffed the air cautiously.

Norah glanced down at her pet. Eddie, who loved everyone he met at Birchwald, let out a low growl, which rose in volume the longer it carried.

Startled, Norah turned her attention to Karanja, who had backed up two steps away from Eddie, as if the little dog was about to attack him. After seeing the hackles spike up on her usually placid dog, Norah couldn't be sure Eddie wouldn't attack someone. She scooped him up, an act that often snapped Eddie out of any odd moods and sent his tail wagging. This time, however, he continued to growl into the room.

"I am not used to dogs," Karanja declared, his eyes shining in the darkness of the room. Norah saw a look of fear within them.

She frowned. "Perhaps now is not the best time for a visit after all," she said to Karanja. She turned to leave the room.

Karanja made sure to stay out of her way as she did so, not saying a word. The moment Norah was clear of the room, he shut the door behind her with a decisive thud.

Eddie wagged his tail and tried to lick Norah's face. She placed him down on the floor and watched as he went back to following his nose with a jaunty step.

She couldn't understand it. Eddie was a fine judge of character and had never acted like that before. She wondered what had upset him so.

The words of Father Berkely filtered back to the forefront of her mind. *If I am being honest, I don't trust his helper.* At the time, Norah had chalked his statement up to simple bigotry. After Eddie's reaction to the room, though, perhaps there had been some truth to the priest's words.

She shook her head. She tried to put the odd encounter out of her mind, instead focusing on visiting Mr. Jamison and Mr. Norris next on her rounds.

Eddie was just a dog, after all. She mustn't read too much into one singular situation.

CHAPTER TWENTY-THREE

Thursday, April 8th, 1915

Norah

Dear Namesake,

My apologies for not writing sooner. I have been wallowing in a deep downcast mood over the amount of horseshit you sent me last time.

Norah choked on the sip of coffee she had taken before beginning to read her letter. With wide eyes, she continued reading.

"LJ sends his love?" You and I both know that is a lie. It has led me to believe the entire letter you penned was completely farcical. And here I thought I raised you better. As far as I know, you've been abducted by Germans and this message was a coded cry for help.

Child, if I want to read for entertainment value, I will stick to my collection of hastily penned erotica. Don't waste my time with your poorly written fiction, especially if it has none of the good stuff in it.

All my love (and for you only. I will not share it with your twit of a brother),

Aunt Nell

Norah put the letter down, needing a moment to absorb what her aunt had written.

Leave it to Aunt Nell to word her grievances so colorfully.

Still, Norah supposed she had a point. She read over the short letter again, this time smiling at the absurdity of the contents, before sitting at her writing desk to pen a reply.

Dear Aunt Nell,

You have taught me the error of my ways. The society we live within, run by men as it is, would have women speak of nothing but sunshine and dewdrops, even if the sun was actively burning us to a crisp and the dewdrops were drowning us. I understand now that as modern women, we must learn to speak the truth, not a fairytale.

Honestly, it's been difficult at times here. I was not accepted as I should have been, initially. But I've made progress in breaking one of the men's curses. And I've learned a great deal more about the others. This by itself has been fulfilling.

I've also gotten to know the president better this past month, and I dare to say we are friends. I will not divulge his curse, as he trusts me alone with the knowledge, but suffice it to say, it has made his life rather lonely. I'd like to break it for him as well so that he can go on to live more fully.

LJ did not send his love. Did you know he calls you "Aunt Smell?" It's rather hideous of him.

As her pen scratched over the surface, a thought came to her. If Aunt Nell wanted truth, Norah wouldn't hold back for the sake of decorum.

I have one rather impertinent question for you. Are you still single? I know it's been half a year since you were last widowed, and sometimes this means the next mister is already lined up. I won't share why I'm asking just yet, in case it's a dead end. But your answer would be most appreciated.

All my love to you,

Norah

There. She would mail that out today, once the ink was dry. For now, she had a question to ask of someone else.

With Eddie trailing behind, Norah made her way to the third floor, where she immediately spied Rodney and Señor Reyes sitting together at a table. The Spaniard had his sketchbook out again, and it would seem that Rodney was once again the subject of the sketch.

Norah leaned over to get a better view of the paper. "Why, Señor, I'm still in awe of your talent. That looks just like Rodney. Well done."

He craned his neck to get a better view of Norah, smiling as he did. "*Gracias, Bella Dama.* Will you marry me?"

"Not today, no."

He shrugged and returned to his work. "Señor Rodney is looking much better, eh? I can see the structure of his bones beneath the curse."

Norah studied Rodney, who turned his blushing face partly away. Señor Reyes was right; Rodney's skin had further cleared, and for the first time, she could see the distinct definition of his facial features instead of a lumpy mess.

"You see?" Reyes continued, flipping back to the last time he had drawn Rodney.

"Remarkable," Norah agreed after comparing the two drawings.

"No, Miss Abernathy. *You* are the remarkable one. A real miracle worker. Will you marry me?"

Norah patted his shoulder and came around to sit in the nearest chair. "No, Señor. But, I have a question for you. Has anyone ever said yes?"

Reyes blinked, taken aback by the question. "Well, yes, actually."

Norah felt her hopes sinking. "Oh? But you are clearly not married."

He shook his head, suddenly shy. "No, it's true. It has only been two women. I do not believe they meant it, so the curse ignored their answers."

"So they only said it to shut you up?"

He nodded, his mouth twisting downward.

Norah knuckled her lips in thought. "Have you no sweetheart waiting for you in Spain?"

"No one, Señorita. I was ... married to my work, before my curse."

Norah understood. She never intended to marry. She was more interested in curses than matrimony. Yet becoming a wife was expected of her by polite society. It was unfair that the practice of working instead of marrying was more acceptable for men than it was for women.

It was time to delve deeper. "Señor ... do you have any interest in marriage?"

Señor Reyes dipped his eyebrows and pondered her question for a moment. "I would not be against it, no. Will *you* marry me, Miss Abernathy?"

Norah narrowed her eyes. This particular proposal felt more personal than his others. She shook her head. "I wasn't thinking about myself with these lines of questions. I am curious to know if a woman agreeing to marry you—with intention to follow through, that is—will break your curse. Would you be willing to test that theory?"

His eyebrows lifted. "With you?"

She closed her eyes and shook her head. "No, not with me. I have no inclination for matrimony with anyone, not at the moment. I'm sure you're a fine catch, though. I do have someone in mind, however. I shall inquire further to see if she is open to this suggestion."

"You will be an angel if you succeed," Reyes commented.

"You may want to hold that thought," Norah replied drily. "In this instance, the cure may be worse than the ailment in the long run."

Malcolm

Back when he had first become the president, Malcolm had flung himself into getting to know each and every member as well as he could. He had no family of his own anymore, not after his mother's death and the burning of Fiona's proverbial bridge. He decided to make the Guild his family.

Of the ten men under his care currently, only four were a part of the Guild before he took over: Rodney, Pablo, and finally Fred and his chicken friend. Rodney was the longest living member of the Guild, having joined in 1901. Pablo came along in 1909, if memory served. And he recalled that Fred and Mr. Norris were fairly new, only having joined Arnold's establishment a month prior to his retirement. Malcolm assumed they were the straw that broke Arnold's camel's back in terms of care.

There were also others at the time of Malcolm's takeover. Two men, both badly cursed, who had since departed this earthly plane. It was a somber reminder of what being in charge of a guild full of damaged men entailed.

It also made it that much harder, in some respects, to get to know the men.

Over the years, Malcolm went from actively participating in the members' lives to viewing from afar. He still interacted with them when needed, and welcomed Ambrose, Hector, Farley, and Marvin in turn when they joined, but beyond a simple acquaintanceship, Malcolm had long stopped trying.

With the addition of Mr. Withers, Malcolm hadn't even bothered that much. He could have excused this lapse with the fact that the man was mostly comatose, or that he already had an assistant—unlike the other members—but one simple fact remained that Malcolm couldn't shake. He had simply given up.

It wasn't until Norah had thundered through the door that Malcolm awoke from his alcohol- and indifference-induced stupor. In his five years as president, he had never once questioned whether these men could be saved. Her insistence on the matter seemed laughable.

Until Rodney's transformation.

Now, Malcolm felt a renewed sense of duty. He needed to make a difference in the lives of these men, and once again connect with them on a deeper level, especially those he had failed to befriend entirely. It was time to put a stop to his indifference. These were men who could still lead fruitful lives.

With this new zest for his position, Malcolm decided to pay a visit to Withers. At the very least, if he could not hold a conversation with the older man, he could get to know his assistant, who had been incredibly shy since coming to live at Birchwald. Surely, the man needed a friend as much as the next person.

And, he reflected, part of his interest in Withers was due to Norah's bizarre account of what happened when she stopped by the other day. Malcolm did not lend much credit to the idea that Eddie's reaction was a reflection of Karanja's character—dogs were simply not that smart, he reasoned. Nevertheless, the description of the room from Norah interested Malcolm.

Karanja and Withers were in this shared room, as usual. The curtains were drawn, blanketing the small space in an eerie darkness. Karanja, who had opened the door and allowed Malcolm in, stooped as if in shame.

"Apologies, Mister. The light can hurt Mr. Withers' eyes."

Malcolm waved it away. "No harm done, Karanja. I understand. How is he doing?"

Malcolm looked at Withers, who sat in his wheelchair, his head slumped forward slightly and a trail of drool escaping his mouth.

Karanja noticed it and wiped it with a cloth. "Same as usual, Mister."

"Please, call me Malcolm." He walked over and bent down, entering the older man's line of sight. "Hello, Peter," he said, hoping he was heard.

Withers moved his head up a fraction at the sound of Malcolm's voice. With great effort, he slowly brought his eyes to focus, making eye contact.

Malcolm leaned closer, delighted to make this connection. "Peter, can you hear me?"

Withers' eyes widened, and his hand trembled where it sat on the chair arm. His lip quivered as a sound escaped, "Ah ... ah ..."

"Good lord, that's remarkable!" Malcolm exclaimed as Karanja rushed over to inspect his ward.

The caretaker nodded. "He has his moments. I must feed him when he gets like this. It is a sign of hunger."

"Shall I ring for some food?" Malcolm asked.

Karanja shook his head. "No, sir. Mr. Withers must eat special food, otherwise he can choke. I make it here." As he spoke, he poured what looked to be cold porridge into an old wooden bowl with a large crack that started at the rim and ran to nearly the apex. He'd never seen it before, so it must have come from Africa with them.

Withers made another sound. Malcolm leaned in again, convinced the man was trying to communicate. "What's that, old chap?"

Another line of saliva escaped Withers' mouth. "N ... nuh ..." His eyes were wide, almost frightened. Malcolm frowned.

"Here, Mister. Eat," Karanja almost nudged Malcolm out of the way to gain access to Withers' face. From his new vantage point, Malcolm watched the cursed man wiggle his head before accepting the spoon of porridge.

"He has a hard time swallowing, sir. When he's awake, it's best to feed," Karanja explained as he spooned more food from the bowl into the man's mouth.

"Of course. Do you know what happened to him?"

Karanja shook his head but kept his attention on his patient. "I knew him in the colonies, and tended to him there, before his curse. But then he came up like this. It was a mystery. I offered to help."

"Do you miss Kenya?"

The question seemed to surprise the man, who swiveled around to gaze at Malcolm. "Why, yes, sir. It is my home. But this is my duty. I will stay here to tend to Mr. Withers."

"But why you?"

Karanja shrugged. "Because I must."

Malcolm let it drop. "Well, good for you. Not everyone would give up their homeland for someone they work for. If you can think of anything that might help us heal Mr. Withers, let us know, will you?"

Karanja gave his full attention back to Withers, who seemed to be losing the spark of consciousness he had displayed only moments earlier. "Yes, sir."

CHAPTER TWENTY-FOUR

Monday, April 12th, 1915

Malcolm

IT WAS JUST PAST one in the afternoon when Norah let herself into Malcolm's office without so much as a knock.

Malcolm eyed her and said sardonically, "Who is it? Ah, Norah, won't you come in?"

Norah smirked as she eased herself into the chair across from him. "I listened at the door. You didn't seem busy, so I let myself in."

"I could have been silently busy."

"And yet, here we are."

He gave his head a little shake of amusement. "How can I help you, Norah?"

She huffed out a sigh. "Mr. Ivey."

"What about him?"

"I cannot seem to find a way in which I can help him. He's shut me out at every opportunity."

"Hm, yes." Malcolm sat back, the wheels of the chair giving a little squeak at the shift in balance. "It's a terrible curse he suffers from. Seeing constant visions of death and destruction is bound to warp a mind. It's no wonder he tries to minimize them."

Norah balled her fists and relaxed them in nervous energy. "Yes, of course. But Malcolm, I'm not even sure what caused his curse."

"Truthfully, I don't know either."

She met his eyes, hers rounding with astonishment. "I thought you knew everyone's story."

"I should," he admitted. "I've allowed myself too much leeway this past year. Mr. Ivey was a tough nut to crack when he joined last January, so I easily gave up."

Norah tsked with mock scrutiny. "Oh, Malcolm. Shame, shame."

He rolled his eyes. "Your satirical debasing is truly befitting of a lady. Thank you for that."

She smiled cheekily. "I think we've already established that I am willing to do things I shouldn't as a lady."

"Like calling unmarried men by their first names?"

"And more."

The tone of her voice caught him off guard. He knew she was going for flippant, but instead, those two words came out lower than her usual speaking voice. It activated the primitive part of his brain. His heart rate kicked up a notch.

"Ahem, yes. Well." The office was suddenly stifling hot. He stood. "Regarding the Ivey conundrum, there's one way to try to solve this."

She stayed seated as he made his way around the desk and held out a hand to her. "What are you doing?" she asked, as if his offered hand was a snake waiting to strike.

He kept his arm outstretched. "*We* are going to go talk to the man. Together."

She smiled and took his hand to help herself up. He grasped it tightly, as if his fingers could memorize how her skin felt touching his. All too soon, though, he let her go.

Together, they walked up the flights of stairs to the third floor and stopped in front of Ivey's room, just past the elevator, at the front of the house.

Malcolm knocked. "Mr. Ivey? It's me, Malcolm. I have N—Miss Abernathy with me. May we come in?"

There was no immediate response. Malcolm shared a look with Norah.

"Shall we try later?" she whispered.

The door cracked open. From inside, Mr. Ivey called out, "Please, come in."

Carefully, Malcolm pushed the door open. Ivey had already crossed the room again, seating himself at the chair by his desk, the only other piece of furniture in the room besides the bed. Malcolm gestured for Norah to enter first.

She did so, walking in until she stood in the middle, while Ivey hung his head and did his best not to look at either of them. Malcolm entered as well, shutting the door firmly and placing himself next to Norah.

"Thank you for allowing us this visit," Malcolm began.

Ivey's shoulders bounced with a chuckle. "I assume it would be something important. It's not every day the president and the guild mistress stop by for a chat."

"Guild mistress?" Norah repeated.

Without looking at her, Ivey held up his hands in placation. "It's not slander, I assure you. I've overheard the others call you that on more than one occasion, and always with affection. It means they view you as a 'den mother,' so to speak, although you are much too young to be considered matronly for us folk."

Norah glanced over at Malcolm, amusement scrawled on her face. Clearly, she liked the term.

Malcolm cleared his throat. "Mr. Ivey, we do apologize for the intrusion. Miss Abernathy and I, we were hoping you would be willing to share your story. How you were cursed."

Ivey raised his head, although he kept his eyes closed. "A bit late in the game for that, isn't it, Mr. Drury?"

"Yes. And I have no excuse for that."

He sighed. "It dredges up some awful visions."

"I can imagine."

"These are different, though," Ivey continued with a head shake. "They are visions of memories. Crystal clear in my mind's eye. But, if you must know, I am willing to relive the nightmares for the sake of your combined curiosity."

"Thank you, Mr. Ivey," Norah said softly.

He made a strangled sound in his throat and thrashed his head back and forth. "Blood and fire. So much blood ... dripping down your breast ... perhaps it's best if you not speak, miss."

Norah's wide eyes turned to Malcolm, a look of horror in them. He quickly spoke for her, "She understands, Marvin."

Ivey nodded and gained control of his mind with a slight pant. "Apologies. Some days the visions come unbidden, even without using my eyes. What did you want? Oh yes. Where to begin?"

"Wherever you want, old chap," Malcolm reassured.

Ivey took a steadying breath. "I was married. She was a goddess. Much too good for me." He tensed his eyelids. Beads of sweat appeared on his balding forehead. "I took her everywhere with me. I was not the type of adventurer to dig up bones or live with natives. I ... *we* traveled for the beauty of the world.

"She lost her wedding ring while we sailed around Africa. She was beside herself. She ... she ... *blood and fire! Fire and death!*" He shouted these last words as he pounded his fists into his thighs. He began hyperventilating.

Norah rushed over, laying her hands on his shoulders. Ivey calmed marginally, but the tears leaked from his shut eyes. Malcolm knew they should not push the subject anymore.

"It's okay, Mr. Ivey. We'll try another day," she soothed as she half-hugged the despondent man.

Malcolm approached, crouching down on his other side to face Norah. "Sorry, Marvin," he said with some small amount of awkwardness. "Some other time, perhaps. Norah?"

She rubbed the man's back in soothing circles as his sobs began to quiet. "I'll stay just a while longer," she said under her breath.

Malcolm longed to kiss her for her kindness to a man she did not know. Instead, he left, knowing that Ivey was in good hands.

Norah

As with the breakfast fiasco, Norah's touch soothed Mr. Ivey, who went from a sobbing, twitching mess to a man who breathed deeply through his occasional hiccup. She wondered why the touch of a virtual stranger would have this effect on him.

"Mr. Ivey?" she ventured after a few minutes. "Are you better?"

He gave a single gasping sob that ended with a laugh. "I don't think it's in my vocabulary, miss," he said. "I'd like to tell you my story still, I really would. I see it all in my mind, but saying the words—it's too hard."

A thought came to her as he spoke, a far-fetched idea plucked from the recesses of her mind. Still, it was worth a try. She patted Mr. Ivey's back. "I'm not ready to give up on you yet. I'm going to get someone who might be of help."

Mr. Ivey nodded and crept up onto his bed, his eyes closed the whole time. Norah marched out of the room, intent on finding the individual in question.

He was not hard to find. Mr. Lyster, Rodney, and LJ were playing cards at the table.

"Just the man I was looking for!" crowed Mr. Lyster before confusion crossed his face. "Now, why'd I say that?"

Norah placed her palms on the table, leaning forward with a crafty smile. "Because those are my thoughts, Mr. Lyster," she replied. "Do you have some time to spare?"

He quirked his mouth to one side and glanced at his cards, before throwing them on the table. "I fold, boys."

Rodney and LJ grumbled about their companion's desertion of the game, but Norah took no notice. She grasped Mr. Lyster's sleeve and guided him toward Mr. Ivey's room.

"Hey, where are we going?" he asked.

She stopped at the room's threshold. "Mr. Lyster, have you ever touched someone while reading their mind?"

He furrowed his brow. "Can't say as I have. Why?"

"We're about to find out what happens. I need Mr. Ivey's story, but he needs help telling it. Can you be that help?"

"I'll do my best. I have all the faith in the world." He narrowed his eyes. "That wasn't my thought."

She smirked before opening the door. "No, it was mine. Come on."

Mr. Ivey was in the same position he had been in when Norah had left. She directed Mr. Lyster to sit next to him on the bed.

"Hullo, Marvin," the Englishman greeted with his usual cheek. "Had any good dreams lately?"

"Behave, Mr. Lyster," Norah gently chided. "Mr. Ivey, I'm going to see if Mr. Lyster can help you tell your story. Perhaps he can say what is difficult for you to say on your own."

"It won't work," both men said simultaneously.

Norah clucked her tongue. "Such pessimism. We shall see. Now, Mr. Ivey. You were telling us that you and your wife were sailing around Africa when she lost her wedding ring. What happened next?"

Mr. Ivey clenched his shut eyelids. "Blood. Fire. Blood ..."

Norah pointedly looked at Mr. Lyster. "Would you place a hand on him for comfort? It seems to help."

Mr. Lyster raised his hand hesitantly, choosing to place it on Mr. Ivey's arm. Mr. Ivey stopped muttering the two words and let out a shaky breath.

Then, to Norah's surprise, Mr. Lyster did too.

"Ohhh, wow," he breathed, also shutting his eyes.

"What is it?" Norah asked in a hushed tone.

The ginger man moved his head from side to side. "I can *see* things. So much blood. So much death."

Drat. If Mr. Lyster became consumed with Mr. Ivey's visions, this experiment would be useless. "Let's focus. Mr. Ivey? What happened to the ring?"

Mr. Ivey stayed still and quiet, other than a small whimper.

Mr. Lyster said, "We were only supposed to stop at certain ports on our sailing trip. But Violet became distraught over the ring. I decided to stop in German East Africa, the closest colony."

Norah held her breath. Her idea actually seemed to be working.

Lyster continued, "We knew no German, or any of the African languages. But there were some people there who spoke English. One was a chap named Metzger, who seemed to be a man of many talents in the town we stopped in. He also happened to own a shop of various and random trinkets."

Mr. Lyster opened his eyes, removing his hand from Mr. Ivey as he did, and let out a heavy breath. "That's disturbing, Norah," he said, his usual brusque demeanor replaced with a shaky nervousness. "I can call you that, right? Malcolm and Rodney do."

She smiled in the low light. "Of course, but only if I can call you Ambrose. What is it, though? What's disturbing?"

He shook his head, giving pause to find words. "I'm used to errant thoughts coming out my mouth, but to *see* them, clear as day. Well, not exactly clear. People, they're fuzzed out. Marvin fixates on his wife, and on certain objects, but the rest is dreamlike."

"When you speak, are you describing what you see?" she asked.

"No. Those are Marvin's words, plucked from his head. That part of my curse stays the same. I'm just not used to the visuals."

He truly seemed shaken up. Norah hated putting anyone in a position like this. She got up from her chair and sat by Ambrose, putting her hand on his. "Are you able to keep going?"

He let out a strangled sound and shot his eyes to hers before yanking his hand away, breaking their connection. "Good lord," he uttered.

Norah felt the blood drain from her face. She had touched him without thinking, even as they discussed Ambrose's discovery. She wanted to kick herself. "What did you see?" Her words came out as a whisper.

"Enough," Ambrose whispered back. He cleared his throat with a shoulder shrug. "It's nothing that wasn't bound to come out sooner or later with me around."

Norah hadn't thought about that before. She was beginning to see why having a man with Ambrose's misfortune around was a risky endeavor. Still, it was not his fault. She had to remember that.

He saw the panic etched into her face. "I won't say anything," he assured her. "It's your secret to tell. I don't blurt out things once I know them. Usually." He tried to look encouraging as he repeated, "It's your secret to tell, not mine."

She nodded and stood, moving back to the safety of her chair. "Thank you, Ambrose."

"I'm ready to continue if you are," he said, hovering a hand over Mr. Ivey's cowering form.

"Mr. Ivey?" Norah asked. "Are you well enough to continue?"

Despite his body language, Ivey gave a definitive nod of his head.

Ambrose placed his hand back into position, the frown returning instantly. "Mr. Metzger was kind enough to find us a ring to replace the one Violet lost. It was beautiful, a large diamond on a gold band.

Much too expensive for us, of course. But Metzger insisted we take it for a trifling of what it was worth."

Norah sighed. "It was cursed, wasn't it?"

Ivey nodded again, the only form of communication he seemed to be able to generate in the moment, but Ambrose spoke his words for him. "Yes. The diamond in question had been collected from the mines by child slaves, and it inflicted a heavy toll upon anyone who would wear it. My poor Violet. She was so young and sweet. She could not shoulder the burden of the ring. Within a week, I found her in our berth, her blood pooling on the wooden floor, her lifeless eyes staring forever at the ceiling."

"Good lord." Norah pressed her fingers to her lips, her heart breaking for Mr. Ivey.

Ambrose continued, "I turned around and sailed back to the German colony, wanting to kill the man who had killed my Violet. He expected me, it seemed. When I told him what happened, he laughed."

Ivey began to sob.

Ambrose's voice grew husky. "He knew the ring was cursed. He knew what it would do. He told me his entire shop was cursed, and then he grabbed me, and ... we fought. There, in the shop. I got a couple of punches in, but I was thrown into tables and touched god knows how many objects. I ended up passing out, and I awoke on a beach, far away from the German colony, with no recollection of how I got there.

"It was through sheer luck that I was spotted by a passing ship and rescued. On our journey, I saw my yacht. It had been burned, just a washed-up shell. And me? My visions began to plague me the moment I spoke with another person. They became worse as time went on. I was no longer able to live my life. In desperation, my family took me here in January of last year. My final resting place."

"No, Mr. Ivey," Norah soothed. "Surely there is hope to grasp onto."

Ambrose opened his eyes and disconnected from Mr. Ivey. "What hope, Norah?" he asked skeptically. "This man has had the worst of it, if you ask me. He doesn't even know what cursed him. Do you, Marvin?"

Mr. Ivey shook his head with a small sob.

Norah pursed her lips. "After what I assume you gleaned from me, Ambrose, you should know I'm not one to give up. And neither should any of you. Mr. Ivey, thank you for telling me your story. I know it wasn't easy."

"I did all the hard bits, though." Ambrose grumbled.

Norah gave him a wry smile. "And thank you, Ambrose, for doing the hard bits. I couldn't have done it without you."

Ambrose waved her words away. "If my curse can bring someone help instead of the usual hindrance, it lightens my load."

"Indeed. You see? Hope. You have some, too." She stood, motioning for Ambrose to do the same. "I will stay with Mr. Ivey until he is calmed again. You may leave if you wish, Ambrose."

He did, and quickly. She surmised the task may have been too much for the man. As she sat by Mr. Ivey, she wondered what exactly it was that he had seen when she touched him.

It worried her.

CHAPTER TWENTY-FIVE

Thursday, April 15th, 1915

Malcolm

MALCOLM DEBATED TAKING HIS work—a loose definition, if ever there was one—elsewhere in order to get some peace and quiet. Norah had a tendency to interrupt him every chance she got these days. In any other woman, this habit would have already driven him mad. But with Norah, she was the only reason he did not fully wish for peace and quiet.

After lunch, as if on cue, she announced herself to his office once again. He smiled at her, but her shrewdness picked up on the tired overtone of the gesture.

"Is something wrong, Malcolm?"

He shook his head and looked down at the papers in front of him. "Norah. Do you recall my ... sullenness over certain calendar dates from our brief history?"

She snorted and settled herself into the chair. "If you are referring to Valentine's Day, it's been burned into my mind."

"And don't forget my fiancée's departure's anniversary."

"That goes without saying. I had a terrible headache from that one."

He chuckled. "Well, in the spirit of me turning over a new leaf when it comes to my interactions with you, let me please give you a modicum of warning."

She leaned forward. "I'm listening."

He turned his full attention to her, the smile he resurrected not quite reaching his eyes. "Tomorrow is the anniversary of my mother's passing."

She leaned back, a worry crease marking the space between her eyes. "I see. That *would* be a distressing day for you. Mercy, this string of months is not kind to you, is it?"

He grimaced. "Precisely."

"Do you have more tragic anniversaries to fill the rest of the months?" she teased.

Her forced insouciance was clearly targeted at lightening his mood. It worked, to a degree. He answered, 'No, not at the moment, anyway."

She gave a slow nod of her head, her mind at work. "What are your plans for tomorrow? What can I do to help?" Her tone was back to serious.

Malcolm sighed as he leaned back in his creaking chair. The fact that Norah was thinking of him first was a balm on his darkening mood. He assumed she meant to help him through this in any way possible.

"I would like to place flowers on her grave," he said after a moment's thought.

"A venture outside, then?"

"I promise it will be brief. But will you attend with me?"

Norah's eyebrows shot up. "You wish for me to visit your mother with you on this somber occasion?"

"Yes."

She paused. "Why?"

Her reticence tamped his mood back down. "Look, you don't have to—"

"Malcolm." His name in her voice buoyed him like none other. He looked at her. She had a knowing smirk on her face, but it was not born of malice. "I would be honored. I assumed you would want to take the day to spend alone, with your mother's spirit, of course."

"That's the thing of it," he said, running a hand down his face. He'd forgotten to shave again, and the rasp was audible to the room. "I've spent the last five years alone with my mother's grave, alone with my thoughts. I don't wish for that this year. I'd like company. I'd like ... you."

As soon as the words left his mouth he wished to swallow them whole, but they were already loose in the room. They made Norah go silent again, her eyes widening fractionally.

He tried to corral them before they could do any damage, anyway. "I mean, I've never let anyone else truly know my predicament. Your confidentiality has allowed you to see *me*. You sleep in my mother's room. You helped me tidy her resting place. I can think of no better person to share my misery with."

She clasped a hand to her heart. "That is quite possibly the sweetest thing anyone has ever said to me."

He eyed her suspiciously. "I can't quite tell if you are joking."

"I am not."

"Then, madam, you have perhaps lived a more melancholy life than even I have."

She scoffed. "I'm not sure where you got the impression that I have had a life of gaiety. My parents died, my brother is cursed, and I was born into a sex that does not allow me to carry out my full potential."

He snapped his fingers. "It's your never-ending optimism in the face of such atrocities, I do believe, that has allowed me to see only the good in your life."

She smiled with a small head shake. "And that is perhaps the second sweetest thing anyone has ever said to me."

Norah

"By the way," Norah said casually as she tried to quell the warmth in her heart over Malcolm's offer, "I did have a reason for barging in on you today."

Malcolm looked back up from his papers. She often wondered what it was he did in this stuffy room. Surely a gentleman with generational wealth did not need to work for a living. And seeing as how he was trapped within the house, there couldn't be much he could do. Still, he never offered to explain, and she never asked.

"What is it?" he enquired with a wry quirk of his mouth.

She fiddled with the hem of her sleeve. "There's to be a doctor coming around in four days' time. A surgeon, to be more specific. I figured, seeing as how this is your establishment, you should be in the know."

He stared at Norah as if she'd just mentioned she was growing another head. She stopped picking at her sleeve to bestow an innocent smile upon him, which made him pucker his lips, a sure sign he was containing a grin of his own.

"And why, pray tell, is a surgeon coming to visit?"

"Oh," she said, suddenly coy, "I've had a thought."

"You have a great many of those, it seems. What is this particular thought about?"

"Well," she began, once more casting her eyes anywhere but on Malcolm. She wasn't sure why she was so nervous to share her idea. LJ certainly would have brushed her off or laughed at her thought process, but Malcolm was different. She could see that now. "It's for Mr. Hunt. He tells me the letter opener has a taste for his blood." She shook her head, suddenly too shy to say the actual plan. Instead, she improvised. "I thought, what if he loses too much?"

Malcolm grunted. "He would die, same as anyone who loses too much blood."

"Yes, exactly." Norah pointed an excited finger at Malcolm. "But the war in Europe has had some breakthroughs in ... oh, I don't know what to call it ... blood care? The point is, the doctors over there are sometimes able to save a man's life by giving him someone else's blood."

Malcolm made a disgusted face. "They can do that?"

"Oh yes. But not just anybody's blood, as it turns out. It must be someone they are compatible with."

"Compatible?"

She shrugged her shoulders. "I'm not entirely sure of the notion, either. Anyway, the reason the surgeon is visiting is to see if Mr. Hunt is compatible with anyone else at Birchwald. Just in case."

"Just in case."

"Yes." His sudden taciturn nature was proving to be vexing in the moment. She was glad she did not bring up her true idea just yet.

He sighed and scrubbed a hand down his face once more, his dark whiskers making a scratching sound against his palm. "Norah, may I be honest with you? I ... have a bit of a phobia."

"Oh?"

He nodded and clenched his neck muscles, exposing his eye teeth on one side. "Needles. I don't care for them."

"Malcolm Drury, brave adventurer, scared of a little needle poke?" she teased.

He frowned. "I do believe we've established I am in fact not an adventurer."

"My mistake. Brave *pretend* adventurer. Is that better?"

He blinked at her, the frown still prevalent.

She chuckled. "I'll be sure to test the other members first, oh brave one. Chances are good we'll find a match with someone else. Including me."

She stood, smoothing out her skirts. "And with that news for you to digest, I'll see myself out. Enjoy your afternoon."

He only hmphed at her as she closed the door behind her.

CHAPTER TWENTY-SIX

Friday, April 16th, 1915

Malcolm

MALCOLM OFTEN DIDN'T LET his curse ruin his existence. For certain, it stifled him, but he was able to lead a productive life, regardless. It was only on days like today that he truly felt the brunt of his misfortune.

His mother had loved flowers. He wished he could have sent out for a hothouse bouquet, but his prudence had won out over the unnecessary expense. Asters were of course her favorite, but it was the wrong season for their cheerful blossoms. As he fixed his tie in front of the mirror, he mumbled, "Ma, why did you have to die in the spring? Couldn't you have waited for the fall?" *Or, better yet, not have died at all,* he amended silently.

She would have been fifty-six years old right now. Sometimes he imagined she was still alive, a vibrant, bustling woman, her steel-gray hair wound upon her head, her dresses of the utmost fashion. Malcolm had inherited her eyes, and upon her countenance, those gray orbs saw everything, hawklike around the help, but always soft for Malcolm.

The ache in his chest intensified.

With a sigh, he stopped fiddling with his tie and left his dressing room, ready to say hello and goodbye to his mother all over again.

In the hallway outside his bedroom door, Norah waited. She turned around at his exit, and with great shock, Malcolm saw that her arms were overbrimming with flowers. Bright yellow daffodils, boughs of forsythia, purple hellebore, and tulips in at least three varying shades practically spilled out of her grasp.

"What is this?" Malcolm asked, his voice lacking in its usual strength.

She blushed and glanced down at the blooms. "I assumed you'd want to grace your mother's grave with flowers. I didn't want you to stay out for longer than was necessary, so I gathered some for you. I only wish I had asters."

"The season is all wrong," Malcolm said, his voice just louder than a whisper.

"Precisely. I hope these will do." She shrugged to draw attention back to the colorful blossoms.

Malcolm felt the tell-tale pricking of his eyes but willed the tears to stay at bay. "These will do just fine," he assured her. "Thank you."

She nodded, apparently at a loss for words. She shuffled the stalks around until one arm was freed. This she held out to him. "Shall we?"

He gratefully took it.

Norah

Norah had never seen Malcolm with such emotion. She had witnessed him drowning out his sorrows with alcohol—something, she realized, he hadn't done in over a month—and she had seen him use his anger as a shield for his anguish. But, in this moment, Malcolm dropped all his façades, allowing his true grief to shine through.

He laid the flowers with reverence on top of his mother's grave, rearranging them into an artful splay. He took a moment to brush a clump of lichen off the top of the gravestone, but otherwise the stone was much the same as it had been when Norah had last seen it. She read the inscription once again: *Paula Maureen Drury, born July 8th, 1858, died April 16th, 1909. She lives on in the memories of her son.*

The last line was odd, in her opinion.

With hands clasped in front of him, Malcolm cleared his throat. A husky quality still remained as he spoke. "Ma. I wish you were still here. You were taken from me too young. It's been six years since you died, and my life has forever changed. I miss you."

Norah's throat was tight as she tried to swallow.

"Wherever you are, I hope you are well, Ma. And I'm okay. I'll never be the same, but I'll survive. I love you, Ma."

With these last words, Norah saw the tears begin to fall from the man's eyes. He did nothing to hide them, only stood in silent grief.

Norah also stood beside him, not daring to break the quiet. She jumped when Malcolm addressed her, though.

"Do you visit your parents?"

She did not look over at him, continuing her vigil over the flower-be-decked grave. "No. I could, if I wanted to. They are buried in Green-Wood Cemetery, in Brooklyn. But I was a young child when they died, and even when they were alive, they did not have much to do with us."

Norah had never questioned this before. Her parents left the raising of their twins to nannies even while they lived. Her father had been ab-sent for much of her first five years, off traveling the globe. And Angela, her mother, had her sweet moments, but overall would have been better off being a vapid socialite with no motherly duties.

Norah's outlook, now that she was truly reflecting upon it, was skewed. She did not feel any love toward her lost parents. All her familial love was reserved for LJ and Aunt Nell. But now that Malcolm was here, with his heart overflowing with love for his deceased mother, Norah for the first time felt like there was something wrong with her.

But Malcolm's words refuted her notion. "It's how I feel about my father, honestly. I understand." He turned toward her, the wetness on his cheeks shining in the spring sunshine. "Norah, thank you for being here with me today. I appreciate this more than you can imagine."

She smiled, the gesture laced with sadness. "It has been my honor, Malcolm. Are you ready to return home?"

He stepped closer, his form towering over hers. His hands reached out and softly touched the sides of her face before he leaned forward. Norah's heart gave a lurch as his lips tenderly brushed her forehead in a small kiss. The lurching was followed by a quick-beat march as she felt a warmth spread from the epicenter of the kiss, enflaming her heart with its afterglow.

On the outside, she tried to remain calm, an undisturbed pool of water.

He straightened and released her face as quickly as he had kissed her. The look he bestowed upon her was of tenderness, an even greater vulnerability than the tears. He smiled at her as he said, "Now I am."

CHAPTER TWENTY-SEVEN

Monday, April 19th, 1915

Norah

ON THE DAY THE surgeon visited, Hector Freeman awoke with a fever.

His curse had been gradually creeping up his legs, and the last time Norah had pried, he'd admitted it was nearly to his hip joints. That was over a month ago.

She was ashamed to admit she hadn't thought much about Hector's condition recently. There was a lot on her mind these days, what with a brooding brother, Rodney's continuing change, and Mr. Ivey's revelations. That wasn't even mentioning the man who encompassed much of her waking thoughts anymore. Still, Hector was ailing, even when he seemed hale, and Norah should have known to check on him more often.

Hector did not blame her one bit. He lounged as best he could in his bed, the sheets tucked around his stone legs. The knees had fossilized at a slight bend, which Norah could see as two gentle hills in the landscape of the bed. Hector still had mobility at the waist, which allowed him to lie otherwise flat. Sweat beaded off his balding forehead as he patted her hand gently.

"I warned you when we met, Norah. I guess my time is running out."

She shook her head in denial. "And I warned you, Hector, that I am not one to give up so easily. How far up does it go now?"

He groaned as he motioned to his hips. "I'm not sure I'll be able to use my chair for much longer. I may have to be bed bound, otherwise I'll be permanently bent at the waist, and I'll be forced to live out my days in the chair."

Norah glanced at the wheelchair in question, sitting sedately by the bed. Without Hector in it, it nearly took on a personality of its own, with two movable legs that seemed like a parody of human legs, large metal wheels, and a rattan backrest. She couldn't imagine being stuck in the thing permanently. Comfort would be lacking.

She did not voice any of this. "Hold tight, Hector," she said instead. "We shall see what we can do."

When the surgeon arrived at half past eleven, Norah made sure to answer the door herself, much to Mathers' horror. She opened the door wide, allowing the small, bespectacled man in tweed to enter.

"Dr. Wrightly. How good of you to come," she greeted.

He looked her up and down, his thick mustache twitching as he set a large black bag down next to his feet. "I take it you are the lady of the house? I have an appointment with Mr. Abernathy."

She quirked her mouth. "I am Miss Norah Abernathy, Doctor. I was the one in correspondence with you last week."

He squinted his eyes. "*N.J.* Abernathy? Beg your pardon, miss, but I was not expecting you to be a woman."

Norah flattened her lips.

From behind her, Malcolm proclaimed, "I know that feeling well."

The doctor turned to look at the new speaker. Malcolm came down the hallway, his suit immaculate, his face shaved without a hint of stubble, and a disarming twinkle in his eye, one that Norah might have mistaken for malice once upon a time. He held out a hand.

"Malcolm Drury, at your service. *I* am the master of Birchwald."

Dr. Wrightly shook it, a smile forming behind his mustache. "Well met, sir. *Miss* Abernathy was most adamant that I come today. Something about you needing my help with blood-related sciences. I do hope you have approved my visit, and my time has not been wasted."

Malcolm, being a head taller than the doctor, glanced over him at Norah, a knowing look reserved for her. "Miss Abernathy is a trusted guest of my home, Doctor. I hope you had a pleasant trip to get here. Might I ask, where exactly did she find you?"

Dr. Wrightly glanced at Norah. "I work in Croton Falls, so it's hardly a trip."

Norah felt the need to chime in, "Dr. Wrightly has had a brilliant career in New York City. I've heard wonderful things about your work in pioneering medicine, Doctor."

The man stood straighter. "Indeed? I wasn't aware I had a fan in such a remote destination."

"It was the reason I reached out to you. That, and your current location. It is most serendipitous."

Malcolm, watching the conversation, cut in. "As a prestigious surgeon, it seems strange to have you stationed so far away from the city."

Dr. Wrightly's glasses slipped down his nose as he puffed up at Malcolm's insinuation, like a cat. "Yes, well. There are *some* in the medical community that look down upon advancing techniques. I ruffled a few feathers in the city. That, and I decided I was due the peace and quiet of small-town living."

Norah knew all of this from her research of the doctor. It did not sway her opinion at all. "There will be small-minded individuals who take every opportunity to look down their noses at innovation, Dr. Wrightly. You'll find no such small-mindedness at Birchwald."

The doctor seemed mollified by her words.

"I assume you are aware of what Birchwald is, Doctor?" Malcolm asked.

The surgeon nodded as he pushed up his wire spectacles. "I believe everyone in Croton Falls knows about the Guild, Mr. Drury. It's God's work you do here, helping the unfortunates."

Malcolm scoffed.

Norah replied for him, "Mr. Drury would indeed do all in his power to see his men be happy and healthy. Which is why I'm incredibly grateful for your visit today. Did you bring the necessary supplies for the task at hand?"

The doctor responded by lifting the black bag again.

She nodded. "Wonderful. Won't you please follow me, then? I'll lead you to the third floor, where the members reside. Some of them have mobility issues."

"I'm well equipped for walking, madam."

A thought struck her. "Oh, may I ask for one more favor? One of the wards is feeling poorly today, with a fever. Could I ask you to examine him when it is his turn to test?"

Dr. Wrightly twitched his mustache from side to side.

Norah added, "I'll compensate you for the extra work, of course."

He visibly brightened. "Of course. Semi-retirement has not been as lucrative as I'd hoped it to be."

Norah nodded knowingly.

Malcolm

Malcolm kept a close eye on the doctor as he approached each patient. He was not used to being around medical professionals, and while he trusted Norah's instincts, he was not fully keen on this particular man, given his apparent fall from medical grace. Still, Malcolm had to admit, he seemed to know what he was doing.

Norah instructed the doctor to use one of the tables in the communal area to set up his equipment while she fetched Farley first. The cursed man came easily enough, although he eyed the large syringe and attached needle with some trepidation.

"Miss Abernathy tells me you are the one in possible need of a transfusion," Dr. Wrightly said with some gentleness. "I'm afraid that means I'll have to take a larger sample from you."

"I'm used to bloodletting, doc. Just do me a favor and squeeze a couple of drops out onto this letter opener when you're finished, if you don't mind," Farley responded, removing said object from his pocket and setting it on the table next to the rest of the tools. He patted the handle with fondness.

Dr. Wrightly raised an eyebrow but said nothing of the odd request.

Within moments, the surgeon had everything set up. Farley sat and offered his exposed arm, around which Dr. Wrightly tightly tied a piece of rubber tubing. "Make a fist for me," he instructed. "That's good, Mr. Hunt. Are you ready?"

Farley looked away. "As I'm ever."

Malcolm also looked away as the surgeon raised the syringe to jab into Farley's arm. His eyes landed on the various small beakers lined up, each one empty. "Say, Doctor. What exactly are we testing for?"

"Steady, Mr. Hunt. I almost have enough ... there. Miss Abernathy, would you be so kind as to hold this gauze here for a moment? Wonderful." Malcolm turned back to witness Dr. Wrightly emptying the bright red contents of the syringe into the largest beaker. "Apologies for not answering right away, Mr. Drury. I wanted to make sure I had my full attention on the job at hand."

Malcolm's stomach gave a little lurch at the sight of the blood. "Quite alright."

Dr. Wrightly picked up the beaker and swirled it, inspecting it closely. "What we are doing here is checking for a crossmatch. There are different types of blood, Mr. Drury, and not everyone has the same type. When one is preparing to give a patient someone else's blood, it is important the two bloods get along. Otherwise, the consequences could be disastrous. Fatal, even." He set the beaker down and turned his attention back to Farley. "Your part is done, my good man. Thank you for your donation."

Farley stood. "Don't forget my letter opener, doc."

Dr. Wrightly picked up the syringe, shaking the tip until the remaining dregs fell on the blade. "I won't ask," he commented.

Satisfied, Farley picked up Bloodletter.

"Farley, would you please send Señor Reyes over?" Norah asked him. He nodded as he departed.

On a piece of paper, the doctor wrote, "Reyes." He tucked this under one of the smaller beakers.

"How does it work, though?" Malcolm asked, intrigued despite his squeamishness. He had never heard of the notion of different types of blood. It all looked the same to him.

"It's simple enough. I will be mixing small quantities of blood together to see if they clot. Blood, Mr. Drury, is notorious for clotting, as I'm sure you are aware."

"Indeed I am. As a matter of fact, won't the blood clot on its own?"

The doctor nodded. "Luckily, last year one of my colleagues discovered that mixing in a little sodium citrate prevents clotting of blood. I added some to Mr. Hunt's beaker, because I did not want his clotting.

Not yet, anyway." He chuckled. "I find blood to be fascinating. I am a huge proponent of cross-matching before any transfusions. Unfortunately, some of my associates don't feel the same way. But despite being pressured out of the medical community for my convictions, I still believe matches are necessary to save lives." He clucked his tongue. "I do hope my European counterparts learn that soon enough, otherwise war casualties will skyrocket."

Malcolm had never thought of this before. He was beginning to see why Norah chose him.

Pablo Reyes appeared and sat in the same seat that Farley had vacated. "What is this?"

Norah took over the explanation. "Señor, we are testing for compatibility of blood, for Mr. Hunt's sake. Can we take a small sample of yours?"

Pablo agreed with the added proposal to Norah, as usual. Dr. Wrightly looked slightly scandalized but stayed professional and said nothing about the exchange.

As soon as Pablo's blood was collected—a much smaller portion, Malcolm noted—it was ejected into the beaker, and the doctor immediately poured a small amount of Farley's blood into the same vessel, giving it a swirl.

"Now, we wait an hour. And in the meantime, we'll test everyone else."

Malcolm watched over each man getting his sample taken—all but Karanja and Withers. Karanja refused politely—stating something about taboos—and he also insisted Mr. Withers could not consent. Dr. Wrightly seemed oddly relieved to leave the two be. Norah went next, stoically sitting still as the needle jabbed into her. Malcolm could not watch the act, but he kept his eyes locked with Norah's and felt a welling of pride for how brave she was.

Finally, it was his turn. His heart pounding, he sat in the chair and rolled up his sleeve.

"This will take but a moment, Mr. Drury," the doctor soothed, perhaps noticing his nervousness.

Malcolm squeezed his eyes closed as Dr. Wrightly's cold hand fastened the rubber tubing in place. He felt the burning sting of the sharp needle, and then a lingering ache, but nothing worse. He let out a breath.

"Very good, Mr. Drury. Just a bit more ... there." The doctor removed the needle, and Malcolm felt the pressure of gauze on his arm. "Very good, sir."

Malcolm opened his eyes, seeing Norah smile at him as she held the gauze in place.

That alone made the temporary pain worth it.

"If that's everyone, we still have ... oh, twenty minutes before the first test is ready," Dr. Wrightly said, checking his pocket watch. "Shall we do a follow-up of Mr. Freeman while we wait, Miss Abernathy?"

They both stood. Malcolm waved at Norah. "Go ahead. I'll stay here."

He watched the various beakers, each holding the deep red blood of his companions. The science still eluded him, even with the doctor's explanation, but he at least had trust in the process. He dared not touch the tests, for fear of inadvertently befouling the results.

When the time came, Dr. Wrightly checked each beaker—starting with Reyes and going down the line—by picking it up and giving it a swirl. Even Malcolm could see the large globs that now floated within the viscous liquids in each beaker. As the surgeon moved down the line of samples, and each one looked the same, Malcolm's hope for a match diminished.

Only the last test, the one labeled "Drury," held no clumps.

Malcolm was a match.

CHAPTER TWENTY-EIGHT

Friday, April 23rd, 1915

Norah

A PART OF NORAH was pleased that Malcolm was the match for Mr. Hunt. It was the subversive side of her, the twisted persona that laughed at the irony of the one person who was afraid of needles being the only one who might just need to be poked in the near future. *Schadenfreude*, as the Germans called it, albeit a mild version.

A larger part of her was annoyed. Now she would need to fully explain her plan to him. None of the other men would have questioned her ideas. Or perhaps they would have, but she had the suspicion they'd have acquiesced anyway. But Malcolm? She wasn't sure.

She joined him in the dining room at lunchtime. Malcolm did not always eat his lunch here, but lately he had been hiding less in his private rooms and taking the time to be sociable. Norah wasn't sure what had changed.

She sat abruptly at the chair to his right, as he went to take a bite of roast chicken sandwich, leftovers from the previous night's dinner. He paused before biting down and reluctantly placed the sandwich back on the plate. "Was there something I could help you with?"

She smiled her best disarming smile. "I hope so. Do you remember earlier in the week, when you were a match for Mr. Hunt?"

Malcolm set his sandwich down, giving her his full attention. "How could I forget? You only forced a doctor to extract my blood. Painfully."

"Hm, yes. Has your bruise faded yet?"

His lips flattened at her frivolousness. "It's yellowed. Almost gone."

"Mine too. Well, I shan't keep you too long. But I did want to let you know, I have a plan for breaking Mr. Hunt's curse. Shall I tell you now, or would you like to eat in peace?"

Malcolm eyed her suspiciously. "I would love to eat in peace, mind you, but you've already broken it with your presence." He grinned to take away the sting of his words. "And I won't know peace until you tell me your plan. But why do I get the feeling it somehow involves me?"

He was shrewd. "Because it does, that's why."

Malcolm sighed as he gazed at his unfinished sandwich.

Norah huffed. "For goodness sake, Malcolm, you can eat while I talk!"

He waited for a heartbeat before picking it up and taking a big bite, keeping eye contact with her while he did.

She nodded her approval. "Very good. Well. Where to begin? Oh yes," she said as Malcolm's eyes became stormy with her delays. "Mr. Hunt's letter opener is attuned to his blood only, correct? He claims it likes the taste of it. Or something equally sinister. But what if we were to give him a transfusion?"

Malcolm stopped chewing and put his sandwich down again. "Are you asking to take some of my blood and place it in Farley?"

Norah scratched the side of her face. "That *is* the definition of a transfusion, yes."

"I don't like it." Malcolm gazed at her, a stray crumb of bread stuck to his lip. Norah fought the urge to reach over and dislodge it. His words crashed around her, breaking her from the impulsive thought.

"What do you mean?" she asked with a hint of whine. She hated that. She did not whine, not even to get her way.

"Norah, have you really thought this through?" Malcolm said, a bit of gentleness seeping from his voice. "The blade could react dangerously to its source being tampered with. It could latch onto *me* instead, and that is not something I want to have happen." He shuddered.

In her excitement over a possible solution, Norah had not quite thought things through. Malcolm had a point, damn his handsome eyes. "We can't be certain those things will happen," she countered weakly.

He shook his head. "We can't be certain they won't either. No, Norah, when it comes to Farley, we must tread lightly. Now," he said, patting her hand, which she had placed on the table, "if Farley is in *need* of a transfusion, if the Bloodletter gets its way and takes too much to the point where his life is in peril, by all means, I am a willing donor. But until then, I will not be volunteering myself to take on another curse. Nor would I want anyone else to do the same. Do you understand?"

Norah looked away, her teeth worrying at her lower lip. "I understand."

He placed his hand solidly on her own, the warmth of it seeping deep into her skin. "I admire where your heart is at," he soothed. "The crossmatch was a good idea, I admit. Without it, the odds were high that he would have gotten bad blood in the event of a transfusion. Because as much as I'd like to say I'd be brave otherwise, given the choice I would not have allowed that doctor to stick me with a needle."

Norah looked back at him, her smile returning. "Thank you."

Malcolm looked up and past Norah sharply, his hand suddenly disappearing from her own. The sudden absence of its heat was staggering. She turned to discover it was Mathers that Malcolm was focused on.

"Pardon the intrusion, sir," the butler said. "Miss Abernathy has a visitor."

"Me?" Norah practically squeaked. "Who?"

Mathers inclined his head. "Your aunt, miss."

Malcolm

As Norah marched ahead with anticipation, Malcolm matched the more sedate speed of his butler. "What time did she arrive?" he asked in quiet tones.

"Just now, sir. I hope it was prudent to announce her arrival while you were entertaining Miss Abernathy. I admit I was not expecting the two of you to be together when I found you."

Malcolm snorted. "I hardly think it matters, old boy. You did well."

They turned the bend and went up the steps to the vestibule as Norah let out a girlish noise of delight and quickly closed the distance to hug the person waiting there. Malcolm only saw a glimpse of the other woman before Norah's height blocked his view. Then all he could see were the stranger's arms, which stiltedly patted Norah's back in an attempt at returned affection.

Norah let her aunt go and backed up a pace, revealing a much shorter woman, pale and perfect. Her black hair peeked from a short-brimmed hat with a see-through veil that fell to her chin, only slightly obscuring her face from view. She was dressed in a hobble skirt of deep blue, and her black travel boots were topped by a velvet of similar color.

"Aunt Nell," Norah exclaimed. "I was not expecting you! How are you here?"

Malcolm could not wrap his mind around this lovely woman being Norah's ancient aunt. She appeared even younger than Norah.

The woman in question lifted her veil, and Malcolm felt his body give a lurch. She was captivating to look upon, her eyes large, her mouth almost button-shaped, and her nose small and shapely.

She crinkled her eyes at Norah. "I made arrangements as soon as I received your letter, gel. A marked improvement over the last, I must say." She looked around, noticing Malcolm for the first time. She remained impassive, awaiting introductions.

Norah turned to see Malcolm as well. "Oh, Aunt Nell, this is Malcolm Drury, the owner of Birchwald. Mr. Drury, this is my Aunt Nell. Eleanora Montmorency, that is."

Malcolm stepped forward to take her hand. Up close, she still held beauty, but her eyes were a tad disarming, with a marked yellowing of the sclera and an overall cloudiness. He also caught a whiff of perfume, sweet to the point of corruption. The legend was true. This woman was not exactly alive. He managed to school his features as he brought the gloved hand to his lips. "Miss Montmorency. A true pleasure to make your acquaintance."

Nell allowed him the old-fashioned greeting as she looked him up and down, her girlish face still neutral. "The president, I take it?" Her voice was raspy and much too old to be coming from someone so youthful.

"One and the same."

"Hm," she said with a sniff. "Mr. Drury, I do hope it wasn't too imposing of me to drop by unannounced like this."

He bowed his head. "Not at all. You are welcome to stay for a visit, if you wish."

"Very magnanimous of you. I trust you are being just as gracious to my niece?"

Malcolm suddenly felt very put on the spot. He glanced beyond Nell at Norah, who had a knowing smirk on her face. "Ah, yes. Of course. Norah has been a welcome addition to Birchwald."

"*Norah* has, has she?" Nell responded, catching Malcolm's lack of formality. "Well, I am pleased to hear that."

"Say, Mathers," Malcolm said as he turned to his butler, needing to take some of the attention off himself, "why don't you set Miss Montmorency up in the Iris Room?"

Mathers bowed and took the one bag next to Nell. She turned and said, "There's one more trunk outside."

"Thank you, madam," Mathers replied as he carried the bag away to set up the room for her.

"Aunt Nell, won't you please come up to my room? I have so much to tell you," Norah asked, her demeanor changing to that of someone much younger around her relative. It amused Malcolm.

Nell fanned herself with her hand. "It has been quite the ordeal in getting here, gel. I'd be delighted to put my feet up for a moment. Lead the way." She looked at Malcolm. "I'm sure we'll see each other again soon."

He could only nod and make noises in his throat as she and Norah walked away side by side. As soon as she was out of sight, he felt his mind clearing. He said out loud, "What on earth just happened?"

Norah

"So," Norah said conversationally as they walked up the stairs, "have you found a new suitor yet?"

She heard Aunt Nell blow out a derogatory breath. "Oh, men always fall over themselves, but you know me."

Norah reached the gallery and turned to wait for her aunt, who walked much slower due to her horrible hobble skirt. The style had already gone out of fashion in the States, she was pleased to see, but Aunt Nell sometimes liked to cling to outdated trends.

She linked arms and led her toward the Aster Room. "I do know you, Aunt. I'm honestly surprised you've waited this long for another Mr. Right to come along."

"Listen, gel. When you are as old as I am, you learn two truths. One, all men are the same. And two, sometimes your personal welfare can be improved by removing them from your life."

Norah grinned but kept her head forward. "I'll agree with you to a point. After living in this house, however, I no longer believe they are all the same."

"Oh no?" Aunt Nell peered up at her as Norah opened the door to her room. "I thought I'd raised you better than that. And which of these fine men changed your mind on that one? Not the stunningly handsome president of this establishment, hm?"

Norah closed the door behind them, her face blooming with heat. "Malcolm is ... nice. A bit of a brute at times, but he has a soft side to him I don't often see in men."

"He can't get it up?" Nell tsked.

"Aunt Nell!" Norah was horrified. "I don't—I'm not privy to that information."

Her aunt gave her a cunning stare. "You've thought about it, though, haven't you?"

This conversation was going from bad to worse. Norah absolutely *had* thought of Malcolm in a state of undress. But despite knowing her aunt's liberties with typically prudish ideologies, Norah was not prepared to discuss this infatuation with her.

Aunt Nell was, as usual, all-knowing. "I have one bit of advice for you. Don't. It's not worth it. You know that, gel. You know how your family is."

Norah blew out a breath. "I know," she responded. "Although if I were to have a bit of fun, I don't think Malcolm is the type to get too involved."

Nell eyed her, clearly not agreeing. "Men are not worth it. Plain and simple. You'd do well to remember that. And speaking of men," she said, an obvious change of topic to lighten the mood, "is your worthless brother still here?"

Norah chuckled. "Yes, he is. And hating every minute of it. He has not exactly been kind to me as of late."

"I should visit and knock some sense into him. Aunt Smell, indeed."

Norah brightened. "There was someone else I was hoping to introduce you to while you're here. A nice man from Spain who has a rather harmless, yet annoying curse placed upon him. I'm wondering if you might be of assistance in breaking this one."

"Oh?" Despite her previous words disparaging men, Aunt Nell perked up. "Is he handsome?"

"Quite dashing. And a true gentleman. I was hoping you'd still be single. I shall introduce you at breakfast tomorrow. In the meantime, I want you to tell me everything I've missed in the city."

"Goodness, gel. Are you that starved for attention?" Nell smiled to disprove her own seriousness. "Well, have you heard of the Red Door on 5th Street? It's all the rage. I began to frequent the establishment once you'd left me in the city ..."

CHAPTER TWENTY-NINE

Saturday, April 24th, 1915

Norah

SHE COULD NOT BE sure why exactly, but Norah felt the flutters of nervous excitement course through her as she guided Aunt Nell to the upper dining room for breakfast. They were running late—Nell was not one for timely entrances—and all the men had preceded them, saving two random seats next to each other at the back table, between Malcolm and Mr. Hunt. Norah took a moment to survey the arrangement before setting her plan into action.

"Gentlemen, may I introduce you to my aunt, Eleanora Montmorency," Norah announced to the group. Most of the members stood, acknowledging the new lady in the room. Norah waited until she made eye contact with Señor Reyes. "Señor?"

His eyes rounded. "*Sí,* Miss Abernathy? Will you marry me?"

Norah smiled at him. "Would you be so kind as to switch places with Mr. Hunt?"

"*Absolutamente.* For you, anything."

As he stood to change his location, Aunt Nell leaned in and murmured, "Are you sure you shouldn't be the one marrying him?"

"Hush. You know my stance."

She snorted, albeit quietly. "Indeed, I do."

Once Señor Reyes and Mr. Hunt had taken their new seats, Norah made personal introductions as she passed each member. "There's Mr. Lyster, Mr. Withers and his assistant Karanja, and Mr. Paulson. At the other table is Mr. Ivey—he's the one keeping his eyes closed—then Mr.

Hunt, Mr. Freeman, and Mr. Jamison with Mr. Norris. LJ, you already know."

LJ, lounging at his seat with an aura of utter detachment, raised a hand in half-hearted greeting. "Hello, Nell."

Aunt Nell hmphed in his general direction before turning her attention elsewhere. "Is that a chicken?" she asked.

Norah nodded as she motioned for Aunt Nell to sit next to her. "That's Mr. Norris. He's quite friendly. And this," she patted the chair next to Nell, "is Señor Reyes. Señor, this is my dear Aunt Nell."

Reyes could not stop looking at her aunt. "Miss Montmorency, will you marry me? It is an absolute honor to meet you."

Nell actually smiled. "Are you this forward with all the women you first meet, señor?"

Reyes blushed and looked away. "My apologies. It is my curse. I meant no disrespect."

At the end of the table, Ambrose shouted, "She's stunning!"

More than a few of the men nodded in agreement. Norah smirked. That errant thought could have come from any one of them.

Ambrose followed it up with, "I wager she's amazing in bed."

The ones who had agreed with his first statement were silent this time, suddenly fixated on the food in front of them.

Aunt Nell laughed, however. "It will take more than a few bawdy words to make me blush. Now then, Señor Reyes, your curse is not offensive to me. As a matter of fact, I'm flattered."

His face fell. "You are truly a vision, *bella dama*. I wish I only proposed to you, and not every woman I see. Will you marry me?"

Nell laughed, and small talk about the table fell silent.

On Norah's other side, Malcolm leaned forward. "Your aunt has a way with men," he whispered.

"She does, indeed. How else can she easily marry every five years or so?" Norah whispered back.

A knowing look passed across his face as he sat back and watched the exchange between Reyes and Nell.

"Señor Reyes, I have a curse of my own," Nell was saying to him. "I have lived since the time when this fine nation was nothing but a string of colonies. I witnessed the revolution in its entirety, and the birth of a strong country. And I've buried countless husbands through the years."

His eyes widened. "You are a miracle, not a curse. Your beauty, it captures me. To end my suffering, I would gladly be by your side."

Nell studied him, her face giving away no emotion. Norah held her breath.

Finally, her aunt said, "Then, Señor Reyes, you should ask me again."

He blinked in rapid succession, as if digesting her words. Then, he came out of his trance. "Madam Montmorency, will you marry me?"

Nell placed her hand over his. Norah noticed a minor flinch at the skin contact before he relaxed into the touch. Nell smiled widely, more emotion than she usually showed men she had just met. "Yes, Señor Reyes," she said loudly in front of the hushed group, "I will marry you."

Malcolm

The remainder of breakfast was a lost cause. The uproar that followed Miss Montmorency's announcement—a cacophonic mixture of disbelief, hearty congratulations, and ribald commentary—was so loud that Mr. Norris screeched and tried to fly up into the light fixture. This caused Fred Jamison to upturn his plate in an attempt to recapture his friend. Marvin Ivey nearly collapsed in on himself in a frightened state, no doubt seeing a slew of dreadful visions. And Ambrose took to spewing whatever thoughts ran through the men's minds in rapid succession.

Malcolm needed to think, and this environment was not conducive to that. He pulled Norah from her chair, dragging her along behind him to make a speedy exit. She had seemed just as flustered by the commotion as he was, but perhaps he should have communicated his actions better, because once they reached the hallway and he released her hand, she had a look upon her face that meant she was ready for a fight.

It pulled Malcolm up fast.

"I'm not angry," he preemptively told her.

She relaxed slightly.

"But," he continued with a hand placed on her shoulder, "was this your plan all along?"

She breathed heavily through her nose. "I did not quite expect Aunt Nell to agree so readily. She took to Reyes faster than I've seen her take to anyone. It was not my intention to cause an uproar."

"Hm, no, that was just your natural inclination taking over."

She sniffed. "Speak for yourself."

Malcolm grinned fondly at her. "Do you think it will work?"

Norah pursed her lips. "Agreeing by itself, no. They'll have to go through with the marriage before he's free, I believe. And he needs to know a few things beforehand. It's only right."

Malcolm had no clue what "things" Pablo would need to know, but he trusted Norah. "I'll go fetch him."

Soon enough, he extracted Pablo and Nell from the dining room, bringing the lot of them into Norah's room, away from prying eyes. He took a look at the newly engaged couple. Pablo was sweating from the commotion but otherwise had a happy glow about him. Nell looked serene as ever, neither frown nor smile marring her features.

"Señor Reyes?" Norah said to get his attention.

"Yes, Miss Abernathy? Will you—" He cut himself off from saying the rest with a determined frown.

Norah studied him like a problem to be solved. In her mind, he was, Malcolm surmised. She turned to Malcolm, interest lighting up her chocolate eyes. "You heard that, right? He stopped himself in the middle of his proposal."

"I did indeed," Malcolm answered.

Pablo's face contorted like he was holding something foul in his mouth. "*Willyoumarryme?*" he blurted out in a rush. Immediately, he clapped his hands to his mouth and turned to Nell. He grasped her hands fervently. "I am so sorry! I do not wish to say it any longer. I am committed to this marriage. Truly, *bella*."

Nell nodded in understanding. "I know, señor. I do not fault you for something you cannot control."

Norah cleared her throat. "As a matter of fact, Señor Reyes, that is a timely remark from my aunt. Before you do commit to such a permanent thing as marriage for the sake of your curse, you should know the parameters of Aunt Nell's curse. You may find your current predicament to be the lesser of two evils."

Malcolm thanked his lucky stars to be present for this discussion.

Pablo looked from Norah to Nell, confused. "What does this mean?"

Nell sighed. "Come, sit." She led the man over to the fireplace, where the two chairs waited. Nell looked at her niece. "Norah, help me out here. I was never good at explaining all of this."

Norah nodded. "Señor, my aunt has already told you she is cursed. She is much, much older than she looks, of which you are also aware. And the reason for that is ... she's, well, dead."

Pablo looked at Nell. "Dead," he repeated.

"Yes. Technically, *undead*, as you can see," Norah pointed out.

Nell splayed her hands. "I don't have a need to eat or sleep, although I can do both of those things. I sometimes smell. And I never age."

"Would the marriage be, ah, consummated?" Pablo asked, his face flushing again.

Nell's eyes held a twinkle that didn't exist a moment ago. "Oh, yes. An active marriage is very important to me."

Norah looked rather repulsed by the notion, much to Malcolm's amusement. Pablo's interest perked up, however.

Norah said, "That leads me to another point. Perhaps the most important of all."

All eyes focused on her.

She continued, "It has not escaped my notice that Aunt Nell's marriages do not last long. And I am not meaning divorce. I do not know why, exactly—I've never pried into my aunt's affairs. But, Senor Reyes, if you do marry, the likelihood of you passing on within five years is acute."

Pablo looked stricken. He turned to Nell. "Is this true?"

She opened her mouth, closed it, and then sighed. "I cannot lie. The longest marriage I ever had lasted six years. I do nothing to kill my husbands. I think not, anyway. Some have accidents. Some get sick. The outcome is always the same."

"I see." he lowered his head, deep in thought.

"It was important that you know the risks, Señor," Nell said, leaning forward. "I want no secrets to be between us. And if this turns you away from the marriage altogether, that is your decision to make. I will hold no ill will toward you."

Pablo looked up, making eye contact with Malcolm, who shrugged his shoulders, a universal sign to the man that it was his decision. Pablo nodded and turned toward Nell.

"Eleanora Montmorency, I would rather have a brief but passionate affair with a beautiful woman and be free of my curse, than live a full life without love. I accept your curse's terms. I will still marry you."

CHAPTER THIRTY

Sunday, May 2nd, 1915

Norah

WITH THE DECISION MADE to wed these two cursed characters together, a plan was set in motion.

Both Aunt Nell and Señor Reyes wanted to marry quickly, the latter for obvious reasons, with the former's reasoning not as apparent. Norah surmised that perhaps with her aunt's curse, it was easier being married, somehow. Again, Norah chose not to pry. Whatever the reason was, the couple had chosen May seventh as their happy day.

The wedding was to take place at Birchwald, on the terrace at the back of the house. It was a beautiful location, with the expanse of spring lawn and birch trees as a backdrop. Norah worried over Malcolm, but he assured her he would survive an hour-long outdoor ceremony.

Father Berkely was to officiate. He met with the couple last week on his usual Sunday rounds, when the engagement was only a day old. Norah could tell he was taken aback by the sudden appearance of a fiancée for Señor Reyes, but he took the news in stride and agreed to the hasty nuptials.

Wedding planning consumed Norah's every moment for the last week. Aunt Nell left for a few days to obtain her gown, leaving Norah—her maid of honor—in charge of making decisions. A steady stream of vendors filled the mansion, discussing wedding cakes, tulles, and bouquets. A tailor was brought on site to attire both Reyes and Norah, and anyone else who was in need of proper wedding attire. Malcolm graciously paid for flowers and catering, his gift to the couple.

Norah knew Aunt Nell did not care what her wedding looked like, in all frankness. She had married so many times in her long life that the pomp and circumstance served no benefit to her. Instead, it was done to satisfy the so-called polite society, since Eleanora Montmorency still positioned herself within the upper crust. Additionally, while Nell personally had no love for the ceremony's trimmings, she cared enough to put on a show for her fiancé, who had never been married before.

Despite this fact, Señor Reyes was not much help in wedding planning, as it turned out. "She could wear a flour sack as a dress, for as much as I care," he said with a shrug.

Given this input, Norah kept things as simple as possible. It was best for her sanity, and that of the others.

Still, even with a modest wedding, there were many details to consider. And now, with five days to go, Norah felt herself slipping into anxiety.

It had been a harder day than others, and Norah's patience had worn to a breaking point. She'd had her fill of a rather pushy vendor who demanded to know which color of tulle was needed for the arch. Norah had replied with white, to which the young man produced three different shades and a lengthy discussion of the uniqueness of each. This was after being harassed earlier in the day by Cook, who wanted to know her aunt's favorite pheasant dish, despite Norah's insistence that Aunt Nell wouldn't enjoy the food, having no sense of taste. After choosing a shade of white at random—which earned her a glare from the vendor—Norah needed a moment to herself.

She escaped to the library, one of the few rooms the wedding madness hadn't consumed, bringing a cup of tea with her. Norah propped her feet up on the low table in front of the unlit fireplace and let her head relax backward, closing her eyes and imagining she was on a deserted island.

The stillness of the library must have lulled her into a semi doze, because she was startled back into consciousness by the door banging open. Norah jerked her head up, catching sight of Malcolm in the doorway.

"Shall I leave?" Malcolm asked, taking one look at her.

"Do I look that poorly?" Norah asked as she sipped her tea. It had gone cold, but she didn't care.

Malcolm paused, assessing her. "You look tired," he said diplomatically.

She laughed and patted the cushion next to her. He took it.

Norah let out a sigh as she placed her saucer down on the table. "This is ridiculous. And slightly pointless. Aunt Nell does not care what she eats, because she can barely taste the food and she does not require it for sustenance. It should not matter what color tulle is on the arch, because she has been married a hundred times before and weddings are not that important to her. And nobody cares how fancy everything looks, because the only people who will witness it are the ones currently living in this house!"

Malcolm listened to her rant, and then picked up her hand, holding it and allowing his warmth to seep into it. "Your hands are always so cold," he remarked.

Norah arched a brow. "Poor circulation. It runs in my family. If it bothers you, you can let go of my hand."

He shook his head. "I never said any such thing. They may be cold, but they are soft, and petite, and lovely."

Norah's insides lit up. On the outside, she tried to remain neutral, like her aunt. "Flatterer."

He chuckled. "Listen to me. I see your struggles, and I do not believe they are in vain. To begin with, this is Pablo's first wedding. He will hold onto the memories of his day, and a little pomp may help to cement them better in his mind. He will feel important in a life spent largely unimportant."

"Yes, I suppose."

"Second, your aunt will see that you care enough to put on a good show for her. Have you ever helped plan one of her weddings before?"

Norah shook her head. She was initially too young to help with any of the previous weddings, and just when Norah had been old enough to be of service, Nell had moved to England and married before Norah arrived.

Malcolm squeezed her hand. "You see? That fact alone will make this wedding more special than her others."

Norah's chest continued to warm, her heart becoming a molten ball. She gazed into his eyes, trying hard not to allow her emotions to spill out through tears of gratitude at his words.

He wasn't done, either. "Lastly, I want to point out that these men living in this house—myself included—have not had a good party in ages. I should have thought of this sooner, to be honest. A ball, or something the slightest bit festive would go a long way to boost morale around here. It took having a pushy woman living amongst us to see the error of my ways." This last line was delivered with the cheeky smile Norah had learned to adore.

"Thank you, Malcolm," she said, barely above a whisper. "You just gave meaning to what I thought were meaningless tasks."

"Just as you have brought meaning into my meaningless existence."

His words splashed around her, making her heart hammer with an emotion she had to pick apart to understand. With comprehension dawning, a worm of dread slithered about her midsection. It was too much. She needed space from him.

She leaned away, carefully extracting her hand and standing as grace-fully as she could manage. "I must go check on my brother," she said, only a half-truth. She *had* been meaning to visit him, as he'd been even more distant than usual with Aunt Nell's arrival. "Thank you for your help."

Without waiting for his response, Norah turned and hurried out the door, her mind once again becoming engulfed in wedding things, but this time glad to be swallowed by it.

Malcolm

He sat, perplexed by Norah's sudden departure. He knew she was at-tracted to him. She seemed open to his small gestures of affection. But why would she react so negatively to his words of endearment? She made no sense.

Norah

LJ was, as usual, in his room, avoiding the other members and the general wedding lunacy that was taking place on the first floor. He heaved a theatrical sigh at her arrival but allowed her entry. Norah walked in,

annoyed by her brother's attitude, but her attention was almost immediately snatched away by the great deal of newspapers LJ had amassed,
which spread out over every flat surface and spilled to the floor in some
instances.

Norah wrinkled her nose. "Have you not allowed Mrs. Bixby in
here?"

He flopped onto the bed with a wince. He smoothed his face out
instantly, but Norah knew when he was trying to hide his pain. "She kept
throwing away my newspapers."

Norah removed a small stack from the desk chair and sat. "Perhaps
she should."

He sat up with a scowl aimed at her. "And perhaps you should stop
sticking your nose where it doesn't belong."

"LJ!" Norah was affronted. "I do not believe I have earned such vitriol
from you. Especially since you've barely spoken to me in weeks."

She watched him clench the hand closest to her in a fist before relax-
ing it. "Perhaps you should take a clue, sister mine."

After the day she was having, LJ's disdain was nearly too much to
handle. Norah held back the tears that threatened her eyes. "What have
I done to deserve this?"

LJ sighed and covered his eyes with his arm as he leaned back on the
pillow. "Why do you still love me, Nor?"

She did not pause with her answer. "Because you're my brother.
You're my only family."

He barked a laugh devoid of warmth. "Am I? I seem to recall I am not
your only family. There's that thing out there you seem so fond of."

Norah bristled. "That *thing* is your aunt. She's a person, with feelings. Just like me. You'd do well to remember that."

"I'm unlikely to forget, with you around."

Norah closed her eyes, giving herself a moment to regroup.

LJ took the moment and broke the silence first. "I want out of here,
Norah."

"As soon as I figure out how to break your curse—"

"This again," LJ groaned. He swung his legs over the side, sitting up.
"Face it, Norah. You've piddled away for months now, and what have
you accomplished? A bit of skin care routine for one person?"

His words sparked a memory from the recent past, when Ambrose recited a similar sentiment. *The nerve. She's not done a single useful thing here and she never will, at this rate. A waste of time.* She had blamed Malcolm in the moment, but she'd believed him when he proclaimed his innocence. Now, thinking back on the memory, she realized LJ had been present at that table as well. "You don't believe I can break it," she accused.

He laughed, a taunting, breathy sound that Norah despised. "You want to know something? I think you're all talk. You have these men eating out of the palm of your hand, but you've produced nothing but air."

It *was* LJ who had thought such uncharitable things about her, Norah decided. For the first time in her life, she felt the urge to hit him, but she contained it. The betrayal coursed through her veins, warring with her despair at the realization.

He was wrong, too. "If you would just interact with the other members, you'd see how misguided your statement is—"

"No," he said with fervor, cutting her off. "I've tried things your way. I'm done. You've made friends here. I haven't. Go and do what you want without me. You don't need me."

She guffawed. "I love you. You know very well I can't live my life without you. I let you go once, and look at what happened."

He swiped a hand down his face. "So, you'll keep me imprisoned? I don't get to enjoy life so that you can? From the sounds of it, one of us loses no matter what, Nor. And that is entirely your fault."

The pressure behind her eyes became too much, and the tears flowed as her chest split open, pouring her anger out along with the anguish. "I'm sorry my heart is such a burden to you, LJ."

"That's not ... Urgh, why can't you understand that I want to live? Truly live, not in this box of a room, but out there? I want to be free."

Norah swallowed a sob. "And what would you do with your freedom, dear brother?"

He glanced at the newspapers. "War is coming. All of Europe is engulfed in it. It won't be long before America is swallowed too."

"What are you saying?"

He huffed. "I plan to enlist."

She stared at him through tear-warped eyes. "You can't be serious."

"Open your eyes, Norah!" he yelled at her. He picked up the closest paper, brandishing it at her. "You may live in your little bubble of ignorance, but out there? People are uneasy. President Wilson is staying neutral, but it won't last. Sooner or later, Germany is going to do something colossal, and it will stir up the hornet's nest that is the United States. And when that happens, Wilson will be outvoted. I'll be ready for that day, no matter if you are or not."

Norah stood. "The war is across an ocean. It's foolish to think it will affect anything here. And wanting to go to war is a death warrant, LJ."

"At least I'll know then that I was truly living."

Norah could not keep arguing with him. The concoction of despair, hurt, and anger exhausted her, and she was already depleted from wedding planning. She hastily rubbed the tears from her face and made her way to the door but hesitated. "Will I see you at the wedding on Friday?"

LJ shrugged. "I would not count on it. But who knows? Stranger things have happened."

She turned to the door. "Very well. I will count on a miracle."

CHAPTER THIRTY-ONE

Friday, May 7th, 1915

Norah

MUCH TO NORAH'S RELIEF, there were no major catastrophes on the day of the wedding. She awoke with only slight bleariness at the tender hour of seven to help set up the chairs and arch for the ceremony. The florist met her at eight to add the flowers to Birchwald, and soon the terrace and the grand hall at the heart of the manor were bedecked with a vast array of peonies, roses, and carnations in shades of white, pink, and red.

Norah met with Cook at nine to make sure everything was in order for the supper feast. The white cake stood in the kitchen, safe until it was to make an entrance.

At ten, she made an appearance on the third floor to check in with the guests and the groom. It was of utmost importance to make sure Señor Reyes had not gotten cold feet. He had not, thankfully, and in fact was in high spirits.

He also did not ask even once for Norah to marry him. Norah took it as a sign.

At eleven, Norah donned her new pale green dress and carefully pinned her hair up. She then turned her attention to the bride, helping her aunt dress in her simple long-sleeved ivory dress ("Not that I'm fooling anyone in this color," Aunt Nell had remarked) and coiffing her hair to fit perfectly with the crown of flowers attached to the veil.

Norah stepped back to survey her handiwork. Aunt Nell's ebony locks peeked through here and there alluringly and shone just as brightly as the pearls sewn into the veil. "You look lovely," Norah gushed.

Aunt Nell blew a breath through her lips. "I expect I do. You have a good eye for detail."

"I learned from the best."

Aunt Nell fixed her with a clouded stare. "Flattery at this hour? I'm not sure it will do you much good."

Norah flopped a hand at her. "Goodness, Aunt Nell. It's your wedding day. I can flatter you all I please."

Aunt Nell rose from the chair. "Well, thirty-seventh time's the charm, I suppose."

Norah stared at her. She had never asked her aunt how many times she'd been married. The number staggered her. For a moment, she worried over Señor Reyes, who she had grown fond of. But, she rationalized, he knew what he was getting himself into.

"Well," she said, holding out her arm, "shall we?"

Aunt Nell took her arm. "Let's."

Malcolm

Pablo twitched nervously next to Malcolm while they waited at the altar. Malcolm wanted to nudge him to get him to stop, but he could understand why his friend might be so nervous. He was about to marry a living legend, after all. And Malcolm still held some unspoken reservations about it. He only hoped Pablo hadn't heard the rhyme Malcolm had grown up with. It flashed through his mind again while they waited for the bride to make an appearance.

Nell, Nell, the widow is swell

She'll marry you quick, and then drag you to hell.

Of course, having gotten to know Nell these past two weeks, Malcolm knew the ditty was not exactly accurate. It helped to calm some of the fears he had been mulling over.

A lone violinist played a lovely tune nearby while they waited. Malcolm let the sweet notes wash over him while he scanned the crowd.

He knew every face, since the only guests in attendance were the people who lived at Birchwald. Everyone, including Leighton, had made an appearance. Mrs. Bixby and Mathers also sat at the back, making the total guest count twelve. A trifling number for such an affair, Malcolm lamented.

Apparently, Nell had no friends, and when he questioned Pablo about any nearby family, he was informed that the only relatives he had lived in Spain. The short timeframe made it impossible for any of them to arrive in time. And barring that, while Spain had so far remained neutral in the war, it was still unlikely any of his family members could have traveled, especially with the German U-boats skulking around and torpedoing ships they deemed a threat. Pablo had not wanted to wait however long it would take to share this moment with his family, which meant only the Guild would witness his union.

At least Pablo seemed to be at peace with the decision, Malcolm surmised.

The violinist changed the tune to the Wedding March. The guests who could stand did so and faced the back of the terrace. Pablo pulled himself straighter. Malcolm craned to see if the bride was coming.

And suddenly, there they were, Norah and Nell walking with their arms linked. Nell looked lovely in her ivory gown, but Malcolm only had eyes for Norah.

She stood straight and proud next to the shorter bride, her dress shimmering in the spring sun. Her dark hair contrasted beautifully with the pale green material. She had tucked a single white peony in her coiffure. Her dark eyes twinkled as she smiled and nodded her head at each person she passed in the aisle.

With dismay, Malcolm remembered his first unflattering impression of her when she first walked into his office back in February. *Skinny.* He'd clearly allowed his ire to command his eyes that day. How else could he have thought such unfavorable things of her? The vision he now witnessed was graceful and elegant.

Norah was beautiful.

At the arch, she took the burgeoning bouquet from her aunt and moved to the side, away from Malcolm. He wished they did not have to stand at opposite ends. He could barely see her from his vantage point.

His only solace was the knowledge that soon the ceremony would be over, and the party would begin.

Norah

There was an advantage to being outnumbered by men at a wedding: unlimited dance partners.

With the ceremony over and the food eaten, the rest of the evening was devoted to celebrating the new couple. The violinist who had serenaded the nuptials had rejoined the three other musicians in his string quartet in the great hall, and they played lively minuets and slower waltzes in turn.

The attendance rate had dwindled by this time. Karanja had wheeled the comatose Mr. Withers back to the third floor during dinner. Hector excused himself once the dancing started, and Mr. Ivey gladly offered to escort him back upstairs, with the help of Mathers. LJ disappeared after the ceremony.

Still, the rest of the members made the most of the occasion, much to Norah's amusement. At the sweet notes of the first waltz, Mr. Jamison plucked Mr. Norris up off his chair and began dancing with the chicken in his arms. Ambrose grabbed Mrs. Bixby by the hand and led her to the dance floor, the older woman protesting weakly all the while, but ultimately falling into his arms. The newlyweds wasted no time in partaking in their first dance.

Norah sat at the table, watching with joy in her heart. She glanced over at Malcolm, who seemed to be brooding in the corner, his eyes already on her. He jolted when their eyes met, and he took a step in her direction before Rodney came between them and broke her view.

He held out a mildly blemished hand. "Miss Abernathy, will you do me the honor?"

He was not the man she wanted to dance with, but she held a keen fondness for Rodney and rebuffing him would hurt his tender heart. "Of course, Rodney," she said as she slipped her hand into his. He grinned widely. Not a single pimple oozed when he did.

Rodney sighed with contentment as they took their place on the floor and began the steps. "Norah, I must say something."

She stopped trying to make their dance smoother—Rodney was a rather lousy lead—and focused on the man instead. "What is it, Rodney?"

"I've spent half my life tucked away because of my curse. I'd given up. Really, I had. But then, you came along and, well, you've changed me. I never once imagined I'd be dancing in the arms of a beautiful lady, but look at me."

Norah's face heated as much as her heart did. "Beauty is subjective, Rodney. There are many men who would not describe me as such."

"It doesn't matter. Your beauty is on the inside, as well as the outside. And I can guarantee there isn't a man here who wouldn't jump at the chance to be by your side. Besides, you were able to see past my flaws, even when I was at my worst. Not many people can. Thank you."

She smiled at the man, his pockmarked face a remarkable improvement over the lumpy and purulent countenance she had first encountered. Even his hair was growing nicely now, a blonde shade that complimented his complexion. He was right. She'd seen through his ugliness to what truly mattered.

As they spun through the waltz, Norah's eye snagged on Malcolm, still lurking in the corner. Only this time, he had a scowl upon his face directed at her dance partner. She frowned back and made a shooing gesture with one hand.

"Pardon me," Mr. Hunt said from behind her, halting their dance. "Miss Abernathy, may I cut in?"

Norah gave a small bow to Rodney, who returned it with grace, before she took Mr. Hunt's hand. Unlike Malcolm, Rodney departed with a smile, happy to have gotten a small moment with her, and happy to share.

Mr. Hunt clearly had more practice on the dance floor. "Miss Abernathy, I just wanted to thank you for everything you've done for me," he told her. "The finger prick is such an economical solution to my bleeding problem. Why, I haven't had a major accident since you joined the house! I'm not sure why I never thought of it before you came along."

She chuckled. "Not all minds work the same way, Mr. Hunt. I'm happy to help. But I would still like to come up with a more long-term solution to your curse."

He shook his head. "You do too much."

"I don't do enough."

The song ended. Norah curtsied to Mr. Hunt. "Thank you for the dance."

He grinned sheepishly. "Oh, I'd ask you again, but I'm afraid Malcolm might do me in."

She blinked and looked past him at the sulking man, who glared at the back of Mr. Hunt. She narrowed her eyes at him. "Pay him no mind. I'd dance with him in a heartbeat if he wasn't brooding."

"Where's the fun in that, eh?" Ambrose chortled, joining them on the dance floor. "Malcolm has a claim on you."

"Says who?" Norah asked him, indignant.

Ambrose shrugged. "Search me. I don't think that was my thought."

She scrutinized the ginger-haired man as Mr. Hunt walked away. "Are you here for a dance as well?"

He laughed again. "And touch you? No telling what thoughts might come streaming out of me. You should have heard old Bixby spilling her guts to me through my own mouth. At least I now know I'm a good dancer. I am a reprehensible man at times. You're right, I am, Norah. But I'm also on the level with you."

She hung her head. "That was not kind of me to think. I'm sorry."

"It's a curse, remember? If it was pleasant, they'd call it a blessing. I am the way I am, but you've also shown I can do more than I thought, so maybe it's not so bad after all. You look like a goddess, Norah."

She laughed at his sudden change in topic. "Your words, Mr. Lyster?"

"No, mine."

She turned quickly at the new voice, nearly running into Malcolm's chest by his nearness. Her pulse skittered.

The music started back up.

"Norah," Malcolm rumbled, "may I have this dance?"

She quirked her mouth to the side. "Are you done sulking in the corner, then?"

"You two have fun," Ambrose said, in a rush to move away from them. No doubt he had no desire to say their thoughts out loud.

"I wasn't sulking," he retorted. "I was biding my time. You haven't answered. Must I ask again?"

She sighed theatrically. "I agree to this dance, Mr. Drury."

She placed a hand on his shoulder as he curled his own around her waist. Clasping their free hands together, Malcolm took the lead, guiding Norah in delicate sweeps of his feet.

"Dance lessons, Malcolm? I'm impressed," she murmured with a teasing smile.

He grinned back, the tilt of his lips sending Norah's heart into an increased tempo as her insides fluttered. "I am a gentleman, after all. That included the best education money could buy."

"This wedding turned out lovely. Thank you for your help with it. I think it meant the world to Señor Reyes."

He glanced over at the wedded couple, who continued to dance and talk with each other. "I admit I had my reservations, but I'm impressed with how well those two get along. I hope it works."

Norah allowed a small frown to wrinkle her forehead. "If he is cured, will you force him to leave?"

Malcolm brought his attention back to her. "I'm not a monster, Norah."

"I know that."

"Do you? I believe you were otherwise convinced when we first met."

She looked into his storm-gray eyes. "We both were different people a couple of months ago. Those people did not enjoy each other's company."

"And now?" His gaze was intense, searing into her as his hand pushed them closer by a fraction.

She fought to breathe properly. "I've reassessed the situation."

"Norah." Her name came out of his mouth with a rumble, and a bolt of desire shot through her. There was no imagining the want she saw in his eyes. It was a good thing Ambrose was not around, after all.

"*Disculpe*, Malcolm, may I cut in? I'd like a word with Miss Abernathy." Señor Reyes' voice cut through the cocoon of intimacy they had wrapped themselves up in.

Malcolm stopped dancing, his eyes still locked with Norah's. They promised that this was not over. Norah nodded, silently agreeing with him.

He stepped back, allowing Reyes space. "By all means."

"*Gracias.*" The Spaniard took over for Malcolm, albeit with much more space between them.

As the Spaniard moved her around the floor, he smiled widely. "You have made me a very happy man," he said.

"Oh?" Norah tried to get her mind off Malcolm and to focus on what was now happening. "Shouldn't it be your wife that makes you a happy man?"

"Oh yes, yes, of course. And she does. But you, you are the one who introduced us, yes? And listen to this. I have not once asked you to marry me."

She nearly stopped dancing as her mind caught on to what he was saying. "You're cured? Truly?"

He let go of her waist to rub his neck. A neck, which Norah now noticed, had no chain around it. She gasped.

"*Sí.* My wife, she took it right off after the ceremony. I am free, Miss Abernathy! No, that is not right," he added with a small frown.

"What's not right?"

He looked at her. "You, me, we are family now. You will call me Pablo, please. But no 'Uncle Pablo;' that feels wrong."

"Very much wrong," Norah agreed. "Very well, Pablo. And you may call me Norah."

"Thank you, Norah. You are an angel. My angel of mercy."

"I'm so happy for you, Pablo," Norah said, meaning every word. "I do hope you will be happy with my aunt. She may be odd, but I love her."

"You love someone else, too?" he asked with a brow waggle.

She narrowed her eyes. "I'm not at liberty to say."

Pablo laughed as he released her. "Very well, very well. We shall see, eh?"

She laughed for show but his words troubled her. She'd always had a knack for keeping an emotional distance from any man, including the classmate she had seduced at Oxford.

But with Malcolm? He intrigued her. She found herself seeking out his company. She enjoyed what he had to say. And that was to say nothing of his physical appearance.

It would be fair to say she was growing an attachment to him.

And it was obvious he was attracted to her. Perhaps she could let her guard down and start something physical with him. After all, he was a man. A man would never be quick to love, if LJ had taught her anything. At best, Malcolm would only form an affection for her. It might be perfect.

Speaking of the devil, he was back in his corner, eyeing Norah like a tiger stalking its prey. A delicious thrill raced through her. As they made eye contact, he gave a jerk of his head toward his office before turning and deliberately walking in that direction.

The song ended, and Pablo kissed her knuckles before returning to his bride. Norah sat again, biding her time, waiting until the rest of the small party no longer paid her any attention.

And then she slipped away.

Malcolm waited in the dark recesses near his office. The faint melody of the quartet still wound through the hall. He stepped from the shadows and held out a hand.

"It was getting stuffy in there," he said with a smirk. "May I have this dance?"

Norah went into his arms willingly, sinking into the feel of his hand in hers, large, warm, and soft. His grip on her waist was firm, possessive, but also protective. They spun in place, not bothering to enact the formal steps in this cramped space.

"Have I ever told you how glad I am that you came here?" he murmured, leaning his head closer to her ear. His voice sent shivers through her.

She smiled. "I don't believe those words have ever escaped you. I'd believed the opposite, though."

"Hmm. Yes. I did come close to throwing you out, didn't I? But then, I never would have gotten to know you, seen your passion, seen *you*. I have very few blessings in my life. Not dismissing you was one of them."

Her heart pounded, an equal measure of excitement and fear. She had to remind herself that men liked to give out sweet nothings that were empty of true meaning, no matter how much she longed for them to be true. If he kept talking like this, though, she might lose her nerve altogether.

She stopped her movement, forcing him to halt as well. "Malcolm," she said, placing her hand on his cheek to get his full attention, "shut up and kiss me."

He stared for a second before cupping the back of her head and lowering his mouth to hers.

The kiss started slow, explorative. A meeting of soft lips and held breaths. Then, as her pulse gamboled wildly and her belly blossomed with butterflies, he deepened it.

She gasped a breath of air as their lips opened further, and his hands braced against her back and pulled her closer. She held his face, not allowing him to back away either. Their kiss took on a frenzied feel.

In unison, they broke apart, panting, foreheads touching and eyes closed. She let go of his face.

"I think ... I will turn in now," she said slowly. The kiss had been amazing, and more than anything she wanted to lead him up to her bed, but the practical side of her told her to wait. To savor the moment.

"Norah?" Malcolm sounded small, unsure. "Was that ...?"

"It was good, Malcolm. Trust me."

He breathed deeply, a sigh of relief if she ever heard one. "Then, goodnight."

She chose the elevator, not wanting to walk through the hall again. She imagined her lips were swollen, and her hair was not as perfectly coiffed as it had been. She did not wish to bring attention to their activities.

As she lay in bed, aglow with her euphoria, she imagined that there was nothing on this earth that could ruin how she felt.

CHAPTER THIRTY-TWO

Saturday, May 8th, 1915

Malcolm

"Sir."

Mathers' voice broke through the fog of Malcolm's sleep, the warm timbre weaving through his consciousness and plucking him into wakefulness. Malcolm stirred and opened his eyes. The light peeking through the curtains seemed normal enough for his standard waking hour of nine, but Mathers hardly ever awoke him in such a manner. Not unless something was amiss. With a start of alarm, he turned over to find the butler standing by his bed, his usually passive face subtly distressed.

Malcolm sat up. "What is it?"

Mathers produced a newspaper from behind his back. "I apologize, sir. I normally would not wake you about a news headline, but I thought it best you saw right away."

With growing concern, Malcolm took the newspaper and unfolded it to read the front page. A grainy drawing of a luxury ship took up a good portion of the cover, along with the title, "LUSITANIA SUNK BY GERMAN TORPEDO, OVER 1,000 LIVES LOST."

The name of the ship was familiar, but it took Malcolm a moment to stitch the fragments of memories together to understand why. Finally, he remembered an event he had originally wanted to attend back in September of 1909—only his curse had prevented it. The Hudson-Fulton Celebration, in New York City, he recalled the name to be. The *Lusitania* had been at the event, and Malcolm had read all about it in the papers following the celebration.

With this insight in mind, Malcolm continued to read the article. The ship had sunk off the coast of England, rather suddenly, from the sounds of it. Among the massive toll of lives lost, one hundred and twenty-eight were American. As tragic as this all sounded, his sleep-addled mind did not quite comprehend why this deserved his immediate attention.

He passed the newspaper back to Mathers. "What of it, old man?"

Mathers cleared his throat. "Sir, the implication is that this act against American civilians will force our president's hand, and we will enter the war post haste."

That was bad news, indeed, but Malcolm knew he personally would not be conscripted. Curses were protected as a disability of their own. "That's terrible, but what does that have to do with me?"

Mathers fidgeted. Malcolm knew when his staunch butler fidgeted, it was very bad news. "Well, sir," he started slowly, as if trying to find the right words, "more than one subscription is delivered here. Many of the other members also pay for a newspaper subscription. And Mr. Abernathy is one of those subscribers."

A dawning understanding began to invade his mind and chase away the sleep-cobwebs. "I see. And he was upset about the news?"

Mathers fidgeted again. "I would not be privy to how he reacted to the news, sir. You see, he's left."

Malcolm paused. "Left?"

"Yes, sir."

"As in, he's no longer here?"

"Correct, sir."

Malcolm palmed his forehead, images of Norah's carefree smile from the night before dancing through his memories. And the kiss. It may as well have been a lifetime ago. "Oh no."

"Exactly, sir."

He looked up at the man. "What about Norah?"

Mathers grimaced. "She is aware, sir. As a matter of fact, she was the one who discovered his absence."

Malcolm moved to plant his feet on the floor. "Are we sure he's left? Perhaps he is elsewhere in the house."

The butler moved farther back to give Malcolm room. "We are quite sure. He left a note."

Malcolm grabbed his dressing gown from its hook, wasting no time. There was no telling what Norah might do, now that she was untethered from her brother.

Norah

Norah sat at the edge of LJ's bed. The covers were thrown back in disarray, a sure sign of his hasty departure. She held the note in her hands, the slight tremor from her frazzled nerves causing the paper to crinkle almost imperceptibly.

She could only stare at the words over and over, her brother's scrawl etched into her memory by now, but she dared not lose this last connection to him.

Norah,

The time has come. The Germans must be held responsible for this atrocity.

I can't stand by and watch the blood of innocents be spilled when I could do something about it. I've given you as much of my life as I can. Now it's my turn to live. The United States will continue to drag its feet even as our citizens are slaughtered. I plan to make my way to Canada and join the fight there.

Do NOT follow me. It's time for you to make your own decisions.

LJ

He had not even bothered to end it with a *Love, LJ.* This last notion undid her. Tears she fought to contain spilled from her eyes and ran down her nose, landing on the paper with a minute splatter.

"Norah?" Malcolm's worried voice filtered through the open doorway moments before he poked his head in. Seeing her, he looked relieved, although the worry never cleared away from his face.

She allowed the tears to continue their flow at the thought of his concern, which of course made his face look even more worried. She bit her lip to try to end the vicious cycle as he sat next to her and pulled her into his side with one strong arm.

"Mathers told me," he said without preamble. "I was afraid I'd find you gone as well."

She thrust the note at him and closed her eyes. "No. He's probably on the train by now. And he would not have wanted me to chase him anyway. He made his wishes clear to me days ago. I should have known this would happen."

"You should have known that a luxury liner would be blown out of the water, sparking an outrage of the American people?" Malcolm asked with heavy satire.

Malcolm's forced levity worked to lift her out of the worst of her despair. A fleeting smile passed over her face. She nudged him with her shoulder. "I was referring to his departure, you dingbat. He was unhappy here and only staying for my sake. He would have used any excuse to leave." She thought of LJ, alone and in pain as he made his way to Canada, and—worst of all—into Europe. "He'll be killed," she moaned, her despondency taking back over.

Malcolm hugged her tighter. "And that, my darling girl, is his prerogative. His choice."

Norah only cried harder, knowing that Malcolm didn't understand. But she was in no mood to explain fully. Right now, his touches, his comfort meant more to her than anything. If LJ was off to live his life—and throw it away—it was time for Norah to stop holding back.

She straightened and wiped her tears before turning to Malcolm. "I need you."

Malcolm tensed within the embrace. "I'm here."

She reached for his face, craning up to touch it. She brushed her lips against his. "I want you, Malcolm," she said as she strained to keep her face near his. "Do you want me?"

His stiff posture vanished and he relaxed into her, bringing his mouth to hers in a full kiss. When he moved back, he replied, "I do want you, Norah. You are exquisite. A treasure. But I won't do anything you don't want."

She smiled weakly. "Right now, there is nothing I want more than to be in your arms, to lose myself in you. Will you take me to your bed?"

Malcolm hesitated before sweeping her into another passionate kiss, one that promised fulfillment. "Yes."

CHAPTER THIRTY-THREE

Sunday, May 9th, 1915

Malcolm

IN THE WEE EARLY hours of the morning, Malcolm lay awake, looking at the sleeping woman next to him. The low light of the lamp flickered over her naked body, half exposed by the blankets she had pushed down as she slept. She was turned away from him, her hair fanned out and glistening like an oil slick in the dance of the lamp's flames.

He longed to run his hand down her curves, from shoulder to hip, but he didn't dare, lest he wake her. She needed her sleep.

Malcolm breathed deeply, feeling for the first time in a long while that he could be at peace. After Norah's heartfelt plea, he'd taken her to this room and locked the door behind him. At first, he wasn't sure what exactly Norah needed from him, and only sought to comfort her with cuddles and kisses. But it was Norah who began to remove his clothes, and it was Norah who searched his body with probing hands, making her full intentions clear.

Malcolm, swept up in the passion of the moment, was only too happy to oblige.

It had been a very long time since Malcolm had last been with a woman. He expected timidity from Norah, but she had surprised him by being an active participant, touching him, communicating her wants, telling him when he needed to do something differently. Her ardor had made for a more sensual experience, which only served to further excite the both of them.

It led to a marathon of lovemaking, with breaks only to hold each other and bask in the other's company. At some point Mrs. Bixby left food outside of the door, which they feasted upon to regain some strength. They then put their newfound energy to good work again.

For a single day, Malcolm's existence had been condensed down to a single need, and nothing else existed outside of it. He forgot about the traditional Saturday breakfast. He neither heard Nell and Pablo leaving for their honeymoon nor did he register when Eddie found his way to the balcony and Norah let him in. No, his only focus had been Norah, and it was sheer bliss.

Now that his fugue had worn off, though, Malcolm grimaced. What they had done together was incredible, but it flew in the face of polite society. And he and Norah would not be the only ones aware of their doings. Mathers and Mrs. Bixby surely knew what had transpired the day before. This did not overly worry him, although it did send a jangle of embarrassment through him. Still, he trusted them. They would neither judge their actions nor would they spread the word of their misdeeds.

Malcolm also wondered about the guild members. Surely it would appear suspicious that he and Norah did not show up for breakfast. He hoped his employees came up with a plausible excuse for their absence.

Whether or not their tryst was discovered, Malcolm felt a modicum of guilt. This may have been Norah's idea, but it was plain that she was not in her usual headspace. She'd taken all her fear, her anger, her sadness, and channeled it into sex. Malcolm knew without a shadow of a doubt that she'd used him as a tool to let go of her brother. And he'd allowed himself to be used without thinking through the implications.

There had been no tender words between them. No talk of courtship, no admissions of love. Malcolm had no idea how Norah truly felt about him. To ease his guilt, he accepted that fully. If she decided not to pursue a relationship, he needed to respect that.

Not that a rejection wouldn't hurt. He was already deeply involved with her before the physical connection.

Norah moaned softly and moved, bringing him out of his reverie. She turned toward him, opening her eyes sleepily and meeting his gaze. She smiled, and Malcolm felt his world crash around him all over again.

"Hello, you," she mumbled.

"Hello. All's well?"

She closed her eyes, but the smile remained. "I'm sore."

"Ah, yes. Well." He was at a loss for words.

She asked, "What time is it?"

He fumbled for his pocket watch on the bedside table. "Just past four. You should go back to sleep."

She rolled over to her side to face him better, her breasts pillowing together temptingly. "I should get back to my own bed."

"Where's the fun in that?" he asked, running a hand lightly over her exposed shoulder.

She shivered theatrically. "Appearances, and all. Although I suppose there's no hope to hide this from the help."

"Mathers and Bixby already know, I guarantee it. But they won't say anything."

She turned serious, a frown line forming between her eyes. "Malcolm, I know we didn't do much talking ..."

He grinned and shifted his weight. "You didn't seem to want to talk. I let you lead the conversation. I still am."

"Yes, well, I ... this doesn't have to mean anything. Nothing has to change."

He let those words settle into him, trying to weigh their meaning before he answered. "Was it that terrible?"

She sat up, pulling the sheets to cover herself as she did. "That is not what I was implying, you oaf." The smile slid from her face, her large eyes deep wells as she studied Malcolm in the half-dark. "There's something I feel I should tell you. You were not my first."

"No?" Somehow, this knowledge did not come as a shock. She had seemed too sure, too understanding of the ways of coupling to be fully innocent.

She pulled her knees up and gripped them through the sheet. "There was a student at Oxford. I chose to have relations with him. It meant nothing. And I have to say, I enjoyed myself much, *much* more with you."

Malcolm chuckled. "Well, thank you. You seemed like you were enjoying yourself. It was either that, or you are an excellent actress."

She nodded her head. "Definitely the former."

He shifted on the bed. "While we are being honest with each other," he said slowly. She turned to look at him. "I've been with someone else as well."

"I would assume so. Most men have."

"It was my fiancée."

This got her attention. She whipped her head around, her eyes wide. "The one you never loved?"

"M-hm. Call it a last-ditch effort to keep her around. Why, I don't recall. Something about duty. It was just after the Valentine's Day debacle. It was incredibly awkward." He recalled Fiona's stiff, unmoving position under him. It had been her idea, but looking back, neither had a good time. "Perhaps our incompatibility in bed was the final reason she left me."

Norah sighed. "Malcolm, we are two broken people. I care for you, but I don't want to hurt you. This—what happened yesterday—can't mean anything. I needed a release, and you gave it to me. For that, I am grateful. But I can't offer more than that."

Malcolm understood. She had been transparent from early on that she had no desire to be in a relationship. A day of passion was not about to change that for her.

If only understanding was the same as agreeing.

"I ... care for you as well," he said carefully, skirting around how he truly felt. "If you want to remain friends, I can accept that."

"Thank you." Norah beamed at him, and his heart both ached at the sight and blossomed with emotion. She threw the sheet off her. "I think it's best for me to sneak away now." She gathered her clothes, quickly throwing on her chemise to hide her nakedness. "Can I escape through the balcony? I'd hate to accidentally run into anyone out in the hallway." She laughed.

Bewildered by the sudden turn of events, Malcolm merely nodded and pointed.

She came around to his side of the bed, leaned down, and kissed him on the forehead, a chaste ghost of the passion he had felt yesterday. "Thank you," she murmured again as she gazed into his eyes. He could swear she was holding back. She did not want to leave. She was forcing herself to go.

A shred of hope lifted his spirits.

"Come along, Eddie," she called softly to the little dog, who sprang to life and leapt off the foot of the bed.

Within a minute, Malcolm was alone again.

He missed her already.

Norah

Falling asleep in her own, chilly bed was difficult, even with Eddie cuddled up against her. He was no substitute for the warmth of a man, especially one who portrayed a sense of protection and caring.

Norah's sleep was further hampered by her traitorous brain, which kept replaying moments of the past twenty-four hours. Her skin would flush hot at the thought of Malcolm, bared to her, his touch, his passion.

It had clearly been a mistake.

Her rational side had said not to get attached. Her heart was screaming something different at her.

Her only consolation was the fact that Malcolm seemed to have a habit of sleeping with women he was not in love with, as his confession supported. And he was amenable to the idea of keeping their friendship at the same level it had been.

Of course, there was that look in his eye Norah had spotted as she kissed him goodbye. It spoke of a longing, a refutation of what was agreed upon verbally. Norah pointedly ignored the remembrance, replacing it with her assumptions in order to ease the burden within her.

Eventually, when the light diffusing through the curtains signaled early morning, Norah stopped feigning sleep and removed herself from bed. She made her morning ablutions, dressed quickly, and went for a walk outside with Eddie, who scampered about like a puppy.

After, she went straight to the kitchen to pilfer a slice of toast, telling Cook not to bother with her breakfast this morning. She ate her toast as she mounted the stairs, not stopping at the second floor but continuing to the third.

It was still relatively early for the members; as gentlemen of leisure, most were used to sleeping in until nine or ten. Norah was certain someone would be awake at this hour, though. She stuffed the last of the crust in her mouth and dusted her hands free of crumbs before seating herself at one of the tables to wait.

She refused to look at the room that once belonged to LJ.

Ambrose was the first to come out of his room, his red hair mussed from sleep and his eyes not yet fully open. He wore his dressing gown with pajamas underneath, not expecting to have company this early in the morning. When he spotted Norah, he stopped in his tracks.

"Blimey, what are you doing here?" he asked with a yawn.

"I needed some company," Norah replied with a smile. "Sit."

He looked dubious but sat. "I take it your food poisoning has passed?"

Norah blinked, her mind trying to make sense of his words. "Pardon?"

Ambrose smirked. "When you and Malcolm missed breakfast, Mrs. Bixby told us you were laid up with food poisoning from the wedding feast."

Bless Mrs. Bixby for covering for them. "Oh, yes. Yes, I'm all better today."

Ambrose's face turned cheeky as he continued to watch Norah. "It was a bloomin' miracle more people didn't come down with the poisoning. We all ate the same thing." There was something in his tone that made Norah's face heat. She hoped he didn't notice.

"Indeed," she agreed, before lapsing into silence.

Ambrose broke it first. "I'm all mixed up in the head," he said solemnly.

Norah snorted. "Was that from you or from me?"

He eyed her. "Could have been either of us."

She sighed and clasped her hands on the table. "I've never asked you how you were cursed."

"Eh, most people don't. They don't wish to be around me long enough to find out."

"Hm. Well, I'm here now, and I have a secret to share with you." She leaned in. "I rather enjoy your company. One on one, that is."

His eyes narrowed. "It's a sad tale of my life, that's for sure. This house here has been better to me than any other I've been in."

Norah studied the man. "Please forgive me, but I couldn't help but notice something during our acquaintance. You don't sound like a gentleman."

Ambrose chuckled. "That's because I ain't. Not a proper one, at least." He looked up at the ceiling, resting his hands behind his head. "I didn't actually get around to any adventuring, either."

Norah raised her eyebrows and waited.

Ambrose sighed and faced her. "Truth is, I'm a bastard. My mother was a scullery maid, and my father was the honorable Lord Sheldon Farthington." He said the name with a mocking deepness. "I lived in his house all my life, and everyone knew my parentage—the red hair was a giveaway—but I was not a part of the family. I was a part of the staff."

He stiffened. "How horrible. Right you are, Norah. I was allowed to have a fairly relaxed childhood, though, and in fact, I played with my sister—half-sister—all the time. We were only six months apart. But Dorothea was legitimate, that was the difference. When I was little, it made no difference to us."

"I imagine that changed at some point," Norah commented.

Ambrose nodded. "Lord Farthington had no legitimate sons. His wife died when Dottie and I were ten, and he never remarried. In my eighteenth year, he fell ill. Dottie was still only seventeen, but she thought the inheritance would fall to her if she married. The old man had a different plan, though. A week before he died, he officially adopted me."

"Goodness. I imagine your sister was not too keen on that."

"No, you could say not. We'd had a bit of a falling out as we grew older, and when our father made the announcement, she was crosser than two sticks. She was already engaged, you see, but I ruined her plans."

He faced Norah with seriousness etched on his face. "I've always been a bit of a loud-mouth, and not one to keep my thoughts in. I said some things to Dottie I now regret. The worst of it was what I had to say about her no-good fiancé. That man already had eyes for anything in a skirt, and I didn't trust the git one bit. But Dottie by this time didn't trust *me*, so she thought I was spreading falsehoods. She was so boiling mad that she cursed me on the spot. I stuck around long enough for her to realize what was coming out of my mouth were truths—not from me, but from him. He made one too many bawdy comments about the women in my presence. It wised up my sister, but she seemed to keep placing the blame on me for her failed engagement. So, as soon as I caught wind of this here guild, I left for it."

"Do you think your sister would be open to reversing the curse?" Norah asked.

"I wish I could say. She's dead now, so it doesn't matter."

"Dead!" Norah spluttered.

Ambrose nodded with a sigh. "I've been here, what, three and a half years? I received word that poor Dottie succumbed to consumption two years ago. My estate sits empty, except for the staff who keep it clean. My god, that is a heartbreaking story."

"You took the words right out of my mouth," Norah agreed. "So, you're simply doomed to speak for others whether they like it or not? Surely, there must be something I can do for you."

Ambrose rubbed his jaw. "I've been giving it some thought. What you had me do, touching someone else. Perhaps there's a way I could spin it into something positive. I haven't figured out how, but I'll keep thinking."

An idea bubbled to life as Ambrose spoke. Norah grasped at it. "Perhaps so. I've been trying to learn more about Mr. Withers. My attempts to befriend Karanja have all but failed, and I still don't know much about their situation. Do you think you could touch Mr. Withers and get his story, like you did with Mr. Ivey?"

"Could be. I'm willing to try, at least."

The sound of approaching footsteps made Norah turn, and the man attached to those footsteps made her smile involuntarily. She could see Ambrose looking at her from the corner of her eye, and she tried to rein in her reaction.

"Good morning, you two," Malcolm greeted. He sat across from Norah, looking almost as disheveled as Ambrose, except for the fact he had dressed himself.

"Why are you lot up so early?" Ambrose complained. "I haven't even had a whiff of coffee yet."

"I had a hard time sleeping," Malcolm replied, his gaze boring into Norah with heat.

Norah looked away from Malcolm, feeling her cheeks warm. She willed herself to keep her mind blank. The last thing she wanted was for Ambrose to broadcast her rather lewd thoughts.

"I was just having a lovely chat with Ambrose, here," she said, trying to redirect her mind.

Ambrose scoffed. "If talk of my dysfunctional family cursing me is lovely, I do believe you are fully cracked in the head, Norah."

She rolled her eyes. "That wasn't the part I was talking about. But if you'd like to compare dysfunctional families, I believe I may be able to give you a run for your money."

Both men chuckled, and the sound warmed her. A sense of peace stole over Norah as she sat with these two cursed people. She had always been an outsider from an early age. Her family dynamic—or lack thereof—coupled with her inherited standing in the upper-class circles made her stand out amongst her peers for all the wrong reasons. When she eschewed social normality in the ways of typical feminine desires, it spelled her damnation in those circles. Norah's desire to pursue an education over marriage was her downfall, and while she truly didn't give a damn what those people thought of her, her friendless status did weigh upon her.

But here, at Birchwald, she had found like people. Each of these men were of high standing, and each of them had been cast aside because of their quirks, their inability to "fit in." After a lifetime of displacement, Norah had finally found her family.

Ambrose blurted, "I love it here."

Norah's heart gave a turn, recognizing her words on his tongue.

Ambrose had barely registered what he's said before he added, "I love you, Norah."

Time seemed to freeze. Those four words hung in the air between the three people like droplets of rain waiting to fall upon them. It was unnaturally quiet.

Norah shot her gaze first to Ambrose, who raised his eyebrows and gave a faint head shake. They both turned to look at Malcolm.

He looked stoically at Norah, his face paler than usual, but his eyes confirmed what his thoughts had said.

Norah felt like she might throw up.

She stood, the loud rasp of her chair breaking the silence. Her action made the men flinch.

Ambrose proclaimed, "I'm going to be sick!" He heaved a sigh at yet another round of stolen thoughts.

She paused through a momentary wave of dizziness from standing too quickly, but as soon as her feet felt steady she moved them. She had to get away from the table. Away from Malcolm. Away from his thoughts.

She should have offered the men some excuse for her sudden departure, but her mind could only replay the words she heard. She left them without another word, nearly tripping over her feet in a rush to remove herself. Eddie did not help things, following his mistress at too close a distance, and nearly getting stepped on for his trouble.

Once she was back in her room, she locked the door, leaned against it, and slid to the floor. Eddie crawled into her lap, ready to shower her with worried kisses, something that almost always cheered her up.

Not this time, though.

Norah had miscalculated.

And Malcolm might pay a heavy price for her mistake.

Malcolm

Malcolm watched Norah as she practically ran from the table, clearly upset but without a word to clue them in. The change from congenial camaraderie to bewildering exit had momentarily frozen him in place.

Once she disappeared down the stairs, his paralysis broke. "What the devil?" he muttered to Ambrose, who had watched the whole scene with wide eyes.

The other man widened them further with a far-off stare and a heavy sigh. He refocused on Malcolm. "Seems to me that something's taken place I'm not privy to," he replied slowly. "And perhaps Norah's not too keen on the repercussions."

"Seems to me some people ought to mind their own business," Malcolm grumbled absentmindedly as he stood. He realized what he said and looked at Ambrose. "Sorry, old chap. Forgot who I was talking to there for a moment."

"Well, *that* certainly doesn't happen very often," Ambrose said. He waved the apology away. "You might want to get to the bottom of this, Malcolm. Things like this tend to fester if not properly addressed."

"Good idea." Malcolm started for the stairs.

Before he could reach them, though, Mathers popped out of the door closest to them. Hector's room. Malcolm startled at the sudden appearance and stopped.

"Oh, sir. I thought I heard your voice," he said, his face hinting at unease.

Malcolm took a step toward him. "What is it?"

"Mr. Freeman's fever has returned, sir. He's feeling too poorly to eat today."

Malcolm longingly gazed at the stairs. Hector's health was important to him, but understanding Norah's mood was of equal importance. He knew the longer he waited, the harder it would be to get to the root of the issue.

"Er, I'll see Hector in a moment, Mathers. There's something else pressing to attend to." Without waiting for his butler's reply, Malcolm bolted down the stairs.

He didn't stop until he was knocking on Norah's door, although in his fervor the knocks sounded more like poundings.

"Norah? Are you in there?"

He heard scrabbling on the other side of the door. Had she locked Eddie inside? But no, within a moment the lock clicked and the door swung open, just enough to show half of her tear-stained face.

His heart dropped at the sight of her. "Norah, what's wrong? What is it?"

She closed her eyes, composing herself, and then opened the door all the way. "Best come in."

He did so, and she shut the door behind him.

Malcolm chose to launch into a hurriedly composed speech before asking again what the issue was. "Norah, I know we spoke at length about how things wouldn't change between us after yesterday. And I agreed. The problem is, things had already changed for me much sooner than yesterday, only I was too much of a coward to admit it."

She stayed silent, her big doe eyes watching his every move.

He raked a hand through his hair. "I wasn't expecting for you to find out from Ambrose, although that was a stupid bet to make in hindsight. But the truth is, Norah, I love you. Before yesterday, and before our first kiss. I can't hide from that fact anymore."

He stopped, waiting to see what she'd say. It was a relief to unburden himself in this way. Now, it was all up to her.

Her mouth quivered as her eyes filled anew with tears.

"Oh lord," he said, reaching into his breast pocket for a handkerchief. "I'm sorry that the prospect of my devotion brings you to the depths of sadness."

She accepted the kerchief with a sob-turned-laugh. "Don't be stupid," she said as she dabbed her eyes. "I *am* sad, but not for the reason you think. Oh, Malcolm, I've been a terrible idiot."

"Why is that?"

She stared at the cloth in her hand. "I don't want you to love me."

He waited to see if she'd add to that revelation. When she didn't, he prodded, "Because?"

She looked at him, a resignation drifting over her face. "I haven't been fully truthful with you. Do you remember when we first met?"

"How could I forget?"

Norah blinked and looked back down. "I wanted membership, and you laid down three criteria before asking me three questions: if I was a gentleman, if I was an adventurer, and if I was cursed. I only answered two of those questions."

He furrowed his brow. "What are you saying?"

She sighed and sat on the edge of the bed. "I'm saying, I'm cursed, too."

Norah

Malcolm did not say anything about what she had revealed; he only stared. She decided it was time to come clean. "It was stupid, not telling you. I see that now. Back then, I never would have believed we'd get to this point, however."

He continued standing there, a stiff statue. "What point would that be?"

She looked at him through eyes heavy with anguish. "Love."

At this, he came alive, a guffaw escaping his throat, the sound piercing her with surprising keenness. "Do you believe me to be that unlovable? Norah, if the thought of my love is so distasteful, then—"

"It's not, you great oaf!" she shouted, shutting him up. She tried to simmer her emotions. "Listen to me. I am cursed. I am here because of my curse. I reacted poorly to your declaration because of my curse. Not because of you."

"I don't understand."

She pinched the bridge of her nose. Her eyes burned with the tears already shed, and the ones she knew were coming. "There are three types of curses in this world. Cursed items, cast curses, and familial curses."

She paused and glanced at Malcolm, who leaned forward as if to absorb her words that much quicker. She sighed. "Mr. Hunt, Rodney, and Pablo were all cursed by items. You have a cast curse upon you. But mine is the third type."

Malcolm walked over and sat next to her on the bed. "Care to explain it?"

"Not much to it, really," she said with a deprecating chuckle. "The curse has affected my family for generations. There seems to be two parts to it. First, every Abernathy has been seized by a desire to be an adventurer, and every single one brings home a second curse from their explorations."

"Like Leighton," Malcolm supplied.

"Yes, like my brother. And like my father, and my grandfather, and so on. Every single man in my family for at least the past two hundred years has died young from a curse. But that's not really the worst part."

"Dying young isn't the worst part?" Malcolm questioned.

"No." Norah twisted the handkerchief in her hands. "The worst part of it is that anyone who loves this adventurer also dies."

Malcolm leaned away slightly, his eyes widening. "So, your mother ..."

"My mother loved my father, yes. And she died because of it. Same for my grandmother. And when LJ dies, I will too, because despite myself,

I love him. Having him here was my last effort to keep him safe and keep him alive as long as possible. I don't hold out much hope anymore. Which is why I chose to be intimate with you, Malcolm. If I am to die, I want to live while I can."

"But?" Norah was sure Malcolm could sense the other shoe dropping.

"But don't you see? I thought you merely desired me, not loved me. I took that chance with blinders on, because I couldn't deny my own wants anymore. I've never been able to get close to a man, for fear of dooming him." She took a steadying breath before finishing her thoughts. "I've doomed you, though, Malcolm. If LJ dies, I die, and you die too. All because you love me."

"I see."

"I can't have that," Norah continued, looking away from the man she cared for. "So—" Norah stood, brushing her hands down her skirts, "I must go."

Malcolm stood as well, much too close to Norah. "Go?"

She kept her eyes trained on the ground. "I must do what I can to save you. I'm not a good person, Malcolm. I went against everything I have lived by to be here, with you. I won't see you die."

He clutched her shoulder, trying to turn her around. "You can't go, Norah." His tone bordered on pleading.

She shrugged him off. "I am not a prisoner, Mr. Drury. You said so yourself."

He quieted. Norah used the bulk of her willpower to stay facing away from him. If she had to see this man shatter, it would destroy her as well.

"Norah. Please." His voice was small, delicate.

A knock sounded on her door, allowing Norah to surface from her web of pain. "Miss Abernathy?"

It was Mathers. Norah was loath to open the door; she was sure she looked a fright from her emotions. She called out, "What is it, Mathers?"

He answered in muffled tones, "I am looking for the master. Mr. Freeman has asked for him."

Norah dared to turn to Malcolm, whose stricken face stared at the closed door. He sighed, a grumble radiating through the exhalation. He marched past Norah, opening the door enough to show his face. "Be right there, Mathers."

He turned back to Norah, a haunted light glistening in his eyes. "Don't do anything rash," he begged. "Take the time to think it through. We can work this out, Norah. Together."

She said nothing, but Malcolm took it as a sign. "I'll give you space. We'll talk tomorrow. Just please don't leave. I can't follow you if you do." He left, closing the door gently behind him.

"I know," she whispered to the empty room. "I'm counting on it."

CHAPTER THIRTY-FOUR

Monday, May 10th, 1915

Malcolm

MALCOLM DID AS HE promised and kept his distance from Norah for the rest of the previous day. He took plenty of time with Hector, who was indeed not feeling well. For the rest of the day, while Hector slept, Malcolm busied himself with guild affairs, duties that he had sorely been shirking since before the wedding. He also entertained Father Berkely for a time, pretending that his head had not just gotten a thorough twisting first thing in the morning. He must have pulled it off, for the priest did not seem to notice the turmoil happening inside of Malcolm.

Busy work kept his mind off what Norah had revealed.

But that night, after he'd settled himself under the covers, the past twenty-four hours came back to haunt him with a vengeance. The memory of Norah's body pressed against his as they dozed between lovemaking sessions rattled about his mind. It was the furthest thing from reality, with his still-cold sheets chilling his skin in the lonely bed, but he could almost pretend she was there instead.

Following the rosy recollection was the shocking one of Norah's confession. He thought back to previous interactions that had puzzled him. He could never understand why she was so tied to her brother, but with the knowledge her life literally depended upon his wellbeing, her motives became clear as day.

Malcolm should have been angry with her. She'd held back vital information, after all. If he'd known loving her was a death curse, would he have eschewed her instead of seeking her out? He couldn't be sure.

He did know that understanding he should be angry and actually feeling anger were two different things. No animosity resided within him, just a vast hollowness.

It was this yawning cavern within his soul that finally allowed him to stop the seesaw between glowing moments and life-changing revelations and get some sleep.

Well, today was a new day. Perhaps Norah would have her own emotions figured out, and together they could come up with a solution.

He decided not to wait for breakfast, dressing quickly and instantly heading for the Aster Room. It was only eight in the morning, but he knew Norah tended to be awake by then. He knocked softly on the door.

Mrs. Bixby answered it, her face paler than usual.

"Ah, good morning, Mrs. Bixby," he greeted with forced cheer. "Is it breakfast time already?"

"Breakfast?" the woman answered. Her eyes looked everywhere but at him, which gave Malcolm a faint sense of alarm. "No, sir. I'm cleaning the room."

Malcolm tried to peer around her plush form. "Oh? Something happened? Is Norah in there?"

"No, sir. She ... left."

"Left." A minute ringing occurred in his ears as he tried to comprehend what Mrs. Bixby was saying. "On a walk?" he added hopefully.

Mrs. Bixby shook her worried head. "Come, sit down, ducky. You look about two seconds from passing out."

She led Malcolm to the chair before the fire, which was not lit. He stared around the room, noticing it was vacant of anything he'd associated with Norah. In a strained voice, he said, "She's gone?"

Mrs. Bixby sighed heavily but nodded. "I'm afraid so, sir."

"When?"

She wrung her hands. "Yesterday afternoon."

"*What?*" Malcolm roared. Seeing his housekeeper flinch at his tone, he lowered his voice. "She's been gone that long? How?"

"Oh, sir, I knew this would upset you." Mrs. Bixby reached out a hand as if to pat his but seemed to think better of it and clasped them together. "Miss Abernathy asked Mathers to call her a cab after lunch. She said she'd packed as much as she could and would send for the rest at a later date. She left an hour later with her dog. She told us not to tell you until today, knowing you'd be in a right fit about it."

"Well, of course I am!" he yelled again, although not at Mrs. Bixby. He grabbed his head in both hands. "This is a disaster."

Mrs. Bixby said nothing, only rubbed his shoulder in matronly affection.

"Did she say anything else?" he asked, looking back up at his troubled employee.

Mrs. Bixby nodded slowly. "She said it wasn't because she didn't want to be here anymore. She wouldn't tell us where exactly she was going, but she had a determined air about her, you know?"

Malcolm did know. Norah and determination went hand in hand.

A sudden overbearing loss engulfed him like a tidal wave. The women in his life always abandoned him. First his fiancée, then his mother, and now Norah. It was hard not to take it personally.

Still, it would not do to allow his emotions to swamp him in front of the housekeeper. Stiff upper lip and all.

He stood, giving the room one last glance, noting with dismay that not only was it absent of the ghost of his mother, now it was absent of Norah too. He focused on Mrs. Bixby. "What's done is done. If you need me, I'll be in my office."

Malcolm hadn't had whiskey since March, when Norah had drank with him. He found he hadn't needed it. But now, it was all he wanted. He was going to cope with this loss the only way he knew how.

CHAPTER THIRTY-FIVE

Friday, May 14th, 1915

Norah

IT HAD TAKEN NORAH a couple of days of sleuthing, but she'd finally found the person she was needing to talk to.

Leaving Birchwald was one of the hardest things she had ever done. Those last forty-eight hours at the house had been a whirlpool of emotions—anguish, satisfaction, euphoria, and utter dread. But no matter what mood surfaced, at the heart of this maelstrom was the conviction that Birchwald—and the people within it—was her home. And now she was turning her back on it.

The abandonment was necessary, however. Norah could not break Malcolm's curse from the confines of the property. Staying at Birchwald would be a death sentence for both of them, and Norah refused to have that on her conscience. The only way to save Malcolm from an early demise was to leave. A broken heart was surely the better alternative over an early death.

The clock was ticking, and Norah keenly heard each second. She would have to break Malcolm's curse, and quickly. There was no telling if LJ would actually make his way to Europe to fight, but if he did, she did not like his odds. She was living on borrowed time, and as long as Malcolm still loved her, so was he.

She tried not to think about the fact that her leaving without saying goodbye might take care of the love issue, at least on his part.

After slipping away from Birchwald, she'd taken the train back to the city, back to her little brownstone townhouse. Now that Aunt Nell was gone on her honeymoon to Niagara Falls, the only other person remaining was the servant Jerrod, who had faithfully worked for the Abernathys for the last ten years. It made for a quiet house, so different from the mayhem of the Guild. Years ago, Norah loved the calmness of her townhouse, with her room on the third floor that allowed just enough light in through the windows, and the sitting room which was always almost too dark to read by, yet had the perfect atmosphere for a day of books. As she walked the hall toward the stairs, though, it now seemed hollow, akin to the void in her soul.

As depressing as the emptiness was, Norah stayed there for two days after her escape, acclimating, feeling like a fish who had gotten a taste of the lake only to be shoved back into a fishbowl. In the between times when she wasn't inactive with moroseness, she ventured out to the library to search the newspapers for a specific name. It was a daunting task.

On the third day, she found exactly what she was looking for: a wedding announcement from six years ago.

It took another half day to determine where the couple now lived, but once Norah had the proper information at hand, she wasted no time in visiting.

As she exited the taxicab, Norah's mind spun to the fateful day in February when she spoke with Arnold Thompson. He'd asked her if she lived on Fifth Avenue, a rather presumptuous assumption, or so she'd thought. But now she stood on the very street, engulfed by the poshness of her surroundings.

The Forsythe mansion was perhaps not as large as the Astors' or as decadent as the Vanderbilts', but it held its own among the elite of New York. Her heart suddenly racing, Norah smoothed out her midnight blue dress with her sweaty palms and made sure her hat was on straight before resolutely marching up to the double doors and ringing the bell.

A butler with combed-back blonde hair and piercing blue eyes answered the door. "Yes, madam?"

Norah thrust her nerves to the side, falling back on her own elite upbringing. "Good day. My name is Norah Abernathy. Is the lady of the house present?"

The butler remained impassive as he scrutinized her. She tried not to feel like a bug beneath his shoe. "She is, but I'm afraid Mrs. Forsythe is not accepting visitors at the moment. May I relay a message to her?"

This would not do. "It would really be best if I spoke directly with her. Is she ill?"

He hesitated. "No, but she is in a delicate way."

Norah nodded. Pregnant. She'd bet an eyetooth on it. "Well, I understand. Truly. But I wouldn't be much of an inconvenience."

He further scrutinized her. "I beg your pardon, but I have not seen you before. Do you know Mrs. Forsythe?"

"Well, no, not exactly—"

"If you have no message for Mrs. Forsythe, I must bid you good day." He began to shut the door.

"Wait!" Norah tried one last time. "Will you tell her we have a mutual acquaintance I wanted to discuss with her? A Malcolm Drury?"

This caused the butler to pause. Norah was counting on him having heard the name before. Staff tended to be invisible when their employers discussed topics, but they heard all.

He opened the door again. "I shall relay the message. Please wait here, but I cannot promise you an audience."

She nodded graciously. "I understand. Thank you."

Norah waited on the porch for no less than five minutes before the butler reappeared, this time opening the door with a full sweep and small bow. "The lady of the house will see you. Follow me, please."

The butler guided Norah through an opulent hallway. It was even more lavish than Malcolm's, although it lacked the warmth and liveliness of Birchwald. He opened a door to a sitting room, and gestured for her to enter.

"Miss Abernathy, madam," he announced to the room.

At first, Norah did not see the woman lounging on the settee in front of the window. It wasn't until she waved a hand to dismiss her staff that Norah caught sight of her.

"Thank you, Stuart. That will be all," she drawled.

The woman sat up, her eyes fierce as she inspected Norah, although her face remained neutral. She patted her bulging abdomen as a small, insincere smile flitted over her pale features. "Miss Abernathy. Forgive me for not standing. It is difficult these days, as you can see."

Norah approached cautiously, feeling like she was entering the realm of a temperamental tiger. One wrong move and she might be finished. "Thank you for seeing me. I apologize for the intrusion. I had no way of knowing your condition."

Another rub of the belly. "How could you? But I've been bored by myself. And we are both women. I don't mind bending the rules of polite society here and there. Especially when my unannounced guest drops that name in my lap. Please, sit."

Norah did as she was told, sitting on the sofa opposite Mrs. Forsythe, née Fiona Yardley. She was tickled to see her prediction of Fiona's hair color to be accurate, the blonde tresses fashionably tucked into an updo. She was a beautiful woman, even with the extra pounds of pregnancy making her face full. There was a sharpness in her eyes, though, that made her beauty turn from innocent to venomous.

"So," Fiona said, her voice that of a little girl's, "you've come from Malcolm's place?"

"Yes," Norah answered. "I am his ..." What was she to him? "Maledictologist."

"Hmm." The tone of this small utterance was telling. Fiona hadn't been fooled by the professional title. "That's right. He's running a charity from his home now, isn't he?"

It was a purposeful mislabeling, Norah knew. "A guild, in fact. For gentlemen. Malcolm is the president."

"And how is he?"

Despite her cool manner while she asked this, Fiona had a glint in her eye, one that spoke of true interest. Norah smiled, a pinch of sadness coming through the expression. "He's well, given his circumstances."

"And what might those be?"

Norah chose her words carefully, not wanting to antagonize the other woman. It would not serve her any favors. "Not to put too fine a point on it, but his curse, naturally."

Fiona sat straighter. "Curse? Malcolm isn't cursed."

Norah furrowed her brow at Fiona. "Of course he is. It's the one you placed upon him."

"I beg your pardon, Miss Abernathy." Fiona's brows lowered, as did her vocal tone. "Was it your intention to come in here and throw accusations my way?"

Norah stumbled over her words in the face of the woman's ire. "Of course not. I don't wish to slander anybody. But I study curses, Mrs. Forsythe, and the truth is, Malcolm has a cast curse upon him. He cannot leave his estate. He told me you placed it upon him when you left. I'm only here to try to reverse it."

Fiona studied Norah with narrowed eyes before letting out a huff of breath. "This is the exact kind of situation my doctor warned me against," she said with another rub of her abdomen. "Too much stress is bad for the baby. I already lost one two years ago. He came too soon."

"I'm sorry," Norah said earnestly. "Have you other children?"

"A daughter, Susannah. She's five years old."

Norah quickly did some mental math, ending on a possible conclusion. Before she could stop herself, she blurted, "Malcolm told me of your relationship in fair detail."

Fiona laughed, but the sound was far from mirthful. "You two must be awfully close to speak of entanglements out of wedlock. I'd be a bit more mindful of the type of information you implicitly give away, if I were you. And to answer your unspoken question, Susannah is not Malcolm's. She's the spitting image of my husband, and she was also born earlier than expected, although not as early as my poor son."

Norah had the grace to duck her head at the chastisement. "I see."

Fiona continued, "After I realized my engagement to Malcolm would not work, I begged my mother to come up with an alternative. She wasted no time and found me a better match within a month. Donald and I were wed in May of that year. We just celebrated our sixth wedding anniversary. And I became pregnant on my wedding night. If you are looking for a scandal, you'll not find it here, Miss Abernathy."

"I do apologize," Norah said. "But, then, what of Malcolm's curse? He said you'd told him to rot in his house before you left."

Fiona chuckled ruefully. "I did, indeed. You must understand, Miss Abernathy. I was angry at Malcolm. He had promised to be a good husband, but the writing was on the wall. I languished in that house. He ignored me in favor of his mother. And his dreams for the future revolved around adventuring, getting away from domestic life, rather than celebrating it with me. That was not the life I wanted. So, I admit, I said some rather cruel things to him as I left. I have a temper, miss. But deep down, I still care for Malcolm. We grew up together, after all. For much of my upbringing, he was like an older brother to me. I suppose it was a bit jarring to pivot into the role of lovers." She sighed. "But I can guarantee you, Miss Abernathy, that I did not curse Malcolm. If he has been cursed since I last saw him, it was someone else's doing."

Norah believed her. Fiona was shrewd and calculating, but honest. She nodded. "I again apologize if I've upset you with my accusations. I do hope I haven't caused you or your baby any harm with my words." She stood. "I wish you well with the birth of your child, and with the life you've created here. You seem content."

Fiona inclined her head in response. "Thank you. I am very happy with my choices. May you be with yours, Miss Abernathy."

CHAPTER THIRTY-SIX

Saturday, May 15th, 1915

Norah

THE ENTIRE CAB RIDE home from meeting with Fiona kept Norah in a muddle. That someone else had cursed Malcom made no sense to her. The theory of Fiona's parting words dooming Malcolm was seamless, yet Norah believed the other woman when she denied the act. Perhaps Norah was wrong, and Malcolm's curse wasn't cast at all. Perhaps one of those trinkets Malcolm's father had brought home was the true culprit.

In any event, she had failed in securing Malcolm's freedom. Even worse, she was out of leads. And even worse than that, Norah finally had to face a revelation she had been staunchly ignoring: she cared deeply for Malcolm, and as much as his declaration of love had pained her, it had also filled a void inside of her, making her feel more complete than she ever had. She'd denied her lovability, and her capacity to love for much too long. Now she realized why she was so adamant about helping Malcolm—it was because she returned his affection. Norah's failure to cure him emptied that void all over again, and in the aftermath of her defeat, the only things that could fill it back up were sorrow and sleep.

This day dawned cheerfully bright, much to her dismay. Norah yearned for weather that would match her mood: dark and gloomy. Sunshine had no place in her disposition, not while she grappled with Malcolm's continuing life-or-death situation.

Inaction would help nobody, and Norah was never one to choose it in any event. But now that she was afloat, in which direction should she go? As she saw it, there were three options. One, she could go back to Birchwald and doom Malcolm by staying with him. She assumed the guilt of eventually killing him would eclipse any happiness she would derive from the choice. Two, she could go back and officially break ties with him completely. Hopefully Malcolm would fall out of love with her, and she could live the rest of her short life in misery. Or three, she could stay away altogether, with the hope Malcolm would forget about her, and—again—live her life in misery.

The choices were not great.

At ten in the morning, the decision fell into her lap. Jerrod knocked on her bedroom door, interrupting her gloomy reverie.

"Madam, I have a telegraph for you," he said as he handed Norah the slip of paper.

She opened it and scanned the contents. A gasp escaped her once she deciphered the meaning.

FREEMAN V SICK AND ASKS FOR YOU PLEASE COME MRS B

"Jerrod," she proclaimed briskly, "I'll be leaving as soon as possible."

Jerrod, who had always been an expressive man—unlike Mathers—rounded his eyes and flopped his mouth open. "But Madam, you just got home."

"I know. But I'm needed at Birchwald." She gazed at Eddie, who lounged on the pillows of her bed. Pursing her lips, she said. "I'm not sure how long I'll be. Do you think I should leave Eddie here?"

Jerrod gazed thoughtfully at the little dog, who thumped his tale at the sound of his name. "I am more than happy to take care of him for you, miss," the servant said. "But I should tell you that Eddie was very unhappy the last time you left him behind. Surely he would not be that much of an inconvenience with you?"

No, Eddie was not an inconvenience. His actions at Birchwald were commendable, with his befriending of Mr. Norris, and his willingness to help Hector. At the remembrance of the old man, Norah made up her mind. "You are right. He'll come with me. Thank you, Jerrod."

"My pleasure, miss," Jerrod said as he rummaged for her trunk.

The trip back to Birchwald was agonizingly slow. The proper train did not leave for another hour once she arrived at Grand Central Station. Once boarded, the slow speed of the train grated at her. She imagined at every small delay that she'd arrive too late, and the guilt ate at her incessantly.

The regret was not just reserved for Hector's condition. She had been in such a rush to leave after Malcolm's declarations of love, she had not said goodbye to anyone other than Mrs. Bixby. There were many loose ends to tie up at Birchwald, delayed by her sudden departure. She had a surprise for Rodney in the works, and she'd left without seeing it to fruition. She had a plan for Mr. Hunt's salvation as well, and without her, it could end in disaster. But she'd given no thought to these matters when she'd fled.

She'd only been thinking about herself. And Malcolm.

And now, poor Hector might be dying. She blamed herself for not being there sooner to help him.

At last, the train pulled into the Mahopac station and Norah hailed a cab for the last leg of the journey. Unlike in February, there was a carriage ready to leave, and Norah thanked her lucky stars that at least one part of her travels had gone smoothly.

When Birchwald finally came into view, she was simultaneously overjoyed to see it and wracked with a sudden anxiety over her upcoming reception.

The cab dropped her and Eddie off in front of the grand doors, and a moment of déjà vu overtook Norah. Before she fully made it up the steps, the door opened, revealing Mathers, whose wide eyes betrayed his surprise at her appearance.

"Miss Abernathy?" he said in a tone of disbelief, so different from his normal, unaffected drone.

"Hello, Mathers," she greeted with a strained smile on her face. "Am I allowed to enter? Or have I been banned from Birchwald?"

Mathers swept to the side instantly, leaving ample space for her to enter. "It is my pleasure to see you again, miss," he said with a twinkle in his eye.

"It's good to see you too, Mathers," she replied as she moved past him. She stopped in the foyer, her face turning stormy. "Is Malcolm ...?"

She wasn't even sure what she was about to ask, but the butler's face filled with understanding. "The master has been rather ... recalcitrant since you left. I do believe he is in his office sleeping off some whiskey at the moment."

"Oh dear." Norah was afraid of that. Malcolm's dependence on the bottle was very much tied to his emotional wellbeing, something she was sure she'd inadvertently stripped from him when she disappeared. "When he comes to, tell him I'd like to talk with him. In the meantime, I came as soon as I heard about Hector. Is he still with us?"

Mathers nodded. "I shall take your luggage to your room for you. You still have use of the Aster Room for as long as you are here. Please feel free to go directly to Mr. Freeman's room."

She handed her valise over. "Thank you, Mathers."

Norah took the steps—so familiar to her now, like old friends—to the third floor. Hector's door was open, and Mrs. Bixby, Mr. Hunt, and Mr. Jamison with Mr. Norris were crowded around the bed. Mr. Norris let out a cluck as Norah approached, and Mr. Jamison was the first to spot her.

"Miss Abernathy, you're back!" he exclaimed, although his tone was muted.

All eyes turned to her, and Mrs. Bixby gave a gasp of relief. "You came, dearie," she said as her eyes shone with unshed tears. "Bless you."

"I'm beginning to believe I never should have left," Norah said as she stepped closer to the bed.

Hector rested there on his back, his torso propped slightly with pillows. His eyes were closed, as if deep in sleep. Despite his plush surroundings, Norah could see the man was not well. His skin was stretched and shiny from sweat, and he had lost weight. His chest strained with each breath.

Mrs. Bixby put a comforting hand on Norah's back. "You came just in time," she murmured as they looked on at the man. "He is not long for this world, I'm afraid."

Norah refused to look away from him. "What's happened?"

Mrs. Bixby made a small noise in her throat. "He'd been having fevers on and off for a time, if you recall."

"Yes."

"Well, it became worse about the time you … left, and shortly after that he stopped eating altogether. We've been giving him sips of water, but the problem is—"

"He can't evacuate, can he?" Norah surmised.

The other woman shook her head. "His last bowel movement was a week ago. He began throwing up anything he ate soon after. And we worry about his bladder bursting if we give him too much water at once."

"Good god." Norah could not imagine a worse fate.

"We are trying to keep him as comfortable as we can. That surgeon of yours came around two days ago and gave us a bottle of morphine to help with the pain. It's kept him mostly asleep for the past couple of days."

"Oh, Hector." He had told her from the very beginning that this was to be his fate, but actually observing it pained her greatly. She longed to see his kindly smile, his optimistic outlook, but all she encountered was a dying man, living out the rest of his life in a sea of pain.

Mr. Hunt placed a hand on her shoulder. "We've missed you, Miss Abernathy," he said softly, the morose atmosphere of the room coloring his voice. A fresh scratch adorned his cheek.

Mr. Jamison nodded as he pet Mr. Norris in his arms, making the chicken coo. "Yes. This place wasn't the same without you."

She stared at the men, a heaviness settling behind her eyes. "But you hardly know me," she rasped. "I've only been here since February."

"Three months is plenty of time to get used to the presence of a new person, and to feel their absence acutely when they are no longer there," Mr. Hunt pointed out, as he stared at Hector's supine form.

Jamison gave a little snort. "Just ask Malcolm."

Norah decided to pretend she hadn't heard that. She turned to Mrs. Bixby. "I'd like to stay with Hector, if that's all right."

"Take all the time you need, dearie. I gather you've not yet seen the master?"

Norah took a heavy breath. "He is not available at the moment."

"Hm." Mrs. Bixby shooed the other men out with her hands. "He's altogether too dependent on letting the whiskey dull his pain when times are bad. You'll stick around, though, won't you?"

Norah looked from Mrs. Bixby to Hector, weighing her options. "I'll stay, for now."

It was the best she could promise with the circumstances. She was not convinced that Malcolm would welcome her back with open arms.

Malcolm

The effects of the alcohol lasted until the evening, at which point Mathers plucked the decanter from Malcolm's hands and clanged it loudly against the silver tray it normally rested upon. The sound resonated like shards of glass through Malcolm's head.

"Bloody hell, man," Malcolm groaned as he rubbed his temples, "that was a bit uncalled for."

"On the contrary, I believe it was just the thing to do. Sir, I am about to be utterly frank with you, at the risk of my position," Mathers replied with zero emotion. No, Malcolm amended—there was anger in his stoic butler's voice. Malcolm looked up into the older man's face, noting disapproval etched upon it.

"Go on," Malcolm urged.

"Your habit of drinking yourself into oblivion is distasteful and cowardly. Life will throw hardships at you, but it is typically better to face them head-on, rather than disappear at the bottom of a bottle."

Malcolm flopped his head back down onto his desk. "You think I don't know that?" he slurred. "I wish I could be strong enough to fix this. I thought I could, too, when Norah was here. But it turns out that on my own, I'm too weak."

"One should never use another human being as a crutch, sir, especially not someone of as fine a caliber like Miss Abernathy."

"She left me, Mathers," Malcolm whined, glancing up. "I'd do anything differently to make her not leave."

"Your grasp of the English language is clearly suffering under the influence of alcohol. But if that is how you feel, I have news for you. Miss Abernathy is sitting upstairs with Mr. Freeman as we speak."

It took a second to piece together what Mathers was saying. Malcolm lifted his head to look at the man through bleary eyes. "Norah is here?"

"She arrived two hours ago."

"And you didn't tell me?" Malcolm leaped up from his chair, nearly losing his balance in the process.

As he hobbled to the door, Mathers called out, "There was no point in telling a senseless man anything, sir. Shall I assume that I am secure in my position still?"

"Fine, fine," Malcolm said as he hurried out the door.

Stairs were tricky, but he navigated them without damaging himself. His heart felt close to bursting with the intense need to see Norah again. As he tackled the second set of stairs, he had a fleeting thought that perhaps she would not want to see him, but it faded by the time he set foot on the third floor.

Hector's door was open, and he lurched to the doorway, pausing to survey the room.

She was there, sitting next to the bed, her head bowed as she held Hector's hand. On his other side, Eddie lay curled up against the man.

She looked like an angel of mercy, coming to take a soul away. Whether it was Hector's or his, he couldn't be certain.

"Norah," he breathed, her name a prayer.

She startled and turned toward him, her large brown eyes wet with tears. They widened at the sight of Malcolm.

"Oh, Norah," he said again, stepping into the room. He opened his arms, hoping against hope she would fill them.

It took longer than he wanted, but she stood and met him in the middle, only hesitating a moment before burying herself into his arms. He relished the feel of her, a sensation he had thought would be absent for the remainder of his time on earth.

"Malcolm," she said, her voice muffled by his body. "You look terrible."

He laughed and only burrowed farther into her hair, smelling the scent of her that he had missed. "I know."

She moved away, and he reluctantly let her go. She studied his face, a concerned countenance about her. "I'm sorry."

"Sorry?"

"For leaving the way I did."

"Oh." He inched back, creating room between them as the old hurt resurfaced. His stomach soured and he fought down a lurch of acid. "Yes, that."

"Malcolm, I only did it to protect you—"

"I would like to remind you that it was never your place to keep me safe," he interrupted, the resentment at his condition—caused by her absence—bubbling to the surface and burying the joy at seeing her again.

She took a step back as well, her shoulders stooping. "I know that," she said weakly. "I—I panicked. I only want what's best for you."

"But that's just it, Norah," he said, calmer than he thought he'd be able to manage. "You don't know what's best for me. You took that choice away from me when you left. And I couldn't even follow you."

Norah glanced at the sleeping form of Hector, who hadn't stirred from his morphine-induced slumber. "I visited Fiona."

The sudden change in topic sent Malcolm's alcohol-soaked brain spinning. "Fiona? *My* Fiona?"

Norah's eyes flashed to him. He smirked. The possessive he'd used angered her. Good.

"She isn't *your* anything. She's happily married and expecting another child. I went to see if she'd renounce the curse. To give you your life back."

Malcolm's insides let out a flutter of hope. "And?"

Norah shook her head. "She didn't curse you."

Malcolm assumed he'd misheard. "What?"

"She was quite clear about her feelings. She may have been angry at you, but she had no reason to curse you. It wasn't her."

Malcolm's head was suddenly too light. He managed to flop into a chair. "Then, who?"

Norah sighed. "I don't know. The point is, you were the reason I left. If I wouldn't allow you to love me, I could at least set you free. You could at least live a long life without me."

As noble as she sounded, Malcolm wanted to cry over her obtuseness. "That's what you don't understand, Norah. Before you came along, my life was gray and dreary. I was trapped in this house with no way to change that. And then you entered that door, and I could breathe again. I finally found a purpose in my life. I found joy in living. When you left, and I thought I'd never see you again, you took the air I breathe with you."

He heard Norah sniffling and looked to see her sitting on the floor near him, wiping her eyes ineffectually. He tumbled out of the chair to land beside her, his knees groaning. He took her hand in his. "What I'm trying to say is, I would rather die tomorrow if it meant being with you for the rest of my life, than be deprived of your company just to become a bitter old man."

Norah sobbed harder, trying to keep it muffled so as not to wake Hector. "I've been avoiding love for so long," she finally choked out. "I assumed everyone else would rather avoid me too. I'm so sorry."

The ache in his heart eased, and he scooped her into his arms, allowing her to cry onto his jacket. "Does this mean you'll stay?" he asked into her hair.

"Yes," she answered immediately.

CHAPTER THIRTY-SEVEN

Sunday, May 16th, 1915

Norah

MALCOLM MAY HAVE BEEN coherent enough for the conversion that evening, but Norah soon shooed him away to sleep his inebriation off fully. He'd been surprisingly eloquent—Norah could admit—but she worried that it was more the booze talking than his true heart.

Morning would tell.

In the meantime, she opted to stay by Hector's side. He neither woke during her and Malcolm's tearful reunion nor did he stir when Mrs. Bixby brought Norah's dinner on a tray at seven. She ate the meal glumly, aware that this was a daily act in which Hector would never participate again. The thought made the food stick in her throat with each swallow.

Eventually, the actions of the day caught up to her and filled her with a bone-tired weariness. She laid her upper body on the bed, keeping her lower half seated in the chair. In this position, she fell asleep holding the old man's worn hand.

A low moan stirred her from sleep. She raised her head quickly, catching the glint of Hector's open eyes in the low light of the oil lamp.

Despite his labored breathing, he smiled at her. "Hello, love."

Norah allowed a laugh-turned-sob to escape. "It's good to see you, too."

Hector gasped around an unseen pain, the sweat beading on his forehead. "I guess I'm dying at last," he said, his words nonchalant.

Norah grasped his hand, her sorrow eating up the air about her. "Hector, I so badly wanted to save you. I failed. I'm so sorry."

He tsked as he patted her hand. "Now, now," he soothed, "none of that. I knew my time was short well before you showed up. I recollect saying something to that effect during our first encounter, you know. If you think you didn't make a difference, though, you're wrong."

"How?" Norah asked, barely choking the word out.

Hector smiled, the expression tightened by pain. "You gave me joy these past few months. You and your little dog. It was the best sendoff I could have asked for."

Norah squeezed her eyes tightly, allowing the tears to fall. She brought his hand up to her cheek, rubbing the wrinkled knuckles across its surface. "I'm glad I'm here now. Both of us." She motioned to Eddie, who continued to sleep in a ball by Hector's side. Her lip trembled. "I should have been here sooner, though."

Hector shook his head marginally, his kind eyes laced with softness. "Never mind that. And no need to carry on. I'm old, and I'm happy with my life. I've met some wonderful people and visited some wonderful places. I should have known better than to take a chunk of that rock. It's magical, you know. Sacred to the Aboriginals. Just plain carelessness on my part." He clucked his tongue. "Point is, I've made my peace. I'm not afraid of dying; in fact, I'm looking forward to it. I'm an adventurer, love. Death is the greatest adventure of all. I'm ready."

"I'll miss you," Norah said between sniffles.

"Well, now. I'll petition hard to be your guardian angel on the other side, and that way, if you miss me too much, you'll know I'm here looking out for you."

Norah heaved another sob but tried to quell her emotions. "Thank you for being wonderful, Hector."

A spasm wracked his body, but as soon as it subsided, he whispered, "You're welcome."

Norah stood, the vision of the spasm making her fully alert. "What can I do to help you, Hector?"

He panted through the pain. "Do you see that little bottle over there?"

Norah followed his shaking finger to the vial on the nightstand. She picked it up. "Morphine. Is it time for your next dose?"

"I have no idea what time it is."

She glanced at the bedside clock. "Just past three in the morning. Do you need a dose?"

Hector coughed wetly before replying, "Yes, please."

She picked up the syringe next to the vial. "How much?"

"As much as you can fit in the syringe."

Norah lowered the bottle to place her full attention on the man. She may not have been a nurse, but she knew not to follow his instruction blindly. "Hector, surely that isn't the proper dosage."

He stared back at her with a stony face, his eyes clear and bright with pain. "Now you listen to me, my darling girl," he said in a voice that brooked no argument. "I've said my goodbyes already. I'll not last another day, I wager. And if I do, I'll either be in agony or I'll be drugged beyond reason. I'm choosing my fate. And I'm asking you as a friend for a little help."

Norah was not religious, but a small voice nagged at her. "Won't I be aiding in murder?"

He chuckled darkly as he stared up at the ceiling. "No. You'll be giving me an act of mercy. No one will need to know here, nor would they judge you for it if they did. And if there is a God, I'll be sure He sees my side of things when I talk to Him. Your soul is too pure for damnation, Norah." He looked at her, determined. "Please. I'm ready to go. I don't want to linger for the sake of seeing another sunrise. I want to fly into it instead."

Norah took a breath. She held it, allowed it to fill her lungs, and she let it go. She picked the vial up, inserted the needle, and drew up the rest of the contents with shaking hands.

"I ... I don't know how to administer it," she admitted.

Hector held out a hand. "I'll do it," he said with a wince.

Norah hesitated, imagining throwing the syringe across the room instead, but handed it to the man. He was right. He had made a choice, and she would allow him to follow through. She watched as he carefully inserted the needle into his arm, drawing the plunger back to make sure he was in his vein, and then injecting the contents into himself.

When he was done, he fell back with a sigh, the empty syringe discarded next to him. "Thank you, Norah," he said almost dreamily.

"Hector?" Norah asked, unsure. "Can I stay with you? Until the end?"

He closed his eyes, but held out his unblemished arm, the arm closest to her. She crawled onto the bed and cuddled up into his side as he wrapped the arm around her shoulder. He sighed, a sound of peace, contentment. "There's nothing I'd like more."

CHAPTER THIRTY-EIGHT

Monday, May 24th, 1915

Malcolm

IT HAD BEEN A week since Hector's death. The morning of his passing, Malcolm had awakened refreshed—albeit with the mother of all headaches—and gone straight to Hector's room, to find Norah asleep in the old man's arms. He had passed in his sleep, a serene tilt to his still lips. Norah was not surprised by his sudden passing and had seemed at peace with it when he awakened her with the news.

That same morning, Father Berkely arrived at his usual Sunday time and immediately took over the details. While death was not a stranger to Birchwald, it had been a while since the last member met his mortal end, and Malcolm's curse did not make it easy to deal with the aftermath. Malcolm was grateful to the priest for his assistance.

Hector's death cast a bleakness over the Guild. The men were slow to laugh, and slothful in their conversations. Ambrose stayed away from any groups, for fear of blurting out something callous or insensitive—never mind that it wouldn't necessarily be his thought.

Norah was lost in her own world, a pensiveness wrapped around her like a new shawl. She once again threw herself into tending to the needs of the Guild as if she'd never left, and Malcolm surmised she wielded her skill like a shield against the worst of her grief.

She refused to discuss her last moments with Hector and somehow acted as if she were partially to blame for his passing, a notion Malcolm found ridiculous. Hector had clearly been at death's door sooner than

Norah's timely arrival. Malcolm assumed the old gentleman had hung on long enough to properly say goodbye to Norah. It was a blessing.

In the between times when Norah surfaced from her cocoon of grief to interact with Malcolm, she was tender with him, showing small bouts of affection, but she seemed unwilling to rekindle what they once had. Even her fiery temper failed to reemerge, and Malcolm missed the easy banter they used to share.

As much as Malcolm ached to shower her with the passion he felt every time he saw her, he restrained himself. He hoped she would come around. Until then, he'd be patient with her.

Instead, he found joy in watching her work with the other members, and in doing so, began to reconnect with them once more.

Rodney had continued to improve with regular nettle baths, so much so that he looked like an average man who had suffered a bad case of smallpox and lived to tell the tale. No new sores erupted, and he hadn't had a bad bout since February. Norah declared him to be mostly cured.

During Norah's absence, Farley Hunt had failed to take proper care of his blood curse, allowing a few accidental injuries to occur. Now that she was back, he dutifully pricked his finger every morning, with Norah's assistance. Malcolm observed a smile on Farley's face when Norah remarked about how nice it was to see all his old cuts and scrapes healing nicely.

Both he and Norah tried to get closer to Mr. Withers, but Karanja, while polite, did little to establish a connection with them, and he would shoo anyone away the moment the older man became agitated.

A letter from Pablo confirmed his curse was truly broken. He wrote to Malcolm about the marvels of marriage. He and Nell were in the throes of happiness, and Pablo made sure to give all the credit to Norah. Pablo also confirmed he would not be coming back to Birchwald but would be moving into the Abernathy brownstone in New York City.

Malcolm was happy for Pablo, even though a tiny grain of sand had wormed its way into the emotion, marring it with a hint of jealousy.

It was Fred Jamison who surprised Malcolm the most. Fred used to walk around with dark circles under his eyes, a testament to his nightmares that plagued him every night. Some days he'd be listless from lack of proper sleep, only going through the motions for the sake of Mr. Norris.

But on this day, when Malcolm greeted Fred, he saw a man who had a vivacity about him, despite the somber atmosphere of losing a comrade. His eyes were clear and free of the usual dark puffiness under them, and the rest of his face glowed a healthy color.

"Good god, man," Malcolm greeted him. "There's something different about you. How do you feel?"

Fred blushed, a pleased smile spreading on his thin face. "Truthfully, I've been worried about telling you. I feel amazing these days. I haven't had a nightmare in about a month."

Malcolm goggled at the admission and mentally kicked himself for being so unobservant. "A month! But how is that possible?"

The tall man shrugged. "I haven't the foggiest. All I know is that I've been getting sleep—glorious, uninterrupted sleep. Until Herbert begins his clucking in the early morning hours, that is." He gazed fondly at the chicken who rested on the tabletop.

The implications confounded Malcolm. People did not simply stop being cursed—not without something to show for it. He leaned in to inspect the positive changes in Fred's pallor. "And you truly have no understanding of why your nightmares stopped? Was it something Miss Abernathy did?"

Fred tilted his head to the side, considering. "I don't believe so, but who knows? Perhaps she's a good luck charm in her own right."

"Perhaps." Despite her own personal drama, Norah *had* brought about beneficial changes to the Guild. Fred might have been on to something. "But why were you reluctant to tell me? This is good news!"

Fred ran a hand down Mr. Norris' back. The bird trilled softly at the caress. "If I am no longer cursed, as appears to be the case, what right do I have to stay in a guild meant for cursed people?"

Malcolm pondered this. "Why, for Mr. Norris' sake, of course! *He* is still cursed, and he needs a caregiver. Besides, you're paid up until the end of the year. You'll still have a place here, old boy. Don't let that fear consume you any longer."

Fred's eyes took on a suspiciously shiny quality. "Thank you, Malcolm."

Norah

Norah did not mean to listen in on Malcolm and Mr. Jamison's conversation, but she heard them speaking as she was about to round the corner, and decided a little eavesdropping wasn't the worst sin she'd ever committed. The conversation was sweet, and Norah's heart filled at the praise sent her way, even if she knew she had nothing to do with Jamison's miraculous recovery.

It reminded her, she still had to solve the case of Mr. Norris. Another trip to the library was in order soon.

But first, she had news she wanted to share with Rodney.

She waited a minute more before bustling around the corner. She spied Malcolm and Mr. Jamison sitting at the round table, with Mr. Norris resting atop it in the middle. Putting on a smile she actually felt for the first time since Hector's death, she waved at them as she walked past.

"Gentlemen, good afternoon," she greeted without slowing.

"Norah, where are you off to in such a rush?" Malcolm asked, swiveling to watch her walk. He'd been overly polite and slightly guarded since her return, and it was nice to hear the ghost of the easy banter they once had in his question.

She slowed but kept moving, waving a letter at them. "I have something for Rodney," she said.

There were no follow-up questions or attempts to slow her, a fact that mildly disappointed Norah.

Rodney was still in his room, the crumbs of his sandwich laying on a plate, ready to be taken back to the kitchen. His widened eyes spoke of surprise to see Norah at his door, but he welcomed her in gladly.

Norah was relieved the awkwardness of the bathroom debacle had finally been laid to rest. With LJ gone, Rodney felt no need to keep their visits quite so properly chaperoned. He seemed to know she was already spoken for, anyway.

"To what do I owe this pleasure?" he asked as he pulled out his desk chair for Norah to sit in.

She took it gratefully. "I have news. I do hope you won't see this as overstepping on my part."

"Norah, for you, I'd forgive almost any transgression. What is your news?"

She unfolded the letter in her hand. "Back in March, after you'd begun to heal, I reached out to the Chinese Consulate. He is located in Washington, DC. No easy task, I assure you." She paused, biting her lip and refusing to look Rodney in the eye. "I ... explained the situation, and asked if China would like to have their cultural relic back, in exchange for your forgiveness."

Rodney stayed silent for longer than Norah anticipated. She finally looked at him to find his eyes rounded and his mouth ajar. "You did what?" he asked, his voice faint.

"He wrote me back, and I just received the correspondence," she continued quickly. "He is sending a delegation here to collect the Tiger Vessel, which indeed holds important historical and cultural meaning for their country. They understand you have paid for your crime already, and do not seek to further punish you. In fact, they have an offer for you."

Still flabbergasted, Rodney said, "For me?"

Norah nodded. "Relations with China are still on slightly shaky ground, ever since the rebellion at the turn of this century. You and your father barely missed it when you left China."

Rodney gave his head a slow nod. "I do recall hearing of it. Anti-Western powers and all that."

"Yes, well, as it turns out, this European war has had a positive influence on our relationship with China. They give their support to America, should we enter the war—and let's face it, it appears to be inevitable." She sighed, as her thoughts spun to LJ briefly. She shook them off. "I'm getting sidetracked. The point is, the Chinese Consulate is thrilled with your forthrightness in correcting your past transgressions, and they have offered to send you back to China along with the artifact, in order for you to explore the country, with local guides this time."

Rodney stared, his lips parted as if to digest her words more fully. "They want me to travel to China? To learn about it? But what about my curse?"

"They seem to be under the assumption that once the Tiger Vessel is safely back where it belongs, it should completely lift the curse. Until then, you would still have access to it in order to continue staving off the worst of the effects."

"Oh, Norah." Rodney ran a hand down his face, his eyes large as he stared at nothing in thought. Norah wasn't sure if he was upset or overjoyed, judging by the expression.

"If you don't feel comfortable in going, you can stay in the States," she added hastily.

He looked at her, a line forming between his brows. "Why would I do that? I've dreamed of traveling back to China my entire life. I just never thought I'd be able to, all things considered. To tour the land, to learn the customs and history, that is a dream come true." He dropped his head into his hand, a small sob escaping as he did. When he looked back up, he was smiling widely through the tears. "Thank you, Norah. I can't believe you not only discovered my cure, you also found a way to facilitate my dreams."

Norah's heart swelled at the praise. "You see? It's never too late to allow hope back in."

CHAPTER THIRTY-NINE

Monday, May 31st, 1915

Malcolm

AFTER A LONG DAY of diplomatic banter with three Chinese offi-cials and a few other governmental bureaucrats, Malcolm watched from his office window as Rodney left with the convoy to make the long journey: first to Washington DC, and then eventually to China, where he would finally part with the Tiger Vessel.

Rodney had been all smiles as he left. Malcolm experienced numerous emotions as he watched the caravan leave the long driveway, taking with it the Guild's longest-standing member: joy for Rodney's bright future, sadness over losing another friend, and jealousy over the adventure laid out in front of the man.

Beside him, Norah sniffled.

He glanced at her. "You aren't crying, are you?"

In response, she glared and dabbed her eyes with a kerchief. "I'm allowed to shed tears over this bittersweet occasion. Not everyone can be an emotionless block like you."

He smirked. The old fire in her had slowly rekindled over the past week, and she'd taken to offering small jabs at his expense again. His world was slowly healing, and Norah was on the proper side of things once again.

"What if I told you that men were just as capable of emotions? For instance, I'm feeling immense pride over this occasion that you single-handedly brought about. Rodney gets to live his life now, scarred but

298

otherwise whole. If you hadn't come along, he'd probably have died in this house."

Like me, Malcolm thought, but kept it to himself.

Still, the words he spoke were true. As Norah gazed at him with joy shining in her glistening eyes, he bent down and placed a tender kiss on her forehead. They still had not resumed any of the passion they'd once expressed—Malcolm lived in fear of scaring her off again—but she allowed small tokens of affection from him. It was his way of telling Norah he was ready whenever she was.

"So," he said, dampening down the urge to sweep her into his arms, "Who is next on your list? I'm losing members at a frightening rate, you know. Soon enough, this guild will be null and void."

She smiled. "I doubt this guild could ever fully disband. You have some tricky customers. I was thinking of researching African curses this evening, to see if I can't figure out Mr. Withers. The poor man, constantly trapped in his body. I can't imagine."

"Couldn't be any worse than being trapped in this house," Malcolm muttered.

Norah heaved a sigh. "On the contrary. You can walk, and communicate, and move your body in whatever way pleases you." She blushed, as if she triggered a memory with her comment.

Malcolm snorted. "Your words, not mine." He wanted to add a bawdy line about moving his body in a way to please her as well, but he did not want to push the matter. "I suppose you have a point. He sees out of his eyes, and most likely has his thoughts, but has no control over his actions. I would go mad."

"Exactly."

"And what of Mr. Norris? Or Ambrose? And Marvin?"

She chewed her lip. "Again, I have been giving them thought. I still am at a loss for Mr. Norris, and frankly, with Ambrose's caster being dead, I don't hold out much hope. And Mr. Ivey?" She blew out a breath through her lips, vibrating them together. "In the end, it might be you, Ambrose, Mr. Ivey, and a chicken holding down the Guild."

Malcolm chuckled, the sound rather deprecating. "What a lovely picture of my future you paint."

She took the initiative and curled her fingers around his, a surprising gesture but one he relished. "Well then," she said with a twinkle in her eye, "it's a good thing I cannot predict the future. That is still very much in your hands."

CHAPTER FORTY

Tuesday, June 1st, 1915

Norah

NORAH HAD FULLY INTENDED to research Mr. Withers' condition last night, but between Rodney's departure and Malcolm being incredibly distracting, she couldn't muster up the energy after all.

But today was a new day, and at ten in the morning, she found herself downstairs in the library with a bracing cup of coffee by her side as she cracked open some rather daunting books.

Africa, for all its size and cultural complexity, was a difficult subject to comprehend. Malcolm's history books told of the Berlin Treaty of 1885, in which the whole of Africa had been carved up amongst European nations like a turkey at Thanksgiving dinner. This opened the door for the spread of white colonialism into the lusher areas.

Karanja had told her he and Withers hailed from British East Africa. Norah knew from the newspaper stories that the war had taken root there as well, and references were often made to infighting between British East Africa and the neighboring German East Africa. Norah's geographical knowledge was woefully lacking otherwise, and she had no clue where exactly these two opposing forces could be found. Luckily for her, one of the books had an illustrated map, and Norah quickly found both territories—BEA, otherwise known as Kenya on the east coast, and GEA directly under it. It was no wonder Africa had been dragged into this war with such proximity.

Still, this did not help her particular search of possible curse origins. By noon, her head spun with knowledge about the "dark continent," but she doubted any of its usefulness. Norah sighed and placed the current book down, rubbing her eyes to ease the strain. Her stomach gurgled, reminding her that breakfast had been hours ago.

She still had one book in the pile left, a rather lengthy tome about Bantu beliefs. The word, so foreign to her eyes, provoked her memories. Ah yes, in one of the drier books she'd scanned; it talked of the different cultures found within Kenya's borders. The Bantu people were one such culture, and Norah believed Karanja to be a part of this demographic, since he surely was not Muslim, the other predominant group. This could be the knowledge she was looking for. She stared at the cover, acknowledging the increasing grumbles of her hunger, but needing the satisfaction of finishing a job—even if it was another dead end.

The book won out over lunch.

Norah immediately chastised herself upon opening it. She should have started with this one instead of the history books. The book immediately regaled her with stories of myriad ways a person of a tribe could be cursed. She pored over each page, filled with descriptions of animal sacrifice to cure a person, or circumstances in which a curse could be placed.

And then, her eyes caught on a small descriptor: *a cracked bowl.*

Norah read the passage. She reread it. Her heart began to speed up.

Lunch was promptly forgotten.

Grasping the book with her finger as a bookmark, she hurried to Malcolm's office, bursting in without a thought to privacy.

Ambrose was there, taking lunch with Malcolm. They both startled and looked at her as she rushed in, brandishing the book.

"I think I have something," she said, breathless from her hurried walk.

Malcolm set his sandwich down to give her his full attention. "What have you got?"

Ambrose answered before she could, "Withers' curse."

Norah spared him a glance. "Yes, exactly. He was sent here without anyone knowing exactly what was wrong with him, correct? Well, I think I know what his curse is."

Malcolm's eyes widened. "Well, what is it?"

Norah opened the book again. "'A Bantu Shaman may place a curse upon an enemy by feeding him from a cracked bowl.' Karanja is Bantu; I'd bet my eyeteeth on it. Isn't there a cracked bowl in their shared room?"

Malcolm stood, his food forgotten. "Karanja feeds him from that bowl. I've seen it myself. You don't think ...?"

Ambrose swore. "I knew there was something off with that fella. He never wanted to associate with the rest of us."

Despite the new evidence stacked against Karanja, Norah still felt the need to defend him. "Be reasonable. He's a foreigner here, and different from the rest of us in both looks and customs because of it. It doesn't mean he's a bad man."

"No, but if he's keeping Mr. Withers cursed, *that* points to a certain wickedness," Malcolm mused as he stared into the distance, a hand absentmindedly rubbing his neck. He focused on Norah. "Right. Let's go and get to the bottom of this."

Malcolm

Malcolm really hoped Norah was wrong. For multiple reasons.

He liked Karanja. Sure, the man was aloof and kept to himself, only participating in the Guild when politeness dictated it. But Malcolm could respect that. And he wasn't the only one to act this way, if Marvin Ivey and even Leighton could be used as examples. Karanja had otherwise been a model houseguest, always polite and helpful.

It was difficult to marry the idea of this shy person with a monster who would purposefully keep someone cursed.

But Norah's words made sense as well. He had only seen Withers eat if Karanja fed him, and it was always from the same wooden bowl.

Ambrose insisted on tagging along, and Malcolm couldn't find it in himself to care. He had become a focused beam, intent upon seeking the truth. Everything else fell away to the background.

The three of them arrived at the bedroom door in short order. Malcolm knocked heavily. "Karanja? Are you there?"

Ambrose snorted. "Where else would he be?"

Norah shushed him sternly.

The door opened a crack, exposing Karanja's face. His forehead pulled into a frown at the sight of them.

"Karanja, we must speak with you," Malcolm said, keeping his voice commanding.

The caretaker backed up a step but did not move to open the door further. "No, sir. I must take care of Mr. Withers now."

His words sealed his fate. Malcolm saw no reason why Karanja would not hear them out. He pushed the door open, forcing the man backward. He marched in, with Ambrose at his heels, and Norah a few steps behind.

Malcolm paused to scan the room as his eyes adjusted to the low light. Mr. Withers sat in his wheelchair as usual, his body hunched forward and his mouth ajar. Behind him, on a small table under the window, sat the wooden bowl, the crack illuminated by a patch of sunlight from a break in the curtains.

Withers' head was downcast at first glance, but now he slowly raised it, the strain causing it to wobble. One of his hands trembled upon its armrest. His eyes slowly moved up to meet with Malcolm's, causing a chill to snake down the latter's spine.

Beside Malcolm, Ambrose let out a small whine, a noise most unlike the brash character. As Malcolm and Norah swiveled their attention to him, he followed up the sound with words that chilled Malcolm's blood: "Help me."

There could be only one man in the room who might think that.

Malcolm turned to Karanja, his anger seeping into his movements. "It's true," he fumed. "You're a Bantu shaman. You're the reason Withers is cursed."

Karanja held up his hands, his eyes rounded and glowing with fear in the dim light. "Please, sir. You don't know—"

Ambrose moved to the back of the room, picking up the bowl. "Is this it?"

"Yes," both Malcolm and Norah said together.

Karanja took a step toward Ambrose but stopped. "Please, you mustn't—"

Ambrose brought the bowl down on his knee, breaking it in two.

The sound of anguish coming from Karanja tugged at Malcolm, creating a great heartache within him. He knew in that moment that Norah's suspicion had been accurate, which simultaneously angered him.

Karanja fell to his knees, the despair emanating from him almost palpable. "No," he moaned as he pressed his head into the floorboards. "It cannot be undone."

Norah rushed over to Withers' side. The man remained unresponsive.

"Karanja," Malcolm stated in his most authoritative voice, "you have deceived us. Are you responsible for the curse that Mr. Withers suffers from?"

Without moving from his low position, Karanja answered, "Yes. I have my reasons." He lifted his head, his dark eyes imploring. "You must listen to me, please."

But Malcolm was not feeling generous. "What you've done is considered a crime. You are a danger to this house, Karanja. I am going to place you in custody for now until I decide what to do with you. The question remains, will you come willingly, or will I have to use force?"

Karanja looked at Malcolm thoroughly, long enough to make Malcolm think he'd need to muscle his way out of this mess after all. Karanja was thin, but tall, and his build showed off a wiry strength. That wasn't mentioning the apparent dark power the man could wield. But Karanja sighed. "I will go willingly. Even if it means I put you all in peril."

The statement sent a wash of chills down Malcolm's spine. "I don't enjoy being threatened," he growled as he clasped Karanja's arm. "Ambrose, bring up the rear. Norah, keep an eye on Withers."

Malcolm brought Karanja to the servant's quarters nearby, choosing a small room at the end of the hall, the only contents within a bed and a chamber pot. Karanja meekly entered, and Malcolm locked the door from the outside, sealing the man inside.

"We shall bring you some supper later," he said before walking away, not bothering to listen to the man's pleas.

"Nasty business, this is," Ambrose said as they emerged back into the communal area. By now, the other members had caught wind of something happening and began to swarm the area.

Malcolm, suddenly winded by the adrenaline running through him, agreed with Ambrose's assessment.

CHAPTER FORTY-ONE

Wednesday, June 2nd, 1915

Norah

MR. WITHERS HAD STAYED his usual immobile self while Norah watched over him all through the previous afternoon and into the night. Norah made sure to feed him a supper of soup, which he willingly slurped through a partially opened mouth. She had no idea if this meal was as messy as his previous ones—Karanja always fed him apart from the others. Still, the old man consumed the spoonfuls readily enough, with small head twitches and flashes of eye contact that lifted her spirits.

At nine that night, Norah recruited Mathers to help her lift Mr. Withers into bed, where he promptly fell asleep. Norah slept fitfully in a chair beside the bed, waking at every creak of the mattress springs, but finding no proof that Mr. Withers was improving.

At four in the morning, he gasped.

The sound catapulted Norah from her light sleep, and she instantly checked the man over. He lay on his back, tears streaming from the outer corners of his widened eyes, the trails glinting in the low light. His upper arms were partially raised, the clawed hands trembling violently.

"Sir, are you well?" Norah asked softly.

The wide staring eyes turned to her slowly, recognition glinting within. His mouth opened and issued a rasping breath, almost a whisper. Then, his jaw moved accordingly, forming actual words.

"Wh ... where ... is he?"

"Shh," Norah soothed, reaching out and placing her hand over one of his shaking fists. "Karanja can't hurt you again. Can you move?"

Mr. Withers wheezed, a sound that scared Norah until she realized he was trying to laugh. "Th-thank you. I ... feel ... better," he said with a stilted English accent.

She patted his arm. "You seem better. I've been worried about you, Mr. Withers. You must rest, though. I'm sure you will continue to recover with proper sleep."

He breathed deeply, settling his arms back down at his sides. The tremors ceased as he relaxed his body, Norah noted with satisfaction. He closed his eyes.

"I'll keep watch over you," she whispered. "Sleep well."

Norah herself got more sleep once she was convinced the old man was in peaceful slumber. It helped to know that despite her misgivings regarding Karanja's treatment, she had helped Mr. Withers with her actions. He would be well again, she knew.

CHAPTER FORTY-TWO

Saturday, June 5th, 1915

Malcolm

MR. WITHERS CONTINUED TO improve, with Norah by his side to help him along the way. She reported every detail to Malcolm with evident delight.

His miraculous reawakening on Wednesday was followed by the gradual ability to control his arms without too much shaking.

On Thursday, Mr. Withers learned to roll from side to side on the bed. It winded him, though, so Norah cautioned about trying too much at once.

Friday saw him able to sit up unassisted in bed, and Norah reported to Malcolm that the man could feed himself for the first time since being cursed.

It was now Saturday, and Malcolm felt a newfound joy floating about Birchwald as the men prepared for the usual communal breakfast. Nearly everyone was there this day, save for Norah and Mr. Withers, who were expected at any moment. Malcolm glanced about at the dwindled seated numbers. With Hector forever departed, Rodney and Pablo cured and gone, and now no Karanja, the table setup seemed almost too large and empty.

Karanja. Malcolm sighed. The only subject that dampened the jubilant mood was the thought of the man, still locked away in the servant's quarters. Malcolm knew he'd have to make a decision soon enough about what to do with him. Authorities would most likely need to be called in. Oddly, Malcolm was loath to do it. He explored this reluctance, reflecting it was most likely due to an instilled protectiveness of the man in his care. Karanja's skin color would put him at a keen disadvantage with the powers that be. Here at Birchwald, he was at least safe from racially charged injustices.

He had also been hoping Mr. Withers could shed some light upon why he was cursed—and perhaps exonerate Karanja in some way—but the old man seemed as confused as the rest of them on the matter. Perhaps his memories would come back as well. Until then, Karanja was as safe as he could be in his makeshift prison.

When Norah wheeled Mr. Withers into the dining room, the table erupted in cheers, which made the old man smile. He inclined his head as if accepting an award, his pale cheeks taking on a ruddy hue.

"Thank you, everyone," Mr. Withers said as Norah situated him at the end of the table and began to fill his plate with food. "It is wonderful to once again be back amongst the living."

"How do you feel?" Farley called from the other table.

"Marvelous," he replied as he stuffed a piece of bacon into his mouth. "It's a wonderful thing to be able to feed myself again."

Norah sat down next to him with a wide smile upon her face. "At this rate, you'll be walking again, too."

He patted Norah's hand in a fatherly way. "And I owe it all to you, my dear."

Malcolm surveyed the table, noting the smiles on everyone's faces, except for Mr. Norris, who was unable to smile, and Mr. Ivey, who must have been having one of his bad vision days. The man was stooped even lower than normal, his eyes squeezed tightly together, and an almost anguished countenance upon his face. Not for the first time, Malcolm wished there were something he or Norah could do to help the unfortunate soul out.

He turned his attention back to Mr. Withers. "How is your memory coming, good sir? Have you thought any more about why you might have been cursed?"

Mr. Withers wiped his mustache upon the linen napkin before replying. "Not the foggiest, I'm afraid. I did have some natives helping at my trade store. They're a brutish bunch, always warring with neighboring tribes. I suppose I might have gotten caught in the crosshairs, so to speak."

"Did Karanja work for you?" Norah asked.

He shook his head and picked up a pastry. "Never seen him before. It was torture, listening to his lies while I remained trapped against my will."

Norah patted his arm, her face radiating compassion. Malcolm's heart warmed with the love he still felt for her. "You're safe from him, now," she told the older man.

"What have you done with him?" Mr. Withers asked, a hint of a wobble sounding in his voice.

Malcolm spoke up. "He's being held in the servant's quarters for now. He'll be removed sometime this next week."

Mr. Withers looked at Malcolm, his expression morphing from concern to contentment. "Good. I'm so glad to hear it."

Fred, sitting next to Malcolm, spoke up. "What's next for you, Norah? Have you looked into chicken curses yet?" He gave Mr. Norris a loving pet down the back for emphasis. Mr. Norris ignored it, gobbling down a biscuit off Fred's plate.

Norah smiled with a hint of melancholy. "I'm still looking into it, Mr. Jamison. I'm afraid between your Mr. Norris, Mr. Ivey's visions, and Mr. Lyster's broadcasting, I'm at a bit of a loss. The only man I have any solid idea for is Mr. Hunt."

Mr. Withers peered about, his watery blue eyes quizzical. Norah patted his hand in her compassionate way. "Mr. Hunt has been cursed by a letter opener," she explained for the old man's benefit. "He must feed it a little of his blood each day; otherwise, a larger catastrophe will befall him."

To illustrate the point, Mr. Hunt held up Bloodletter for Withers to see. "Indeed," Withers responded with a nod.

Norah turned back to the group at large. "I haven't given up yet on the rest of you, though."

"Nor should you," Malcolm chimed in, his reward a gratified smile from Norah directed at him only. "Of course, if you keep this up, the Guild is doomed to fail spectacularly."

"I wouldn't worry too much about that," Norah assured him with a cheeky twinkle in her eye. "As long as there are men out there in the world foolish enough to mess with things they have no right to, there will be cursed individuals to direct to Birchwald."

Malcolm laughed, as did the others around him. "In that case," he said, raising his glass of water, "a toast to foolish men!"

"Here, here!" Ambrose said, clinking glasses with Farley.

Norah

Given how old and frail Mr. Withers was, Norah felt it prudent to insist on an afternoon nap in order for the man to regain his strength faster. He did not object, readily agreeing with her assessment.

Norah wheeled him back to his room and helped him into the bed. The room had been cleared of everything belonging to Karanja, just in case. It gave the room an unlived-in atmosphere, which made Norah strangely melancholy. Her thoughts once again traveled to the African man, locked up in the servant's quarters.

"How did you come to be in Africa?" Norah asked as she tucked the covers around Mr. Withers.

He sighed and wiggled a little to make himself more comfortable. "Misfortune has been my lot. I was orphaned as a child and sent to live with relatives. As soon as I turned eighteen, I joined the army and eventually wound up in Africa. I've been there ever since."

The story was short and lacking in details, but Norah knew he was tired, and a lot of talking was probably difficult. "We have some things in common," she mused. She stood and closed the curtain. "Get some rest. I'll check in on you in a couple of hours."

"Thank you, my dear."

On her own again, Norah made her way to the balcony, hoping to find the master of the house. His presence was a comfort, although a strain still existed between them.

Malcolm was indeed out on their shared balcony, a small glass of sherry in his hands and a thoughtful expression on his face as he stared into the scenery.

"I've been thinking," he said by way of greeting.

She sat next to him, close enough to feel the warmth of his body emanating into hers. "Should I be concerned?"

He gazed at her, his lip tilted up in a half-smile. "I'm not known for my brains, you know. Nothing too dangerous could be born of them."

She leaned back with a contented sigh, happy to have regained the old camaraderie. "On the contrary, an ignorant brain can be one of the most dangerous things in the world. You give yourself too little credit, though, Malcolm, so I'm not terribly concerned. But I've derailed you. What was your thought?"

He exhaled slowly. "We've not given Karanja a chance to explain his side. Do you think we should?"

"Do you really want my opinion on the matter?"

"Of course I do."

Norah hmphed quietly to herself. "I think you should have given him a chance to explain when you first accused him. Instead, you and Ambrose strong-armed Karanja into his little prison without allowing him a word."

"And you're just telling me this now?" Malcolm narrowed his eyes at her as he sat straighter.

She threw her hands up. "I doubt you would have listened to me. You seemed to be acting on some primal male instinct. A lowly female such as myself would have been ignored in such a situation."

Malcolm goggled at her. "My word, you really have it out for me sometimes, don't you?" He shook his head. "You might have a slight point, though. I was not thinking too clearly that day. What say you and I rectify my primitive male mistake?"

She smiled wryly and placed her hand on top of his. It was cool to the touch. "Let's."

Within moments, they made their way to the door in the servant's quarters. Malcolm knocked softly with a clearing of his throat. "Karanja, it's Malcolm. And Miss Abernathy. We would like to talk to you. Will you be civil?"

Norah lightly slapped Malcolm's arm over his choice of words. "He's not an animal," she hissed.

He rubbed his arm. "No, but he's certainly capable of causing harm. I have your safety to think about, after all."

His words softened her. Turning to the door, she called out, "Karanja, we only want to hear your side of things. May we talk?"

From behind the door, the man's deep voice called out, "Come in."

Malcolm unlocked the door and opened it, caution paramount in his movements. Karanja was on the other side of the room, sitting on the small bed. The room smelled of stale sweat with an undertone of used chamber pot. Norah wrinkled her nose momentarily before schooling her features.

Karanja glistened with sweat in the stuffy room. Deep circles around his dark eyes belied a lack of proper sleep. He looked terrible, and Norah felt an instant pang of regret for not checking on him sooner.

Once in the room, Malcolm shut the door and stood in front of it. "Mr. Withers is healing nicely," he stated.

Karanja closed his eyes. "You don't know anything about him."

"Only what he's told us about himself. He's a harmless old man," Malcolm stated.

Karanja looked up at Malcolm, a new fire behind his eyes. "I know a much different story, sir, but I doubt you will believe me."

Norah took a step closer. "Then tell us, Karanja. I at least am open to hearing what you have to say."

Malcolm shot her a look. She ignored it.

Karanja shook his head. "It will not look good for me to tell you that I have withheld truths from you. But I must tell you that."

"You lied to us," Malcolm paraphrased. "We already knew that. You are right; it does not instill a great amount of confidence in this scenario."

"Hush," Norah admonished. To Karanja, she said, "Go ahead."

Karanja took a breath. "I am not from Kenya, nor any of the British-owned territory," he began. "I lived farther south."

Norah's previous geography lesson helped her piece together a rather large fact. "You lived in German East Africa?"

Karanja nodded. "We call it Tanganyika. Close to the border with Kenya, but yes. And Mr. Withers also lived there."

Malcolm scoffed. "Are you implying that Peter Withers is German? The man sounds as British as the king of England."

"I know not where he came from originally, sir. I only know where he ended up."

"Did you curse him, Karanja?" Norah asked, getting to the point.

He shook his head. "I did not. My father did. He is a *mganga*. What you would call a shaman. Baba instructed me to keep Withers under thrall."

"But why?" Norah pressed.

Karanja splayed out his hands. "Because he is a bad man, ma'am."

"Withers?" Malcolm interjected. "Or your father?"

Norah heaved a breath. "Withers, obviously," she answered for Karanja. She turned back to the other man. "But *why* is he a bad man? Karanja, surely you can see that people's ideas of morals can vary. The concept is simply not black and white."

Karanja dropped his head. "My father, he kept his eyes on this man, this *shetani*, for many years. My father is a good man; he kept my family safe, both from tribes who would hurt us and from the white men who thought they owned us just because they moved to our land. My father worked alongside this … wizard. To keep him close, to make sure he did nothing bad."

"Keep your friends close and your enemies closer," Malcolm mused.

"Exactly that," Karanja agreed. "I asked to help, but Baba said no. He would not even give me the full name of the man. Only his first name."

"So, your father watched over Withers, worked alongside Withers? And then what?" Malcolm asked.

"Withers left for many months. When he came back, he bragged to my father. Something he had done, an unspeakable act. My father decided he was too dangerous to allow free will any longer, and he cursed him. The act weakened my father, though, and he could not keep the curse alive."

"And that is where you came in, I take it?" Norah asked.

He nodded. "I offered to take over keeping him in thrall, and to further help Baba, I moved away from our home, to go where no one would recognize us. I traveled toward Mount Kilimanjaro with Withers, but I was too close to the British border. With the white men riled like ants, there were more soldiers on patrol, and we were taken in by the British army. They questioned, why was I traveling alone with a white man? I worried they would think I was a spy, so I told them the man had employed me in one of the British colonies, but he'd become ill with a curse and I was seeking to break it. Baba never told me the cursed man's full name, so I named him Peter Wizard. The British men misheard me and changed the name to Withers. They offered to send me here, and to protect my father, I accepted. That is all."

Malcolm rubbed his chin. "Quite the story, Karanja."

Norah agreed, although with slightly less cynicism than Malcolm's tone suggested. Karanja seemed earnest in his tale, however far-fetched it seemed. She still could not see Mr. Withers as anything more than a harmless old man.

"Perhaps your father was mistaken about Mr. Withers," she suggested. "You never actually saw him do anything bad?"

"I did not. My father would not allow me to get close. Only after the curse was placed."

Norah nodded and met eyes with Malcolm briefly. "Thank you, Karanja. We have much to discuss."

"I'm afraid I'll need to keep you in here a bit longer, old chap," Malcolm added as he ushered Norah out. "No hard feelings."

Karanja only sat on his bed, his head hanging low, as the door was shut and locked again.

Once back in the main area, Norah turned to Malcolm. "Well, what are your thoughts?"

Malcolm sighed heavily. "I'm unsure. It sounds off to me. His father never let him know *why* Withers was bad? It's his word against Withers'. I say we keep an eye on the old man and go from there."

"But what about Karanja?"

He grimaced. "That's a bit more of a pickle. Technically, he imprisoned a man against his will for no discernable reason. And he lied to us in the process."

Norah couldn't help but point out the hypocrisy. "*You're* imprisoning him against his will."

"Yes, I'm well aware." Malcolm ran his fingers through his dark hair. "Very well. I'll call on the authorities tomorrow. Karanja should be moved."

CHAPTER FORTY-THREE

Sunday, June 6th, 1915

Norah

BREAKFAST HADN'T YET BEEN served in Norah's room when Malcolm knocked on the door.

"You're up early," she remarked upon letting him enter.

Malcolm flashed a customary smile, but she could see the strain behind the brief gesture. "There's a bit of an issue," he said in low tones.

Norah closed the door, her stomach clenching at his words. "What's wrong?"

Malcolm ran his hand down his face, a sure sign of his agitation. "Farley came to me first thing this morning." He paused. "It seems he's misplaced Bloodletter."

A rush of dread coursed through her. "Oh dear. He's done this before though, hasn't he?"

He nodded. "Yes, but not since you've come along."

Norah made a noise in her throat. "Has he bled yet today?"

"No."

That was one bit of good news, at least. "Let's try to keep it that way, shall we?"

Malcolm raised his eyebrows. "And how do you plan to enact that? The man can cut himself on dust in the air, it would seem."

"I'm not sure, but the sooner we act, the better." Norah, still in her robe, began to head to her dressing room as she spoke, shucking the outer garment off as she did with only thoughts of haste spurring her forward. She forgot she'd worn a rather skimpy nightgown overnight, but the sound of Malcolm's strangled inhale reminded her. She stopped in her tracks and began to pull the wrap back into place, thinking of propriety much too late.

Malcolm's hand touched her bare arm as she did so, a pleading sort of caress. "Norah ..."

She placed her own hand over his before turning. "I must dress if I'm to be of use to you and Mr. Hunt."

He looked lost as he gazed into her eyes. "We haven't discussed what happened—what's happening—between us."

She nodded, dropping her sight to their connected hands. "You're right. And we should, once the danger to Mr. Hunt has passed. But Malcolm, now is not the time."

Malcolm tilted her head back up with a gentle finger under her chin. She met his eyes again, a new light, one filled with hope, shining within. "Just this, then," he said, and then leaned down to brush his lips over hers.

The same ignition in her chest as before lit her up from within, erasing the misgivings caused by the falling out. Norah kissed him back, although only long enough to make an unsaid promise to him. He let her go, a wry smile gracing his lips.

"I'll be just a jiffy," she said before running into the dressing room, her heart a strange mixture of lightness over Malcolm and dread over Mr. Hunt.

Malcolm

Farley was rummaging frantically in his bureau when Malcom and Norah arrived. Clothes littered the floor of his room like oversized confetti, and as they watched, the man grabbed another armful and threw it out of the drawer in an uncaring manner.

"Any luck?" Malcolm asked.

"Gah!" Farley exclaimed with a jerk, pulling both hands out of the dresser and swearing. He cradled one hand in the other.

"What's happened?" Malcolm demanded, rushing over to see.

Farley extracted his hand, a long, ragged gash marring its top. Malcolm watched in horror as the wound welled with blood.

"There was a splinter on the side," Farley said. "It caught me when I jerked my hand away just now."

"Well, so much for keeping him safe until we've found the letter opener," Norah said, the ire in her tone evident. "How long before something worse happens if we don't feed the blade?"

"Er, usually a couple of hours, tops," Farley said. He sat on the bed with a thump. "What do we do?"

Malcolm, adrift with his mixed feelings of concern and annoyance over causing the injury, tried to gather his thoughts into a coherent answer, but Norah was quicker. "We mobilize the rest of the household to search for it," she declared, sitting down in the only other chair in the room. "When was the last time you saw Bloodletter?"

Farley rocked back and forth for a moment. "Yesterday morning. I've been in the habit of placing it on top of my bureau every day, in the same place. I pricked my finger as usual yesterday and placed the blade back. At least I thought I did. But it was not there this morning."

"You used to place it down in odd spots before Norah came along," Malcolm reminded him. "Where else could you have placed it?"

"I've checked the bathroom already. I suppose it could be in the dining room, from breakfast. I overslept and didn't have time to feed Bloodletter until after the meal."

Norah stood and turned to leave.

"Where are you going?" Malcolm asked.

"There is no time to waste," she answered, pausing at the door. "I'm going to rouse the others, and I'm also sending for the surgeon. Just in case." She left without waiting for any follow-up questions.

"Well, at least we know she's competent in emergency situations," Malcolm said. "Come along, Farley. We have a cursed relic to find."

Norah

After rousing the troops on the third floor—consisting only of Ambrose and Mr. Jamison; Mr. Ivey was oddly not in his room, and Norah did not want to tax Mr. Withers, whom she assumed was sleeping in—Norah rushed down the stairs to find Mrs. Bixby and Mathers. Mrs. Bixby had been setting up breakfast trays in the kitchen with Mathers, but she sprang up to go about the hunt, knowing the danger of the blade. Before Mathers could also assist, Norah pulled him aside.

"I need you to run into town and fetch Dr. Wrightly," she told him. "Please tell him to bring all his transfusion supplies. Nothing has happened yet, but he should be here in case we aren't timely enough."

Mathers gave a stiff nod. "Very well, Madam."

With Mrs. Bixby in tow, Norah came back to the third floor and began the search in earnest.

By eleven in the morning, Bloodletter was still at large, and the entire floor had been picked apart. Malcolm decided it was time to search the second floor, as unlikely as it might be.

Mathers still had not returned with the surgeon. Norah's pulse throbbed to the beat of her agitation, a measured tempo to count down the sword of Damocles dangling above her. She expected disaster at any moment, no matter how much she told herself to be calm. At least she presented an outside appearance of control, instead of the ever-increasing internal distress she truly felt. It would do no good to further panic the others.

Each man took a room on the second floor, fanning out to search. With the multitude of bathrooms and dressing rooms, plus the spaciousness of the bedrooms, it proved to be a larger task than the whole of the third floor.

Norah searched the Iris Room to the north of her own room, planning to make her way down the hall once she was finished with it. As she peered under the bed where her aunt had slept before honeymooning with Pablo, she heard a mighty crashing sound, muffled by walls and distance.

The unexpected discord jangled her to her feet. "What on earth?" she said to herself. She ran to the hallway.

At the other end of the hall, Malcolm stood in his bedroom doorway, equally confused. "Did you hear that?"

Norah nodded as she walked toward him. "Something broke. Something large."

He glanced at the door to the Aster Room, which was ajar. "Was there anyone in your room?"

She shook her head, alarm bells racing through her stomach at seeing the open door. She was sure she'd shut it. "I'd planned to search it next myself. You don't think ..."

Malcolm did not wait for her to finish her thought but marched into the room. Norah followed.

A pleasant summer breeze greeted them, a most unexpected sensation, given that Norah left the windows closed. But the sight that came next made Norah gasp. The window directly in front of them was in tatters, completely broken, with flecks of red gracing the tips of the jagged window shards.

They rushed forward in unison.

Careful to avoid the broken panes herself, Norah poked her head out of the large hole and surveyed the immediate area. There, resting on the roof of the solarium with a halo of broken glass surrounding him, lay Farley Hunt.

Norah nearly dared not look at him, for fear he was dead. After all, he was perfectly still, his back aligned with a metal rib of the roof—and probably the only reason he did not fall through the glass. His arms splayed out limply at his sides, reminding Norah of religious iconography. Running down the solarium's windowpanes was a small stream of ruby blood.

But Mr. Hunt groaned softly and stirred. She let out a choking gasp.

"He's alive, Malcolm," she breathed, turning to the man beside her. "We have to get him down from there."

Malcolm, his face white, straightened and yelled, "*Mrs. Bixby!*" at the top of his lungs before striding out of the room.

Norah continued to watch Mr. Hunt, knowing that time was running out for the man, as surely as his blood was.

Malcolm

Getting Farley down from the roof of the solarium was no easy feat. Malcolm procured a ladder straight away with Mrs. Bixby's help, and, ignoring his own curse, departed the mansion through the front door to get the man down himself.

Ambrose and Fred came as well, having investigated the ruckus and learned of their comrade's perilous state. Mr. Norris ran about the front yard, chasing after grasshopper nymphs and other tasty invertebrates, and largely ignoring the rescue attempt. Eddie also cavorted about, happy to be outdoors with so many of the people he adored and oblivious to the upsetting undertone of the occasion.

Norah watched from the destroyed window.

With Ambrose holding the ladder steady, Malcolm climbed. He thought the natural rounded slope of the roof would make his job of procuring Farley easier, but the injured man stuck fast the moment Malcolm tried to move him. He soon figured out the reason: a small, curved piece of wrought iron had pierced the man's side, close to the kidney, keeping him pinned in place like a bug in a shadowbox. Malcolm's only course of action was to climb higher up the ladder in order to fully grasp Farley and lift him off the metal.

As soon as he was free, blood began to flow in a fresh gush. Malcolm suppressed the urge to gag at the sight.

"Do be careful!" Norah needlessly instructed from her perch above him. Malcolm ignored her, intent on his task.

Now that Farley was no longer impaled, his limp form easily slid on the smooth glass surface.

A little too easily, Malcolm was dismayed to discover. It took all his strength to prevent the man from completely sliding off the roof. A fall like that would surely kill Farley.

Fred, having noticed Malcolm's struggle, crawled up the ladder behind him. Taking Farley's legs, he helped Malcolm guide the unconscious man down to the safety of the ground, the blood meanwhile coating all three men in sticky gore.

Norah made a cry from the second story, a sound that grated at Malcolm. He looked up at her, but she was gone. Ignoring any other background noise, he stripped his shirt off and began to tie it around Farley's midsection in an attempt to stop the bleeding.

It was during this arduous task that the surrounding sounds filtered back. "... in need of immediate assistance," Norah was saying.

"Good god," someone else said, a voice Malcolm did not recognize. He looked up to see Dr. Wrightly staring at the gruesome scene before him. He rushed over to Malcolm's side, placing his fingers at Farley's neck. "What happened?"

Malcolm gave the doctor more room. "Seems someone defenestrated him. He's lucky to be alive."

"I'll say. And I do believe his guardian angel is working overtime about now. It's pure providence I arrived when I did. Come, no time to waste. He'll need a transfusion."

Malcolm felt a wave of pain travel through his body as his curse reared its spiteful head. "Can we move this indoors?"

Dr. Wrightly paused, rolling the thought around. "I suppose. We must act quickly, though. He's lost a lot of blood already."

Mathers, who had arrived with the surgeon, quickly bent to help Malcolm lift Farley. Together, they entered Birchwood and set him down in the grand hall. Dr. Wrightly immediately began unpacking his tools.

Malcolm grimaced. He saw a lot of needles in his immediate future.

Norah

Norah thanked her lucky stars she'd had the forethought to summon the surgeon. As it was, he'd nearly arrived too late, and it was still much too close a call for anyone's comfort.

The doctor wasted no time in setting up his tools. Malcolm looked a bit green as he stretched out on one of the sofas—brought into the hall by Mathers and Ambrose, who fetched a second for Mr. Hunt's unresponsive form. Eddie jumped up next to Malcolm, cuddling into his side as an offer of physical comfort and emotional support. Warmth spread through Norah's chest at the sight.

While Dr. Wrightly began the procedure, Norah beckoned for Mrs. Bixby to follow her back to her room. There was no point in hanging about uselessly downstairs when there was work to be done, and her room was a complete disaster. She could continue the search for Bloodletter as well, even though the matter was no longer urgent. It was a bit like locking the barn door after the last horse was stolen.

"What a mess," Mrs. Bixby said as she began picking up pieces of the broken breakfast table.

Norah agreed. Much of the window debris had naturally been blown outward, but some bits of glass and window trim littered the floor, not to mention the hunks of table and chair, which had also been a casualty of whatever had transpired. She picked up a broom and began to sweep the debris into the center of the room.

"What do you think happened?" Mrs. Bixby asked as she added wood hunks to the pile.

"I can't even begin to imagine," Norah replied as she swept. "I wish we could ask Mr. Hunt. It's possible his curse caused him to lose his balance near the window and fall through. I'm not sure why he was in here in the first place, though."

The housekeeper only made a small noise as a response.

It was incredible how far the glass spread out. Her bed even had shards about it, and upon cleaning up the biggest of the pieces, Norah decided to move the bed farther away to check for any shards that might have traveled underneath.

She pushed with all her might but only ended up shifting the mattress from the heavy frame. Sighing, she lifted the mattress to move it back. As she did, a piece of paper wedged in the frame caught her eye. She grabbed it out before letting the mattress fall.

The paper was folded in half. Norah opened it, and a small bundle of flattened dried leaves and flowers tumbled out. Ignoring the botany for a moment, she studied what was written on the paper.

Please keep Malcolm safe from harm. Keep him protected in his own home forever.

Those two short sentences sent a shiver through Norah. Her eyes widened as she took in the implications.

"Mrs. Bixby?" she called out, hearing the tremor in her voice.

The older lady approached immediately. "What is it, dearie? You look as if you've seen a ghost."

"I think I have." She held the paper out for the housekeeper to inspect.

"What's this?" she asked as she looked at the paper. Her eyes also widened as she read it.

Norah inspected the dried bundle. Asters and marigolds, if her eyes did not deceive her. She accessed her Oxford teachings. Marigolds denoted protection. Asters too, but there was also a personal connotation with that particular flower, one that would have given this curse an extra strength.

"Mrs. Bixby," Norah said with a new strength to her tone, "do you recognize the handwriting?"

Mrs. Bixby nodded. "It's Mrs. Drury, as I live and breathe. Where did you find this?"

"Under the mattress. Did you know about this?"

The anxiety in the housekeeper's eyes as she shook her head spoke to her truthfulness. "I had no idea. Mrs. Drury loved her son like no other. She did always worry about him taking after his father and being lost to adventuring, though. Still. I can't believe she'd curse him."

Norah pursed her mouth. "Perhaps she did not mean to curse him per se, but the impact is what matters, not the intent." She frowned at the implications that continued to tangle together the more she pondered them. "Poor Malcolm. He'll be heartbroken."

Mrs. Bixby handed her the note back. "What are you going to do?"

She stuck the note in her pocket. "Tell him, I suppose. He deserves to know why he can't leave his home." She thought for a moment. "Be a lamb, Mrs. Bixby, and go see how he's doing? I don't wish to disturb him if he's feeling poorly." She shot her arm out to take the other woman's before she could stand. "Don't mention *this* to him yet," she cautioned. "It might come as a shock, and with his current blood loss, I'd hate to do more damage. I'll keep cleaning in the meanwhile."

Mrs. Bixby nodded and left promptly, and Norah once again began sweeping.

The repetitive action opened her thoughts, allowing them room to breathe. She let out a sigh. This day should have been like any other, but instead it had been a complete disaster. How had things gone so wrong? First Mr. Hunt and his near-fatal accident, and now this, the discovery of Malcolm's curse origins in the form of someone he clearly adored. Her heart yearned to be with him at this moment, but she had sent Mrs. Bixby like a coward instead.

But then again, now that she knew the basis for the curse, she had a good shot at breaking it. And if she did that, the best course of action would be to leave him, in order to allow him the life he should have. Coming on the heels of the promising kiss, it was nearly too much for Norah to handle.

The door opened again behind her. Malcolm must not have been doing well at all for Mrs. Bixby to be back already. Norah began to turn. "How is—"

It was not Mrs. Bixby standing in the room. It was Mr. Withers.

"Goodness," Norah said breathlessly. "I wasn't quite expecting you, Mr. Withers. Are you well?"

The older man smiled. "Fine, fine," he answered as he slowly stepped closer, inspecting Norah's sweeping with a puzzled look upon his face. "And how are you, my dear?"

Norah placed the broom down and motioned for the gentleman to take a chair. "You're walking! Are you sure you don't require your wheelchair?"

Mr. Withers scowled at the suggestion and ignored the proffered chair. "I've had my fill of that wretched contraption, thank you very much. It feels good to be on my own two feet again."

"Of course," Norah stammered. At a loss for words, she blurted, "I do hope we haven't disturbed your peace too much today. I'm afraid it's all gone rather poorly around here."

Mr. Withers chuckled as he craned his head about. "Quite the *katzenjammer* out there, isn't it?"

The strange word jangled at Norah. She'd heard it before—anyone who had read the newspaper comics had—but coming from the mouth of the old man, it took on a different flavor from the antics of two cartoon characters. Karanja's implication that they came from German territory, not British, clanged about her head. A slight alarm shot through her already frazzled nerves, but she quelled it externally.

"Y-yes," she replied, her thoughts slowing to a crawl. "It's been an odd day. Poor Mr. Hunt fell out of the window. We are hoping he'll pull through. Are you sure you shouldn't sit?"

Mr. Withers looked about the room with apparent boredom. "Oh, I'm well. Just dandy. My strength is all returned. No more bed for me, my dear. So, Mr. Hunt is still alive?"

Norah's senses sharpened as if a dangerous predator had just entered the room. The phrasing of the question he directed at her caused the mild alarm to intensify. "He is. He's downstairs with the surgeon."

Mr. Withers sighed as he slowly approached Norah. She backed up closer to the broken window, leaving space between them. She stopped shy of it, her self-preservation telling her not to approach it too closely.

There was something about Withers' locomotion; it was too smooth, too easy for a man who could hardly walk just a day ago. She realized now that she had only assumed Mr. Withers to be asleep in his room all morning—she had never actually checked.

He stopped coming closer and gazed at the hole in the wall behind her. "I assumed a quick trip out of the window would be sufficient," he said with nonchalance.

Norah's heart pattered too quickly. She backed up further, the window behind her a prominent reminder that she was not safe. "Mr. Withers—" she began, hating the timid catch in her voice.

"That is not my name," he snapped, silencing her. He fumbled into his vest pocket as he began speaking again. "I am tired of hearing that name. I may have been immobile during my curse, but I could see and hear it all. Do you have any idea how much torture it is to be trapped in your own body with no escape, no means of communicating with the world around you?"

Norah, sensing he needed a response, quickly shook her head as she darted her eyes about for an escape from this nightmare.

He chuckled. "No, I could hear every conversation around me with stunning clarity. I knew it was Karanja's father who had gotten the better of me. I thought him to be a weak old man, but I was wrong for once. When Karanja was detained at the British border, they asked for my name. He did not know it fully, of course. His father only referred to me by my first name, or as 'the wizard.' That was the name Karanja gave, only those idiot soldiers misheard him. 'Peter Withers.' It has been my name ever since. But I was born with a better, stronger name."

He took another step closer. Norah's throat closed over a swallow, producing a small whimper.

A new voice came from behind Withers at the door, full of righteous anger. "Dieter Metzger," it boomed through the room.

Withers—Metzger—turned to the new interloper. Norah peered around him as best she could.

It was Marvin Ivey, his green eyes fully open and fixed on the older man, and his face in a scowl.

"Mr. Ivey?" Norah squeaked, hoping his appearance was one of fortune.

"Let her go, Metzger," Ivey growled. He squeezed his eyes shut for a moment, his face contorting to pain. "Fire and blood!"

Metzger turned back to Norah, a wry grin gracing his face. It chilled her. "How fortuitous that you and I ended up in the same safe house, Mr. Ivey. I never forget a face, and I've seen yours ever since I got here, even if I couldn't react to it. But you ... you never saw me, did you? Too afraid to open your eyes to the visions."

Ivey relaxed his face to meet Metzger's gaze. "I knew it was you from the moment you spoke yesterday at breakfast. It was your voice. It's haunted me ever since I lost Violet." A tear escaped his eye as he turned toward Norah, still not daring to look at her. "I apologize for disappearing, Miss Abernathy. I should have warned you, but I was afraid. I knew if I stayed in my room, I'd be the first to die, and I needed time to collect myself. But now I know what I need to do. Let her go," he repeated, this last line directed back at Metzger.

"I think not," Metzger responded, a cool demeanor demonstrating he was in charge. "While I am grateful to her for saving me from my curse, Miss Abernathy meddled in things she should not have. Now that she has broken mine, I don't wish for her to help anyone else. She must go. As a matter of fact, I don't think I can allow anybody in this house to live. I've already dealt with Karanja, that little grass snake. I thought I had Mr. Hunt taken care of, but alas, I must be losing my touch. No matter, I'm free now and have the luxury to take care of things. Starting with you," he ended with a growl at Ivey, the mustache Norah had once thought grandfatherly twitching menacingly. "I'm curious, though. How on earth did you survive this long with what I cursed you with?"

Norah watched this interaction with a muddle of emotions, fear being at the forefront, with despair at releasing this monster overpowering the anger and sadness in the background. Through it all, her natural curiosity overrode everything else. If Norah was to die, she'd do so with as much knowledge of the situation as possible. "Who are you?"

Metzger moved to the side, to allow both her and Ivey to remain in his sight. "I am a person of consequence, although until now I've worked from the shadows. I have a knack, you see. I am attracted to curses. I enjoy sniffing them out, finding the cursed relics, and using them when they'll be at their most advantageous."

As he spoke, he once again reached into his pocket, this time extracting a familiar blade. Bloodletter. Norah could only shake her head with sudden clarity, mentally cursing her previous obtuseness. Ivey took a small step back.

Metzger studied the relic before meeting Norah's eyes with a cunning stare. "I was rather short with you about my history when you asked yesterday," he said conversationally, as if he hadn't just threatened to kill everyone in Birchwald. "What I told you was more or less true, but I left out many a fine detail. Such as the fact I was born in Germany to parents who didn't care if I lived or died. I was just a mouth to feed. A voice to ignore. A hide to whip when they truly were tired of me, and that was often. So, when I was eight years old, I lit the house on fire, with them in it."

He lifted his eyes heavenward and sighed theatrically. "Had I known I'd be forced to leave my beloved homeland, perhaps I would have done things differently. I was forced to go to England, to stay with my uncle. He was not much better than my parents, but I had the element of sympathy on my side. You see, no one knew the fire was my fault."

Metzger looked at her again, ignoring Ivey who still skulked on the side. "The act of killing my parents had changed me. I was filled with glee—no, with *Schadenfreude*. Did you know there is no good English comparison for that word? The English language is sorely lacking." He clucked his tongue before smiling. "I wanted more of the feeling, and the more I sought out the darkness, the happier I became. I thrive on chaos, you see. I can sniff out curses, and I bask in their presence like a pig in mud. Now that you know my story, do you still think we have a lot in common?"

No, Norah could say she did not still feel that way. Norah's life may have been difficult, but she did not want to tear the world down because of it. She stayed silent, however.

Metzger grunted, taking her silence as an acceptable response. He continued, "I had to temper this affinity while I was young, but as soon as I could, I traveled the world, bestowing little acts of unkindness as I went. I also collected cursed relics. They seemingly had no effect on me. I eventually settled in Africa and opened my little shop, so I could curse the tourists at my leisure, like I did with Violet Ivey. My shop was one of horrors for most, but it brought me great delight." He sighed at the memories before facing Norah with a gleeful glint in his eye. "But all the while, I dreamed of a greater mission, one that would unleash a suffering unlike any other. When I caught wind of strife brewing between Austria and Serbia over a year ago, I knew at last my calling had come."

"What are you saying?" Norah asked.

"Germany will always have my allegiance, despite living in Africa for so many years. Even from my little perch in the dark continent, I've kept my finger on the pulse of the world. I'd heard about the increasing discontent of the Serbs under Austrian rule. My contacts told me the time was ripe to pluck that restlessness and mold it into a tool. All it would take was a push in the right direction. And then Germany would have no choice but to declare war in the name of Austria."

"Surely you're not claiming what I think you're claiming," Norah said.

Metzger eyed her. "You are quite the outspoken young woman. Most would—I don't know—faint or scream in the face of the villain. In other circumstances, I'd admire your fortitude, my dear." He studied the letter opener for a moment. "But yes, I *am* claiming that. *I* traveled to Serbia. *I* joined the dissenters. *I* gave that young man the cursed pistol that ended the archduke's life. And I started the war to end all wars."

"And then you scuttled back to Africa like the spider you are," Norah practically spat. This was the horrendous deed Karanja's father had cursed Metzger for. Norah felt like a fool for having undone it.

"I merely needed to bide my time," Metzger continued. "But that meddlesome witch doctor somehow discovered what I did." He frowned before smoothing it over. "No matter. I succeeded in the end, despite not accomplishing everything I'd hoped. I would rather more countries join the fray, but I have no doubt that will still happen."

"But why?" Norah pressed.

Metzger considered the question. "Call it my curse," he replied with a shrug. "Sowing the seeds of destruction and malcontent. It is positively *delicious* to me. And a full-out world war is an absolute banquet."

"You won't succeed," Ivey said.

"I already have, you *arschgeige.*" Metzger turned to Ivey, who backed away slowly, toward the unlit fireplace. Norah realized he was drawing the older man away from her. But she refused to leave just yet; Ivey was in as much danger as she.

Metzger's smooth voice filtered through her panic. "Do you have any idea how delightful it was to curse your wife? That ring had sat in my little shop for years, just waiting for the right woman to come along. And your Violet was perfect."

Mr. Ivey flinched, as if from a sudden headache. "Blood, so much blood," he moaned as he clutched his head.

"Mm, yes, so much blood, Mr. Ivey," Metzger purred as he withdrew Bloodletter.

Norah acted on instinct. She grabbed the oil lamp base by her feet and rushed forward, striking Metzger over the head.

He roared in pain but did not crumple. Instead, he lashed out, backhanding her across the face. Norah spun and fell with a yell of her own.

A trickle of blood wound its way down Metzger's balding pate. He smeared the flow across his forehead, looking at his fingers for the evidence of her attack. His responding smile redoubled her already overworked heart.

"And here I thought ladies knew to play by the rules," he said with a gleeful sneer. "If you wanted to end your life so soon, Miss Abernathy, you only needed to ask." He took a step toward her.

"Blood and fire!" Mr. Ivey yelled as he launched himself toward Metzger, allowing Norah to crawl backwards a couple of paces. The two men collided together, wrestling for control of Bloodletter.

They careened about the room with the blade held high, their heavy breaths and grunts of anger punctuating the room. Metzger punched his opponent squarely in the jaw, but Ivey's proximity meant the blow landed too softly to be of detriment. In retaliation, Ivey pushed Metzger toward the fireplace, taking himself along until the older man thudded into the wall. His shoulder bumped into the gas nozzle, and Norah heard the sudden hiss from the unlit fireplace.

Metzger growled and tried to push back, but Ivey was slightly stronger, keeping him pinned to the wall. In the commotion, Ivey had loosened his grip on the man's hand which held Bloodletter. With a nasty smile, Metzger twisted the letter opener free and pivoted the hand down, stabbing it into Ivey's side.

Norah cried out upon witnessing it.

Mr. Ivey groaned with pain and staggered back a step, away from Metzger.

"Detestable whelp," Metzger growled. "I should have ended you when I had the chance."

His head hanging low, Ivey mumbled to himself. Norah could barely make out the words. "So much blood ... a river of red ..."

Norah noted with horror the crimson stain blooming at Ivey's side in a halo around the hilt of Bloodletter.

Metzger straightened his body, a look of satisfaction upon his face as he panted. "Better late than never, I suppose."

Ivey kept mumbling, his hand grabbing hold of the hilt where it stuck out of his body. The stain spread wider as Norah watched, her terror rooting her to the spot.

"Silver linings. You'll soon be united with your wife, I suppose," Metzger continued, the vindictive smile still present. "Your insufferable Violet."

At this, Ivey stopped the flow of his words and lifted his chin to stare at Metzger. Norah watched as he looked darkly upon the older man, before pulling Bloodletter from his side in a sudden jolt. In one swift motion, Ivey arced the blade up and brought it down squarely upon Metzger.

The blade slid into the space between Metzger's neck and shoulder with a sickening crunch. The man bellowed in pain and rage and crumpled to his knees in front of the fireplace. Mr. Ivey continued to hold the hilt, pinning the older man to the ground as the latter began to thrash below him.

"You'll not be done with me that easily," Metzger said with a pained sneer.

Mr. Ivey stumbled forward as he continued to hold the other man down. His side now dripped blood to the floor. Norah knew there was truth to Metzger's words and began to approach to help in any way she could.

"No, Norah," Ivey called out to her.

She paused.

With his free hand, Mr. Ivey reached for a long match where they lay ready for use. "You need to run, Norah," he panted, the arm holding Metzger down beginning to shake.

Confused, Norah examined the scene. The hiss of the gas from the fireplace sharpened her wits and she stared at Ivey with eyes wide. "You can't!"

Ivey groaned. "I'm still cursed. I see it all. So much death, so much blood and fire. My visions have never come true, but maybe ... just maybe, if they did, I'd be free. Go. Now, Norah. Out the dressing room. I can't hold him any longer."

Metzger laughed, the cackle an insane one, and began to lurch to his feet, the blood streaming from his shoulder.

Norah fled. As she reached the door to her dressing room, she heard the unmistakable sound of the match being struck upon the fireplace, along with the last words uttered by Ivey: *Fire and blood!*

Malcolm

Malcolm was entirely fed up with lying on this sofa in the great hall. His arm hurt fiercely from being pricked so many times, as Dr. Wrightly had to fulfill the transfusion one syringe-full at a time. But he knew the importance for Farley, who was still unconscious on the other sofa facing him.

Fred, with Mr. Norris in his arms, lingered behind the sofa, casting worried glances at his injured friend. Ambrose stood farther away, muttering to himself and refusing to watch the proceedings. Mathers assisted Dr. Wrightly with any task he demanded.

"How much more, doc?" he asked as Dr. Wrightly extracted another vial full. The pain of his arm was beginning to be replaced by a general sense of malaise, most likely from the blood loss.

The surgeon patted his good arm. "I think this ought to do it. Otherwise, I'll need to find some blood for you next."

From the other sofa, Farley said weakly, "I do appreciate your donations, Malcolm."

Malcolm's anxiety lessened. The young man had been out cold until now. "It's good to hear you're still kicking, Farley."

Farley groaned. "A straight-up miracle, you mean. I thought for sure I was a goner when the old man pushed me out the window."

Malcolm tried to sit up but ceased his actions to keep the dizziness from setting in. Still, the man's words had grabbed his attention. "What do you mean?"

Farley let out a small moan as the doctor placed his hands on his shoulders to push him back down. Dr. Wrightly admonished, "You're heavily injured, Mr. Hunt. Please lie back."

Malcolm's patience was at an end. He was about to bark a demand for an explanation, but Farley began talking. "It was Withers. I'd gone to Norah's room to search for Bloodletter, and he came up behind me, unexpectedly. When I turned to ask him what he was doing, he pushed me out the window."

"Good god." Withers, the kindly old man who couldn't yet walk, a would-be murderer? *Karanja must have been right after all.* Malcolm felt a stab of remorse for not believing him. He would have to make it up to the man as soon as soon as possible. Withers *was* a bad man, and now his guild was paying the price of ignoring the warning. "Mathers," Malcolm called weakly.

Mathers was by his side in an instant. "Sir?"

Malcolm gestured toward his office. "Ring up the constable. There's a madman on the loose."

"Yes, sir."

He heard his butler's footsteps retreating. Malcolm closed his eyes, a deep weariness blanketing his mind. As he drifted away, he thought again of poor Karanja, locked away upstairs. Norah had been right about him. Karanja's motives had been on the right side. Norah was so wise.

Norah.

The thought of the woman he loved caused alarm to shoot through him, clearing his mind again. "Where is Norah?"

The voice of Mrs. Bixby answered him as she approached. "Upstairs in her room, lovie. She sent me down to see how you were doing."

Malcolm relaxed. He trusted Norah's judgement. She wouldn't be as unsuspecting as Farley had been. "Other than feeling like a human pincushion and being dead tired, I can't complain."

She rounded the sofa and patted his hand. "And our Mr. Hunt?"

"Still alive, Mrs. Bixby," Farley said from his position.

There was a look upon Mrs. Bixby that Malcolm couldn't place. Concern, certainly, but not about his current condition. "Everything all right?" he asked her. Perhaps he should send Mathers to check on Norah as soon as he finished ringing the police.

She smiled, but it was strained. "Nothing to worry about in the moment," she said.

"Good heavens," came another new voice from the foyer. "What on earth is happening here today?"

Malcolm groaned internally. He'd forgotten it was Sunday in all the hubbub. "Father, my apologies for the mess you've found yourself in."

Father Berkely entered his line of sight, his pale face a mass of confusion. "Think nothing for me, dear boy. I was simply confused as to why no one was answering the door. I do apologize for letting myself in. And now I see I've walked into quite the scene."

"Mr. Hunt had a bit of an accident, Father," Malcolm explained. "Although now that he's awake, it wasn't an accident at all. Someone tried to murder him."

"Is that so?" the priest knelt to gaze at Farley.

"He'll be better, now that he's got some blood in him," Dr. Wrightly proclaimed as he put away his syringes.

Father Berkely seemed dubious. "If you say so. Might I inquire as to where Miss Abernathy is? I'm rather surprised she isn't by your side, Mr. Drury."

Malcolm chuckled. "I think it was too much for her. She went upstairs to clean up her room—it was her window Farley was flung out of."

"My word. It's been a momentous day around here, hasn't it been?"

Malcolm grimaced. "You could say that."

The priest began to say, "Who could have possibly harm—"

A loud explosion rocked the mansion, shaking the ground. Mrs. Bixby screamed.

"What the hell?" Malcolm shouted, uncaring of the religious man next to him. A cloud of smoke crept over the balustrade from the second-floor gallery. The sight sent his stomach deep into a pit of hell. He sat up, uncaring of his condition.

"Mr. Drury, you must stay seated!" Dr. Wrightly insisted.

Malcolm ignored him and tried to stand. His vision instantly went fuzzy, and his head grew light. He sat back down. "I need to check on Norah," he said, trying to shake the dizziness away.

"I'll go," Father Berkely said, running for the stairs before Malcolm could protest.

Norah

The explosion pushed Norah away from her room faster than she could run, causing her to sprawl on the dressing room floor. She lifted her upper half up, shaking off the disorientation, and then turned around.

Fire belched from where the door used to be, licking up the sides and quickly spreading.

"Oh no," she murmured, before forcing herself to her feet.

Norah dashed to the relative safety of the balcony before entering Malcolm's room. In a recess of her mind, she noted this was how Withers—Metzger—had escaped their detection after pushing Mr. Hunt out the window. She allowed the thought to drift away again, intent on warning the rest of the household.

She was out of the room within seconds. The smoke was already massing in the open space of the gallery, much to her dismay. She leaned over the railing, noticing the group of people down below in the hall. "Malcolm!" she yelled down. He turned his face up, searching for her. It was good enough. "The house is on fire! We must evacuate!" She paused, counting the people. Mr. Hunt, Mr. Jamison, Mr. Norris, the surgeon, and Mrs. Bixby were present. And yes, there was Ambrose farther away. Eddie, the good dog he was, still cuddled up to Malcolm on the sofa. Who was left?

"Where is Mathers?" Norah yelled down.

"Gone to make a telephone call," Dr. Wrightly yelled back.

Norah nodded, still trying to remember if there was anyone else she was missing from her mental roster. Cook and her scullery maid would still be tucked in the kitchen, most likely unaware of the danger. Metzger and Mr. Ivey remained on the list, but they were now gone—Norah felt a pang of loss at the thought of the latter. That was everyone.

Except ... with a stab of panic, she remembered Karanja. Metzger had claimed he'd "taken care" of the man, but Norah would not leave this house without knowing for certain. She yelled down one more time, "I'm going to get Karanja! Everyone else, get out of the house, and don't forget the kitchen staff. I'll meet you outside."

Malcolm surely had begun to protest, but he was already being picked up by Mathers, who had finished his telephone call, and besides, Norah knew she couldn't waste any more time. She could feel the heat of the fire behind her.

She made for the stairs, only stopping when she heard the huffing of Father Berkley's breaths coming down the hall toward her. He stopped, red-faced, to catch his breath.

"What are you doing here, Father?" she asked him.

"Your Malcolm wouldn't rest easy until he knew you were safe. I heard what you said, though, and I'm determined to follow through with his wishes."

Norah shook her head before marching resolutely up the stairs. "I won't leave until everyone is out of this house," she warned.

"I wouldn't expect otherwise from you," the priest agreed as he took the steps behind her. "Which is why I'm coming with you."

Norah wasted no more time talking.

The door to Karanja's prison room was open, and all was quiet within. Norah gasped as she entered, seeing Karanja laid out on the floor, the man supine and unmoving with smatterings of blood upon the carpet.

Father Berkely rushed over and felt for a pulse. He let out a gusty sigh. "He's alive."

"Thank heavens for that." Norah hurried over to help the priest lift the man. "How an old man could get the drop on the likes of Karanja, I don't know," she added with a strained grunt.

Malcolm

The conflagration was picking up speed, Malcolm noted with a heavy heart from his vantage point at the head of the driveway. Dr. Wrightly had instructed everyone to stay here, a long distance from Birchwald. As such, Malcolm had a top-notch view of his home going up in flames.

Almost everyone had made it out safely—all who had been stationed in the great hall, and Cook and her scullery maid as well, that was. Only Norah, Father Berkely, and Karanja remained inside.

Another boom shook the area, and the flames belched from the broken windows of Malcolm's suite. The rooms belonging to Fred and Mr. Norris also displayed the rosy glow through the windows, which meant the fire had spread to the third floor.

The wait was killing Malcolm.

"Mathers, go in there and help them!" he demanded.

For once, Mathers refused to heed his master's orders. "It's foolish to risk any more lives, sir. You can sack me if you need, but I already risked myself by staying to ring the fire brigade."

"Damnit, man," Malcolm growled, trying once again to stand up. The dizziness had lessened, but his body felt as weak as a kitten's.

"I highly recommend not going in there in your condition," Dr. Wrightly warned.

"Stuff it, man. I need to know she's alright," Malcolm said before lumbering down the drive toward the house.

He'd felt brave, noble even, going against doctor's orders to save the woman he loved. But within the first few yards, Malcolm recognized the foolishness of his pursuit. His heart hammered, and a cold sweat broke out on his forehead as he slowed to a march instead of a jog.

Much later than he cared to consider, he pushed the double doors open. Thick smoke had already permeated the first floor, and it belched from this new opening, swamping Malcolm with its foulness. He coughed and cried out, "Norah! Where are you?"

The smoke confused his eyes with its dancing contortions. He thought he saw his mother for a brief second, her familiar shape dominating the foyer. He blinked, and she was gone.

New shapes took her place as he bent over to let out a racking cough. He tried to yell one more time, but the tainted inhale choked his words. He turned to escape to fresh air, defeated.

He was no hero. He'd failed to save Norah.

At the steps, he breathed a lungful of mostly untainted air. Only then did he hear the sweetest sound imaginable: his name spoken by Norah.

Malcolm spun, seeing the shapes he had been so confused by seconds ago reform into Norah and Father Berkely carrying a beaten and barely conscious Karanja between them. As soon as they were free of the interior, Norah secured Karanja with the priest and rushed over, falling into Malcolm's arms.

"You weren't about to go in there after me, were you?" she asked. Her face was covered in soot, her eyes red from the smoke.

He smoothed back her hair. "Is it so unbelievable that I have a shred of chivalry in me?"

"No, not at all," she said.

Norah

By the time the fire brigade arrived an hour later, the conflagration had taken a firm grasp of the entire house. The firemen ran their hoses and gave it their best, but Birchwald was beyond saving. Norah and Malcolm held hands as they watched the entire structure burn, leaving only a few outer walls to mark where once a grand estate stood.

Norah glanced over at Malcolm, who continued to witness the destruction of his only home. He was weak from blood loss and in shock most likely from the turn of events, but he was standing on his own without looking too ill.

"How are you feeling?" she asked softly.

He grimaced. "I feel like my heart's been ripped out and stomped upon."

She squeezed his hand. "I understand. But that's not exactly what I meant. How are you, physically?"

"Oh." He paused, taking stock of his body. "I thought my curse was acting up when I went to rescue you, but I believe it was just the transfusion. I'm still a little weak, but I feel fine otherwise. How long have we been outside?" He withdrew his pocket watch.

"At least a couple of hours."

He made a small noise in his throat. "Long enough to start feeling the effects." He glanced behind him, away from the destruction of his home and toward the start of the drive. "Shall we put it to the test?"

Norah took his hand, and together they walked to the edge of the property. Malcolm paused.

Norah squeezed his hand. "I'm here if you need me to drag you to safety."

He snorted. "Until today, I might have doubted your strength. But now, I'll never doubt your capabilities ever again."

Her heart lifted like a withered potted plant getting its first watering. She said nothing, however, only taking the first step across the threshold, urging Malcolm to take that leap of faith with her.

He did.

After a moment, he stayed standing.

"It's gone." His voice was filled with incredulity, wonder, excitement. Norah's potted plant of a heart wilted slightly with the implications.

Malcolm was free.

She immediately felt like a cad for the feelings of desolation this revelation brought about. She should be happy for Malcolm. He could continue to live his life.

Once again, she kept all this to herself. Outwardly, she smiled. "You're free."

He picked her up, spinning her in a circle before dropping her like a stone, both of them tumbling to the ground in a burst of laughter.

"I forgot about my current limitations," Malcolm confessed as he picked himself back up. "How? How am I cured?"

Norah's mind spun with what to say. She honestly didn't know if she had broken the curse simply by disrupting the bundle his mother had hidden, or if the destruction of Birchwald was the culprit. Perhaps it was both.

In the end, Malcolm only had his fond memories of his mother left. What good would it do to strip him of those as well?

"Birchwald is gone. Without the house to anchor you, I imagine the curse had no choice but to dissipate," she told him. It was as close to the truth as she dared go.

CHAPTER FORTY-FOUR

Friday, June 11, 1915

Norah

WITH THE LOSS OF Birchwald, the Guild was officially homeless. A hasty decision had to be made as to what to do next. Father Berkely offered to take them to the rectory for the night, and like lost lambs they followed the priest home.

However, a more sustainable solution was desperately needed. Norah offered her own brownstone townhouse in New York City, and everyone accepted.

They left the very next morning on the first train out. The other passengers had not expected a disheveled, smoky ragtag band of travelers, one of which was a small dog and another a white hen wearing a diaper. Many curious looks were cast their way, but the misplaced group was too downtrodden and exhausted to care.

Aunt Nell and Pablo had returned from their honeymoon only the week prior. They'd taken up residency in Nell's basement apartment. To say they were surprised by the Birchwald crew at their doorstep was an understatement.

Norah's brownstone was much, much smaller than Birchwald. It had taken some adjusting on everyone's part to adapt to the close living arrangements.

Jerrod had at least been grateful for Mathers, Mrs. Bixby, Cook, and the scullery maid. With more mouths to feed and people to tend, he would have otherwise been stretched quite thin.

Any time Norah felt gratitude for their numbers being smaller than when she first joined, the feeling was chased by an immense reaction of guilt and loss. After all, she may have helped cure the likes of Rodney and Pablo, but three of the previous members were lost forever, two of which to her own carelessness.

Farley Hunt healed quickly from his injuries. Dr. Wrightly had traveled with them to New York City, and stayed long enough to ensure those who survived the events would thrive—physically, at least. Bloodletter had been an official casualty of the fire, and both Norah and Mr. Hunt were sure that he had been released from its curse. Whether this was from the destruction of the letter opener or from the replacement of much of his blood, they couldn't be sure.

Karanja also healed from his beating that had left him nearly dead. Norah suffered terribly from guilt over his treatment at Birchwald, considering he'd been in the right for keeping the evil man Metzger locked away in his own body. To help atone for her past inadequacies, Norah personally tended to him, with a little help from Dr. Wrightly. Karanja assured her that he held no ill will toward her or Malcolm, however. After all, Karanja was not fully blameless, given he had lied to them and broken their initial trust. He understood how his actions had led to misgivings.

Ambrose, Mr. Jamison, and Mr. Norris grouped together more often than not. Ambrose still broadcasted anyone's thoughts, but those reflections must have been more subdued than normal, for nothing lewd or outrageous graced his lips. Mr. Norris still acted like the chicken he was, and Mr. Jamison stuck by him with the same devotion as always.

Eddie was of course delighted to be home, which happened to be wherever his people were. He was single-handedly a beacon of light for the weary outcasts, devoting much of his time to cheering the others up. The little dog showered everyone with affection, including Karanja, who, after getting over an initial shyness, took great delight in the dog's cheerful antics. Not once did a growl ever escape from Eddie when he spent time with Karanja, and Norah now knew for certain that the day Eddie had reacted so unfavorably in the room, it was directed at Metzger.

Malcolm was quiet, pensive. Norah only knew this about him from small, occasional encounters; she avoided his company whenever possible, another faction to add to her increasing guilt.

It pained her to treat Malcolm in this way, but now that he was free of his curse, she wanted him to live his life. She refused to be a dead albatross about his neck. As much as it troubled her, she needed to give him space. Perhaps then they could begin to separate their intertwined feelings for each other.

Even now, five days after the destruction of Birchwald, ignoring Malcolm felt like she was depriving herself of air.

Aunt Nell, ever sharp-eyed, noticed her niece's moping. At lunch, she invited Norah to her basement for a private meal.

Norah knew an inquisition was coming.

Aunt Nell was not one to waste her breath. As Norah sipped her soup, the undead lady eyed her critically. "What's wrong with you?" she finally asked.

Norah put her spoon down, careful not to make a loud noise against the bowl. There was no point in trying to eat now. "I'm not sure what you mean."

"You've been mooning over that boy ever since you came back. I may have clouded eyes, gel, but I'm not blind. He's no longer beholden to his house. Why doesn't that make you happy?"

Norah huffed. "Why would it? At least when he was still cursed, he didn't care about dying young. And I still felt guilty over my curse affecting him in this way. But now? He has a chance to live, to travel like he always dreamed. If he continues to love me, he could die within the year. He doesn't deserve that, Aunt Nell."

"But he chose you before. What makes you think he won't choose you again?"

"That's just it, though!" Norah practically shouted. "I don't want that burden on me. I want my own happiness, of course. I'm almost selfish enough to take it. But Malcolm deserves to have a life. LJ has a death wish, as much as I tried to keep him safe. He doesn't care enough about me to change that. I know what it's like to be on the receiving end of someone else's selfishness. I won't do that to Malcolm, even if it destroys any chance of happiness I might find."

Aunt Nell was silent, staring at her bowl of uneaten soup. In a voice softer than Norah thought she was capable of, she said, "You really do love him, don't you?"

A tear tracked down Norah's face. "I do. I love him enough to let him go. I love him enough to destroy myself doing that, if it means he will live on after I die."

Nell snorted softly, but not unkindly. "Love. Do you know, with all my husbands, all my years, it's been something that alludes me? Even Pablo—kind, sweet Pablo. He loves me, there's no doubt. But I find it utterly lacking in me. I care for him, sure, but no, I don't love him. I think ... in this world, love is a rarer commodity than we humans let on. Perhaps that's why so many curses exist, and blessings are hard to come by."

Norah wiped the stray tear away. "I love *you*, even if the feeling isn't mutual," she assured her aunt. "Perhaps it's enough for the both of us."

Nell patted her hand. "Perhaps."

CHAPTER FORTY-FIVE

Saturday, June 12th, 1915

Norah

"Norah?"

Pablo's voice came from far away, an interloper into her dreams. She heard him a second time, at which point she roused enough to open her eyes in the real world.

It was still fully dark out. She must have dreamed he was calling her name. She closed her eyes again.

"Norah."

This time there was no denying the reality. Pablo was here, in her room. She sat up, discombobulated. Finally, she saw the dark mass of the man hovering over her bed.

"Pablo? What time is it?" Her words were slightly slurred, her mouth refusing to work properly just yet.

"It's two in the morning. I'm sorry to wake you, but it's important."

She yawned. "What is it?"

He paused. "Nell is dead."

Norah froze for a moment and then let out a relieved chuckle. "Of course she is."

"No." That single word was filled with frustration, despair. Norah's heart clenched at the sound. "She is truly dead. Not undead."

"What?" Norah threw back the covers, reaching for the bedside candle.

"Here, I have a lamp in the hallway. Come with me," Pablo said, taking her hand in the dark.

Norah followed him, through the upper hall, down two flights of stairs, into the basement she had converted just for Aunt Nell. Pablo did not stop until they entered the bed chamber. All the while Norah's mind seesawed between incredulity—Aunt Nell couldn't die—and crushing finality.

The ripeness of rot assaulted Norah's nostrils. It was nothing new for Aunt Nell, although it was stronger than usual. She wondered how Pablo could stand it. Or any of her previous husbands, for that matter.

Her aunt was under the covers, lying on her back, eyes closed. Her long black hair fanned out amidst the pillows. Her face was serene, with almost a hint of a smile.

"Aunt Nell?" Norah leaned over her. The woman didn't move. Norah couldn't check for breath, because Aunt Nell had no reason to breathe under normal circumstances. She had no reason to sleep either, although she often went through the motions for her husbands' sakes.

Norah touched her cheek. The waxy paleness of it did not change. She did not open her eyes or smile as if she was pulling a joke. She was completely motionless, and cold to the touch.

"She's gone, *mi bella*," Pablo said softly behind her.

Norah gasped then, the enormity of this fact almost causing her to sink to her knees.

"How?" she asked, the word choking her.

Pablo handed her a sheath of folded paper. "She told me to give this to you last night before we retired. She gave me one as well. I thought nothing of it at the time." His face was drawn, anguished. He felt her death as deeply as she did.

Norah accepted the papers, unfolding them to see her aunt's neat handwriting. *This is the last letter I'll ever get from her,* she thought, and felt undone all over again.

"You're shaking. Please, Norah, sit. I'll go fetch a brandy for you," Pablo insisted, guiding Norah to the chair in the corner of the room.

She sank into it, grateful to no longer be reliant on her legs. She flashed a ghost of a smile at Pablo. "Thank you. Please, wake Mathers for me? We'll need to ... do something ... with the body." She closed her eyes, the pain intense. *The body. Aunt Nell.*

Pablo must have felt it as well, for his throat bobbed over a difficult swallow as he nodded and left without another word. Norah was now alone with only her thoughts, this letter, and her aunt's corpse as company.

Wasting no time, she carefully unfolded the papers, smoothed them out, and began reading.

My dearest namesake,

Don't be sad.

Knowing you like I do, though, it's probably too late. Your strength of emotion has always been deep.

I, Eleanora Montmorency, being of sound mind, have made the choice to give up my so-called life, to renounce this corporeal body.

Norah, I have been incredibly unfair to you, and you have not even known it. When you were little, you used to try to ask questions about my past, and I always shut you down. The truth is, I was ashamed.

I know full well that the origin of my curse has gained a life of its own. I've heard the whispers of how I was the seductress of my stepfather, cruelly flaunting our relationship in front of my mother as she lay on her deathbed. It would certainly explain why I deserved such a curse.

The truth is another matter.

I was ten when Ernest Abernathy married my mother. I was eleven when she had his heir. After that, she'd have no more children. Ernest's eyes began to roam as soon as it became apparent my mother's "usefulness" was over. And, as I blossomed into womanhood before him, his eyes landed on me.

I did nothing to spur him on, yet as soon as I was of age he pursued me. By this time, Mother was very ill. Ernest assumed she'd never learn of his debauchery, and as soon as she died, he'd marry me, transforming me from a stepdaughter into a much younger and prettier wife.

That is not how it happened, however. Mother found out.

It should have been obvious he was the guilty party, yet she blamed me! That much the rumors got right. She cursed me, killing me yet forcing me to live on with an insatiable need for men, one that would kill them to keep me fresh. She cursed me with her dying breath, leaving none of the condemnation behind for Ernest, the true culprit.

I was enraged. I was angry at my mother, certainly, but deep down, I knew who was truly to blame. And this weasel of a man had gotten away scot-free, while my life was irrevocably changed forever. I hated him.

And this is the part, my dear niece, in which I feel the most shame, although at the time, I only felt vindicated.

You see, you were led to believe that the curse upon your family had been placed by an object of Ernest's. I allowed you to believe that because I didn't wish for you to think differently of me.

The truth is, I placed the curse upon your family.

I cursed the line of Abernathy men to always be struck with the need for adventure and thus find themselves cursed at a young age. And I cursed your family with death for anyone who dared to love an Abernathy.

All because an Abernathy led to my curse.

Ernest effectively killed any respect I had for men, despite my curse inflicting me with desire for them. I wanted Ernest to hurt as badly as I did, and I did not care one bit for any of the men who followed in the Abernathy line. And there were many of them. All boys throughout the generations.

And then you came along. A girl. The first girl born to the Abernathys since before I was born.

And after your parents' death, as I came into your life, I learned that my heart wasn't quite as shriveled as I once thought.

I grew to love you. And in doing so, I began to hate myself, just a little bit.

What you said to me yesterday, about needing to stop being selfish in order to let others live, it resonated deeply in me. And I realized that I've been incredibly selfish.

I've allowed you to suffer in order to continue my way of life.

I'm sorry.

I think my curse has shifted over the years. I'm sure my mother did not intend for my own curse to continue for this long. I do believe I've been living solely on spite at this point. I feel like if I just stop forcing myself to be here, I can finally be at peace. I can finally die.

I intend to release you from an old family hurt. I can't continue watching someone I love suffer simply because I'm selfish. The only way to release you, dear Norah, is to release myself.

It's past time I forgive. Forgive my mother, and that old lech Ernest. They both have been dead for generations. And it's time I forgive myself too.

I only hope you can forgive me as well.

Be free now. Live your life on your own terms. I demand it.

All my love,

Nell

By the time she got to the end of the letter, Norah's tears freely flowed. She placed the pages down in her lap, marveling over what her aunt had divulged.

So much pain. Generations of suffering. Nell's anguish, her disdain of men, made perfect sense now. They all reminded her of Norah's ancestor, who took a girl's young life and squashed it with his careless actions. It was no wonder Nell had cursed him. But if what Aunt Nell had written was true, it was over now. Norah had been freed from her curse.

If only she didn't have to lose the one family member who cared about her to do so.

Love was a heavy price.

CHAPTER FORTY-SIX

Tuesday, June 15th, 1915

Malcolm

NELL'S GRAVESTONE WAS ERECTED next to Norah's parents in the Abernathy section of the Green-Wood Cemetery. The grave itself was empty, for Nell had asked in her letter to Pablo that she be cremated, and her ashes spread in her birthplace, a quaint estate in England where she lived as a small child before being moved to New York in the 1700s.

The morning's funeral was small. Only the inhabitants of Norah's house attended.

The June weather was perfect, a stark contrast to the somber mood. Malcolm expected rain clouds at a funeral, not bright sunshine and a pleasant breeze. Thunderclouds would have been more apropos than the cheerful birdsong he heard instead.

As much as it pained him to admit, the outside world was too intense for him, after years of forced enclosure. Malcolm felt too exposed in this vast outdoor space, and he spent the morning glancing about, confronting a sense of doom about the event that he knew only existed in his head. Of course, the gloom of the affair did not help with this sensation. He struggled through the service wordlessly, eager to be back indoors once again.

Norah and Pablo were the only two people who seemed upset by the woman's passing. Norah allowed herself to cry openly during the symbolic burial, and Pablo had a lost look about him. Despite only being married for about a month, he'd apparently fallen in love with the undead lady.

After the funeral and back at the Abernathy brownstone, everyone went their separate ways. Malcolm returned to the security of his guest bedroom, soaking in the comfort of the four walls. He expected Norah to disappear for the rest of the day, and did not bother to chase her. She had been distant since the fire, and Malcolm had known well enough to give her space, despite his heart yearning to do the opposite.

This was why he was shocked to find Norah in his doorway an hour later, clutching her aunt's letter to her chest. Her eyes were puffy from crying, but otherwise she looked remarkably put together. Malcolm waited for her to speak first.

"I want you to read this," she said simply, still standing in the doorway.

Malcolm stood and gestured to the chair he had occupied. Norah crossed the threshold, handing the letter to him as she sat.

He read it, his eyes widening as he came to the end. He looked at Norah.

She smiled with half her mouth. Her eyes looked as if she might start crying again. "I had my mind made up to let you go," she said. "While you were stuck at Birchwald, I was prepared to be with you and doom you along with me. But then you were cured, and your whole life opened up. I couldn't have been happy knowing you were going to die after my untimely end, now that you could do whatever you want. I told this to Aunt Nell, and this was the outcome."

Malcolm opened his mouth to speak, to tell her she was being foolish, that he still wanted to spend his life with her, no matter how little they might have.

"Please don't say anything yet," she said with a hand raised. He closed his mouth. She continued, "My aunt could see how much this initial decision was destroying me. She chose to break the curse for me. She gave up her life for me. I would be a fool to waste this opportunity, so I shall say this to you once, and if you feel otherwise, I will leave you alone." She took a deep breath, let it out, and focused her beautiful brown eyes upon him. "Malcolm Drury, I love you. I don't love easily, but you have wormed your way into my heart, and I cannot pretend otherwise. I would like to be by your side and explore the world with you, if you are agreeable to that."

Malcolm stared, his insides frothing in a pleasant way.

She pursed her lips. "You can say something now."

He grinned. "I know. I was just stunned speechless. I thought for a moment hell had frozen over."

She huffed a breath. "Drury, I swear to—"

"I love you," he said quickly, interrupting any tirade that might escape her mouth. "God, Norah, I love you. I've loved you probably since you barged into my office in the middle of the night demanding to stay. You make me want to be a better man, and I wouldn't have ever left this house without you. I want to travel with you, make love to you, marry you—"

"Let's not be too hasty," she interrupted.

He laughed. "No, I know you are a thoroughly modern woman. I can wait. A little."

"Let's be sure we won't want to murder each other first," she agreed. A crease formed between her eyes. "And I cannot say for certain that my curse is lifted. We may still die."

"There's a war overseas. Our lives cannot be taken for granted, whether we are cursed or not. After all, now that I am uncursed, I may be enlisted if the US joins the war, in which case my chances at a long life are affected. Darling, life is never a guarantee. We must make what we have count."

The tears now tracked down her cheeks, but she smiled through them. "Thank you, Malcolm. Whatever happens, it will happen to us together. Curse or no curse."

He reached for her, pulling her off the chair and into his arms. He ran his thumbs through her tears with reverence before leaning in and kissing her, finding the truth behind her convictions. He'd kissed her before, but this time he found her completely open, giving. He admired the strength of her love.

Norah

Later, after proving just how much she loved this man in the confines of his room, Norah and Malcolm joined the rest of the household in the parlor. Mr. Hunt, Mr. Jamison, and Pablo sat at the small table by the window, a game of rummy in progress between them while Mr. Norris pecked at some crumbs on the carpet. Eddie also snuffled about, stepping on his long ear fur as he tried to beat Mr. Norris to the biggest crumbs. Ambrose leafed through a book by the unlit fireplace.

Norah held Malcolm's hand as they stood in front of the sofa. "We have an announcement," Norah proclaimed, waiting until all eyes were on her. A hush fell over the room.

Malcolm gazed at Norah, the look filling her with love and gratitude. "Norah and I are officially courting," he said without much pause.

The hush grew into a lengthy silence.

"That's it?" Ambrose snorted loudly. "There's not a man in this room who didn't already know that. If you are trying to shock us, you've failed spectacularly."

A rumble of chortles and noises of agreement filled the air before the men stood and offered hearty congratulations in the form of hugs and handshakes.

With the well-wishes coming to a conclusion, Norah flopped onto the sofa, Malcolm already having done so with a satisfied grin on his face. Eddie ran over and jumped into her lap, adding his own brand of felicitations. She hugged the small dog to her, her heart close to bursting with the love she felt in this room.

The doorbell rang. From her spot on the sofa, Norah heard Jerrod open it and speak to someone in low tones. A moment later, the servant cleared his throat at the entrance to the parlor.

"Miss, there is a caller for Mr. Jamison," he said.

Norah stood, dislodging Eddie. "Mr. Jamison?" She exchanged glances with the man in question, noting the quizzical frown on his face. "By all means, send them in."

Jerrod nodded and retrieved the person. When the stranger—tall, thin, deeply tanned with white-blonde hair—made his appearance, Mr. Jamison gasped and turned white, to Norah's interest.

"Herb?" Mr. Jamison asked, his voice rising an octave.

Norah grasped at the name, trying to remember why it was so familiar.

"Hello, Freddy," Herb said with a shy smile.

Jamison leapt up, rushing to the man. He threw his arms around him and kissed him quickly on the mouth. Norah was only slightly surprised by this reaction.

"It *is* you!" Mr. Jamison exclaimed, reluctant to let the other man go. "But how? I thought—"

"I've been living with the tribe all this time," Herb explained. "At first, I was unable to leave. After you escaped, the Dayaks were first angry you had slipped away, then they were laughing and pointing at me as if I was some big joke. I was initially angry with you for leaving me behind."

"But I didn't—" Mr. Jamison started to say.

Herb held up a hand, cutting Jamison off. "I know. At first, they guarded me vigorously. Then, they gave me more leeway. I wasn't as brave as you, to flee in the night, so I stayed. And I learned their language, and I began to make friends with the Dayaks. They grew to like me too, and eventually adopted me as one of their own. I only learned last year that they had cursed you with nightmares. I asked them to undo the curse, which they finally did. They also filled me in on your great escape. It was at this time I realized you didn't leave me after all. And I missed you terribly. So, I asked to leave, which they allowed immediately, since I was no longer a prisoner. I've been halfway around the world looking for you. I thought I'd lost you all over again when I tracked you down to Croton Falls and only found a burnt shell where the Guild should be, but a priest at the rectory told me I'd find you at this address."

Mr. Jamison stared with wide eyes. "You've been with the tribe this whole time? And you're the reason my nightmares vanished? Oh, Herb, this is wonderful! I—" He stopped himself, turning to face the gathering group with a bashful smile. "Everyone, this is Herbert Norris."

The silence that followed was deafening. Ambrose blurted out, "Wait! If *that's* Herbert Norris, then who is this?" He pointed to the chicken.

Herb frowned and cocked his head to the side. "*That's* a chicken from the Bornean tribe. They're everywhere in the village."

The hen, unaware that all eyes had fixated on her, stretched her neck and said, "Cluck-cluck-cluck-ba-*gawk*!"

CHAPTER FORTY-SEVEN

Saturday, May 27th, 1922

Norah

IT WAS A BEAUTIFUL spring day in Oxford.

Norah stood nervously in line, her foot tapping to ease some of the energy she possessed. The world fogged in and out about her as the line inched forward, her sole focus on the man at the podium reading out names.

"Dr. Norah Jane Drury," he said at last. The audience clapped.

Norah leapt to action as if stung from behind. She willed her feet not to trip as she crossed the stage to receive the rolled-up paper from the man. He shook her hand.

"Congratulations, Dr. Drury," he said to her. She smiled in response, her palm itching as it held the object she'd long treasured.

Two years ago, in 1920, she'd heard that Oxford was finally allowing women to graduate. She wondered if it was mere coincidence that the decision corresponded with the year she was at last granted the right to vote. Whatever the driving factor was, she'd not been one to waste an opportunity. She convinced Malcolm to move to Oxford—taking over the house her aunt and the merchant had owned, since she'd inherited everything from Nell—and re-enrolled into Oxford to finish what she'd started so many years ago.

And now, with her degree in hand, Norah had everything she'd ever wanted: a prestigious doctorate in Maledictology and more equal footing in this men's world. She also still had Malcolm, who—after years of waiting—had insisted they finally marry before moving to Oxford. He'd been patient enough with her modern ways, so Norah readily agreed. Father Berkely performed the ceremony the day before their ship left the New York City harbor.

Life wasn't perfect, but it was pretty damn near close.

And it had certainly been a journey to get to this point, Norah reflected as she waited for the rest of the ceremony to finish.

Malcolm had officially closed the Guild after the destruction of Birchwald. With only Ambrose still cursed, and uncertainty overseas strangling the prospect of new members, he decided it simply wasn't worth keeping open. Instead, he and Norah traveled about the United States for two years, answering inquiries about curses and doing their best to help the cursed people break them. They had a fairly positive success rate.

Because of their nomadic lifestyle and the lack of a grand estate to tend to, Malcolm gifted both Mathers and Mrs. Bixby with incredibly generous severances, more than enough to retire on with all the human comforts. To Norah's amusement, the two retired people decided to cohabitate in one house, although she suspected it was a relationship built on friendship and not romantic love. Any time Norah and Malcolm found themselves back in New York, they made sure to visit these cherished chosen family members.

The Great War had dragged on for longer than anyone in 1915 would have guessed. In 1917, the United States joined the war, and Malcolm was indeed drafted—as he had predicted— thus ending their domestic travels. Because of his status as a formerly cursed individual, however, he'd been lucky enough to stay off the battlefields, instead being shunted into a more clerical role far from danger. He never once saw the true horrors of the war. Still, Norah worried over his security, stuck as she was in New York.

Not everyone who entered the war was granted the same privilege of safety. Back in 1915, Norah's brother LJ had successfully joined the Canadian army—clearly having hidden his curse—and gone overseas in 1916. He wrote to Norah on occasion, speaking of battles he'd fought in, the numerous close calls he experienced, and the horrid conditions on the front line. Despite the unsavory topics, his letters were always saturated in eagerness, as if he was thriving on the chaos. It was a far cry from the petulant miser LJ had been back at Birchwald, and Norah could no longer refute that her brother was happier in battle than he was tucked away like she'd wanted to keep him.

His letters came to an end in the fall of 1917. Norah instead received a telegram, a simple statement that LJ had been killed in action during the Battle of Passchendaele, the third battle of Ypres, in Belgium. He'd died a hero's death that so many others shared with him. It was the type of ending he would have wanted, Norah reflected: one of action and bravery.

LJ's tragic loss weighed on Norah, although not as much as she once thought it would. Along with the crushing sadness, there was a balancing peace in her heart over his death. And oddly, she took great comfort in a single notion brought about by the passing of her brother: the Abernathy line, one of heartache and destruction, effectively ended with Norah, and would continue no farther.

In 1918, as soon as the war had officially concluded, Malcolm returned home, miraculously unscathed. And Norah was still alive. She had spent the time after LJ's death wondering if she would still succumb to the family curse after all, but reuniting with Malcolm had convinced her of the opposite, lifting the last great weight off her shoulders. She was truly free of her curse.

As the guild members parted ways after the demise of the Guild, Norah did her best to keep track of their whereabouts over the years. Rodney Paulson sent regular letters from China, where he now permanently lived. During his initial travels, he'd gained the acquaintance of a paleontologist who had discovered a treasure trove of dinosaur fossils. The call of paleontology spoke to Rodney, and he had ended up becoming an apprentice. He'd also fallen in love with a Chinese girl, married her, and according to the last letter Norah had received, Rodney now had a son.

Farley Hunt was indeed cured after his blood transfusion and the loss of Bloodletter to the fire. He returned to his family after fully healing, resumed his business, and even married the woman he'd been originally engaged to, as her first husband had died.

Fred Jamison and Herbert Norris, happily reunited, rented an apartment in New York City while they waited out the war so that they could continue traveling and exploring together—after promising they'd not get into any more trouble, that is. They also kept the chicken as a pet, since Jamison had grown so fond of her over the years. He did rename the hen, settling on the name Norah as a tribute. Norah was flattered. Her namesake lived another three years before succumbing to old age, a noble death not often granted to her species.

Pablo Reyes mended his broken heart slowly after Nell's death. Eventually, though, he decided to continue his archaeological work, finding fascinating jobs in the States while the war raged. After peace was proclaimed, he moved back to Spain, where he continued to be happy and unmarried.

Karanja stayed in America during the war as well, becoming good friends with Norah and Malcolm and accompanying them on various trips before 1917. As soon as it was safe to venture overseas, he bid them farewell, eager to be reunited with his homeland. Norah could not blame him.

The only member of the Guild who Norah failed to cure was Ambrose Lyster. It was the one shortcoming that initially haunted her, but Ambrose had a way of turning rainclouds into rainbows. He discovered a knack for theatrics, and took his curse on the road, showcasing his talent for reading people's minds. In a time when the average folk needed some levity, Ambrose became wildly successful.

All in all, the people who had survived the demise of the Guild seven years ago had found their niche in life. Norah couldn't have been prouder of the old guild members.

And now, with her new diploma clutched tightly in hand, she could add herself to that list of successes.

As the ceremony wound down and came to an end, Norah found Malcolm in the crowd, a wide smile on his face. He held Eddie, who wagged his tail with happiness for his accomplished mistress. At nine years old, Eddie showed his age, but he still had enough vigor about him to last a couple more years, as well as enough love for his little human family to last a lifetime.

Norah rubbed Eddie's face before being swept into a one-armed embrace and passionately kissed by Malcolm. A year shy of forty, Malcolm was still as dashing as ever, only with a few extra gray hairs. Norah couldn't complain; she liked the dash of salt, and besides, her own brown hair was showing a few grays these days as well.

Malcolm ended the kiss and released his wife. "Dr. Drury," he mused with his usual sardonic grin. "I like that."

"I expect you to call me that all the time," Norah responded, trying to hide her own cheeky smile.

As they walked away from the crush of people arm in arm, with Eddie prancing ahead of them on his lead, Malcolm let out a contented sigh. "Well, you've done it. You are officially graduated. There's no need to stay in Oxford any longer."

Norah bumped him with her body. "Has the wanderlust finally taken hold?" Malcolm had admitted to her years ago that adjusting to outside life had been harder than he'd imagined. Their trips about the States had often been more than enough for him to cope with.

He nodded thoughtfully, staring off into the distance. "It's possible. I've been giving it some thought while you've been staying up half the night studying."

"Yes?"

"I've been reading about Egypt. There's a man there, Howard Carter, who has been excavating in the Valley of Kings for many years now."

Norah stopped their walk. "Your father died from an Egyptian curse, didn't he?"

Malcolm nodded. "That's right. They're quite common there. It would seem that Carter hasn't found anything big yet, but he's bound to soon, wouldn't you say?"

Her blood sang with the unknown. "I *would* say. What are your thoughts on you and I taking a well-earned vacation to the Valley of Kings? Just in case?"

"We can make it a celebration holiday for your hard work. It would be fortuitous if your skillset were to come in handy while we were there as well."

"Mm, I agree," Norah said, snuggling into her husband's side as they resumed their walk. She felt the rightness in this decision with every step she took.

Acknowledgements

Once upon a time, I was pregnant with my first child, and she decided to be ten days late in entering the world. While I was approaching that tenth day, I began to believe that I was always going to be in a state of gravid discomfort, that I would never encounter the fruits of my labor (pun intended). Basically, my brain convinced me that I was going to be pregnant for the rest of my life, and that this was my new normal. Obviously, my brain was incorrect, and said stubborn baby is now thirteen.

This book had a similar genesis. I had multiple surprise delays along the way, through nobody's fault, and I watched my projected release date get pushed back time after time. Once again, I began to believe this book would never see the light of day, but would instead reside in some sort of limbo until the end of time. I even stopped telling people about it, in case my fears came true.

I was wrong, obviously and thankfully. It was a lesson in patience, and one that I apparently needed! This book may not have had the release date that I was wishing for, but here it is, and I'd like to think that the wait made it all the better. After all, I had a lot of people in my corner doing their parts to help me polish it along the way.

My husband Matt is the first to be thanked, mainly because not only is he my alpha reader and he gives me the confidence to show my work to others, but because he supports my dreams unequivocally.

To my beta readers: Rachel, Angelee, Jillian, and Cay, I appreciate you so much! Thank you for taking the time to read my stuff and offer your feedback. And to my sensitivity reader, Kyle Dixon, I offer my sincerest gratitude for your help!

Deep appreciation goes to my editor, Tina S. Beier, for her hard work in getting this manuscript off the ground and giving it wings. Tina, you are always a joy to work with, and I always look forward to future projects with you.

Likewise, I thank my proofreaders Cynthia Ley and Nanci Remington for their eagle eyes. I'm only human (as is everyone who worked on this book), and mistakes were bound to happen!

And Angelee van Allman, thank you for another wonderful cover design. I love our brainstorming sessions and how easily you are able to read my mind. I hope we will have many more covers to brainstorm together.

On a personal note, I'd like to thank the various people in my life who were forced to listen to me talk about this book for a year and a half while it came to fruition. In the writing community, I have nothing but love and appreciation for my Scribblers Club peeps, who lift me up when I'm feeling down. And those thanks also go to my friends and peers at Northwest Writers Association (NIWA). I have learned so much from everyone and it has made me a better writer. To my family members, thank you for your support and love you give to me on a regular basis. And to my friends, thanks for being the best type of listening ear.

Lastly, to my readers: thank you. The fact that my books reach strangers from all over the world still boggles my mind. If you've read this book, or any of my other books, you are the reason I keep going. You are the reason I do what I do, and for that, I am eternally grateful.

About the Author

R. Lindsay Carter grew up in the coastal forests of Oregon, where she developed a deep love of nature and animals. Her writing subjects clearly reflect her remarkable childhood upbringing, with plenty of woodsy scenes and quirky characters that aren't always human. Ms. Carter currently lives in Milwaukie, OR with her husband and two daughters, as well as a menagerie of pets. In her spare time she creates art, reads, plays cozy video games, ignores most household chores, and continues to dream up more stories to eventually share with the world.

Books by R. Lindsay Carter

Series:
The Familiar's Legacy:
Unfamiliar Territory
Relative Truths
Chasing Tails
Curtain Call

Standalone:
The Gentlemen's Guild for Cursed Adventurers

Connect

Follow R. Lindsay Carter for all the latest news!

Social Media:
https://www.rlindsaycarter.com
https://www.facebook.com/rlindsaycarter
https://www.instagram.com/author_rlindsaycarter
https://www.tiktok.com/@author_rlindsaycarter

Newsletter:
https://www.rlindsaycarter.com/newsletter/

www.ingramcontent.com/pod-product-compliance
Lightning Source LLC
Chambersburg PA
CBHW020226010826

48973CB00006B/1387